TARIN SANTOS

Dagger Eyes

Due to the complete independence and length of this project, there may be both grammatical and formatting mistakes throughout this piece of work. Please do not mind these mistakes and discrepancies as this is more a passion project than a professional one.

First edition

Cover art by Tarin Santos
Editing by Sage Lidzbarski-Lahti

This book was professionally typeset on Reedsy.
Find out more at reedsy.com

Dedicated to my Grandfather, Bob Santos, who always gave me the confidence to have faith in my identity and pursue my passions. Though we never got to write a book together, he will always be my driving inspiration to keep telling my stories.

And to Jayden Jenner, who passed before either of us could complete our goals.

Contents

Foreword iii

Map of Mordenla vi

 1 The Mother 1

 2 An Old Friend 14

 3 The Duel 26

 4 Shifted Fate 41

 5 Escape 53

 6 The Girl With the Red Hair 64

 7 Of Blood & Wine 81

 8 Silver Secrets 95

 9 Unbroken 108

10 Path of Destruction 121

11 Amethyst Gardens 137

12 Raven Crown 149

13 The Maiden 162

14 Question of Love 176

15 The Archer 191

16 Priorities 204

17 An Absent Farewell 219

18 The Crooked Flickers 233

19 Wolves & Hares 248

20 Crossroads 262

21 Honor Among Thieves 274

22 The Prince & the Knight 287

23 A Warm Welcome 301

24 The Fox's Den 315

25 What Once Was   326

26 The Crone   338

27 Human Nature   350

28 Bound   361

29 The Truth   371

30 Loyalty Within Lies   387

31 Redemption   399

Epilogue   410

Acknowledgments   416

Q&A with the Author   418

Dagger Eyes Tracklist   425

Foreword

Hi. Not a very authorly to start a book with "Hi", is it? But I suppose enough of that can be forgiven since it's this author's first book. As far as forewords go, it's also my first of those. Though, I guess foreword may not be the word for this. An Author's Note, Letter to the Reader, or perhaps a Thanks for Deciding to Read this Book, I Wasn't Even Expecting to Get It This Far would be a better title than Foreword.

I'm getting off-topic, aren't I? Let's start over.

Thank you for picking up this book and giving it a chance. For that, I am grateful to you. Dagger Eyes started out as a dream. And no, not a fantasy of "I wish to be a famous best-selling author". A dream that you might have on any other night. I can't quite recall the exact details of such a dream, but I do remember sitting in my parents' room reciting it to my mother while she did her morning routine.

"Maybe you should write it," was the response I got. I had heard that response time and time again as I told people about the stories I spent my days and nights imagining. A few people had gotten me journals so that I could "Write down my stories".

And each time, I ignored them, coming up with a number of excuses. "Too much work", "I don't know how to type", "My hand gets tired", "It'd be nice if someone else wrote it for me"

Little did I know, a few days later, I opened up a document on my computer and began writing. The date was December 25th, 2014. Yes, the first memorable date I have for Dagger Eyes is Christmas. I'm not sure what prompted me to write that day instead of playing with whatever I had gotten from my stocking, but I'm grateful I did. I mean, look where we are now.

The next known date was July 1st, 2015, where I first 'published' Dagger Eyes to the teen writing website Wattpad (Now that I think about it, July 1st is my parent's anniversary... I feel like the fact that I did these things when I should have been celebrating with my family says something). From there on, the adventure began. A year later on June 25th, 2016 I finished the first draft.

Cool.

...

I don't know if you know this, but at the time of publishing, it's the year 2022. Yes, it took me seven whole years to write this book. Now you know why I have so much gratitude for anyone who has decided to try and read it.

I don't mind if you don't like it, or if you decide it isn't for you in the first few pages (though I would prefer if you stick around for at least chapter four). Heck, if you end up hating it, that's alright too! What's important is that you took the time to even consider giving this story a read. Because what I can tell you, is that in these seven years, I have found that this isn't my favorite story. Not out of all the stories in the world, and certainly not out of my own. There are a dozen other stories in my mind that I love and cherish the idea of sharing with the world more than this one, but we all have to start somewhere, and I have decided to start with this (And hey, if you stick around, perhaps you'll find a story I hold even closer to my heart. This is just the beginning, after all).

Dagger Eyes has been with me through so much, not just as an outlet of my creativity, but also a crutch of when I felt everything else was too much. When I felt hopeless in my own reality, I'd come here and write out a reality I could escape to... Even if I may not prefer to live in a reality that has the technology of the middle ages and people constantly trying to kill you.

There were times where I loved wrapping myself in the world, and there were times I absolutely hated it. I am not afraid to admit that there are times I cried out of frustration at it. Nevertheless, it was always there.

I have wanted to give up on this a lot. I've wanted to shut my computer and walk away so many times, that I'm pretty sure it adds up to more than the number of sales this book will get, but in the later half, I realized it would be really useless to give up after spending so much time on it. And my stubborn self was not going to waste that much time only to result in a failed project. So I pushed through, and here we are.

I understand there is room for acknowledgments at the end, but I want to take this space to share my gratitude, not only with you but with all of the other people who helped me on the way. From beta readers and peer editors who gave their feedback, to those who did whatever they could to help me promote this book before a physical copy was even in the works... From my mom, who pushed me over the years to the point of even bribing me to finish my chapters, to my dear friend Sage, who answered the phone each and every time I needed to spit out plot ideas for book two...

So many people helped me on the way here. And each of them has a thousand thank-yous from me for it. I truly couldn't have gotten this far without any of them.

With that, I do believe I've rambled on for a little too long, haven't I? At this point, I'm sure anyone who was reading the foreword already either put the book away or just skipped ahead to the good stuff. In any case, I do have more writing to do, a statement I fear (and hope) will be true for the rest of my life. So with the consideration of how diverse my other ideas are, if this book isn't your cup of tea, I hope to someday write one that might be. One chapter at a time, though.

P.S. If you don't like Alanitora, don't worry, I often don't either. The amount of times I've yelled at her is insane, to say the least.

Enjoy!

-Tarin Santos

Map of Mordenla

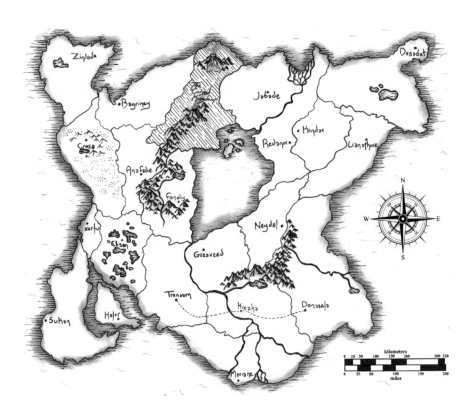

1

The Mother

His eyes were glossed against the fire of the torch, golden flecks of flame among a dull gray. Alanitora didn't think he would have the audacity to look upon her face—not after denying her entry to a place she had every right to be in. His excuse of after-hours be damned.

She pressed her eyes shut to gain composure, and then shot them back open, meeting his gaze with hers. A jolt of fear shot up his spine, and the castle guard looked away in embarrassment. A small clatter of metal followed, but the princess had no desire to waste her attention on such little things. Quite frankly, she could have done far worse to the man, but the tiresome day had numbed her need for satisfaction.

Alanitora waited for the rusted creaking of the large oak doors opening, revealing the misty night sky. She stepped down off of the rug, listening to the echo of her heels on the cobblestone. The outer courtyard was empty. No dogs ran about, nor were peddlers holding up exquisite jewels, waiting for nobles to gain interest. She preferred it this way. Without the bustling crowds of the high class, she didn't have to be the definition of perfect and poised. She didn't have to straighten her back and step in accordance with those around her. To the princess of Trenvern, accepting obeisances every few moments from lords and ladies was tiresome. Etiquette constricted her higher abilities—her abilities to fight.

In battle, there was freedom. The dancing of blades. The anticipation of one's opponent. The sweat and blood. The rest of the world faded away when there was a weapon in her hands. For others, the objective might simply be to inflict pain, but for her, pride came with her opponent's realization that he was no match for an experienced warrior such as herself.

"Good evening, your excellence." Alanitora bolted away from her thoughts towards the voice. A commander was passing by with a soft smile. He likely had just finished the security rounds for the night. She didn't know his name, but based upon his medallion, the man must have been a favorite of her father's court.

"Good evening." She forced a small curve of her lips and nodded. Not wishing to converse any longer, the princess quickened her step towards the grand oak tree that rested against the castle walls.

When she was out of sight, Alanitora gathered her skirts in one hand and reached for a branch a few feet above her head. She pulled herself up with one arm, planting her feet against the trunk. With no time to waste, Alanitora released the hem of her skirts, searching through the folds to find what she needed to get to the top. The dagger held a few uncleaned spots of blood from a previous encounter with an escaped prisoner the other week. She stabbed it into the tree, not worried that it would dull the blade. There were plenty more where it came from.

Using the protruding hilt as a boost, Alanitora was able to reach the cluster of branches raised far above the ground.

She wasn't supposed to be climbing trees, stargazing, or walking unaccompanied. She should have been inside, having an evening bath, or eating the meal that she had skipped earlier. People wanted her to be a princess of composure. One who blushes at a compliment, or dreams of attending the upcoming cotillion. But Alanitora didn't care about any dance, nor did she care for the compliments made only on the basis of her status. Her head was filled with weapons and battle tactics, not mannerisms and delicate social graces.

It wasn't as though anyone was around to tell her what she *should* be doing, and even so, only someone who knew absolutely nothing would dare do such. The exception to this, of course, being her parents. Alanitora might be lucky that her mother enabled her to practice the art of war, but her father? When he wasn't ignoring her completely, he was scolding her for things any other had the freedom to do. Her father was clueless when it came to her abilities, hypocritical too.

She pushed aside such pessimistic thoughts, reaching for the last branch to breach into the clear sky. Alanitora didn't understand why so many people despised the night. She'd rather be awake and lively in these times than any other. Darkness, they'd say, is a terrifying thing. That within the folds of trees, and the obstruction of moonlight, there resided an ominous shadow. But that night, everything was clear. An amethyst sky sparkled with stars the way sunlight might reflect upon a rippling stream. And while the moon was on the other side of the castle, it was clear its shine touched the atmosphere of her surroundings.

This was peace. These moments in time were rare for her, moments where she could think, she could ponder. Alanitora's mother claimed that other people, whether royalty or not, didn't think as the princess did. Not with the same constantly running analytical mind. A mind that, though brilliant in observation, could not rest. Even when the situation called for her heart instead.

Her mother also claimed it to be a gift, but that didn't explain why or how. Some said it was because she was mature, others that she was smart. But more often, people said it was different—and not necessarily good. Snide comments and whispers followed her, telling her that people thought her cold and calculating. The words intelligent and composed would be her preference, but she paid no mind. Their unwillingness to speak with her was a claimed sign of Alanitora's superiority, and perhaps it was so. It was to the point where she couldn't recall a time where walking into a room had not elicited comments behind her back.

A rustle sounded in the windless night, something impossible for her to ignore. Alanitora peered through the thick canopy, scanning the top of the walls for a possible intruder. A flicker of amber light flashed across Alanitora's eyes from below, revealing a figure in a cloak walking towards the archer tower next to the tree.

Without hesitation, Alanitora grasped a small throwing knife from her ankle and swung down as silent as an owl in flight. She lunged at the suspicious person, attacking from behind in hopes of catching their cloak. There was a shriek of metal and at the next moment, Alanitora saw that they had turned and blocked her blow with a blade of their own. Hair wisped in front of her heaving breath as the princess forced down her beating heart.

"Oh, it's you." Her melodious honey voice rang deep in Alanitora's ears. "My goodness my love, you mustn't give one a scare like that."

"Mother?" Alanitora lowered her weapon, relaxing her shoulders.

"I will have to say that was an excellent downward stroke." The woman's warm pink lips curved into a satisfied smile as she took off the hood of her cloak.

Queen Elena's eyes were confident, with dark circles underneath. Her long brown hair was pulled back into a braid, golden threads intertwined among the strands. Her arms opened wide, welcoming Alanitora into them.

The embrace was one of a warm hearth. It wasn't just the smell of lavender that brought her there, it was the fondness from the only person she had ever looked up to. The bond between a mother and her child was strong, but the connection she and Queen Elena shared was more than that: it was a sense of belonging.

Alanitora stepped back. "What are you doing out so late? Shouldn't you be in the castle going through finance, or whatever else Father has you do nowadays?"

She chuckled, so bright that it gave Alanitora's heart a flutter of elation. "I'm off to make rounds in the village. King Ronoleaus needs input from the townsfolk regarding the food supply for the upcoming winter." Something strange hung on the edge of the queen's words.

Their eyes met for only a few seconds before Elena darted hers away. That alone told Alanitora something was being hidden from her. She didn't know why she could read people's emotions through their eyes, but the only person it didn't work on was her mother. Yet there were rare times when her mother's nervousness allowed Alanitora to see past the complexity of her irises. Like now.

"Are you sure that's all? You seem… unsettled."

"Don't be silly." Elena shook her head. "You know better than anyone else that when your father requests for you to do something, you can't help but be nervous. I'm not afraid to admit that's how I feel at the moment."

"I could always come with you—"

"No no, you don't worry about that." Elena pulled her into another tight hug. "You need to stay here, safe and strong."

Alanitora trusted her mother, but a foreboding feeling lingered in the air still. Before she could ask any more questions, her mother had kissed her on the cheek and turned to continue on her way, the torch flickering on the stone wall once again.

Having pushed the last of her evening energy into the potential battle, all of the day's events came tumbling off her shoulders, dragging her feet and eyes as though they were attached to a ball and chain. Deciding not to let sleep escape her that night, Princess Alanitora carried herself through the castle, upon the corridors, and into her chambers. Her feet were sore from the heels as much as her back was to the tight bodice that bound her waist. She kicked off her shoes and sat in a chair to unbind herself from the constricting dress, but her eyes wouldn't follow the command of her mind as they drifted downwards into sleep.

The morning sun had shifted upon her, and while it enshrouded her with warmth, the blinding light was too intense for her shut eyes. Alanitora shifted her position to find that she was still within the ostentatious chair, its blunt engravings pressing into her skull. She frowned and sat up, craning her neck to relieve the tension.

After allowing the rest of her body to wake up, the princess turned her head back towards the sunlight, gazing past it yearningly at the bed she had deprived herself of. Various colored cloths lay upon it.

"Korena, Gwendolyn!" Alanitora called out.

A series of rushed footsteps could be heard just before her bedroom door opened for two young girls. A surge of their energy pulsated towards Alanitora like a tidal wave. She sighed and gestured toward the bed.

"What are these?" the princess asked, standing up.

"New shipment from Elisan," Korena chatted, her straight blonde hair bouncing with each vowel.

Alanitora didn't have the patience for Korena's bubbling energy. She had no idea how Gwendolyn was able to stand it for as long as she did.

The two were inseparable, and not just because it was their duty to keep each other and the princess company. The three of them were brought together a little over five years ago when Alanitora turned twelve. Neither were fit with the job of a maid beforehand, but their background didn't matter, as they were appointed more so as companions to the princess. The serving duties made sure to provide pecuniary compensation to their families. Alanitora hadn't been the one to choose them but was satisfied with their company nonetheless.

Previous occurrences where they talked about their pasts had revealed that Gwendolyn's family used the money to help her twelve-year-old invalid brother, whereas Korena's father used it for his own purposes. Apparently, serving at the castle was the only way her mother could think of to keep Korena away from the drunkard.

"Your Highness?" Gwendolyn's voice broke her from her thoughts. She looked up and into her soft brown eyes.

"Yes?"

"Which would you like to wear today?"

She looked down at the garments of various colors. Their embroidery was beyond exquisite, yet the contrast in hues was slightly unnerving. Unfortunately, such brightness was conventional to their origin, an origin that also made them the flawless fit for her figure. Such dresses were sourced from the kingdom of Elisan, where her measurements had been taken and perfectly calculated years after her singular trip there. The memory of this trip stayed fresh in her mind, perhaps because it was the only time she had ever left Trenvern's borders. She could vividly recollect the landscape of lakes through the carriage window as they rode into the walls of the kingdom's capital. Then instantly, as though snapping from one dream to another, there were hanging tapestries and textiles of color at every turn. It had been such a shock for the young Alanitora to see such unfamiliar wonders.

"None of them," the princess replied, coming back to her present reality. "Save them for next spring."

A smirk crawled across Gwendolyn's face. "Told you," she said, looking over at Korena.

With a sigh, Korena pulled a few coins from her girdle and dropped them in Gwendolyn's hand.

"Help me get dressed, something less… bright."

Without hesitation, the ladies-in-waiting began to prepare her for a proper fitting, replacing her partially removed undergarments. The dress they chose was a deep maroon laced with gold accents. The skirt was neither large nor constricting and waist-above formed perfectly around her curves, only loose past the elbows, which faded out into long bell sleeves. The material was a thick velvet, meant to hold warmth without excessive layers underneath.

"What are your plans for today, Your Highness?" Korena asked, pinning up the hem of her skirt to keep it from dragging across the floor.

"I don't have any specific plans, although I would like to find my mother. She was acting unusual last night, and I'd like to discuss some other topics with her. Do either of you know where she might be?"

Gwendolyn frowned, shifting her gaze to the sky. "I certainly couldn't tell you about her whereabouts, but perhaps we should take a small walk and visit the courtyard performers. It seems a wonderful day has been bestowed upon us. It might be the last of the year."

"Or we could get different items from the kitchen and have a tasting party!"

7

Alanitora subsided her companion's suggestions. "I'd rather be in the presence of Queen Elena." she sighed, placing herself back in the ornate chair. "I'll call for you if I need to, you can leave if you'd like. Once I gather up my things I'll head out of my chambers so you may clean," she ordered, watching as the ladies turned on their heels and walked out of her bedroom.

Some of the advising lords and ladies she came across said she treated her ladies-in-waiting too harshly. It wasn't that she didn't care about them—she did. However, it wasn't her role to do so. To Alanitora, it felt futile to concern herself with individual people's well-being. When one opens an emotional connection, they allow themselves to be taken advantage of. She couldn't give a single excuse for someone to prod at her vulnerabilities, not when so many were eager to spill the blood of the crown, or at least taint it.

Alanitora had learned that the hard way. Enough people had tried to get close to her to win her favor or alter her fate. Why should she put her trust in anyone, if only to find herself a victim of another deception? And while she was certain of her ladies' loyalties, there was no telling what information others would be able to pull from them if she allowed them to get any closer to her. It simply wasn't in her best interest to allow a *genuine* connection.

After cleaning and equipping her weapons, Alanitora exited her room to reveal the long hallway of her chambers. There were many rooms, some housed servants specifically assigned to her, others were designated with activities to help her pass the time. In past generations, her tower of residence had housed many offspring of the crown, but her mother and father had only ever had her.

It always baffled her why this was the case. With only one heir to the throne, it was easier to apprehend Trenvern. In addition, not a single girl had ever ruled the kingdom. Could she be the first to do so? And if not, why hadn't her parents had at least one more child?

"Princess." It was an unfamiliar voice that snapped Alanitora into her abnormal surroundings.

Her eyes scanned the hall, which was unusually bare. It was routine for six guards to be posted, but only two stood before her now. She could have cast aside this irregularity if only one had not spoken. Guards and soldiers had no place to speak with her unless she addressed them directly.

She looked at the man standing guard outside of her bedroom, a smirk upon his fair-skinned face. His chain mail hood wasn't upon his head, leaving his dark hair tousled in a mess. He was young: not much older than Alanitora herself.

"Where are the others?" she asked.

"Erm." Her head swiveled towards the other guard, who stumbled over his words with a quivering lip. "They, uh… King Ronoleaus called for a meeting, a dispatch of soldiers is currently being arranged." He paused but continued after her stare suggested his information was not sufficient. "Rumors have spread that the kingdom of Fonolis is planning on attacking the capital of Trenvern in the coming week. All knights are being posted around the borders, and a fresh batch of squires have completed their training in hopes of supplying enough defense."

"That's us," said the darker-haired one, bowing almost mockingly. "All squires above the age of sixteen arrived this morning." The boy grasped her hand, kissing the back of it. "Say, princess, aren't you only a year older than that?" His face contorted into a perverse smile as he gripped her wrist tighter.

Alanitora raised her chin, examining his sickening boldness. "Remove your hand from me."

The boy jerked her towards him, placing his other hand on her waist. She watched his eyes brighten, a rush of excitement buzzing in them. The princess then looked over at the other guard, but she knew he would be too timid to intervene. Useless. That's what they were. Useless and ignorant. She looked back at her apprehender.

"Oh, don't give me that daring look, princess. We've heard the rumors. Although, now that I see you in the flesh, you seem much more… fragile than they say."

"I'll give you one chance to unhand me or—"

"Or what?" He cackled, bringing his face inches from hers. "As I'm sure you've noticed, it's just us." The hiss of his tongue lingered with his last words.

Her lips curved into a curt smile, and she watched as his eyes glossed over with bravado as he opened his mouth to speak again.

Alanitora rammed her head forward, slamming her forehead into his nose. It may not have been the best call, as she could feel the pounding rise in her temples, but it was enough to shock him. She clenched her nails in the skin of his forearm, forcing him to loosen his grip. In a swift movement, the princess twisted his arm until pain pulsed in his shoulder. Then, she grasped the blade hidden at her waist and slashed at the back of his arm. The cut ran deep and long, though not enough to cause severe blood loss.

The boy yelped in pain, backing away to grab his bleeding nose. "You little—"

Alanitora punched him in the stomach with enough force to knock the wind out of him, rendering him speechless. After pulling a few stray hairs out of her face and smoothing out her dress, she turned to the other guard, who had remained in the corner.

"What's your name?"

"H-Howard."

"Howard, let your commanding officer know your comrade needs bandages and ointment to dress his wounds."

She walked down the hall, stopping only to wipe her blade on the fabric of the gaping boy's clothing. Perhaps that would teach him that standing by idly in such a confrontation wasn't in his best interest.

"What should I say happened to him?" Howard called after her.

"Whatever you want. You could break whatever ego he has left, or spare him the embarrassment. I don't care."

"What if—"

But the princess had already shut the stairwell door behind her. She nodded at the soldier posted there before gathering her skirts to descend.

"Queen Elena? No, I'm afraid I haven't seen her, Your Highness."

"Very well, thank you."

Alanitora watched as the maid scurried off to her duties. She had been searching the castle for nearly two hours, but there was no sign of her mother anywhere. Was it possible her mother was at the meeting the guard talked about? It didn't seem likely, considering all of the decisions were made solely by her father. Holding a royal title meant several privileges; a say in politics was not one for the princesses and queens of Trenvern. It was one of the reasons she rarely had the chance to leave the capital.

Finding no alternative options, Alanitora entered her mother's residency, which lay a few stories beneath her own. The two shared a staircase, but entry to each other's chambers was not permitted. Keeping all three royals in different locations was a rule put in place by King Ronoleaus as a precautionary step to ensure the safety of the throne.

However, as she approached the door, Alanitora saw that there was no one standing guard. She stepped further towards the doorway with caution, pulling at the engraved iron handle.

"Hello?" she called out.

No response.

Alanitora made her way into the well-lit hallway, confused as to why it was empty. Even if the queen wasn't there, it was routine for there to still be someone guarding the space to ensure no one tampered with her room.

The carpet was much more worn than her own, dulled with dust tucked in the edges. No tapestries or decorations hung from the walls, leaving the stretched room bare. This was odd, as Trenvern had a sumptuous amount of shipments with ornaments of wealth from across the land. It looked almost as if it had been abandoned sometime before. Queen Elena had never been keen on details, but surely her mother wasn't this plain.

Alanitora continued down the hall to her mother's bedchamber. The door opened with a simple press of her hand, revealing a cold room, the only sign of warmth emanating from the bright embers of the fireplace.

So this is where her mother spent the majority of her time.

The room contained various items and stationery trinkets along the surfaces, and yet it remained more simple than that of Alanitora's. Besides the curtains and sheets, there was no colored fabric to bring the room to life. No rug upon the bare floor. The chairs were without embroidered cushions. Even her garments were folded away in a neat pile. If it weren't for the smell of sweet smoke and lavender, she would not have guessed it was her mother's room.

The only thing that remotely resembled the personality of Queen Elena was a small chest at the foot of her mother's bed.

She peered at the chest. It seemed familiar, like something from a distant memory. A memory. That's what it was. Alanitora recalled her mother talking about that very box. She remembered her saying it was the only thing she brought from home.

Home.

She used to ask her mother where her home was, but the only answer Alanitora got was a soft smile and sad eyes looking back at her with... an inexplicable fondness, as though there was a longing deep within her that she could never share.

Without thought, the princess placed her hands on the chest, pressing her fingers along the grooves of its carved wood. It was rough, jagged, and yet somehow soothing. With a careful nudge of the clasp, Alanitora released the binding that held it shut. Her curiosity filled to the brim as she lifted the lid. A folded slip of paper slid from the crack in the opening and glided across the floor, under the bed.

The inside of the chest was even nicer than the outside. The lid held ornate carvings, the walls were lined with a teal velvet, and there were small dividing walls for different kinds of items. Several trinkets lay within—a wreath of golden leaves, a bundle of feathers, a dragonfly pin, a shining thimble—the collection was boundlessly beautiful.

Before she could further examine the jumble of objects, a distant rumble passed through Alanitora's ears. The deep vibrations of the bell tower striking the hour were enough to send a chill through her body.

The hour was eleven in the morning, meaning it was time to eat lunch—despite, of course, it being her first meal of the day. If there was anywhere she would see her mother, it was now. The two of them always ate together, away from everyone else. This was seen as unusual across the land. In most neighboring kingdoms, all lords and ladies of a castle dined together, with royalty at the head table.

Alanitora closed the box, not bothering to collect the slip of paper. She needed to talk to her mother, and now.

The importance of being punctual was something that she glossed over in her etiquette lessons. There were rarely any consequences for her absence, considering her presence was rarely necessary.

"Terribly sorry I am late," Alanitora announced as she stepped into the dining room, but there was no one waiting for her, only a few maids lined up against the wall. It had only taken her fifteen minutes to reach the private dining hall, surely Queen Elena would have waited. "The queen, is she here?"

A look was exchanged between the maids, and one opened her mouth to say, "No, Your Highness."

"Was she here?"

"… No, Your Highness."

A guttural sound of frustration escaped Alanitora's throat as she turned on her heel to leave.

She was out of breath, out of time, and out of patience. The queen was nowhere to be found, and everyone had their noses too deep in their work to know where she could be.

There was only one person left that might know where she was: Alanitora's father.

2

An Old Friend

Howard had said King Ronoleaus was hosting a meeting among the soldiers for dispatch; therefore, he must be in the Great Hall. She couldn't help but feel like the castle was simply a dream as she made her way toward the Great Hall. Could the minimal presence of guards have made that much of a difference? The solemn silence was thick in the air around her, and it felt almost tangible. Her heels clicked on the cobblestone without the satisfaction of power. Everything felt... there, but not truly present. Not truly rooted in reality.

Hollow. Hollow was the word for it, Alanitora decided as she cut across the second courtyard towards the Keep. She knew the Great Hall was between there and the Throne Room. The three of them: a cluster of sections cut off from her reach—too dangerous, they would declare. Between volatile prisoners and explicit discussions of war, she was always strongly advised to stay away from the political discourse of the castle.

Omitting the sounds of moans and growls that escaped through cracks in the foundation of the Keep, Alanitora continued her way down the dark corridor, the thick carpet silencing her stride. The princess approached the grand oak doors that blocked her from the meeting inside. There were no guards or soldiers on the outside, most likely so that all could be addressed.

"Idiotic," she spat under her breath. If there were minimal guards around the castle, that meant they were susceptible to an ambush. Was her father that foolish? Alanitora made note of this as a precaution to her eventual reign.

She pressed her hand on the door, pushing its heaving mass inwards to unleash the myriad sounds of chatter. She could almost feel a waft of bravado washing over her. Tables lined the room from front to back, all seating over two dozen men hacking away at their food. Others were standing around them, blocking any view of the front, where her parents might be. Large green curtains hung drawn from the ceiling, exposing tall mosaic windows, an owl with its wings spread designed on each of them. In addition to the natural light from outside, the hall was riddled with torches, providing boundless—and slightly stifling—warmth.

Alanitora couldn't help but wonder what this place looked like abandoned, being that she had only ever seen it when an important event was hosted that required her attendance. Nevertheless, she focused her mind back to the issue at hand.

The princess slammed the door behind her, causing a few loud cackles to reduce to hushed tones. Heads turned toward her, and a nearby guard spun around to look at Alanitora and spoke in a panicked tone.

"Your Highness! You shouldn't be here." The man stepped in front of Alanitora, unsure how else to stop her.

She looked up at him. He was at least a head taller than her, and most likely weighed twice her size. A fight without additional variables would result in her loss, but she was lucky enough that the man wouldn't do anything about the matter. Alanitora looked at his irises, the green in them wouldn't be too bad to look at if he didn't have so much pride in them. A pride that could easily be broken.

Move. The words didn't come out of her mouth, but her intention was clear just by the way her threatening gaze lingered.

The man's dismissal seemed to silence more people, as more eyes focused on the princess.

After a moment to soak in the bewilderment surrounding her, Alanitora stepped forward. Her heels echoed louder than they ever had before, regaining the power they had lost in empty halls. She kept striding, even when another man stood dazed in the middle of her path. She let her shoulder push his arm aside as if she was a specter walking through walls. Where she stepped, silence followed in a wave of unsettled consternation.

It was then that she heard his voice, quiet but forceful, like a viper's bite. "What is the meaning of this?!"

The rest moved out of the way, realizing they were mere onlookers in this encounter.

She raised her head to the center of the head table, where her father sat nobly.

"Alanitora Nayana Leland of Trenvern! What are you do—"

"Where is she?"

King Ronoleaus' eyes grew dark, the circles underneath holding storm clouds of rage. "What?" he spat the word out forcefully.

"Mother." The princess swallowed the lump that had formed in her throat. She needed to keep herself collected if she planned to confront her father. It had always been difficult. "Where is she?"

The king stood from his chair, letting it scrape the floor behind him. His knuckles whitened as he pressed his fingers into the wood. His face turned red, twitching violently. "You dare enter this room without permission?" The words shot at her like arrows, plunging themselves into her confidence. "You dare interrupt a meeting of importance to ask a childish question?!" His voice crackled with aggravation, bouncing off the walls with the force of a hundred lightning bolts.

She swallowed. A part of her had anticipated this from the moment she decided on the idea, but she hadn't expected it to go further than her imagination. Alanitora took a breath, allowing the tense feeling to release slightly. "I would like to know," she said.

Ronoleaus banged his fist on the table, causing her entire body to jolt. "Somebody take the princess back to her chambers and keep her there until I say otherwise."

The silence was held for what felt like forever as guards and soldiers looked at one another with uncertainty. One of the helmeted men positioned at the sidewall stepped forward in mute agreement. Why he was in full armor, she didn't know. What exactly was her father planning in here that required armored soldiers?

The king sat back down in his chair, staring at Alanitora as the soldier grasped her forearm, turning her towards the door. She wished she would have resisted, but the princess was treading on thin ice with her father, something she usually avoided in fear of the consequences.

She kept her mouth closed until they left the room, the door shutting behind them. Alanitora yanked her arm away from the stranger, walking ahead of him towards the tower. She wasn't a child anymore. There was no need to have supervision or an escort to her room. Doing her best to ignore him, she entered her chambers, going straight to her room after passing through the empty hall.

Alanitora sighed, throwing the dagger from her sleeve into the bedpost. "You can leave now," she said to the soldier, turning to face him.

"I see you haven't changed." His voice was muffled by the helmet, a metallic echo following.

"Excuse me?" Alanitora spat.

"Still as stubborn and demanding as always." His confidence and informality took her by surprise. She stared at him in silence. "Nitora, it's me," the man said, taking off his helmet.

Her eyes were immediately drawn to his fiery hair, sticking out in spikes like pine needles. His face was riddled with freckles. Blue eyes stared into hers with immense excitement. Alanitora looked away as a wave of memories crashed into her. Him, after all these years. "Don't call me that."

"But Nitora," he said, grasping her hand in his. "It's me, Owen." His smile was sickeningly jubilant.

She relaxed her face, gaining her composure once again. "Yes, I can see that. Now remove your hand before I cut it off."

So it was him. The boy she grew up with, who she trusted more than anyone for ten years, who she even shared a birthday with… Only to become the boy who abandoned her. And here he was, grasping at her wrist as if she was a lifeline.

After a moment of deafening silence, Owen's grip faded. The smile on his face was drawn back. "You... don't remember."

Alanitora sighed in annoyance. What a dunce. "Are you suggesting I don't remember the simple boy that followed me around like a dog for years?"

Owen moved to wrap his arms around her "I'm so glad—"

"What are you doing?" She sneered, pushing his torso away from hers.

"I thought—"

"You didn't think. As usual." She backed away from him, a frown upon her face. "What were you expecting? That I'd welcome you in, after a half a dozen years?"

Owen and Alanitora were born on the same summer afternoon, only hours apart. His mother was a lady-in-waiting for her mother, allowing for the two of them to grow up together as best friends. Throughout much of her childhood, Alanitora was focused on becoming the strongest heir in the history of Trenvern, and Owen had supported her the whole way: assisting her in pursuits of knowledge as well as mischief. For years they were inseparable, often found sparring in the courtyard, or leaving hidden messages in the gallery. She was different then—happy, carefree. She didn't have to worry about the constant target on her back or the desires of everyone around her.

At ten years of age, the two were separated to pursue their natural duties. While Alanitora further studied to become a legitimate member of royalty, Owen was sent to the kitchen under an apprenticeship to become a servant of royalty. Though there were various opportunities for them to reunite, she hadn't seen him since. Alanitora assumed he'd been promoted to a key position of personnel or discharged to another region.

To see him now, standing in front of her, knowing that he'd had the ability to contact her the entire time, made her stomach churn in vexation. She looked back at his face, slightly contorted with pain. His eyes reached out to her like a beggar's, asking, pleading for something to attach to.

"You left me." There wasn't much else she could say.

"I didn't."

Lies. "You did." Alanitora bit her lip in hesitation, trying to hold back a fervent outburst. "You were the one who said nothing could tear us apart. You were the one who said you'd do everything to keep seeing me, that we would find a way. Broken promises. All of it!" Her voice was beginning to quiver. She swallowed the lump at the back of her throat.

"I couldn't." His words came out fragile.

"You could've tried!" she shouted. "You know—knew—that I very well couldn't. So what? You sat around idly, ignoring my existence as though I were an old figment of your imagination? Years I waited for any sign of you. Years. Not once did your face appear among the array of servants bringing food from the kitchens. Not once was there a note at my door, or word passed through others. There were a million ways you could have found means of communication. Was I that insignificant to you, that you took the first opportunity you could to abandon me?" Her mouth shut close as water sprang to her eyes. Alanitora sighed, trying to compose herself. Any more and everything would come surging out.

It was funny. She'd spent years mentally reviewing what she would say to him if they ever came face to face. At first, this message was one of happiness, but time had turned it bitter, and now she hadn't a clue what to say at all.

A stillness filled the room as Owen stared at her, some form of pity in his eyes. Perhaps he wasn't lying.

"Alanitora. I'm sorry. I tried to see you, I did. But…"

"But what."

He drew in a breath, averting his eyes from hers. "Just as planned, I was assigned to the kitchens. But something happened. After only a month of being there, I found out that one of the assistant cooks was poisoning you and your mother's food. At first, it was small, just a drop here or there, and I figured it was just a form of seasoning. Over time, he began putting more in when no one was looking. I wasn't positive, but after examining the particular ingredients myself, I began to doubt his intentions."

Alanitora remembered being sick for some time after their separation, but she had just assumed it to be because of the health conditions of their environment, not the malcontent of any particular person.

"Not only did I collect the evidence, but I confronted him myself." Owen pulled down the fabric around his neck, revealing a long wrinkled scar on his collarbone. "My bravery was rewarded with a proposal: A chance for me to become a squire."

She looked him up and down. So that explained the attire and the reason for his prolonged absence. He must have been sent off to the training camps for the past seven years. Trenvern squires were usually employed at a much younger age to ensure their allegiance. How could he have risen the ranks so quickly, though? She assumed his reappearance coincided with what the feeble Howard and his friend said earlier about soldier dispatches.

The look on her face must have suggested that she figured as much, for Owen continued after a moment. "Don't you see?! Now I can truly protect you! Everything we had always dreamt of can come true. That's what kept me going all those years. Six years and five months I've waited for you." His eyes were hopeful again. It seemed his feelings fluctuated like the year's harvest.

"I don't need you to protect me, Owen. I never did, and never will," Alanitora raised her chin to look down on him like she used to, but alas, he had grown much since their last encounter. The princess forced the feelings that had arisen in her back down, gripping her stability by thinking of anything else. Her emotions were to get the best of her no more. After a few moments, she broke the stare, walking away towards her weapons chest. "When can I leave?"

"The meeting should end an hour after noon. I'm sure King Ronoleaus will send a messenger to summon you after then."

She sighed, lifting the heavy lid to reveal her most valued possessions. "In that case, I'll wait. I assume it's futile to try and make you leave."

His silence affirmed her queries. Owen may constantly think of her as stubborn, but the same thing could be said about his persistence to acquiesce with her.

Alanitora kneeled on the floor to distance herself, reaching her hand into the collection of weapons she had accumulated over the years. Many were either sheathed or wrapped to conceal the sharp blades. The chest itself was big enough to fit Korena, perhaps herself if she tried hard enough to stuff herself within it. Among her tools of combat were a collection of trinkets and valuables near the bottom, some untouched for years. The princess pulled out her set of bronze throwing knives that rested underneath her longbow.

"Is that my toy sword? You said the hunting dogs ate it!" Alanitora looked up at Owen, following his gaze towards the small wooden play-sword that was sticking out on the side.

"No," she retorted.

"Uh, yes it is. My name is on the pommel," Owen protested, crossing his arms.

Alanitora picked it up to examine the edge of the handle. Sure enough, in jagged strokes, the name 'OWEN' was carved into it. "Nevermind that." She tossed it back in and picked up her polishing tools. Ignoring his presence and the emotions that were swirling around her mind would be harder than she thought.

Sitting at the end of her bed, Alanitora unwrapped a cloth that surrounded the knives, revealing dull blades that matched the color of her hair. She had gotten this particular set on her thirteenth birthday, a gift from the southern kingdom of Mariane. She had seen them as impotent for their lack of use in combat, given that they were much weaker than iron, steel, and other alloys. Regardless, the blades were a beautiful texture and color, which meant they were better kept in pristine condition.

Polishing and sharpening her weapons wasn't something Alanitora did often enough. While she excelled at the use of them, her upkeep and care were lacking, which could be seen in the blood left on them. However, when there were times she needed relaxation, or a chance to idly think about something, the menial task allowed a safe escape and excuse to do so.

In this case, the thing she was pondering was in the room with her. Owen Conlan. A part of her had always hoped, always believed he'd come back. For months after their separation, Alanitora thought of him every day, even talked to him as if he could somehow hear her. But time was not kind to her. The person she was, the person he knew, was gone, like a leaf taken away by the river.

She needed to figure out what motivated her to forgive him, and if she *would* for that matter. There was no logical or tactical reason to. His friendship did not grant her any favors, nor was there validation to gain. So why did she feel inclined to? Certainly not just the nostalgia—that had been filled with bitterness. The inability to solve this was like an unreachable itch.

It certainly didn't help her conscience that he tried to strike up a conversation more than once, unable to stay silent. Perhaps to him, the sound of her sharpening and polishing a variety of weapons was unsettling, but she didn't care. He was the one who was insistent to stay in the room, guarding her like a robin guarded its eggs.

When he asked what she was doing, she ignored him, and when he began asking personal questions about the last decade, she turned him down, explaining how she didn't want to hear about his heroic squire duties. After a few more failed attempts, he shut his mouth.

"*Alanitora!*"

The princess shot up from her seat. The sound was faint, but she was sure she had just heard her name.

"*Alanitora!*"

She snapped her head towards Owen, who looked perplexed. "Are you alright, Your Highness?"

"My mother."

"What?"

"My mother. She just called my name." Alanitora stood still for a few more seconds. Her mind couldn't be playing tricks on her. She had just heard her name, *twice*, and it was Queen Elena's voice.

Owen chuckled. "That's impossible, you couldn't have heard the queen calling for you."

"And why is that?" Alanitora asked, placing her hands on her hips.

"Because... the walls are too thick."

"I know what I heard. It sounded like my name!"

"You probably heard, I don't know... 'A lawn of flora'."

She stared at him blankly. "That is utterly ridiculous. Why would anyone say that?"

"Well, would you rather it be 'All yawn in torture'?" The boy smiled.

Alanitora turned away, stifling a burst of laughter and holding her mouth in a tight line to keep from returning a grin.

"*Alanitora!*"

"There it is again!"

"What?!" Owen exclaimed.

She whipped around toward him again. "Oh, I swear if you are pretending you can't hear that I will take this dagger and make sure you don't hear anything ever again!"

Owen raised his arms defensively. "I'm sorry, but you're incorrect. These walls are too dense for you to be able to hear anything."

"Are you sure about that?"

"Yeah, I would know. During our strategic training, I learned about the castle's defense. The walls of this castle, especially your walls, were built and reinforced with the strongest materials to prevent collapse if an enemy attacks with the use of catapults.

"I'm aware. I was taught that too, you dunce. Heir to the throne, remember? Anything you learned in your silly training camps was probably taught to me as well."

Owen crossed his arms, opening his mouth to fuel a rebuttal, but she cut him off. "Look behind me and tell me you don't see a window right there."

When he opened his mouth again to provide a ridiculous response, Alanitora tossed her half-sharpened dagger onto the chair and turned toward the wall between it and the door. She kneeled, pressing her hand against the wall. After a small appliance of force and the dissipation of dust and stone rubble, she pushed the stone into another room. "Here is

23

the space that I used to pass notes to my ladies-in-waiting after hours.

"And this." She stood and walked past Owen to the other side of the room. Alanitora reached up and lodged her fingertips into the cracks of the cobblestone and pulled, dropping the slab to reveal a space between walls. "This is where I keep an extra dagger in case of exigency." The princess reached in and pulled out the plain blade, spinning it between her fingers.

"Now, if you would please allow me to leave, I need to respond to the summonings of my mother."

"I can't do that, Nitora. You need to be patient."

"Don't call me that, and do *not* lecture me about patience! The meeting supposedly ended an hour ago. Do you expect me to keep sitting here like a caged bird? Move."

"No." Owen stepped in front of the door.

Alanitora stepped forward. "Don't make me use this," she said, holding the blade offensively.

"You wouldn't."

"I will. In case you haven't noticed," she huffed, "I have changed beyond your comprehension. You seem to have this idea implanted in your head that I am the same person, the person you want me to be. I am not. If you are so blind that you can't even see that, then I doubt your ability to hold the mantle of something as noble as a knight." Alanitora looked into his eyes. He was shielding his emotions, the sight of it tying a knot in her stomach.

"I can't."

"Why?!" She didn't have the time for this. Her patience was running thin.

"Your mother, the queen, she—"

"She what?" Alanitora pressed the dagger to his skin, her hand shaking from the intensity of her grip.

He sighed, "Queen Elena has been banished from Trenvern."

The world froze at that moment. Alanitora's arms dropped to her sides, her grip loosening enough to allow the blade to clash onto the floor. Her shoulders relaxed, like a puppet with cut strings. Her eyes couldn't help but dart around as she tried to process the impossible truth. The princess swallowed a wave of air and opened her mouth to say something, anything. "How— why?"

"I don't know," Owen said, meeting her eyes again. His stare was like a warm blanket, there to comfort her sorrows. She pushed it away, a frown setting deeper into her features.

Alanitora took in a sharp breath, closed her eyes, and exhaled, regaining her composure once more.

"Let me through, I need to speak to the king."

The knight stood for a moment, a collection of somber feelings around them. He stepped aside, yielding to a maiden who would soon find herself in the hardest confrontation one could imagine.

3

The Duel

Alanitora pushed past Owen, swinging the door open out of her way.

"She emerges!" a familiar voice drew her eyes up towards the ignorant boy from earlier, this time with bandages wrapped around his arms. "Oh, and with an armored soldier. What did the two of you do in there? Anything interesting?"

"Uldin!" Owen barked from behind her.

"Owen, my man!" Uldin chuckled, turning his attention back towards her. "Wow princess, you really could have done better than this pig... unless farm scum is what you're into."

Owen stepped forward. Alanitora gazed down at his clenched fists, his white knuckles. She placed a gentle hand on his arm as a warning and continued walking. The princess reached for the door handle, giving it a quick pull.

"Oh, that won't work," Uldin chirped.

Releasing her grip, she turned around. "And why is that?"

"Howard!" Uldin leaned against the wall, an amused look on his face.

A few seconds later, a feeble knight came running out of the storage room, nearly tripping as he tried to slow his momentum. "Yes?" He took a moment to examine the room, his eyes laying in Alanitora's direction. "Oh, they locked it."

"What?" Owen asked.

"Yeah, they said you needed to stay here."

"Since when is there a lock on the door?!"

"Oh, I don't know Owen, how about sometime in the past *seven* years?" Alanitora rolled her eyes at her childhood friend and looked back to Howard. "Give me the keys, I have urgent business to discuss with the king."

The look on his face suggested he didn't have them. She turned towards Uldin. "I don't have them." He raised his hands defensively. "Since we are stuck here, if Owen can... get to know you, surely I can too. Hey, maybe your ladies-in-waiting can join."

Alanitora flinched at the mention of Korena and Gwendolyn, who were resting in an adjacent room. She opened her mouth to belittle his pride but was taken aback as Owen swung his right fist across Uldin's face.

"Seriously?!" hissed Alanitora. She shoved Owen away from the boy, causing him to release his grip.

"He was disrespecting you!"

"So? What makes you think it's your role to fight my battles?! I certainly do not need anyone to defend my pride."

"As a knight of Trenvern, I am sworn to protect members of the royal family!" Owen retorted, shaking out the pain in his wrist.

"You aren't a knight," Uldin intervened. "You haven't even been accoladed. I'm sure the princess would love to—"

"Shut up!" Owen and Alanitora snapped in unison, a small smile beginning forming on Owen's face as they did.

"I don't have time for this Owen," Alanitora sighed, stepping back to collect her patience. "You two," She signaled to the soldiers. "Figure out a way to get me out of here, I don't care if you have to break down the door. I'll be in my bed chamber."

Alanitora relaxed her shoulders as she walked past the three boys.

"Nit—" Owen paused to correct himself. "Your Highness, I think I know a way out... The old maid's quarters. It used to have a secret passage to the Throne Room."

"Show me," she said, turning around, throwing all doubts aside as desperation set in.

The old maids' quarters were untouched for years. It had been abandoned as soon as Ronoleaus assumed the throne, and continued to be even when Alanitora was born. There was no need for two sets of maids' quarters for one royal, so they closed off the area, allowing for rats and spiders to claim it as their home.

Alanitora had heard rumors from her nurses that there was a young maid who took her own life in the room during King Ronoleaus' upbringing, though she never ascertained further details or if it was true. Regardless, the young princess avoided it like the plague. The idea had quite frightened her as a child.

With some effort, Owen got the door open, revealing the dark interior. The light of the hallway illuminated a small area, but otherwise, the walls were engulfed by darkness. Alanitora took a step forward, but froze in the doorway, staring into the emptiness.

"You scared?" Owen whispered into her ear, leaning downwards. He was aware of this past fear.

"No."

"I'd venture to guess you're still jumpy about it." Owen prodded her in the ribs with his finger, causing her mouth to squirm into a grin.

Suddenly, a pang of similar memories rushed through her mind, and her smile faded. Things had changed. Alanitora cleared her throat and stepped through the room.

Cold, damp air surrounded her instantly, the presence of mold prickling at her skin. Her eyes took a few moments to adjust, a small amount of light seeping from neighboring rooms through the cracks of cobblestone. The room was empty, save for a few items: A small, crooked, dust-covered rug. A knocked-over chair with a missing leg. Small shards of shattered glass spread throughout the room. And lastly, the remaining pieces of a broken broom.

"Supposedly, your great grandmother had a tunnel made from some-where in here to the Throne Room during her first pregnancy to ensure access to her maids if she went into labor on court duty," Owen informed, stepping behind her.

Alanitora drew in a deep breath, tilting her head. "Well then, let's find it." The two of them took separate sides of the room to start their search.

"Is that it right there?" Alanitora did not have to turn around to know that Uldin was standing in the doorway.

"Out!" Owen barked. She turned to face the foolish boy. Perhaps the eeriness of the room contributed, but she could have sworn she saw a glint of true fear in his eye before he scurried back down the hall to join Howard.

"I know my great grandmother was a very clever woman. I think I have a puzzle box that she gave to my father."

"Okay... so do you think she might have made it some kind of puzzle?"

"I wouldn't put it past her. Check each of the stones for a possible trigger, if not, there will be something between the cracks."

"Well if she was pregnant, I would hope she didn't make it a *hard* puzzle."

Alanitora examined each stone with her fingers, digging her nails into the crevices, looking for any sort of vertical crack or a loose stone, but all she received were cobwebs, mold, and a wave of frustration

She had just finished the right wall when Owen's shoulder bumped into hers. The princess couldn't see his facial features, but she knew without a doubt that he was wearing an apologetic look. "Have you checked the floor?"

Owen sighed and nodded, leaning his back against his wall in defeat. "Two walls and a floor, and you're still attached to one."

She rolled her eyes. "I happen to check and investigate with a thorough procedure."

Owen stayed silent for a moment, a silence that suggested he had thought of a good idea.

"What?"

"How about the ceiling?"

So maybe his idea wasn't so good. "Don't be daft." Alanitora looked up regardless, straightening her back when she saw the darker rectangular area near the center of the room. She walked over to it, feeling his eyes on her. "Owen, come here, I need to use your shoulders."

He nodded, kicking himself off the wall and rushing over to assist her. Owen bent down, propping his hands in front of her feet for a boost.

Alanitora disregarded them and pulled herself up to his shoulders instead. Planting her feet near his collar bones, she reached up, digging her fingernails into the outline of the shape. She then smoothed her palm along the cool metal of the trapdoor, feeling for a handle of some sort. Her fingers brushed over an engraving that at first touch resembled a mix between the letters X and T.

"Careful, Your Highness, I can only hold you for so long." Owen wobbled underneath her weight, clutching her ankles tightly to provide her the best stability.

She found the rusted latch just in time for Owen's falter. Alanitora gripped it with both hands, pulling herself off of Owen. With a quick swoosh, she swung the door open, dropping herself inches from the wall opposite of their entry.

Alanitora patted down her skirts and turned around to see the silhouette of Owen, standing motionless with fluffs and dust sprinkled upon his head. Gray flecks rested upon his freckled cheeks, falling like snowflakes to the floor below. She held back a chuckle and walked back towards him.

"Go get a torch while I figure out how to get up there," she demanded, peering into empty space.

Upon the emptiness, she saw a small piece of rope hanging from the edge. With Owen away, Alanitora had limited height to reach it. She frowned. This would take some effort.

Withdrawing a dagger from her left waist, the princess positioned herself opposite from the rope. She tossed the blade upwards in hopes of it catching a part of it but stepped away when it clanked against the ceiling stone and fell back to the floor. On her third attempt, she managed to hit the coil, resulting in a slight drop, albeit the loss of her weapon to the darkness above.

It was upon Owen's return that she was able to pull down the rope with a strip of her undergarments attached to another dagger. A ladder hung down from the opening, swinging slightly in response.

"What took you so long?"

"I was removing the *copious* amount of dust from my hair and garments," Owen said, extending the torch out to her.

"Turn around."

"...What? Why?"

"Just do it!" He obeyed. Alanitora stood on her toes and squinted at his scalp. "There," she said, sweeping the remaining particles off of him. "You can turn back now."

He snapped his head back towards her in confusion.

"What?" she glowered, you looked far too unkempt with all that dust in your hair.

Owen blinked in surprise at her comment, before shaking his head and turning back to the rope ladder. "Why would a pregnant woman make such an arduous path?"

Alanitora shrugged, testing the strength of the rope with her weight. Another interesting question was how the architecture supported such a system. How could one create a route to the Throne Room through the ceilings? Especially so long after the castle was constructed. The Throne Room was a far distance across the castle and below their current point. Regardless of such doubt, curiosity piqued her interest further as she climbed the ladder upwards

She looked down at Owen and signaled for him to hand her the torch. Once in her hand, she heaved herself into the hole and began pulling the ladder back up.

"Wait! What are you doing? I'm coming as well!"

"You aren't."

"Your Highness, it's dangerous!" Owen's face resembled that of an abandoned puppy.

Alanitora held back a sigh and leaned towards him. "You are staying here. I don't trust your good friend Uldin with two sleeping ladies, and Howard is too feeble to defend them. I need you to watch over them.

"But—"

31

She shut the metal door inwards.

Looking around the area, grabbing her lost dagger when she spotted it. The princess then gathered her skirts and began to crawl, holding the torch out uncomfortably to see the direction she wished to head. It was cold and wet, only made worse by the accumulation of spiders and their homes. Alanitora really hoped the whole path wasn't this cramped.

Thankfully, it wasn't. After a few long minutes of making her way through the crawl space, the floor began to descend at a downward slope, with the ceiling staying level to where it previously was. A little after that, it was tall enough for her to stand; the ceiling started to run parallel to the slanted path.

Even in her layers, she felt cold. The fire did its work in warming her face, yet was too uncontrolled to hold it near her garments. She could feel her toes begin to dampen within her shoes, which slowly numbed them to her surroundings, each footfall less sure than the last.

After what felt like a quarter of an hour walking downhill with twists and turns every once in and awhile, Alanitora reached a fork in the path, with a faint oak sign in the middle. She hadn't been keeping track of what direction she was turned to, and it looked as though the sign may have directions. She leaned closer to it, wiping the dirt and grime off to read the scrawled writing upon it. Was this her great-grandmother's handwriting? It was terrible. A symbol lay in the bottom corner, one she recognized to match the engraving on the trap door. A wide 'X' with a vertical line descending from the crossing point. She tried her best to decipher the writing, but eventually gave up and went with her gut.

"Right it is."

Her instincts proved correct when Alanitora caught a glimpse of light up ahead. It was white and wavered on the floor like a ribbon. Once the tips of it touched her slippers, it was clear that the light was from behind some sort of curtain.

Alanitora rested her hand on the heavy, velvet fabric, carefully pulling it aside. Bright light flooded into the hallway, outshining the torch she was holding. The back of her parents' thrones faced her, their extreme height casting shadows upon the ground in front of the curtain. She rested the torch on the ground, careful not to let it touch any of the drapes. The flame would die out with time.

"Of course, I'm going to tell her!" Her father often had an irritated ring in his voice, but this time, he sounded furious. It made her skin tingle. "I just have to wait for the right moment."

She stepped out from the evergreen-colored curtain to observe the area. Her father was not visible from where he sat. A lone chamberlain stood in the middle of the room, looking up at the king. She could have sworn his hands were trembling in fear, but if they had, they stopped when his eyes drifted up to her. The young man bowed.

"What are you...?" Ronoleaus stood up and followed the chamberlain's gaze. When he saw her standing there, the King's emotions seemed to move from consternation to anger in a matter of seconds. "Alanitora! How did you get in—"

"Where is she?"

"Excuse me?"

"Where. Is. She." Alanitora slowed her words, making sure her father did not squirm away this time. He'd evaded her once, not again.

He sighed, turning back towards the front. "Chamberlain, leave us."

The man scurried away with a small squeak of acknowledgment, shutting the grand doors behind him. Echos clapped across the room, leaving the two of them in deadly silence. Despite the high windows casting an afternoon light into the green-carpeted room, the entire area seemed to darken.

Ronoleaus fell silent, making sure the chamberlain was far enough away from the Throne Room. He began pacing the room. For a second Alanitora hoped he would just open his mouth to reveal the answers she desperately wanted. But she knew this hope was futile.

"You ignorant girl! Do you believe that you can come in here at any moment you wish and demand anything from me? You have no sense of respect. You will not do this again, Understood?" His voice crackled like an oncoming storm. Anger radiated off of him in a thick, gripping presence.

She squeezed her eyes shut for a moment, taking a deep breath and pushing her fear down. As she felt the air leave her lungs, courage and strength welled up inside her and she spoke a word she seldom dared to say aloud to her father. "No."

Ronoleaus stopped in his tracks, took a moment to process the word thrown at him, and turned around to face her. "Since you are feeling *ever* so defiant, you will get more than a warning this time." He placed his hand on the hilt of his sword, pulling it out in one sweep.

Alanitora narrowed her eyes and held her ground. If she ran, she was cowardly, but if she did anything to insult him... Well, she had no idea what he'd do. He had never threatened her like this before.

She bit her tongue. Perhaps this was a bad idea.

Ronoleaus marched up to her, raising the tip of the sword to her chin. "You want answers? Fine... However, you must prove you are worthy of receiving them." He withdrew the blade. "We will test this with a duel. If you win, I'll tell you what you want to know. If you lose... there will be severe consequences." He pushed the sword into her hands. "Deal?"

Alanitora nodded, taking the long sword in her grip. It wasn't her weapon of choice, but there was no given alternative. She was able to relax in the idea that he at least recognized her strengths.

It had been a long time since she and Ronoleaus had dueled. The last was at the age of fourteen when she asked to participate in the biennial knight tournament. Her father gave similar conditions back then. If she won, she could participate. If she lost, she wasn't allowed anywhere near it.

That duel lasted mere moments, resulting in Alanitora's failure. She had since practiced with various weapons and styles, mastering whatever she could to prove her worth someday...

Today would be that day.

Ronoleaus plucked another longsword from its display on the wall and moved towards the center of the room, prompting Alanitora to make the first move. She was well aware that this was a strategy to notice the patterns and mannerisms of her technique.

There was no backing down.

With a moment of consideration, Alanitora pounced over the gap between her mother and father's thrones and descended the steps, charging towards her father for an upward left stroke. Her eyes met his as she swung the sword towards him, planting her feet on the ground for stability. His sword met hers, the clash of metal echoing as it bounced across the stone walls.

The duel had begun.

She jumped back, breaking away from the pressure of his strength. If she could just keep her wrist straight, Alanitora may not have to worry about his physical advantage. The long sword was difficult to wield for someone of her size, which was the reason why she typically chose daggers and knives.

That moment of divided focus nearly stopped her from blocking Ronoleaus' thrust towards her torso. A move that, if not blocked in time, could have impaled her. She continued to block moves from her father as he took the upper hand in the offense, but the further he continued, the harder it became for her to counter. Alanitora caught his downward stroke with the hilt of her sword, swinging it around and away from her. He backed away as predicted, and she began her own round of attack.

Careful not to give her father the upper hand, Alanitora turned her wrist to different angles at each stroke, trying her best to not revert to any habits. Ronoleaus was observing her, and it was only a matter of time before he figured her out.

The two switched between defense and offense, both examining each other discreetly. Then she saw it: his falter. Each time Ronoleaus switched to offense, he started with an upward left stroke across her shoulder. His mind must have been so focused on following her moves, that he left no consideration for the possibility that she was doing the same.

Upon the next switch in dominance, Alanitora watched as he raised his arm the same way, and instead of blocking, she ducked out of the way and thrust her sword to the side of his chest. Stopping him from completing the stroke.

While this caught him by surprise, the king also immediately recognized his mistake. Which meant he knew she was using the same strategic analysis as him. There was no point in keeping their analysis secret now, it would do them no favors.

"You've... gotten better!" he said through heavy breaths. His praise held no real admiration.

"I know you're trying to distract me." Alanitora dodged another blow, separating herself from him slightly.

His frown intensified, filling her with small satisfaction. She took his momentary distraction as an opportunity and kicked him in the side, holding back a little. The princess assumed that this would shock him further, but instead, anger bubbled in his eyes. Ronoleaus lunged at her without hesitation, as though he intended to kill her.

It was Alanitora's turn to be surprised as she jumped out of the way. The sword ran through her long hair, slicing away a few ends. Their eyes met once again, and she could see the fury and frustration within them. There was something else beneath it. Sure, there was a slight embarrassment, but even deeper than that was something stronger.

Arrogance.

By the time she figured out what was planned, it was too late. Ronoleaus swung at her already strained position, causing her to lean back further. Her balance was disrupted and the princess fell to the floor, the back of her skull hitting the ground hard enough to make her head spin.

Ronoleaus stood, towering over her like an owl swooping down on its prey. His face held a sickening grin as he raised his sword to her throat. She brought hers towards his torso, but he hit it away in a quick motion.

"It looks like I won." Ronoleaus' laughter was filled with pride.

Alanitora smiled. Her father was blind. Too blind to see that there were more possibilities. Too ignorant to know that she had grown beyond his imagination. This was not the end of the duel.

Alanitora clamped her hands around the sword, paying no attention to the edge that buried itself into her flesh. She tugged it downwards to the left of her face into the thick carpet, cringing at the fresh blood running down her wrists. Then, Alanitora wrapped one foot around the back of his knee, and the other on the outside of his ankle, pushing the two together and knocking him to the floor.

The princess rolled to the side and stood up, kicking him onto his back while he winced at the pain. She took both swords in her hands and stabbed them at an angle on each side of his neck, creating a scissor-like contraption.

"No, it looks like I won," Alanitora sneered, blowing a stray strand of hair out of her face.

Ronoleaus grunted, nodding in acceptance of his defeat. She removed the swords and handed him his, placing the other in its respective place as Ronoleaus returned to stand by his throne.

She took a moment to remove a strip of cloth from her undergarments so she could wrap her hands. The bleeding wasn't bad, but her ladies would kill her if she got blood on another dress. He took the time to calm his breath, checking himself for any unnoticed injuries.

"If you must know, Queen Elena was banished from Trenvern. There are high suspicions that she was working against our kingdom, selling information to the Fonoli."

Alanitora shook her head. "No. That's impossible." Her father met her eyes. There was no doubt in them. "Show me the evidence! I can prove it wrong! She wouldn't do that. She wouldn't put us in danger in any way!"

"I am not at liberty to show you evidence, just as you are not entitled to raise your voice at me!" he snapped.

Alanitora fell silent, looking down at the ground, and back up to him. "We had a deal," she said, holding back her impudence.

"I told you what you wanted to know"

"I wanted to know how— why? Was there no case held for the Council? Did she even have a chance to defend herself?!"

Alanitora knew that she was in denial. She knew that, logically, her father's actions were right. However, deeper into her heart, in a place she was not aware of, the princess knew that something was truly awry.

"She was a danger to all of Trenvern! Every second that she stayed here was another piece of information sold to the kingdom of Fonolis!"

Fonolis was a neighboring enemy kingdom that had been at war with Trenvern for generations. The reason for which was most often rumored to be a long distorted dispute; almost no one could recall the exact details. In this day and age, the war between the two kingdoms had become dormant, though animosity remained strong.

She didn't know much of them besides this, save for the cascading mountains and cold that surrounded their capital, as well as the fact that their animal was—fittingly—a mountain lion All she knew of them besides this was much of their land was a snowy landscape of cascading mountains, and that their animal was a mountain lion.

For what reason would her mother sell information to them? How long had this been happening? If it was only recently, why now? And if it wasn't, how had Alanitora not realized it?

Ronoleaus sighed and sat down on his throne, rubbing his temples. "I don't know what your mother's intentions were, all I know is that it is my duty to protect, as well as be, the future of this kingdom. It will be a long time before anyone else will sit in either of these thrones."

Alanitora froze. Was her father that obstinate? His answer, his heir, was standing right in front of him! What did he mean by a *long time*? Surely, now that her mother was gone, a coronation would be put in place for her to become the crown queen. That was how it had worked in previous generations, with the next heir inheriting the throne when one of his predecessors passed away.

As though her mind had been invaded, Ronoleaus answered her ponderings.

"Alanitora." He waited until she met his eyes before he continued. "I have news for you, and since we are speaking of ruling and such, it is time I tell you."

Was this it? Was this when he answered her lifelong question as to whether or not she was to be the first ruling queen of Trenvern? "Tell me what?" she tried her best to keep the excitement out of her voice.

"Tomorrow morning, you will leave Trenvern and travel to Donasela, the infamous war kingdom in the far east of the land."

38

"Donasela? As in one of the kingdoms we are in disharmony with?" She, unsurprisingly, didn't know much about that situation either. The only bit she could recall was that Donasela and Trenvern's systems of rule were contrasting. Donasela, a kingdom built on old power and now rebirthed into the modern era, frowned upon several opposing views. They were said to scrutinize those untraditional, yet opposingly scold anyone who wasn't willing to be progressive.

And defying them was something no kingdom wished to do. Donasela had the best military across all of Mordenla. Their tactics and technology were far advanced, to the point where they were able to monetize the production of military goods for export.

Ronoleaus smiled. "What do you think your arrival there is for?"

"Are you saying I have the privilege of signing the early documents of the alliance between Trenvern and Donasela?

Ever since she had a small taste of the political affairs that Trenvern had with the other kingdoms of Mordenla, Alanitora had hoped to someday participate in the union of one. Such documents were crucial for the history and future of Trenvern, and the thought of such an honor caused her heart to jump.

He shook his head. "Alanitora, *you* are the alliance."

"W-what?"

"All of your things should be getting packed by now. Before you rudely intruded, I had just put in the order for them to be collected.

"What do you mean I am the alliance?!" Alanitora could feel her core twisting and turning with unease. She tried to control her breaths. Now was not the time to show weakness. Not in front of him.

Ronoleaus took a deep breath. "Prince Daruthel, Crown Prince of Donasela, has asked for your hand in marriage. I have agreed to the marriage in return for an alliance and supply of resources. The wedding is scheduled for three weeks from now. As soon as it is officiated, you will be the queen of Donasela, and the alliance will be sealed." A smile came to his face. The joy expressed his hope in her. One she had no idea the king had. "Alanitora, you are going to make history."

Alanitora froze completely. A ripple of emotions crossed her heart as her fingers numbed. This wasn't happening. It couldn't be happening. Owen, her mother, now this? She knew that she would be married someday, but had never anticipated it to be so soon. It seemed like a sea and a star away.

Despite her sudden loss of hope, despite the new, sinking weight of her heart, all Alanitora could do was force an obedient smile and nod in agreement, turning away as Ronoleaus settled into his throne with satisfaction.

He must have thought this would be a great joy to her. A surprise she would bask in. But he did not know her at all, and she would not tarnish his pride in her just mere moments after gaining it.

Having forced her feet to walk away, she pulled open the door and stepped through, stopping for a moment to release her breath. Alanitora shuddered as she realized that her father had won the duel. It hadn't been a physical fight, it was mental, and her sword just melted to molten steel. All of that preparation and she'd lost yet again. Her mind was weaker than her body, after all.

A wedding, the first wedding she would ever attend, was her own.

4

Shifted Fate

T
he guards posted outside the Throne Room shared a quick glance
of confusion as Alanitora closed the doors behind her. She
had begun to walk back towards her room when a prickle of
realization came to her. Perhaps it would be easier to go the way she came.

No, the dark dampness of that passage would allow her thoughts to be
louder than everything else. She needed the distance of daylight. Then
again, it didn't matter, she knew that Ronoleaus would check the area she
appeared from, and he would likely block the passage. So much for a secret
path to use...

Alanitora mentally halted again. Nothing about the passage mattered.
She was leaving anyway. No use was going to come from it if she wouldn't
be living there anymore.

Her arms ached as she pulled her skirts up to descend the courtyard
stairs. The princess was exhausted. She had barely spent an hour with
her father, and she already wanted to take a nap. Not only was her mind
racing with questions about this new 'arrangement', but she knew her
social skills would be put to the test as she cut across the open courtyard.
Nevertheless, she would rather make it through a million conversations
than walk around the entire castle if it meant getting to her bed faster.i

Lords and ladies of the court frolicked around, applauding the performers and peddlers that peppered the perimeter. Many turned and greeted

her, others bowed and curtsied until their chests nearly brushed the floor. At this point, she would have to stop and smile until they raised themselves again. Her mother told her to wait until they were finished if she wanted to be respected.

Though if her mother was truly a liar, perhaps she shouldn't follow any of her advice.

Alanitora was just about to enter the stairwell to her chambers when someone tapped her shoulder. "Excuse me, Your Highness, sorry to bother..."

She turned around and looked at the man, his cheeks plumped on either side of his toothy grin as he stared up at her. "What do you want?" she asked, addressing the desperation under the folds of his brown eyes.

"Ah, sorry. I'd like you to take this pendant. Free of charge, of course!" The necklace dangled between his fingertips, its brown striped surface shifting in the cool sunlight. "It's a tiger eye. A clever stone for a clever princess."

After the man continued to hold it out to her, Alanitora grasped the crystal with a brief thank you before turning away. When she looked back, he had stalked off back to his stand and was talking to a lady about the ring she was holding.

The princess gave a weak smile to the guard in front of the stairs as she slipped the pendant into the hidden pockets of her dress that Korena insisted on making. She climbed the spiral staircase towards her chambers with speed, well aware she'd be drained either way once she reached the top.

She came across the door to her mother's chambers and stopped for a moment. Could it be true? Was Queen Elena a traitor? How long had she been selling information to Fonolis? Alanitora had heard about spies' incredible ability to invest themselves within the lives of others, all to end up betraying them. But could that really be her mother? The woman who raised and nurtured her, the woman who taught her benevolent morals, taught her to defend herself...

Feeling the lump in her throat, Alanitora continued up the stairs, pushing thoughts of her mother out of her mind. It was all too much.

As she approached the top, the princess was surprised to see that no one was guarding the front door of her chambers. Exactly *how* many soldiers had been dispatched to war?

Alanitora took the key off its hook and opened the latch to unlock the door. The hallway was empty once again, the only sign of movement was the flicker of flames on the wall.

As she shut the door behind her, Korena's voice pierced through the silence like a bird at the sight of dawn. "Your Highness, is that you? We're in here!"

Alanitora followed the voice, agony washing over her when she realized they were in the old maids' quarters. She really didn't want to go back in there. She peered through the doorway at the scene. Gwendolyn sat on her knees facing the princess, a circle of five candles in front of her, with another ten surrounding her and Korena, who sat with her legs crossed, watching the flickering light in front of her.

While the glow that was cast upon their faces was certainly eerie, there was something about the warmth of the candles that made the room more inviting. Alanitora stepped in, looking past her ladies-in-waiting to Owen, who was leaning against the wall, frowning at the four cards in his hand.

"... What is happening here?"

"Witchcraft!" Korena beamed.

"You do know you can be hanged for practicing magick, right?" Owen pushed himself off the wall and straightened his back.

When Korena's whole body twitched at his words, Gwendolyn intervened, a frown upon her face. "Shush Owen. Korena, dear." Her tone changed from stern to gentle, placing her hand lightly on the blonde's arm. "This isn't witchcraft. I'm not casting spells and curses. I'm simply telling fortunes." Gwendolyn's eyes met Alanitora, inviting her to sit down.

The princess grasped her skirts and stepped over the outer candles, slowly lowering into the same position as Gwendolyn. Alanitora placed her hands in the girl's outstretched palms, smiling as her old friend gave them a quick squeeze.

Korena leaned in. "Oh! Oh! Can I do it this time Gwendolyn?"

"No, last time you did, you told Gwendolyn she had bread for breakfast," Owen said.

"And was I wrong?"

"You ate breakfast *with* her this morning." He crossed his arms. "Plus, it didn't even relate to the card she chose."

"Yes, it did! It was the herdsman, and when I listened to the card as she told me to, it said 'Let us get this bread.'"

"You—"

"Enough Owen. Now give me those cards back, I need to shuffle the deck," Gwendolyn demanded.

Alanitora stayed silent, observing the cards within the smaller circle of candles in front of her. The backs of each were painted in a deep water blue and were the same shape and size as those used as playing cards, although their faces were lightly painted with pictures of creatures and humans alike. Alanitora saw small connected dots glimmering in the light and immediately recognized them as constellations.

Gwendolyn grabbed the pile on the floor and began to lace the cards together, shuffling them over and over until she seemed satisfied. Careful to not touch the fire, she placed them in the center, spreading them out towards Alanitora with the palm of her hand.

"Before we begin, do I have your full consent of spirit and mind to unveil your fate? You may not like the results."

Curious as to what Gwendolyn could be referring to, Alanitora nodded with a small amused smile.

Gwendolyn met her eyes again before speaking. "Pick four cards and keep them in the order of selection. Do not overthink it, and do not doubt yourself. Choose what you feel is right."

Alanitora tentatively scanned the deck before her. Her fingers seemed to grasp onto some with no thought, beckoning for her to choose them. She picked each card as though they were cracked glass on the verge of shattering, and held them out towards Gwendolyn.

The maid took them into her care, scanning them before presenting the first to Alanitora. "Virgo: The Maiden. This card represents a past of solitude. Virgo is a woman held back by the bounds of mankind from her true potential. She holds both the symbol of purity and fertility."

Gwendolyn placed the next card on top of her palm. Alanitora recognized this as one of the cards Owen held. "Orion: The Hunter. This card represents your present. Orion is a fearless hunter who made the mistake of letting his guard down in a time of vulnerability and desire. He shows strength and defense.

"Ara: The Altar. This card holds various possibilities for the future. Ara is a place of worship and unity. It can represent the following of a terrible fate or the union of a spiritual path.

"And lastly," Gwendolyn said, turning the fourth card over. "Corona Borealis: The Northern Crown. This crown of fate is the heavier of the two and holds both burden and power. Take care in wielding it, for while its perceived outcome is a life of fortune, many crumble under its weight." A smile returned to Gwendolyn's brown face as she held the cards back out to the princess.

Alanitora took the cards into her hands, her eyes scanning them with curiosity. Could there be truth to them? They sounded accurate. Then again, Gwendolyn knew her well. Alanitora had picked each card herself, but in the light of her betrothal, the Altar couldn't have been coincidental.

"Gwendolyn?" Her lady-in-waiting perked up at the mention of her name. "How do you choose what to say about each card?"

Her brown eyes flicked over to Korena, then back to the princess. "Well, it's not a matter of choice, I suppose it's more what feels right. They... speak to me."

"Speak to you?" Alanitora questioned.

"Oh, nothing of worry! Not like voices or whispers. More along the lines of intuition."

"So you just... guess people's fortunes?" The tone of Owen's voice suggested disbelief.

"No, never. It's just a pulling feeling I get, directing bits of knowledge to me through the cards." Gwendolyn shuffled the cards and put them to the side. "Oh, never mind. I don't know how—"

"A feeling in your stomach, telling you to follow through with a certain action. I get it when I'm in combat," Alanitora said.

The smile on Gwendolyn's face said it all. She did have an intuitive direction. But how could that be so specific? The princess' thoughts wandered back to the cards based on constellations. She always disliked the meaning of Virgo. *The Maiden* seemed so frail. It wasn't that she didn't like femininity, she just didn't like the Virgo interpretation of it.

On the other hand, Orion was always one of her favorites. She and Owen used it as a spotting point when they had begun learning about constellations. His story also intrigued her, in that the object of his affection was a goddess of the hunt.

This brought her to Ara once again. "Gwendolyn, could Ara have something to do with the betrothal?"

"The what?" Owen's head whipped up.

Gwendolyn bit her lip. "Believe me when I say I wasn't expecting the card to be chosen either, but it appears so, yes."

"Wait," Korena chirped. "How do you know about the betrothal? Gwendolyn and I were just informed last night and instructed not to tell you."

"What betrothal?"

Alanitora ignored Owen. "My father told me about it after explaining that my mother was exiled. The two of you knew about that as well, didn't you?" Gwendolyn averted her eyes. Korena nodded, her head hung. They looked as though they were ready for a long-winded beratement. The princess couldn't help but pity their position. "Well, you were simply following orders in not telling me. Next time, I hope you find yourself coming to me. I'd rather have heard it from you."

Korena's eyes glittered like a puppy who had just been offered steak from its owner. "Oh, Tora! I've heard so many great things about Donasela. Wealth, luxury, and sun! Lots of sun! Gwenie and me were so nervous as to how you would react."

"We started packing your things when Owen told us you were off to talk to your father, everything should be finished and ready to go by tonight, though the rest will probably be dealt with by the guards."

"Pack? Pack what? Nitora, where are you going?" Owen asked.

She was about to scold him for calling her Nitora again when Korena practically jumped out at her. "I've also heard that Prince Daruthel has quite the looks. Although... that peddler from the east did say he was a little bit desolate, whatever that means. Oh! But once the two of you get married—"

"You are getting *what*?" Owen's voice echoed through the dark room.

Great. Did he really have to barge back into her life now? Forget now, why did he have to re-enter her life at all? The disbelief, the frustration, the anger in his eyes only reflected how she felt towards him. Alanitora did not want to deal with this right now.

"Korena, Gwendolyn, blow out the candles and head to my room. You can clean this up later."

She watched them work in rapid silence. The two shared a knowing look as they followed Owen and Alanitora out of the room, before continuing to her bedchamber and shutting the door behind them.

Alanitora took a deep breath as the door closed behind her, and she was alone with her childhood best friend, the boy who left her... the boy who came back. She sighed, and placed her hand softly on his arm, guiding him away from the doors. She sighed. Where should she start?

"Yes. I am betrothed to Prince Daruthel of Donasela."

"You're getting married?!" The anger ran through his voice in a way that Alanitora had never heard, and her skin tingled with shivers. All this time she had been concerned about him not accepting her change, but she had never even considered the possibility of his. Owen had always been too sweet and too nervous to raise his voice. To Alanitora, his voice sounded so rough and wounded when he yelled. And even if he was more surprised than mad, it felt as though he was blaming her for something.

She drew in a heavy breath. "Yes, but you have to understand that I just found out as well. I'm just as startled as you."

Owen turned away from her. The soldier ran his hands through his orange hair, frowning as he pressed at his temple. Abruptly, he turned around, his face softening. "Nitora, you don't have to do this."

She didn't even bother correcting his use of her nickname. She looked into his eyes, they were now so... empty. He had been shattered like glass, and now the shards protruded from his icy irises.

Alanitora caught her strength fading. She was becoming vulnerable. She took a breath and composed herself.

"Do you think I want to do this? Do you think I have a choice? I don't want to leave the life I have here. I can't just run off and do whatever I want. You have no idea how hopeless I have felt today. I found out that my mother is a traitor, and that she's been banished for treason. I was told that I am leaving my home, my life, and being married off to some man that I have never met. I found that my best friend never truly abandoned me." He flinched at her words, and she softened her tone. "Owen."

He avoided her eyes, but the silence slowly prompted him to look at her: he couldn't help it. The boy was trying his best to hold back the emotions he was feeling. She was always so good at reading him, but if he let her now, she'd know the emotions he had—still had—for her.

The only way she'd get him to understand was if she matched his emotions.

Her lips curved into a comforting smile. "Look, I'm glad you're here. I'm glad you're okay, and I'm glad you are still the same person from all those years ago..." The smile fell. "But I am not, and that's why I have to do this."

When he finally spoke, his voice was frail. "I just found you."

Alanitora's shoulders dropped. "I know, and maybe that's okay. Maybe this is the closure you need to move on."

Owen tried his best to smile. To show her that he understood, yet his eyes only watered. "And I always thought I was the tougher one," he said, wiping the tears away with the back of his hand.

They both laughed at that. "Oh please, you were always the sentimental one."

"Kind of ironic, huh? That you leave once we have a reunion."

"No kidding—"

A series of crashing noises from her bedroom cut her off. Alanitora pulled a dagger from her waist and rushed to the door, leaving Owen to exchange looks of confusion with the two guards that popped their heads out from another room.

The princess tried to open the door but found some resistance. With a rush of worry, she slammed herself against it in hopes of stopping the threat.

Her entrance was greeted by an annoyed-looking Gwendolyn near the bed, followed by an "Oww" from behind the door.

"Prowler of the century everyone." Gwendolyn threw her arms up, motioning behind the door.

Alanitora stepped through the doorway, allowing Korena's upright legs to push the door closed. The blonde was sprawled out on the floor, the contents of one of Alanitora's garment chests dumped around her.

The rest of her room was just as disheveled. Old clothes hung from furniture, her storage chests stacked on the south side of the room. As for the floor, instead of her familiar green rug, the cobblestone was covered with downy mattress feathers from her now bare bed frame. It looked like a wind storm had come through in her absence.

"What in the world is going on here?!" Alanitora wasn't sure which lady to look to for answers.

"Well, besides Korena trying to listen to your dramatic conversation," Gwendolyn said, placing down the pile of clothes in her arms "We are packing for tomorrow."

Alanitora froze. It hadn't truly hit her until now. This was happening. She knew it, she understood it, but it was finally feeling real. She was leaving everything she had ever known.

Korena must have noticed a shift in the princess' mood, for moments later, she had gotten up and rested her hand on Alanitora's shoulder. "Hey, it's okay, me and Gwendolyn are coming with you!"

She smiled at this, but another question swirled into her mind. "Did either of you consider that I need a place to sleep before the morning?"

While Korena shrugged, Gwendolyn's face contorted into puzzlement

49

as it often did when she was thinking. Her eyebrows rose a few moments after.

"How about Queen Elena's room? The servants may have already cleaned it out, but it is worth a try."

Korena squealed in excitement, grasping Alanitora's wrist in her hands and leading her out of the door.

Gwendolyn followed, and as the three girls ran past him out of the chambers, Owen was left standing in their dust. He smiled, looking around at the room that had changed much since he was younger, and was now changing again. The boy approached Alanitora's weapon chest, opening it up to see his toy sword upon the top.

"Someday, Nitora, you are going to hurt yourself with this childish weapon," Owen chuckled. He slid his hands across the rough surface, allowing small flakes of wood to fling off of it and onto the floor.

He couldn't accept this as closure, not when he had just found her. With a small smile of determination, Owen left the room as well.

Gwendolyn's concerns were correct: much of Queen Elena's personal items had already been moved out, save the stationary on her vanity desk.

Alanitora swirled her name on the paper, careful not to let the ink splot anywhere. She then wrote letters of farewell. Not to anyone in particular, but her past. It helped her process what was to happen and keep going. She had been doing this for hours, too preoccupied to get supper or roam the castle one last time.

Her thoughts and scribbles were nevertheless interrupted by the reappearance of her ladies, who rushed into her room without bothering to knock. A bad habit she thought they had overcome.

"Milady, we have terrible news!" Korena said.

At this point, Alanitora placed the quill down and turned.

"The guards took away the chests... All of them!" Gwendolyn joined in.

"And that is terrible because… ?"

Korena's face dropped in a mix of disbelief and grief. "We can't show you your wedding dress!"

Alanitora shook her head. The two were always worked up about the most random things. Well, Korena normally was, but chaos ensued when she convinced the usually demure Gwendolyn to join her.

"Since the two of you are here, do you mind helping me out of these clothes and into a nightgown?"

Korena and Gwendolyn stopped squabbling and got to work. Dressing Alanitora for the day was their normal routine, but the princess often undressed herself—much to Korena's dismay, as she often found a way to tear important seams.

Unfortunately, wearing one of her mother's nightgowns meant Korena still had to do patchwork. Gwendolyn, in the meantime, undressed Alanitora's first few layers and began brushing out her hair.

"So," Korena began, pins in between her lips. "Hab you heard who's comink on your drip to Donaseya?"

"The two of you? It's been mentioned a few times, Korena."

"No! I mean a cer'ain someone is a guard in de entourage."

Before she could process who Korena was talking about, Gwendolyn intervened. "Oh heavens no! Does he have to?"

Alanitora stood as Korena raised a finished nightgown. Taking it in her hands, she stepped behind the divider and changed, still pondering who it was.

"Wait." Alanitora stepped into view. "You don't mean Owen?"

Korena nodded gleefully, motioning Alanitora to spin around so she could examine her work.

"Of course…" Alanitora rolled her eyes. Not that she had been around him much recently, but it was typical of the Owen she remembered to insert himself.

"Trust me when I say that I'm not happy about it either," Gwendolyn added, smoothing out Alanitora's waist.

"What's your deal with Owen anyway?" Korena asked.

Before Gwendolyn could answer, a rustle could be heard from outside. The three turned towards the door, expecting some sort of assassin to burst in.

Moments later, Owen came in, the swing of the door sending a thick, scented air into the room with him.

"Ugh, speak of the Devil," Gwendolyn groaned, putting her hands on her hips. "What do you wa—"

"Owen?" Alanitora stepped in front of the ladies towards her old friend. "What's wrong?"

His eyes were filled with fear, water lining them. He looked at Alanitora as if he had seen a ghost. He looked terrified. With much effort, the princess shifted her eyes to his head. There were a plethora of gray flakes in his orange hair and on his shoulders.

Something was wrong. Something was very wrong.

"Oh my God." Korena quivered.

Alanitora looked back at her. A gray substance blocked her view of the lady-in-waiting, whose eyes watered as well. Alanitora's vision blurred and was clear within the next second, a streak of moisture sliding down her cheek. She should have recognized it as soon as the pungent suffocating smell reached her nose, but that was the last to hit her.

She turned back to Owen, her lips shaking as the word came out of her mouth. "Fire."

5

Escape

"Korena, Gwendolyn, we need to go. Now." Alanitora reached her arms back to the ladies, her eyes locked with Owen's still. When she only felt Korena's soft fingers intertwined with hers, she broke her attention from him to Gwendolyn, who stood motionless upon the forming smoke. "Gwendolyn!"

Owen coughed, someone screamed in the distance, a crash could be heard nearby, but Gwendolyn didn't look up. She stared feebly down at her feet.

Alanitora let go of Korena's hand. "Owen, get Korena and the other guards out of the tower."

"But—"

"Just do it!"

The princess didn't even bother to make sure they left, instead, she turned to Gwendolyn, stepping towards her lightly. The girl's eyes ran back and forth, as though she was processing something.

"Gwendolyn."

She didn't respond.

"Gwendolyn, look at me." Alanitora pressed her hands to the girl's cheeks, raising her eyes to hers. "We need to go."

The lady's brown eyes softened, focusing on Alanitora. Slowly, she nodded. Her attempts to come back to reality were all but secure.

The two girls ran out of the corridor, practically busting down the door to get to the staircase. Alanitora's eyes stung and her throat thinned at the excess debris.

Owen ran up a few stairs to meet them, waiting until Alanitora and her ladies were ready to follow him before descending again.

"I told you to get Korena out of here!" Alanitora croaked as the four rushed down the stairs with as much caution as they could.

"There was no way in hell that I was leaving you, you know that. I sent the others to check for anyone else up in your chambers. The structures are starting to collapse."

"That doesn't—"

A large wooden plank fell from the top of the staircase, ridden with flames. They nearly froze when the sound of it hitting the bottom of the shute clattered their ears, sending up a puff of ashes.

Alanitora covered her mouth in response to Korena's fit of dry coughs and continued to lead Gwendolyn down the stairs.

Their visibility of what was below continued to decrease, and they had to slow down to avoid any fallen objects. It wasn't long before the sound of frantic footsteps could be heard behind them.

"Was there anyone up there?" Owen yelled out to the two guards he had sent up.

"One, his leg was crushed by a beam, but everyone else seems to have left besides 'em. Thomason is providing him support up here."

"Thank you, do me the biggest favor of helping Her Highness' ladies."

One replied with a grunt of confirmation, and Alanitora looked back to get a good look at the three guards. The smoke was so thick, however, that she could barely see an arm's length in front of her. Not wanting to leave Gwendolyn behind while she was still unresponsive, the princess continued to look for them.

She could only faintly see the figures when Owen shouted out.

"Alanitora!" He had pressed her against the wall, his chest covering her. Before she could react, he yelled out a shrill of pain as a metal part fell on the step below him. She couldn't see it well, but it appeared to be a scrap of a support beam.

Beads of sweat rolled down from Owen's forehead as he grimaced. He removed himself from guarding her. "Are you alright?"

"Yeah." The word could barely come out from her hoarse throat. Alanitora looked over at her ladies to see that the guards had caught up to them and one was leading both of them down the steps.

Nearly at the bottom, they all reserved their breaths, the only sound being the occasional whimper from Korena, who flinched at every fallen object. Gwendolyn was in better focus now, but her expression was a sorrowful blankness, one that worried Alanitora.

Owen flung open the door to the courtyard, holding it open for everyone else to step through. Alanitora took a deep breath as fresh air reached her lungs, kneeling to catch more of it and cough out the ashes in her throat.

"Gwendolyn! Where are you going?!" Her head jerked up at the sound of Korena calling her best friend.

Owen rushed into the door and dragged Gwendolyn out moments later.

"Let go of me!" The sharpness in her voice was foreign to Alanitora's ears.

The girl squirmed out of Owen's grasp and back into the stairwell, only to reappear seconds later. This time with an item clutched between her hands. Alanitora couldn't see it well with the ash that covered its features, but it appeared to be a sewn doll. The right arm was partially burnt away, but other than that it remained intact.

The fire was spreading. No time could be wasted on details. Alanitora broke her gaze away and ushered Korena and Gwendolyn to the center of the courtyard, ignoring the passing faces of lords, ladies, and peddlers as they watched the black smoke rise to a pink sky.

"Princess, ladies, head toward the east exit of the castle, but don't leave the walls until I meet back up with you. You two," Owen pointed at the guards, "with me."

Korena yelled out. "Where are you going?"

"To get the carriages ready, we need to leave. Tonight!" With that, Owen ran off into the distance, his figure leaving a small trail of clear air before it was engulfed in more smoke.

"Oh, I hope no one was hurt too badly…" Korena picked at the hem of her sleeve with a needle, threading an invisible string in the way she would during a hemline adjustment.

Alanitora was only listening slightly, her attention more focused on the people evacuating. Luckily, the fire hadn't spread past that particular tower. A few guards had rushed past them minutes before with pails of water, one of which was stopped by Korena for a brief discourse before running back to his duties.

Something seemed off. What was the origin of the fire? If it was small, how come no one noticed until it had built up enough to engulf the entire top level? However the fire started, it must have been large to begin with, possibly intentional…

"Do you think our stuff made it out fine, Gwendolyn?"

Alanitora turned to look at the exchange, not surprised to see Gwendolyn silently clutching the doll, not responding or making eye contact with her dear friend.

She shared a glance with Korena. The blonde's eyes looked for guidance, to which Alanitora gave a small shake of her head. Hopefully, Korena understood to give Gwendolyn space.

Two men strode in the nearby open corridor, undisturbed by the chaos. "Seems the castle fire is contained."

"Yes, though I hope King Ronoleaus dispatched more soldiers to take care of the other, I'd hate for my favorite bakery to burn down."

"I suppose it would bake all the bread."

The two laughed, their jolly echoes leaving Alanitora with piqued curiosity.

"Stay here you two, I need to check something out real quick. I'll be back." It seemed Gwendolyn's desponding hope had spread to Korena, as the lady just gave a small nod instead of her usual shoutings to be careful.

Alanitora pressed open the door to a small stairwell, climbing her way up until she reached the inner bailey. She wasn't usually allowed up there for her own safety, but she had to know if her suspicions were true.

The inner and outer wall connected at the northeast point where her father's tower was located. She certainly didn't have time to run a whole league just to switch over, so Alanitora rushed toward the inner south wall instead, hoping it gave a high enough vantage to see where she assumed the fire was. Multiple guards were lined among the outer bailey.

She had no idea how far or how fast she was running, but it felt as though the distance to the southern wall wasn't changing. Smoke rising to the sky only contributed to her suspicions as she neared.

The fire blazed. Her eyes watered. It didn't matter if it was the smoke or her emotions. The debris rose like a shadow of death, and she could see the Grim Reaper collecting bits of her soul with everything else that burned. Everyone else that burned.

The capital of Trenvern was ablaze. The town that she had peered out at on gloomy days, watching all the people and children run about.

The fire was speckled across different buildings, as though raindrops landed on the map of it, pinpointing where to strike. This was no mistake. Someone sparked this. To think of all the people who smiled at her. The people who sent gifts to the castle on her birthday each year. The people she had hoped to lead someday. Alanitora didn't even know their names. Her anger burned brighter than the flames.

Shouts and screams echoed toward her. Some areas were saved by a line of guards and citizens alike throwing buckets of water, others blackened further by the second.

Princess Alanitora was watching her home burn, and she couldn't do anything to stop it.

Right now, she needed to focus on the task at hand: leaving it behind. If King Ronoleaus and her both burned this night, there would be no hope for the future of Trenvern. Alanitora needed to leave. She needed to get to Donasela so they could keep her kingdom intact.

Picking up her skirts once again, she ran back towards the center of the east wall. She tried her hardest to decipher the events around her, but it was as though her mind was as blocked as the night sky.

"Is everything ready?" Alanitora asked as soon as she exited the stairwell.

Korena nodded vigorously, squeezing Gwendolyn's hand. The brunette seemed to be slowly coming back to her senses, as Korena didn't need to communicate anything for Gwendolyn to rush out towards the carriage with them.

A half dozen covered wagons tailed the carriage waiting for Alanitora and her ladies, another half ahead of it. Soldiers led them on the right side, rushing them forward with such haste that Alanitora almost expected Korena to trip on her skirts. The carriage itself was rather plain, seeming to specialize more in size than decoration. It was meant to hold four people, but with the size of the girls, all three could sit squished together on one side if they wished to.

The second they got in and the door was shut, the wagons in front of them started moving, causing their horses to lurch forward.

All of it. Every sight, every motion, every sound was so rushed. Everything moved faster than her thoughts could process. Only one thought persisted through it all: she had to escape.

Alanitora looked across at her ladies, following their gaze out the window as they watched their home increase in distance. So this was it. No goodbyes. No closure.

The carriage came to an abrupt stop. If this was how the entire ride was to be, Alanitora would certainly be sick before Trenvern's capital was out of sight.

"Forget about the wagons at the end, protect the middle! They don't care about stuff, they want what's really valuable!" Alanitora narrowed her eyes at the commands of a nearby officer.

She pulled back the curtain of the left window, but couldn't see past the collection of soldiers standing in front of it. She grunted. She was missing the action.

"Korena, where did they take my weapons chest?"

"Huh?"

"My weapons chest," Alanitora repeated. "Which wagon did the guards put it in?"

"I don't... I don't know."

"The one behind us." Gwendolyn's voice was hollow.

Alanitora nodded and opened the door, looking around to see if there were any adversaries before turning to grab onto the top of the carriage.

Korena shrieked "You— You're not thinking of going out there, are you?"

At least her uneasiness had returned. Alanitora gave a small apologetic smile and hoisted herself up onto the carriage. The brass plate covering it seemed sturdy enough to support her weight, even though she could feel the shift of wood beneath it as she kneeled onto a weaker point.

She strained to see in the distance. There was a crowd of conflict on the road ahead, but the commotion was too hectic for her to see the opponents. Alanitora focused her attention on the field to her left. Hopefully, none of the soldiers on that side of the carriage noticed a person standing on top of the royal carriage and shot without hesitation.

The gray of the smoke drifted among the grass fields, causing her to stand idly by until her eyes adjusted enough to see. There was a soldier on a horse, holding a banner above his head. The colors slowly emerged, first a bright yellow color of dandelions. The second...

"No," Alanitora could hear creeping out of her throat.

The second was blue. Yellow and blue. The colors of the northern neighboring kingdom. Fonolis. Trenvern's long-time enemy. It was them who had started the fire. Which meant... her father was right. Queen Elena had sold them information. Her mother was a traitor.

Alanitora could feel her hands start to tremble. Everything that had happened today was tearing her apart. At this moment, the smoke had taken her breath, but this sucked out her lungs completely.

Stop.

Breathe.

She needed to focus. Alanitora picked up her skirts and backed towards the front of the carriage to get her a running start. Jumping off the back, she launched herself over the horses and onto the abandoned coach seat of the covered wagon. Her feet moved light and fast as she ran across the wooden structure to the back, ducking into the wagon's contents.

Dark oak wood with silver linings. Dark oak wood with silver linings... Alanitora rushed to her weapons chest, unlatching the clasp as fast as she could. She'd scold herself later for how aggressively the hinges were forced open. The princess grabbed her bow and quiver, closing the lid and jumping out in little time.

The smoke was still heavy, but this time around, Alanitora could make out shapes enough to aim her arrows at the correct adversaries. In addition, the armies had come much closer. Many on foot, Alanitora looked past them towards those on horses. Commanders. They raised their banners ever so pridefully. She narrowed her eyes and pulled out the first arrow.

It had been so long since she'd used her bow that her fingers fumbled to rest the nock on the string. When it stabilized, Alanitora pulled it back aiming carefully at the horse, aware it would shoot upwards when she released.

"Or not," she growled as the arrow struck the horse in its chest. It may have deterred the commander's mobility, but harming a horse, who'd been born to follow the rules of man, did not feel right to her.

The horse collapsed on its front knees, causing its rider to tumble forward. Using the opportunity of the man fumbling to release himself from the horse, Alanitora aimed again, smiling as the arrow struck him down.

"Your Highness, what are you doing?!" A soldier had rushed up next to her in a frantic worry.

"Helping." She shot another officer down after a few tries. So maybe she wasn't as good with a boy and an arrow as she thought she was. Ranged weapons were not her forte, that was for sure.

"But—"

"Protest and the next arrow goes in your chest, go help the front."

Alanitora aimed at the third and last commander, cursing at herself when the arrow flew right past his shoulder. She readied the second arrow.

"Your Highness!"

With a huff of annoyance, Alanitora turned to her left, expecting to see another distraction. Instead, she witnessed a collection of Fonoli soldiers huddled around a singular figure. The voice yelled out again, and Alanitora was able to match it to a girl in the center of the huddle. She redrew her bow, shooting one of the men to get a better view.

Red hair peeked through, nearly as intense as the decreasing flames dispersed across the town. The girl made a quick second of eye contact before striking one of the soldiers next to her. She had no visible weapons in her hands, and yet yells of agony were released with each debilitating hit.

Alanitora was able to shoot a few more back before it became more likely she'd hit the girl. She needed to be in a closer, more consistent range. She dropped her bow to reach for the throwing knives in her skirts.

"Damn." She was wearing a nightgown—she hadn't even noticed until now. Weary to take her eyes off of the girl, Alanitora jumped back into the wagon and opened the chest with haste, unrolling a cloth of spare throwing knives. She grabbed a handful and jumped back down, rushing over to help.

"Get down!" Alanitora yelled. Once the girl followed the command, the princess threw the handful at the remaining three.

One collapsed onto the girl, the other two staggering back. Alanitora rushed forward, incapacitating one of them.

"Princess Alanitora!" The girl wiggled her way out and eagerly gave her a bow. "It is an honor."

The girl's red hair was pulled back and tucked into her shawl. She wore commoner's clothing, but the elaborate gemstone that hung from her neck suggested she was a member of nobility. Freckles dotted her fair skin, which was clear besides the fresh scratch on her left cheek.

Picking up a bag from under one of the collapsed men, the redhead ushered herself and the princess away from the battle.

"The pleasure is mine. You've done well." Alanitora smiled. "What's your name?"

"Diane, Your Highness."

"Diane," Alanitora repeated. "How did you incapacitate so many of them?"

The girl smiled. She pulled out a collection of needles, similar to those Korena used to pin her dress. "They don't do lasting damage, but it's enough to hit points that immobilize them until I can get away."

Alanitora chuckled. This girl was most certainly smart. She pointed to Diane's cheek. "Does it hurt?"

Diane pressed her fingers to the wound, pulling them back to examine the blood, and shook her head. "It doesn't sting too much, but it might leave a scar.

"Ah." Alanitora nodded, pulling back her hair and turning her head to the left so Diane could see the scar that ran across her cheekbone and jawline. "Didn't hurt much either, but a fun story to tell."

A horn sounded in the distance, causing the two to turn their heads towards the sound. The Fonoli were retreating, many of their own lying dead or injured across the field.

"Oh thank goodness," Alanitora hung her head back in relief. "We can relax."

"No!"

Alanitora looked over at Diane in confusion, her ocean blue eyes overflowing with panic.

"Princess, you have to leave now!"

"And why is that?"

"The Fonoli, they are here to kill you."

Alanitora paused. What did Diane mean? "Me specifically?"

Diane nodded vigorously. "I can't explain now, I fear there isn't enough time. You were the target of the attack. They have reinforcements coming and it is vital that you leave immediately."

"Then come with me." If Diane knew information, specifically information about her own life, Alanitora needed to know. "If what you say is true, then I'll need you to tell me."

"I— Are you sure that's alright?" Diane croaked.

"If they have reinforcements as you say, I could certainly use someone like you to help defend me on the road ahead."

A confident smile arose on Diane's face. "If you think I'd be useful, then I'd love to."

6

The Girl With the Red Hair

Alanitora guided Diane to the carriage, checking around them for any more adversaries. The girl was beaming despite the fact that their home was still on fire behind them and half a dozen men had just tried to kill her.

The carriage door practically slammed open when Korena saw them approach, and Alanitora had to quickly introduce Diane before climbing in next to Korena.

"Diane helped fight off the Fonolis from the eastern entrance. I thought it would be kind to offer her the opportunity to travel with us," she explained.

"That is very brave of you." Gwendolyn smiled. She must have been feeling better. Her hand still clutched the burnt doll, but it was good to see her responsive again. "How old are you?"

"Fifteen," Diane replied.

She nodded in response. "Well, if Tora says you are okay to travel with us, then you may come along however far you'd like. You and Korena look about the same size, so if you need any clothes, let us know."

"Speaking of," Korena interrupted, "Did the guards say anything about when we are leaving?"

"Shouldn't be long now. He said they needed to reinforce their resources as fast as possible so we can get away from the castle. They aren't certain if the second batch of Fonoli are on their way yet, so it's best to get some distance."

Alanitora gave Diane a weary look. She wanted to know what the girl had been talking about before, but not in front of her ladies. Such information was delicate.

It wasn't as though she didn't trust them. She did, but Alanitora had always tried her best to keep any violent affairs away from her more fragile ladies-in-waiting. Gwendolyn hated violence, and Korena was too squirmy for it. In addition, she knew they had a certain sense of security when around her. If they were aware of the dangers she faced, they could find themselves in the middle of it all.

The carriage door swung open again, and Korena screeched. Owen was sheathing his sword as he climbed in, absentmindedly seating himself next to Gwendolyn, who looked uncomfortable as she moved closer to Diane to make room.

In relation, Diane was stiff as a board, her posture up straight, her head pressed to the carriage as though there was a dog on her lap trying to kiss her face. Her mood had completely changed.

Owen waved to the man outside the carriage, who Alanitora assumed was the coachman, and they began to move again.

"Why is it so squished in here?" Owen asked, shifting in his seat.

Korena gestured to his right, where Diane shook her head fervently "Oh! Owen, this is—"

"Diane?!"

She smiled wryly at him.

"What are you doing here?"

Alanitora looked between the two. So they knew each other somehow. And based on his reaction, whatever had happened between them did not end well. Perhaps they had courted one another at some point… "She helped fight off the Fonolis, I invited her to join us," Alanitora repeated, hoping to dispel any outbursts.

"Yes, Owen. I helped. What are you doing here?" Diane sneered.

"My job!"

The carriage jolted over a bump, rattling everyone within.

"Well," Korena said. "Since we are all acquainted, why don't we enjoy ourselves and talk? It'll be quite a long ride."

Diane scoffed. "Acquainted is one way to put it."

"Oi!"

"Owen." Alanitora shook her head in warning, to which he relaxed his shoulders.

"It appears we will be traveling all night, so feel free to sleep if you can," Gwendolyn added.

"I know I certainly can't. It's far too bumpy to get a wink of sleep," Korena said.

Alanitora gave a satisfied smile. Korena and Gwendolyn were excellent at calming any negative situation, even if it meant becoming too energized and practically sucking the life force out of Alanitora. If there was a negative past between Diane and Owen, it would soon be fine.

And if her life was torn apart, she'd get through this. She would be fine. She had to be.

Alanitora opened her eyes, her vision focusing on the light outside the window. The sky was a light gray. Puffs of clouds rolled over the horizon like fresh-baked bread. The land itself was bare, yet lively with a field of grass spread across hills. A forest lined the outskirts of an empty field, various colors sprucing from their leaves.

She turned her head and saw a warm greeting in Gwendolyn's eyes. Everyone else was asleep. She wasn't sure how long she'd been out, but it had to be at least eight hours… Better sleep than she'd usually get.

"Good morning." Gwendolyn's hair was pulled back into a low braid, small curls peeking out to frame her face. Her hands held a small collection of flowers, and she was wrapping them into an arranged bouquet.

"Where did you get those?" Alanitora asked, gesturing towards the slightly wilted petals.

"Six hours ago or so. We stopped in the middle of the night for a small break. Since all you girls were asleep, I thought I'd stretch my legs and leave you be."

Alanitora sighed, stretching out her legs as much as she could with the limited room. Upon looking at her lap, she noticed she was still wearing her nightgown.

Gwendolyn examined her movements. "If you need a moment to stretch your legs and change your clothes, I'm sure they wouldn't mind stopping."

She shook her head. It wasn't that bad. Besides, she would have to wake up Korena to get out, who didn't handle her slumber being disturbed well. Alanitora patted down her thin skirts. Goodness, she'd been so distracted by the previous night's events that she hadn't once concerned herself with the fact that her thin chemise was improper attire for a lady of her position to wear in the presence of men. She'd change later when everyone else woke up.

Her hand ran over a lump at her waist and she paused. Alanitora hadn't realized there was something in her pocket. Reaching her hand inside, she pulled out the striped-stone pendant given to her the day before. Her fingers pressed over its smooth surface, running along the lines that wrapped the edges. It was heavy, dense, and it felt like her fingers were being pulled down at its touch. She lifted it to the light, admiring with awe as the golden color shifted.

"What's that?" Gwendolyn was staring at her fingertips.

"Oh, it's just some pendant a merchant gave me the other afternoon." What was its name? "Eye of something..."

"Tiger's Eye," Gwendolyn stated.

"Yes, that's it."

"May I see it?"

"Of course," Alanitora said, dangling the necklace towards her.

She gathered the pendant in her hand and pressed a finger on the stone, closing her eyes. After a moment, Gwendolyn frowned and opened them again, peering closely at the stone.

"What's wrong?" asked Alanitora, who was quite curious about Gwendolyn's actions.

Gwendolyn shook her head. "Nothing. Who did you say you got this from?"

"Just some random peddler." She shrugged.

"Did they say anything when they gave it to you?"

"Not really..." Alanitora looked at her lady pensively. Why was she asking so many strange questions? It wasn't usual for Gwendolyn to pry. The curious one out of the two was Korena. "Just said it was a clever stone. Why? Is there something wrong with it?" she asked again.

Gwendolyn's eyes blinked as though she had just been in a trance. "Not at all, it just looks a little dull for a piece of jewelry given to a princess. Is it alright if I hold onto it for a little? To clean it."

"Mhmm." Alanitora couldn't help but notice that Gwendolyn's chocolate eyes sparkled peculiarly. She hadn't seen so much charisma in them before.

Alanitora averted her eyes. She was overthinking things. Surely Gwendolyn was being herself, she always did have a fascination with earthly things, how was this any different?

She looked back out the window, letting her thoughts drift. Alanitora wondered what Donasela would be like. She knew about their weapons and riches but wasn't sure of the scenery, the atmosphere, the customs. Did certain kingdoms have personalities? If it was up to her, she'd say Trenvern was silent, almost shy, but solid. It was intelligent and wise, but not all-knowing.

Maybe all kingdoms were like that. In Donasela, her life could be the same tone, with different characters, or completely chaotic in change. She didn't know. She wouldn't know until it was too late, and Alanitora hated that.

Korena was the next to wake up, and like a morning songbird, she announced her presence proudly. Both of the rivaling redheads snapped awake at this, and silence no longer surrounded the carriage.

"Morning everyone... Owen," Diane acknowledged, her eyes scanning around the area.

"Good Morning!" Korena beamed.

"You seem to be in a cheery mood." Alanitora smiled back at her lady-in-waiting.

"Of course I am! It's such a beautiful morning, after all."

There was a rap on the moving carriage door that caught everyone's attention.

Owen leaned forward, pushing it open, and groaning at the sudden results.

Alanitora stretched her neck to see past Korena, nearly hitting Diane's head in the process as well. It was that boy, Uldin.

"Good morning, Your Highness." He began, such politeness in his tone. "I apologize if I interrupted anything, but I came to let you know our next stop is fourteen hours away. It's a known village near the border of Trenvern. We will be staying there for the night.

"In the meantime," he continued. "You may request us to stop at any time you wish, and food can be delivered to you whenever." The boy dismissed himself and guided his horse away from the carriage door.

"Thank you!" Korena sang a little, shutting the door behind him with a smile.

Alanitora blinked a few times. What had just happened? Was that the same boy who threatened her decency only a day before? "Whatever happened to that peasant for him to suddenly hold a tongue of respect?" She hadn't even noted herself saying it aloud until Diane responded.

"Actually." The redhead raised her hand matter-of-factually. "Trenvern conduct states that men of a low class are not permitted to become soldiers or knights unless under siege or war. I would know, my brother is training to be a knight."

"Is that so?" Gwendolyn asked. "I wonder if Owen knows him."

Owen huffed. "Yes, I do, and he is quite valiant. Much more than Uldin."

"Sure he is…" Diane raised her eyebrows.

Alanitora shot Owen a warning glance when his mouth began to open for a rebuttal. She wasn't in the mood for bickering.

"He's actually an okay person." Everyone turned to Korena in curiosity, intrigued for her to elaborate. "Uldin. I talked to him the other day, turns out he—"

"Korena!" Gwendolyn set down her flowers. "You know the rumors that surround the likes of him, it is unwise for a respectable young lady such as yourself to converse with him."

Gwendolyn was right. If any of the things her ladies had heard corroborated with her own experiences, then the boy certainly had ill intentions. He could even be pursuing them now.

Korena waved her hand at her friend. "No no, I was fine. William and him are good friends! In fact, William even confirmed so, and I trust him. Uldin may be misguided, but I believe he is a good man at heart."

"William? William Tabyer?" Owen asked.

"Yep!"

He gave a small hum of contemplation. "My experience with that boy hasn't been the best of times, but the fact that William approves of him must mean something. William is a fine man. Graduated two years earlier than the rest of us. He gave me his old longsword when he left camp. I'm glad to call him an acquaintance."

"Well if William is both friends with you and this Uldin character, he obviously is a terrible judge of character." Diane interluded.

"Oh…" Korena hung her head, and Alanitora could see water forming in the corner of her eyes.

So fragile, that girl. The princess knew Diane meant nothing malevolent by that, but knowing Korena meant the blonde would take it to heart. She had to admit that such soft skin annoyed her at times, and another part of her was urged to comfort her lady.

Then again, there would be no toughening of that skin if the girl didn't defend herself. If she didn't teach herself to not be weak. That fragility was her choice.

So Alanitora watched her carefully. Korena would either break or become stronger at this moment.

"It's alright dear, Diane didn't mean it that way." Dammit, Gwendolyn.

"Hmm?" Diane looked up. "Oh, I'm sorry if I hurt you, I'm not very careful at selecting my words."

"Goodness I hadn't noticed..." Owen murmured.

This left Gwendolyn having to lean far back in her seat as Diane swiped at the boy. Lord, they bickered a lot. What in the world had happened between them that caused such bitter and childish behavior?

Korena, still a little down, did respond to this with a small giggle, which was a good sign. Maybe Alanitora wouldn't end it just yet. At least until Gwendolyn pleaded for escape.

Conversations released into the background as Alanitora drifted into her thoughts. Everything was so strange. It felt like a dream, really. Her mother, her father, Owen, the fire, Diane.

The princess couldn't help but look at the girl. She was so inclined to trust her. What did she see in those eyes that reminded her of something, of someone? And what was it that Diane had to tell her? It didn't matter how often Alanitora distracted herself, her thoughts kept circling around to the same point. It wasn't like Alanitora to just accept someone into her closed circle so quickly. What was different? Was it because she had strange information?

No. She needed to stop thinking about it. Alanitora would figure all this out with time. Right now, she needed something to break her mind from the repetition of useless questions.

"Owen?"

"Hmm?" He lifted his vision from glaring at Diane.

"Can you have the entourage stop for a little while? I'd like to eat and change out of these clothes."

"Oh, yes, I'd be relieved to do so, too," Korena chimed in.

As expected, a pause in their journey was needed. Alanitora noticed such upon their reentry to the carriage, as an unfamiliarity settled the air. Everyone's clothes had been changed, their hunger appeased, and their moods considerably lightened.

This stark difference made the trip pass faster in time. Conversations were light and elongated, with subtopics and tangents in every direction. It was any matter of trivial things from news around the kingdoms to personal food preferences.

When encountering casual conversations such as these, Alanitora did her best to approach with the mindset of a game. In this instance, the princess kept conversations going because to her the goal was to never stop talking, to avoid the risk of awkward silence.

It bore her, but it was worth it for the positive outcome of both occupying her time and pleasing her companions. And by making the right moves, the conversation could shift into more interesting topics.

"Every weapon?!" Diane leaned forward.

"Yes," Alanitora replied. "All that Trenvern has to offer."

Owen interluded. "But… but that's impossible! Sir George Thurman, our weapons master, has tried such, but cannot for the life of him figure out the war hammer. Surely someone as small as yourself couldn't wield a sturdy blade!"

"Well, you should certainly believe it." Alanitora chuckled.

She could see Korena nodding her head in affirmation next to her, which was hilarious to the princess, as the lady was clueless about weapons.

"That sounds like an exaggeration to me…" the fiery-haired girl replied.

"Oh, I've been meaning to ask." Gwendolyn clasped her hands together. "You must be good at combat Diane, if Alanitora invited you along for your skills. What is your weapon of choice?"

"Here we go…" Owen rolled his eyes.

Diane jumped up with glee. "Needles!"

"What." Gwendolyn's eyebrows furrowed in confusion.

"Like… *Needle* needles?!" Korena pulled out her sewing pouch.

Diane opened her own. "Mhmm! I attach them to the folds of my gloves, and when they least expect it or are going to stab me, I poke them with the needles in sensitive places!"

Owen crossed his arms, puffing out a breath of air. "It isn't very effective or efficient to do so. You wouldn't hold up well in an actual battle."

"And you would?"

"I've been trained to use *honorable* weapons of combat, not silly little dressmaking things. In battle, it's important to face your opponent with a strong, large blade."

"Is it now?" The girl crossed her arms. "Would you expect someone as small and feeble as me to hold a cumbersome weapon?"

"That's why you shouldn't bother going into battle!"

Alanitora raised a brow at this comment. Sure, it was better to be muscular and stable in a battle of strength, but sometimes it was better to be swift and light on your feet.

Diane voiced this opinion well. "I'd argue the opposite. If you appear small and innocent to your opponent, then it is most likely he will underestimate your abilities. This allows for a precise plan of action if you use their heftiness against them."

Alanitora smiled satisfactorily as Owen yielded to Diane's arguments.

"Still," Gwendolyn began. "I don't understand how you are able to hold your ground. Is it not just a simple series of pricks?"

Diane folded her hands in her lap. "It is, but the smallest of pricks can be the most painful. There are certain places to aim for that cause severe pain and possibly immobilize your victim."

"Like the eyes!" Korena looked excited to finally know something.

"Most of the face, yes, but also the joints."

The conversation began to die down, and soon, so did the carriage. As it rolled to a stop, Alanitora felt a wave of exhaustion roll over her. Goodness, she needed some time alone.

The princess peaked out the window at the landscape. They were currently set in front of a small farmhouse, but up ahead there was a collection of buildings that Alanitora could only assume was the stop Uldin spoke of.

The opening of the door took her attention away from the late afternoon sky as her eyes met with an older guard.

He bowed. "Greetings, Your Highness, I am Sir Corwyn. I was assigned as the head of your travels to Donasela." The man paused for a moment, a small sign of worry washing over his square face. "I do apologize for not introducing myself earlier. We left in quite a hurry and the rest of the way I had to map out our path to effectively lead the entourage.

"No worries," she reassured him, a small smile upon her face. His eyes were kind-hearted. Soft and weathered.

"May I?" He reached his hand out to her.

Alanitora glanced around at her companions before taking Sir Corwyn's hand and stepping out of the carriage.

It was much brighter outside, the sun slowly approaching its resting horizon. The town in front of her looked like a tight-knit village. The buildings brushed their shoulders together, all circled around what looked like a plaza. The long line of wagons restricted her view, however, so she couldn't be sure.

"Quaint, isn't it?" Corwyn asked. She could hear the smile in his voice. "The town's name is Hearthshire, the only residential community in the land of Lord Darick. I was born and raised here, so on behalf of the people, I humbly welcome you to our home."

"Thank you Sir Corwyn. For the hospitality and for taking on such an important role."

The man laughed. "It is a pleasure. Come with me."

Alanitora's legs were numb from sitting idle for so long, and it took a small effort to bring her attention away from them and into maintaining a sense of patience.

The two of them walked to the front of the train, where a group of soldiers stood side by side to create a pathway of travel. Alanitora could hear the excited cheers and shouts from the crowd on the other side, and luckily the enthusiasm hadn't turned to violence. She wearily stepped forward.

Corwyn seemed to notice the change in her composure and shielded her from that side of the path, mumbling something about the town's excitement to have a royal pass through.

The precautions he took for her safety were comforting, and she felt at ease around the knight for some reason. Perhaps it was because she did not detect any ulterior motives for his actions. It was strange to meet someone so... genuine.

The path led them to a robust cobblestone building, one Alanitora could see was the tallest in the entire town, though it only raised three stories. Corwyn opened the door for her and led her inside.

The walls were jagged, but ultimately the tapestries and carpets made the area more welcoming. Candles were strewn across the walls in a pattern that illuminated the entire room. It wasn't as docile as she wished, but Alanitora at least felt a bit of comfort.

"Not that we've had the chance, but normally we would house royals in Lord Darick's estate north of here." Corwyn walked up behind her. "However, it would be inconvenient for our trip, as the Trenvern-Kreaha border is the other direction. I fear this may have to suffice in the meantime."

Alanitora smiled. It wasn't her preference, but how could she say no to such hospitality. "And the entourage?"

"Ah, Hearthshire is known as a checkpoint before the border, we have a lot of inn and tavern space for visitors. I'm sure everyone will find themselves a bed to sleep in tonight."

She turned around to face him. "Thank you."

"Of course, Your Highness. I'll leave a soldier posted outside the door. You may ask him if you need anything, and he will fetch it for you."

The man turned on his heel and departed the building, closing the door behind him.

The seclusion was refreshing. The princess had spent the last several hours pent up in a small space with four other people, so being able to walk around the cobblestone building gave her the wings of a sparrow. There wasn't much to explore, but it was a pleasant change of setting regardless.

It wasn't long before her ladies came bustling in, exclaiming things about a feast and music before cornering her away from the door.

Korena told Alanitora about a festival that was in production to celebrate her visit while Gwendolyn laid out a series of dresses for her to wear.

All of this was overwhelming to her, and it took all of her energy to not commence in an annoyed outburst with the two. Ultimately this composure worked, as Alanitora was able to settle into a new dress quick enough for her ladies to scurry away without a task, and leave her in solitude once again. Only the sounds of rising music for the festival remained.

After peaking outside to watch the townspeople prepare the lights of the event, Alanitora moved towards the vanity.

She checked herself in the mirror and sighed. The deep cerise dress fit her well, but she wasn't used to the flare and flow of it. A wavy curtain of silk surrounded her figure, leaving an open section in the front for her to extend her legs as she pleased. Her modesty was retained by the seal of its cut just before her knees.

Knowing there would be festivities soon, her energy came back just in time for the signaling knock on her door. A quick readjustment here and there, and Alanitora was ready to go.

She opened the door, and couldn't help but smile as a gust of wind blew back the wisps of her hair. Owen stood on the other side with a bright smile and an extended hand.

She tentatively took it, and suddenly felt a rush of excitement. The sky had turned dark, the stars glowing ever so radiantly. As for the light on earth, a series of lamps lined the doorway towards the center of the plaza.

The wall of guards had stopped her from seeing it before, but now that Alanitora could peer at the town, it became clear why she felt such a rush of welcoming. The streets felt like they were closing in for a welcoming hug, and a fiery warm light rested upon the paved pathways.

A crowd of people stood to the opposite side of the plaza, there was a mix of members of her entourage and townsfolk, all with such bright faces. A few cheered when she stepped into view, others stared in awe.

She and Owen moved towards the long table at the center. There was a single chair, its back facing Alanitora, welcoming her to sit.

Owen slowed his steps and raised her hand slightly. He drew in a deep breath. "Presenting Princess Alanitora Nayana Leland of Trenvern."

He had barely finished when the crowd erupted into applause. Upon their appraising shouts, Owen led the princess to her seat, pulling it out for her to sit.

In full honesty, she hadn't the faintest idea of what was happening, but rather than worrying about what protocol to follow, she chose to live in the moment.

A group of young children was the first to catch her eye. Some hung onto their mother's skirts, others had to be held back from investigating the princess that was receiving so much attention.

It was quite endearing, as Alanitora wasn't used to interacting with children. It was only ever lords and ladies of the castle, perhaps a soldier or maid here and there. Nevertheless, the collection of people were more aligned with those who lived on the outskirts of Trenvern's capital. Alanitora was sure they were dressed in their best clothes, but the simple and near-colorless garments showed that many were local farmers and working class.

They began to line up in front of her, one family approaching after another, offering obeisances and placing small gifts and products on the table. Some would introduce themselves or compliment her, a few would trip over their words and leave the table with red cheeks.

The princess did not usually enjoy the systematic attention towards her, but this didn't feel forced. Strangely, it felt genuine. It felt real. It felt human.

After the cultivation of gifts, a lively tune began to play to the side. It took a stern mental scolding to tear her attention away from the glee of the townsfolk to examine the presents on the table. She wouldn't be able to accept all of these, but with the number of goods on the table, it must have been much of the people's best work. If she couldn't make use of it, Alanitora would be sure to share it with the entourage.

"Care to join them?"

Her attention bolted upwards at Owen, who was standing beside her. His hand was extended to her again, and it took an examination of the crowd to understand what he was referring to.

They were dancing. It wasn't anything formal like a waltz, but their movements were in a free-spirited organization. Pairs of people stood opposite of each other, turning and twisting themselves around each other while also circling the plaza as a whole.

She looked back at Owen, his icy blue eyes holding the question. Alanitora shook her head and averted her eyes "I couldn't…"

"Why not?"

She looked back up at him. Alanitora wasn't expecting for him to ask such a direct question. "Because… I wouldn't know what to do."

He smiled. "Come on." Owen tilted his head toward the plaza.

She looked down at his hand then back up. Taking it for the second time that night, Alanitora allowed her old friend to lead her near the center, where people moved slower than their outer counterparts

People made room, and a few others slowed down to stare with curiosity. Alanitora tried her best not to mind.

"Raise your hand to mine." Her attention came back to Owen as she cautiously followed his instructions. "It is not much different than the dances you have already learned. First, find the rhythm of the music, and set your heart to sync with it."

Alanitora wasn't exactly sure what he meant, but she tried her best.

"Now," Owen pressed her hand towards her waist so they were parallel to one another. "Mirror my moves."

He began to move his hands around the air, slow enough for her to copy the movements with her own. Owen gradually began to incorporate the rest of his body, moving his feet as well. It was difficult to keep up. Dancing was sort of like fighting, but instead of counteracting each other's moves, you were supposed to unify them.

"Relax. Don't analyze, just feel it."

She closed her eyes for a second, centering herself with Owen's words, then opened them back up. Her feet moved in unison with him now, their movements swift and soft. She understood why this was the design of the dress Gwendolyn wanted her to wear.

As soon as the two were comfortable pairing with each other, Owen ambitiously guided her towards an outer circle, where the entire area moved together.

The world around her both fell away and took root in her movements, integrating instinct away from observation.

She felt free. The lack of routine allowed for expression, and with Owen as her partner, Alanitora felt no need to be self-conscious of how others would see her.

The princess couldn't help but laugh. "Is this what they teach you in your noble training?"

Owen shrugged, matching the small flourish of her arms. She had taken the lead now. "Sort of."

"What?" She wasn't expecting that reply.

He smiled at her. "We are encouraged to take up a hobby for the times where there are no battles to fight. I choose to study music—both dance and instruments."

She jokingly averted her eyes, drawing in a sharp breath.

"What?" he chuckled.

"Well… it's quite unfortunate, considering your *interesting* singing voice as a kid…"

"Hey!"

The two laughed, joining their hands back together as the song came to an end.

It was hard to stop her feet as the skirt brushed against her legs. Her giggles ended with her head hung and she looked back up at Owen. The applause had overcome the rest of the crowd, but her hands were still joined with his.

His eyes were soft and warm, and like the dance, she could feel herself reflecting them.

Alanitora stepped forward.

"Mind If I cut in for the next one?"

The two separated to see Diane smiling brightly.

"Of course," Alanitora stepped back, motioning towards Owen.

The soldier offered his hand to the other redhead, to which she rolled her eyes "Not you, idiot. The princess."

Owen raised his hands in defense. "My bad."

Alanitora's eyes followed Owen as he departed. The music began to start again, and she looked at her new partner. But instead of being met with the cheerful prospect of dancing, Diane's eyes were cold and serious.

"Pretend like we are enjoying the dance. Act casual, and don't look around at others."

Alanitora had to stop herself from stepping back in shock. The princess swallowed. It appeared her heart had been uncovered temporarily. This was a stark reminder of why she should never let that happen. "Understood." Alanitora met the girl's eyes with the same gravity.

"Princess Alanitora. From now on, you need to be careful. Don't dance with strangers, don't accept their food or gifts, and don't speak with them."

Alanitora frowned, but quickly relaxed her face and the thought of Diane's original warning. "Why?"

"Because. People are trying to kill you. They have been for years, and they've nearly succeeded before."Alanitora looked at the girl. Her eyes scanned the redhead's face over and over, looking for any sign of doubt. "And now that you are out in the open, you have given them the opportunity to finally carry out their plans."

7

Of Blood & Wine

"Wat are you talking about? *They*?! What plans?!" Though her voice was quiet, Alanitora couldn't help the forcefulness of it.

"Calm down."

Calm down? How was she supposed to calm down after Diane said something like that?! Alanitora thought the extent of people trying to kill her ended at the Fonolis attack, but now this girl was telling her that there had been assassination attempts for years, that there was an organized group dedicated to it.

"Tell me everything."

Guilt filled Diane's face. "I can't. Not here. Not now."

"That is what you said last night."

"I know, I'm sorry, but there is too much of a risk. They could be anyone of any status anywhere. Watching and listening at any time. Be careful, don't eat any of the foods given to you by individuals, don't communicate with townsfolk, and don't dance with anyone. Just go back to my brother."

"Your brother?" Alanitora asked.

"Owen."

What.

Alanitora froze in the middle of the plaza. Owen and Diane... They were siblings? That's why they were so bitter to each other? Not because they had any sort of romantic fallout, but rather a basic sibling rivalry.

The song neared its end and Diane broke her hands away from Alanitora's.

"Wait." The princess grasped her sleeve. "Just—" she paused. "Tell me who *'they'* are."

The redhead bit her lip, looking around. "The Men of the Blood Dragon."

The fabric slipped through her fingers as Alanitora watched the girl go. She tried to focus, forcing her mind to decipher the words about her adversaries. But only one thing repeated itself in her mind. Over and over. An endless loop.

"Excuse me." Alanitora made her way through the crowd of people, avoiding eye contact. She approached her temporary residence, the table in front of it now adorned with food.

"Are you ready for supper, then?" Sir Corwyn's voice emerged the second her eyes met the meals.

She peeled her eyes from the ground, meeting his. There wasn't a slice of malice in them. "Yes," she said softly, relaxing her shoulders.

But in full honesty, Alanitora wasn't the least bit hungry. She didn't want to force any food into her when her insides were twirling in their own dance. Everything suddenly felt large, as if she had shrunken to a little girl. One who the monsters and demons could grab for a snack.

The princess ate among her entourage. The princess ate among her entourage, cautious to bite anything that others had yet to try, Diane's warnings ringing in her ears. Yet she was too preoccupied to focus on sustaining her bodily needs. The core of her focus was her mind.

Alanitora replayed her conversation with Diane over and over again, greedily gripping each word as though it might slip away from her.

She'd learned from the conversation that people were hunting her. No, that was nothing new, it was a constant fact of her life. People were always hunting her. She had to be careful of that every day. She didn't have to worry daily about her old friend having a sibling.

Owen and Diane were brother and sister. This was a fact. A fact Alanitora knew nothing about.

How? How could she have gone all these years without knowing Owen had a sister? She scraped at her memory to find any instance, any indication that she had encountered the younger sibling. How could Owen and her have grown up together for ten years, and Alanitora hadn't known—or couldn't remember—anything about a sister?

The more she thought of their features, the more they looked alike. Red hair was an obvious resemblance, but also the slight puff of their cheeks, the way their noses protruded forward from at the tip. They certainly had the same lineage.

Based on Diane's age, they would have been two or three years old when she was born, meaning there were *seven* years of reason unaccounted for. With the frequency of time spent with Owen, she assumed there would be overlap with Diane as well, but there was never a redhead girl in her memory. If she was asked what siblings Owen had, she would have said none without hesitation.

Dinner goes by fast when placed in the background of one's mind. While trying to remember her past, she did not remember the events from eating until getting ready for bed. She had a faint recollection of feeling tired among trivial conversation, but anything more than that was a blur.

"Are you alright, dear?" Gwendolyn's hand upon her shoulder allowed her to emerge from the waters of the past, her words were no longer muffled and distant.

She wasn't drowning in memories of Owen and her childhood anymore. Alanitora could breathe again. "Mmm." She nodded, her head becoming clear. "Were you two aware that Owen and Diane are siblings?" If there was anyone to console her, it was her ladies.

"Oooh," Korena said with the sight of an epiphany. "I thought they were quarreling lovers."

"As did I," Alanitora noted.

Gwendolyn moved from the partition they had brought with them. "You did? I thought it was clear that they are blood relatives."

"I dunno, there are a lot of redheaded people in the world. If that is the case then I am probably siblings with Howard." The blonde waved her hair

83

in front of her own face.

Gwendolyn finished patting down the ends of Alanitora's nightgown. "Right! I forget neither of you have siblings."

Well, that explained the reasoning behind Gwendolyn's keen observation skills. "You have quite a few of those, don't you?" Alanitora teased, sitting on her bed and slowly brushing out the waves of her hair that had become quite tangled in her frolicking.

"Two older sisters and two brothers: one older and one younger. I knew the moment they began making snarky comments towards each other in the carriage. The constant fighting was all too familiar for me to miss."

This was shocking, considering Gwendolyn's peaceful behavior. "Don't tell me you—" Alanitora began.

"Oh, goodness no!" Gwendolyn seemed to catch right onto her insinuation. "Similar to how it was with the redheads, I was always in the middle of it."

The two laughed, and Korena joined in. "I'm not sure if that explains your mediator behavior, or if it is the other way around."

Gwendolyn shrugged as if she was shrouding herself in mystery.

The sun reached its zenith before they came to their fifth abrupt stop. The entourage had left the warm welcome of Hearthshire at dawn and had been stopped at the border for nearly an hour.

Alanitora's urge to sleep only increased, as she had found herself unable to rest the night before. Her mind had been processing everything in the darkness despite her best efforts to silence it all. 'It', of course, had shifted away from the Conlan siblings and to the mysterious Men of the Blood Dragon.

Unfortunately, now was no time to sleep, as she was informed that border officials would send someone to debrief the customs of entering Kreaha.

"How much longerrrr," Korena wailed.

"Korena." Owen leaned back. "As I explained earlier, crossing through the border takes a lot of time, especially with a party of our size. Each cart has to be thoroughly checked by officials. Plus, we have to replenish our supplies to help us with our journey ahead."

Korena kicked her feet forward in retaliation, nearly knocking the book Gwendolyn was reading out of her hands. Diane leaned back as she readjusted, her own activities of embroidery almost interrupted.

Their pause didn't last long, as the carriage soon lurched forward again... only to stop a minute after.

Gwendolyn sighed. "Lost my page... again."

"Wait, do you all hear that?" Diane shushed everyone and sat still.

There were muffled voices outside of the carriage, and they were coming closer. Before they could investigate, the voices stopped, and a knock followed.

Owen gave Alanitora a knowing look and opened the door.

Two men stood in front of it. Alanitora recognized one as a lower rank member of their entourage, and the other was a large man in full armor, helmet included.

"Good evening ladies, gentleman... Your Highness." the armored man's helmet made his voice echo within the metal. His head shifted to Alanitora's direction, and he gave a deep, stiff bow. "Your Highness, I presume. If you will give me the pleasure of coming to our base so we can review Kreahan customs."

She nodded, unsure if he could actually see the motion. The princess used Owen's outstretched hand to make her way out of the carriage, a polite smile on her face. She brushed down her skirts and double-checked to see that she hadn't left anything in her seat.

However, upon checking the carriage, her eyes flicked to Diane's. So silent, so cold of a glare that it concerned her more than she wanted to admit. Something was wrong, Diane was trying to tell her that.

The girl's eyebrows inclined as she nodded towards Alanitora's direction slightly. Her eyes then shifted and locked on something past her waist. Following her gaze, Alanitora turned to the armored knight. Diane seemed to be referring to the fact that the man's hand was resting upon the hilt of his sword.

Not to worry her, she gave the girl a small smile of affirmation before turning to the knight and began to walk with him towards the fort. Her mind replayed Diane's warning from the previous night for the hundredth time. She was obviously telling her to be careful, but of what exactly? Was it the man in particular, or a general statement?

Alanitora looked over to her walking companion. None of his posture or actions were out of the ordinary. She concluded that Diane may not know this, and was possibly being overly alert. The princess took comfort in the concern regardless.

"I apologize for using up your time, but it is a standard procedure that all nobility are debriefed in the laws of Kreaha before crossing over."

Alanitora gave a small hum of agreement. "Thank you, Sir..." She gestured for his name.

"Sir Devante, knight of the eastern district of Trenvern." They walked past a market of tents along the wall separating the two kingdoms. "Right this way."

Sir Devante motioned toward the entrance of a tent, where four soldiers stood guard. They moved out of the way with their approach, and he opened the curtain for her.

Alanitora stepped through, awed by the decoration of the tent. There was a map and diagram to the left that was as long as two men were tall. It held details depicting the wall she had seen outside. On the right, there was a collection of seats and cushions, each piece lavish and colorful. The walls held papers of notice and tapestries depicting mythical tales. And lastly, a large desk sat to the back in the center of the tent, two chairs on either side facing the paper-filled surface.

Devante rounded the desk, taking his gauntlet off and then his helmet, and placing them on the desk as well. "Sorry about that. In the case of ambush, I am supposed to wear full armor upon any form of correspondence. If you ask me, it is quite overbearing, but alas, you can never be too cautious," he huffed.

"That's alright." She gave him another polite smile.

The man had light brown hair that grew both on the top of his crown and along his jaw. He looked around his mid thirties. His deep-set eyes had crinkles at the edges and a brow bone that hung over them like a hood. His cheeks were filled, but tight enough that she could tell he had a sharp jawline beneath his beard.

"Please, sit. I'll get you a fine drink. One I've been saving for a special moment."

She tentatively sat in the chair opposite to his, and immediately felt small in it. The armrests were far apart and caused her to raise her elbows more, and the back of the chair rose above the top of her head. It was extremely comfortable, though.

Sir Devante took two chalices from the cabinet behind him and placed them on the desk. He then popped the top off the glass bottle and poured it into the cups, giving one a little extra splash. "There you are." He placed the fuller one in front of her.

She picked up her chalice and gave the liquid a little swirl. Wine. Her preference of anything alcoholic. The fermented bittersweet smell of the drink was refreshing, and it awakened her senses a little.

"I heard about the attack on the capital, and I offer my condolences. But on a positive note, I would like to toast to your safe travels up to this point, and a long life ahead of you."

He raised his glass, and in return, she did as well. Bringing the chalice to her lips, Alanitora took a gulp of the liquid, stopping for a second then continuing when she saw that Devante was drinking his entirely.

The wine was similar to that Alanitora often had, but with a much more sweet sensation. It was a little too sweet for a typical wine, which was odd to Alanitora. Having drunk about half and set back at the taste, the princess placed her drink in her lap.

The aftertaste was just as strange though, a tangy sensation settling around the edges of her tongue, a hint of unfamiliar bitterness.

"We should go over some familiar laws of Kreaha." Sir Devante began. He pulled a key from his pocket and opened a drawer to his desk, drawing out what Alanitora assumed was a set of Kreahan laws. "Basic illegal activities of Trenvern are the same sort. This applies to murder, thievery, other things I'm sure you won't have issues with." He laughed.

She smiled. "I'll be sure to not commit any crimes."

"A big thing that most royals aren't aware of is something less of a formality though." She took a small sip of her wine as he continued. "Though you are a royal, you may not be treated with as much respect. The diplomatic nature of…"

His words drifted off as the princess felt a small seed on her tongue. She rolled it forward across the roof of her mouth, bringing her fingers to take it out. It was small and black, round and firm, but not unbreakable, as her nails were able to split it in half. She frowned. It wasn't a grape seed.

"Is something wrong?" Sir Devante interrupted, snapping her out of a small trance.

She flicked her head up to him. "No, sorry about that." She had just been distracted for a moment, that's all.

Alanitora met his eyes to tell him to continue, but he looked blurred, distant. Her eyes felt dry, but her vision was watery. Small lines seemed to wave around the figure that was Sir Devante. Her senses tingled.

She looked down at her chalice. It didn't taste like wine, not any wine she'd had. Something was wrong with it. Very wrong. "What exactly is this wine made of?" she asked, looking up at him, trying desperately to see straight.

He gave her a look of confusion. "I believe it was made out of marionberry."

She slammed her eyes shut, then opened them back up, her eyesight a little clearer now. Alanitora met the eyes of Sir Devante. They were cold, proud. Like black consolidated clay that morphed in and out of shape, hidden behind stained glass.

Her stomach rumbled, causing the princess to double over in her chair, leaning over the side. Alanitora, trying not to let her eyes trick her too much, brought her hand to her mouth. Then, enclosing her lips around her knuckles, she jabbed at the back of her throat, shooting her hand back out as she felt the contents of her insides come up and out of her mouth, onto the grass below.

She raised her chest back to the chair, spitting the leftover acidic composition out of her mouth. "Poison!" Alanitora hissed.

"Damn," Devante cursed, setting down his chalice with force. "No way you are that clever."

No. How had she not seen it before? The malice in his eyes must have been so clear, and she missed it completely.

Alanitora pressed her hands on the arms of the chair, hoisting herself to stand up, but her right arm collapsed under her weight, forcing her down again.

The man who claimed he was Sir Devante sighed heavily. "I suppose we will have to do this the messy way." He began to make his way around the desk, and despite how slow he seemed to walk, Alanitora couldn't bring herself to get up.

She coughed fervently. "You aren't the real Devante, are you?" her voice came out as a scratched growl.

He laughed, cackled even. "Oh, Your Highness, I assure you that I very much am the real Sir Devante." He leaned in front of her, close enough that she could feel his warm breath on her cheek.

Alanitora strained her neck away. "Help!" she shouted out, but her voice betrayed her. It was small, frail, just above her typical volume.

"How cute," the way he dictated his words disgusted her. "The guards outside? They have no intention of intervening in this. "

Her thoughts raced. So fast, so unorganized. The dagger closest to her was in the fold of her skirt past her knee. If she could just reach it...

Alanitora leaned forward, reaching towards her toes, but her delirious nature led her to fall upon the ground. The grass was dry and sharp under her hands.

Devante grasped her bicep and picked her up, slamming her against the chair. "Oh," he cooed. "Such a pretty face, too bad it'll go to waste." From there, he made his way around the back of her chair, her chin grasped roughly in his hand.

Tears came to her when she saw the blade out of the corner of her eye. She had been rendered defenseless, weak at the mercy of a prideful man. This was it.

No.

Alanitora wouldn't go down without knowing she'd fought. Tactics didn't matter anymore. Calculations of what to use were of no advantage to her. Not in this state.

She flung her arms up, using her hand to feel for Devante's face. Then, with a quick grasp of his cheek, she dug the tips of her fingers into his skin, ripping them down back toward her. It was sloppy, but she knew there was a success when crimson dripped onto her lap.

Well, that and the bloodcurdling scream that came from Devante. Diane was right, the smaller things did tend to have the most impact. She could feel an accumulation of Devante's skin beneath her nails. His hands released her to respond to the cool air burning his cheek and she quickly bent forward, grasping for a chance to get the dagger out from her skirts.

She had nearly succeeded when she heard the sound of fabric ripping. Alanitora shot her head up in a panic to see a sword protruding from the fabric of the tent to the right of Devante's desk.

A rush of relief tingled every bit of her when two redheads emerged from the hole with haste, weapons drawn.

That relief didn't last, however, as soon after she heard a rush of footsteps entering behind her from the traditional tent entrance.

"Guards!" Owen shouted, gripping his sword with both hands. "This man is trying to kill the princess, apprehend him quickly!"

Oh Owen, if only you knew the half of it. She met his eyes with a pleading look. Sir Devante wasn't stupid enough to conspire a royal killing while surrounded by soldiers of the crown. She gripped the handle of her dagger as her sight began to swirl again.

Owen rushed forward with a downstroke towards Devante, but one of his soldiers blocked the attack, sending a large ring of metal to surround the princess' ears.

"Your Highness, are you okay?" Diane's voice was just as detached as everything else. The girl was kneeling in front of the princess, nudging her leg in an attempt to check if she was alright.

Alanitora wanted to tell her to go, to fight, to not worry about her. She wanted to tell Diane she was fine, that she would be fine. But a grumble and roll of her eyes could not communicate that.

The girl seemed to know what the objective of the moment was: eliminate the impending threat. This, unfortunately, was a plan Devante must have signaled to his people too, as one of them charged Diane with such speed that Alanitora was sure she was done for.

Diane slid under his swing and jumped forward, blocking Alanitora from the adversary. She threw a punch forward as he prepared to swing again, and the man stumbled backward.

Alanitora felt so heavy, and yet her mind was floating away. She felt like there was barely a twine connecting her mind to her body as she turned around in her seat with as much force as she could. She had to watch out for her friends if she couldn't stand beside them herself. Devante had backed up to the entrance of the tent, a scowl on his face at the violence between them. He clutched a handkerchief to his cheek.

Coward. Hiding away when things were closer to a fair fight. Alanitora pitied him. He had to rely on lies and deception to kill someone. There was no pride in that.

"Owen, down!" Diane's voice powered through the tent, the clearest sound in a cloud of confusion. Alanitora watched as she rushed toward Owen, who was dealing with two soldiers at once.

She slashed her hand across the back of one of their necks, kicking the same man back when he turned toward her. Owen stabbed the man in the gut, then turned to immediately block a blow cast by another.

Another man charged toward them, and Diane took the opportunity to leap off the ground and grasp his neck, a move that risked her getting stabbed, but was clearly worth the risk when she successfully boosted herself off his left arm and around his back, using all her small force to close her arm around his throat.

She took her other hand and stabbed one of her needles through the fabric of his sleeve, a chain of yells consuming Alanitora's ears. She watched as he blundered into the grass before she had to close her eyes.

The banging in her head. It was too much. The colors, the movements, the noises: All of it clawed at her mind, tearing apart the reality around her.

A firm hand gripped her shoulder, causing her to open her eyes again. Was it over? But a looming figure towered above her, his head looking down over the back of the chair she sat defenselessly in.

"Diane!" Owen yelled out.

Both Alanitora and Devante swiveled their heads towards the action, where Diane ducked at one of the last two apprehenders. She reached for the desk and grasped Devante's helmet off of it, swinging it around into the man's head. Nearly missing, Diane rolled to the other side of him to escape a raging downstroke.

Alanitora did not see the rest of her fight though. Not with the pending situation at hand. Things were suddenly clear, and Alanitora took the chance to flip her dagger into a reverse grip hold and raise it as far above her head as she could, before thrusting it down on Devante, somewhere near his shoulder blade.

For the second time, he screamed out, this time around more pain in his voice. Alanitora dug her hands into her skirts, clenching for something as the screams erupted in her mind. They echoed even when they were reduced to grunts, and Alanitora knew the next part was something she needed to brace herself for.

Her head still spinning, the princess looked up. Devante had pulled the dagger from his shoulder, blood gushing out ever so violently, and was now holding it high above his head. Alanitora's eyes aligned with the blade tip that threatened to plunge into her.

She didn't have any more energy. Her hands and legs felt like a heaving anvil, solid on their ground and unable to lift. With a simple breath, she prepared herself for the inevitable. She closed her eyes.

There was a deep inhale by the man who threatened her life, then another growl, and a thud.

"Nitora." Hands gripped the sides of her arms, shaking her vehemently. "Nitora!"

She lifted her lids. Orange. Like fire. Like early fall leaves. And blue. The same you'd see in a painting of a calm sea, next to a sandy landscape. A sandy figure.

Owen. He held her head in his hands as her vision of him focused. He was kneeling on one side of the chair, his eyes moving between hers. "It's over. It's over. Are you okay?"

Aware of his worry, Alanitora nodded, looking around the room. Her eyes focused on the sight of blood. It was Owen's, a steady stream trickling down from his bicep. She reached toward it, the frown quite intense on her face.

Owen followed her vision. "Don't worry about it. It's just a cut."

She shook her head. He was a silly boy. Dumb, really. Alanitora leaned over, ripping a part of her underskirts and sitting back up, taking the cloth towards his wound.

Owen's hands interjected her process though, as he took her hand in his, lowering it. "We can do that later. It's okay."

"Owen..." Diane warned. "Enough of the sentiments. We don't have time. Let's go."

The boy nodded to his sister and turned back to Alanitora, moving around the chair to pick her up.

She held onto his neck, though it probably didn't help much. He held her back in one arm, and her legs in the other, lifting her into the air.

"What are you doing?" the vibrations of Owen's chest when he spoke comforted Alanitora as she rested her head against it. She looked around.

Diane was opening Devante's drawer with haste, tousling the contents with one hand, and holding both a sword and Alanitora's chalice in the other. Her size certainly justified her preference against swords. "I'll explain later, We gotta get out of here before reinforcements flood this place." She rushed to their makeshift opening, holding it open for the other two to go through.

8

Silver Secrets

"I can walk," Alanitora said when Owen gave a small grunt.

"No. You'll slow us down."

Her breath was ragged, too ragged for her to properly argue against him. "You carrying me will slow us down—"

"Shush. I'll put you down soon, okay?"

She closed her eyes. The turbulence of him running with her weight in his arms gave her a headache. Alanitora couldn't stand to keep them closed as she watched them rush along the border wall, stopping only to hide before they might have been spotted.

"Go," Owen nodded at his sister, who rushed ahead at their approach toward the gateway.

Diane stopped in front of the posted guard with the sword and chalice behind her back, striking up a casual-looking conversation with him. While he was distracted, Owen and Alanitora slipped behind him to the other side of the border before picking up the pace until the carriage was reached.

Owen slowly set the princess on her feet, offering his arms out for support. Alanitora felt weak. She was, having ingested poison, but it still bugged her. Diane wasn't far behind, and as soon as she reached them, Owen handed Alanitora over to the girl.

"Help her into the carriage. I'll alert the entourage. Be ready for anything."

95

Diane's mouth opened, rebuttal ready, but her brother had already descended into the distance.

They made their way to the door, Diane nearly yanking it open before helping Alanitora in like an old lady.

"My goodness, what happened?!" Korena gasped.

Diane closed the door. "They poisoned her." She held up the chalice. "Not sure with what though."

"Can I see?" Gwendolyn asked, a frown upon her usually tranquil face.

Alanitora watched her lady-in-waiting grasp a handkerchief from her girdle and scoop up the contents of the chalice. The midnight purple skin of a berry spread across the cloth when Gwendolyn rubbed her fingers against it. The wine left a wet reddish residue, a more maroon color underlying it. There were small seeds that had been in the bottom of the cup, now scattered upon the liquid and berry skin.

"Atropa Belladonna." The name rolled off her tongue. "Also known as deadly nightshade. It's highly toxic to humans."

"Oh my," Korena gasped.

Diane bit her lip. "She threw it up though. Surely..."

Gwendolyn nodded pensively in response. "Based on the ratio of wine to that of the berry, drinking all of it would have killed her, but if that is the case, then her body never processed the amount taken. Her Highness will be a little sick, but nothing more.

That was good, Alanitora concluded. At the moment, she hadn't been sure whether or not regurgitating the contents would save her. There was no rush of relief upon hearing Gwendolyn's words, but there hadn't been any impending dread in the first place. She just felt indifferent. An indifference, Alanitora thought, probably wasn't usual to dying.

Just then, the carriage began to lurch forward, her stomach almost bursting with it. Owen opened the door and climbed through, placing himself next to Alanitora. Gwendolyn took this chance and tossed the handkerchief out of the open door before he closed it.

"What was that for?! We could have used that!" Diane vociferated.

"There is no use for something that only grants death," Gwendolyn said calmly.

Owen waited until their exchange was over before speaking up himself. "I've told them only the base of the story. I made sure to leave out *who* did such, in case loyalties are questioned. Sir Corwyn is doing everything he can to ensure Alanitora's safety. How is she?"

"I'm fine," Alanitora said, tired of people speaking for her. The horses of the carriage must have been moving at an accelerated trot rather than the normal walking pace.

Silence folded around them for a long moment, Diane finally breaking it. "That knight... What was his name?"

"Diane, we can talk about this later. Right now—" Gwendolyn was cut off by a gasp from Korena.

"Your Highness! Your wonderful hair, there is blood in it!" Her dramatic lady-in-waiting began pouring water from a canteen onto her handkerchief and wiped away at the princess' scalp before Gwendolyn, quite visibly annoyed, placed a hand on her arm.

"That's enough. We need to leave Alanitora alone. I'm sure she's tired from her fight, and her body needs to recuperate from the effects of poisoning. Let her sleep."

A pang of protest hit Alanitora from inside, but Gwendolyn was right, she desperately needed to sleep.

"She's right," Owen's soft voice whispered, winding its way into her ears. She had barely noticed that he was brushing her hair aside so that it didn't stick to her sweat-ridden cheeks and forehead.

Slowly, Alanitora leaned into the support of his arm, her head resting softly on the padding of his shoulder. She realized that since dropping her off at the carriage, her soldier had changed out of his bloodied armor. The cloth of his sleeve was soft, the warmth of his body seeping through, soothing her mind.

Alanitora's consciousness ebbed in and out like a tide, sleep faltering like a flickering candle. She could feel the support of her weight under her knees and upon her back, the rest of her body hanging below it with a slight swing. Her head rested against a vertical surface. One that had a steady rhythm beneath it.

A zap of realization struck the princess: someone was carrying her.

Pulling herself from sleep as fast as she could, Alanitora opened her eyes, ready to see another adversary.

But above her was nothing of danger, it was Owen, his eyes set ahead in the direction in which he was carrying her. She relaxed. There would be no need to fight at this moment.

Alanitora let her eyes scan the rest of her surroundings. They were in a clearing, already adorned with camp materials. A few groups of men were rushing around to set up the tents in the area, a forest beyond the clearing. The sky above was turning dark with the subtle approach of night.

She drew in a deep breath, one she hadn't realized she'd been holding back. Her stirs were enough to draw Owen's attention, as he looked down at her with a soft smile.

"You're awake."

Giving a hum of affirmation, she shifted her chest. "I'm all fine to walk, thank you."

Owen nodded, bending down so she could slide from his hold and onto her feet. Grass tickled past the edges of her shoes, sending a small thrill up her spine.

Alanitora brushed down her skirts, which were considerably disheveled. She turned to Owen. "Please retrieve my ladies as well as your sister. There are heavy subjects for us to all discuss."

"My sis—" Owen paused. "When did you figure that out?"

"It doesn't matter, bring them all to my tent in five minutes."

Something was very wrong. None of what had happened to her recently could possibly be a coincidence, not with what Diane had said to her in Hearthshire. Whatever information that girl was holding, she needed to tell them. They all did.

Alanitora turned. She could only assume the large tent was hers, as the other ones were either still being set up or were shambolic in nature. She made her way towards it but stopped at the large bonfire in the center of the camp when she noticed there was no light emanating from inside.

Alanitora entered the tent with the torch, lighting the four standing ones within before placing it back outside.

The tent was set up as a permanent room would be, with furniture from her own back home, most notably her desk and ornate chair. There was a cot on the right edge and a corner for her weapons chest. On the other side, there was a leisure chest next to a dresser that she assumed held materials for her ladies to use in maintaining the temporary area.

Reciting the contents in her head, Alanitora made her way to the leisure chest. She hadn't used it often, hence the reason it was always tucked into a corner of her room back home. There were books inside, along with ink and parchment and a few rolled-up diagrams and maps.

She sifted through the contents, settling on the map of southern Mordenla and some clean leaflets.

Clearing the desk of the pitcher of water and bowl of fruits, the princess rolled the map out. She then rushed back to the chest to retrieve a few books that would weigh it down.

"Princess this, princess that. Make sure she has that, make sure you put this in her tent." Korena had entered the tent, a pile of sheets higher than her head held in her arms. "We have to sleep on the floor with tiny sheets while she gets enough blankets to warm a pack of bears— Ah!" The girl had just put the sheets on her bed when she made eye contact with Alanitora, her ears beginning to turn a deep shade of pink.

"Just so you know, Korena—" Alanitora began, setting a book on each edge of the map.

"Your Highness! My greatest apologies, you see I was just—"

"Korena."

"—and I wasn't thinking of whether or not you would be present—"

"Korena!" Alanitora raised her voice, silencing the blonde. "First off, a group of bears is a sleuth, not a pack, and second—"

"I'm sorry!" Korena interjected.

Alanitora took in a sharp breath. "Second, you have every right to complain about your situation, just know I don't have the ability, nor the intention to change them," the princess said softly, waiting until her lady's flesh was rid of its rosy color. "Third, Owen and the girls are on their way. I asked them to collect you as well, so please stand outside and usher them over when you see them."

The blonde nodded and rushed out of the tent with haste.

Alanitora smoothed out the map, going over what she'd say to everyone. She'd never debriefed someone on such a subject before, and it wasn't as though she had ever expected to. Everything that was happening was generally unsettling, and the biggest of her worries right now were formulating words that would maintain a calm composure.

The princess had nearly rearranged the entire set up of the desk three times before her companions filed in. She walked around to the front of the desk and leaned back slightly on it, resting her hands in front of her.

Gwendolyn met her with kind eyes. "Are you feeling alright?" she asked. It was comforting to see her lady concerned for her health.

Alanitora gave her a small smile before letting her face drop back down. "Yes, I am alright, but that isn't the important part right now. The important part is why I was not alright in the first place. Owen, check to see that no one is listening in, the four of you are the only people I consider trusting."

She waited for him to check before continuing. "Something is happening. There have been far too many attempts on my life in the past few days for it to be a coincidence, as well as a plethora of new and intriguing information that points to a possible conspiracy." Her eyes instinctively flicked over to Diane.

"It's time we clear up all of this, and while some of you have seemingly nothing to do with it, I believe it is important that we hold a shared universal knowledge regarding this matter. If my life is in danger, so is all of yours for being close to me." She felt a small chuckle rise in her throat. "I understand this is a dramatic thing to say, but it is true."

Alanitora looked around the room, anxiously gauging everyone's reaction. Korena and Gwendolyn immediately looked at one another, and the princess wasn't sure if it was confusion or concern on their faces. Perhaps both.

Owen, on the other hand, peered straight at Alanitora, his eyes narrowing as though trying to ask her directly what she had figured out without speaking.

She pinned her attention back to her own words. "Let me make this clear: Each one of you has kept vital information from me in the past few days. With the events that have occurred, I believe the best course of action is full transparency with one another. If there isn't, I won't hesitate to dismiss you from your duties."

Korena's eyebrows creased. "But Your Highness, we would never do as you accuse us of! We are your sworn maidens, meant to—"

"Is that so?" Alanitora interjected. "Despite claiming to be my closest friends, neither of you told me of my mother's betrayal, nor my betrothal." She paused, sighing away the tension in her shoulders. "I am not trying to invalidate years of companionship, but I don't know who to trust."

There had been attempts on her life before, but none like this morning. Devante not only used his position of authority to try and kill her, but he joined with five other guards to execute it. It was too organized to be a small act of mutiny.

After a long moment of silence without protest, Owen spoke. "I'm sure your ladies didn't mean to keep such things from you. They must have heard whispers of it as castle gossip with nothing to confirm its credibility."

Alanitora's patience was running thin with their defenses. She held up her hand, stopping him from continuing. "Don't. Don't you dare give me excuses. Do not forget that you withheld the same information from me until I threatened to slice it out of your throat. Our secrets will kill us if we don't reveal them. So I ask you all to take this time to lay out whatever you may be keeping from me on the table."

Owen stepped forward. "I swear on my life, Nitora, none of us would ever do anything that in any way would cause you harm."

"Well, you certainly aren't doing anything to stop one from harming her,"

Diane spat, the break of her silence bringing everyone's attention to the girl.

Owen frowned, facing his sister. "What are you talking about?"

"How do you expect her to trust someone who can't even keep their promise?"

Gwendolyn looked between the two siblings. "What promise?"

Alanitora, intrigued as well, pushed herself off the edge of the table. "Yes, what promise?"

"You don't mean…" Owen stepped back.

"You know exactly what I mean. You left. Someone had to protect her," Diane sneered.

Owen's voice raised. "I left to protect her! What are you saying, that you took the mantle on at the age of seven?!"

Alanitora brushed back the stray hairs from her face before clenching her hands in the air. "Enough! Just— Diane. Clearly, this has something to do with whatever we've talked of. Tell us what you know."

Diane looked around at the rest of the entourage. "I don't think they should—"

"Like I said, transparency. It goes two ways."

The redhead sighed, looking over at her bewildered brother before turning her attention to Alanitora as she took her bag from around her shoulder and placed it on the table. She turned it over, letting the contents spill out before she arranged a few, including a collection of papers and weapons.

"Over the years, I've encountered a number of people embedded in positions of power around Trenvern who have used their advantages to try and kill you in particular. Devante is the fourth confirmed member that I have stopped." She turned to face everyone, crossing her arms. "These attacks are getting more frequent. I think something big is being planned."

Gwendolyn tilted her head. "Member? How do you know they are correlated?"

"Because," She lifted some parchments in the air, unfolding them to smooth out against the table. Diane lined up three in a row. "These."

Alanitora stepped closer to look at each of them. They all held similar, strange lettering. It was a cursive-like structure, the alphabet tossed randomly among the writing. There was a possibility it was a different language, but pronouncing anything phonetically was impossible. "It's some kind of code," she examined out loud.

"Look at the seals." Diane gestured toward the table.

At this point everyone else had congregated at the table, looking over Alanitora's shoulder with piqued curiosity.

On the bottom right corner of each page was an ink symbol that held a dragon. A single wing towered over its silhouetted body. One of its claws was wrapped around a sword, the end of which pointed to an orb-like circle wrapped within its tail.

She looked between the three. They were all the same pose, but the dragon was not quite the same. Some of the details were different: one more scaly, another less neat. Regardless, they all appeared to be hand-drawn rather than stamped. The handwriting, ink, and supposed contents of the letter were different as well.

In fact, the ink color itself, regardless of which one, was peculiar. It wasn't pure black ink. Instead, it had a murky brown tone to it. She looked closer. Putting aside the darkness of actual ink, the liquid looked familiar. Her mind scanned what it could be before the thought of dried blood came to her conscience.

Alanitora's head shot up, her eyes meeting Diane's as she remembered her words of warning from last night. "Men of the Blood Dragon."

Diane nodded grimly.

"What is it? What's going on?" Korena asked.

Diane, ignoring the blonde's question, began again. "I was on my way to deliver this evidence when the Fonoli attacked. That last one was in Devante's drawer. And get this-" she reached across the table and brought the knight in question's longsword over, turning it so the handle was visible. A metal dragon wrapped around the handle, a small red crystal in its mouth. "Two of the other men in power I stopped had dragon-adorned weapons. Other Trenvern officers didn't have them though."

So that was why Diane had looked down at Devante's hand when he retrieved her from the carriage that day. She was trying to tell her to look at the handle.

"Alanitora, I believe a corrupt system is embedded within Trenvern."

Owen stepped toward his sister, towering over her. "Why didn't you turn these in? It could have helped protect her!"

Gwendolyn scoffed. "You dunce, did you not hear what she just said? People in positions of power at Trenvern are the ones to blame. How could Diane possibly put her trust in one of them?"

"Do *you* hear what you are saying? A conspiracy? Seriously, Diane! Trenvern officials promise their entire lives to the crown, not one of the men I know would dare to defy this oath, not even those with generally twisted morals," Owen spat.

Korena wrapped her arms around herself. "He's right, *my* love would never do something as vile and terrible as what you are suggesting."

"You're biased." Diane stood her ground.

"I'm honorable," Owen replied.

Alanitora could feel her insides seeping out. Raw and vulnerable. "What did they do to you?" Owen's eyes flicked to hers, silence folding over him. She couldn't see him, but a stranger. It wasn't the Owen she knew, it wasn't *her* Owen. Her Owen didn't trust authority. Her Owen always sided with her, even if it was just to impress her. Her Owen was smart. This wasn't him.

The princess sighed, rubbing at her temples. It was all too much. After a deep breath, she raised her head again. "Alright, is that all the information you have, Diane?"

The girl bit her lip. "Unfortunately, factual and physical wise, yes. I still have accounts of the times I prevented the attempts, but more importantly, there are theories and assumptions I—"

"No need," Alanitora cut her off. "Is there any other information anyone is withholding from me at the moment?

When her eyes scanned her companions, Alanitora saw no secrecy within their eyes through the fog of silence. Save for Diane, who seemed as though she still wanted to share her heroic events. "Very well, please leave me be then. Thank you for bringing up these concerns. You may go."

Alanitora watched them depart, taking a deep breath as the curtain of a doorway closed behind them. What the hell was happening?

Darkness often feels like an entity. Whether it's a blanket of serene sorrow to hug, or a foreboding shadow watching from a distance, it's always there.

That night felt different. That night, as Alanitora lay restlessly awake in her tent, the entity of darkness was not there. It felt like a statue. A hollow impostor. A numbing abyss.

Agitation bit at her as she looked up into the nothingness.

She felt idle. Like a puppet left on a shelf in the corner of the room, strings action-less, waiting for someone to pull at them, to pull her fate.

It felt like an eternity without rest, and Alanitora sprung from her bed, pressing her feet to the grass beneath, guiding her toes lightly across the area of the tent to her weapons chest.

The slight light emanating inside the tent from the large fire outside barely allowed her to see what was in front of her as she felt her way around the latch that held the large chest closed. Slowly, she lifted the lid, aware that it was often quite creaky.

Alanitora lightly guided her fingers down toward the center of the chest, careful enough so she wouldn't find loose blades slicing at her fingertips. Most of her weapons were indeed protected with a sheath or cloth, but caution was still kept as she guided her way past a sword and toward the bottom, where her fingers soon brushed across a thick wool fabric. Resting her other hand lightly on the weapons that lay above it, Alanitora began to pull the folded garment out, putting it aside and securing anything from clattering within the chest.

She was lucky she had wielded her bow a few days before when leaving Trenvern, otherwise the princess would have had to retrieve it from the bottom of the chest, the risk of the string catching on any number of objects. Instead, Alanitora plucked the bow from its resting point and loaded her quiver with arrows before putting both aside and closing the trunk.

She cast the fabric over and around her shoulders, a smile of satisfaction creeping onto her lips as the cloak's edges settled around her figure. She clasped it, gliding her fingers across the hood to pull it up.

Alanitora swung the quiver over her back, gripping the bow as sweat came to her palms. She wasn't nervous, but rather thrilled. The princess would hunt for the first time in forever tonight.

The only issue, of course, was getting out of camp without raising suspicion. After the events with Devante earlier that day, there would no doubt be vigilant eyes watching over the camp. Alanitora's tent was in the center, which probably meant there were guards posted around the perimeter of the entire campsite rather than just her tent.

Regardless, Alanitora stepped lightly towards the opening, peering out at the landscape before her.

Adjusting to the bright flames of the fire made things difficult to see everything else at first, but with enough concentration, she saw that there were only a few guards in the center. Two of which faced the other way, while the one closest to her lulled away. Typical. This was why Alanitora was glad she knew to fight. No man could properly defend her, even though it was their job.

The crackles of embers did well in masking any sounds Alanitora's feet might make as she crept around the side of the tent, around the sleeping guard, and to the shadows of another tent. Her heartbeat pattered in an addicting tempo. A thrill of adrenaline rushed into her. She took a moment to catch her breath as she turned to the woods ahead.

Alright, so her theory about a heavily guarded camp had been incorrect. It took her much effort to banish thoughts that perhaps there were Men of the Blood Dragon within the entourage itself, instead focusing on her goal at that moment: getting away from everyone else.

A few guards were posted between her and her freedom, but her luck held that they were trying to prevent people from coming in, not out.

Alanitora kneeled, her eyes on the men while her hands searched around for a projectile to use. There was indeed a rock, but she wasn't sure it was dense enough to fulfill her desires of intent.

She stood slowly, bending her knees slightly and looking into the distance past the guard. She only had one shot at this. Checking her right to be sure no one was there, Alanitora grasped at the stone, planting her feet in the ground and chucking it over the guard and into the canopy.

As anticipated, their eyes flicked over to the sound in alert awareness. She didn't have time to double-check or doubt her action before bounding herself across the small clearing between the camp and the forest. She ran as fast as she could into the covering of the trees, slowing herself upon touching the ground foliage, to not make a sound.

Now in the shadow of the trees, Alanitora turned back to look at the guards.

She smiled. Their immediate reaction after hearing the stone was to turn towards the camp to look for any intruders, giving the princess the perfect opportunity to slip into the night without suspicion or notice.

Coming back into camp would potentially be a problem, but for now, the night was hers.

9

Unbroken

Moonlight cascaded through the silhouetted trees and onto the forest floor. Thankful for her nocturnal adjustment, the scenery around her brightened the deeper Alanitora ventured into the woods. It was silent too. She could hear nothing but her light footsteps, and perhaps her thoughts by extension.

It was peaceful. This silence was like basking in the sunlight on a windless afternoon... though the princess supposed this was quite the opposite.

After traveling far enough from camp that the animals would be undisturbed in their natural lives, Alanitora paused at a clearing. She wished to continue, but getting lost was not an option, and the panic that might arise if someone noticed her absence was enough to hold her back from freedom. Instead, she looked around the area.

Ferns and shrubs covered the floor. In the distance, she could see the outline of a fallen tree. These spots could hold small skittering creatures that would stay hidden if she continued to walk around. A quick survey of the trees left a particularly large one with a number of lower branches. Early to autumn's embrace, a scarce amount of leaves were left on it. Enough to conceal her while allowing for a view of the area. That would be a good vantage point for sure.

Not to make too much commotion, Alanitora didn't give herself a usual running jump, instead pulling herself up from the lowest branch and making her way slowly higher up until she was satisfied with the position. She had a good view of the landscape and a path to jump down if needed. It was perfect.

Now to wait. Patience was needed for these things. Probably why most royals she knew of didn't enjoy the activity unless in a group with other experienced hunters. She was able to admit she was not an experienced hunter herself, but that didn't rule out the possibility to be.

There were small rustles every once in a while, many of which she either couldn't place or attributed to rodents. She was grateful that there were no owls nearby to call out and deter the smaller animals. After all, even a rabbit would suffice.

Doubts had started to fill her mind when she saw it out of the corner of her eye: the rustle of shrubbery. It couldn't have been large, due to the size of the bush, nor was it small when considering the amount of movement. Perhaps it wasn't something impressive like a deer, but it was better than nothing. Alanitora searched her quiver for an effective arrow, readying her bow before she lost sight of the small creature.

However, as she drew back the string, another sound followed from an area not far away from her target. Feet padded at the ground, rushing towards the creature. There was a growl, and Alanitora saw it. It was a faint figure at first, her eyes unable to take in motion within the dark.

But one thing was clear: This was a predator of the night. Massive and ducked low to the ground, with wild hair upon a sleek body. The silhouette of its tail a sparking flint.

The thump of its forelegs hitting the ground came seconds before the low squeal of the prey, followed by a low growl of grotesque satisfaction.

Alanitora's eyes glimmered at the sight of such a magnificent hunter as it came into view of the moonlight. A wolf. She had never seen one in person before. It was glorious.

A few moments later, other padded footsteps followed, and a half-dozen of others joined the first one to help devour the victim. She watched as they surrounded the dead creature, chewing at its flesh with a series of guttural sounds.

One wolf in particular stayed behind, its ears pulled back as it tentatively tried to find a spot in the circle, walking around them and peeking its head between their hides.

There was something odd about it. At first, she thought it was observing the hunt, but its constant shift in weight suggested impatience. And when the lone wolf finally had a clear path to the food, the victorious hunter began to growl before snapping at it.

The lone wolf jumped back, cowering as the others turned to it for a few moments before returning to their food.

Alanitora frowned. She understood there may have been a system to the wolves that she did not know about, but how they treated their companion didn't feel right to her. She watched the scene pensively as the wolf continued to wait for a small portion of the food. Passage of time revealed to her that the pack had no intention of sharing with it, and the princess raised her bow again. If the natural world didn't act against selfishness, she would.

She raised her weapon again, putting her aim on the hunter. Her fingers tightened around the embedding of the bow as she steadied her hand. With a strong pull of the string, she released, sending the arrow through the air with a thwack. It zoomed past the foliage between her and the pack, embedding itself in the ground to the left of them.

They paused looking around with sly detection… only to go back to their meal. Seems scaring them away wasn't going to work. Holding back her frustration, Alanitora aimed again. Grip. Pull. Release.

This time her target was hit, knocking it to the floor with a loud thump. The barks of the other wolves rose as they scattered about in different directions.

She jumped from the tree, bending her legs to catch her weight before the ground. Her cloak flapped around her, sweeping in the cool air before it deflated on the floor. She stepped over the ferns and twigs, no concern for the commotion she made now that her hunter's ambition was released.

The wolf lay alone on the floor next to the scraps of what looked to be a groundhog. Its feet twitched slightly in moments before the end. A fight to stay among the living. Moonlight illuminated the body, and Alanitora found herself surprised at the size of the canine. She hadn't realized a wolf would be so large in comparison to the hounds that roamed the palace.

She watched as its life and spirit slipped out from the wolf's wound into the blood-rich forest floor. When motion ceased, when life was gone, Alanitora kneeled down and pressed her hand to its body. Its hair was coarse, dried blood from more of its victims tangled in. Small scars and scratches riddled its body, the pads of the wolf's feet torn and rough.

Alanitora knew she should feel bad for taking a life she knew nothing about, a life that could have been innocent.

She didn't.

Just as the princess was about to pick up the corpse a rustle sounded from behind her. Her hand shot to the dagger at her waist. Alanitora darted around to see the lone wolf flinch, cowering an arm's length away from her. It stared into her eyes unblinkingly. A look of loneliness, a desire for belonging. An expression of curiosity and hope.

She reached her hand out, putting her dagger back in its place.

The moment of silence was filled with tension as the wolf looked between them and their surroundings, before stepping forward slowly. Its cold wet nose touched the palm of her hand, leaning into her touch more and more with every passing moment. She took her gaze away from the wonderful eyes and to the rest of it, captivated by the way the wolf's fur shined silver in the moonlight. Gray outlined the features of its face and a charcoal color weaved into its coat near the hind. Its tail faded from silver to white, save for the tip, which was black like a brush dipped in ink. The wolf's glimmering colors left her breathless.

"Hello there." The wolf flinched at her words, but stepped forward again, sniffs audible as its neck craned to smell her face. After a singular lick of her cheek, the wolf sat down obediently.

"So you're a he, huh?" His tail wagged slightly in an unusual form of response. Alanitora gave him a scratch on the cheek like she did the dogs in the castle. "And you're okay with the fact that I just killed one of your own?"

He tilted his head, his eyes filled with jubilant innocence.

"Your leader was that bad, huh?" she looked at him with pity, her eyes scanning over his coat again. Silver in the moonlight. Silver Moon. She chuckled at the idea of the name, aware naming an animal might attach one to it.

With a heavy sigh, she stood. The wolf's ears perked as Alanitora gathered her things preparing to head back to camp with the dead wolf. "I believe it is time for me to go, little one." she gave him one more scratch before turning to walk back towards camp, stepping carefully with the heaving mass in her arms. After a few paces, she turned around. The wolf was slowly following behind her from a distance. Alanitora smiled, it was quite cute. Luckily his curiosities would cease.

But he continued following her, only stopping when the forest did. She readjusted the body onto her other shoulder, giving a small smile of goodbye to the strange animal before turning away from him for good.

Getting back into camp was painfully easier than getting out. This was something she wasn't sure she could give credit to her luck or the guard's stupidity. There must have been a few of them on break when she returned, for there were half as many around the perimeter and the ones there oscillated back and forth from opposite sides.

She rushed with the mass in her arms to the shadow of one of the tents before heading to her own after it was clear. The guard out front had now fully nodded off to sleep, soft snores coming from his hung head. At least he was alive.

She slipped past him and was nearly in her tent when Owen came out of it frantically with a panicked look on his face, nearly running right into her before consternation overtook his features.

"Where the hell were you?! And why do you have a wolf?!"

Alanitora held back her annoyance, instead looking around to be sure no one heard him before pushing him into the tent, not bothering to close the curtain behind her.

"I couldn't sleep." She explained calmly, placing the corpse down on an uncarpeted area of grass. Hopefully, he'd take the hint of her serenity and relax.

"Couldn't—!" He stopped to lower his voice, no less riled up than before. "Couldn't sleep?! So after someone tries to kill you, you decide to go on an excursion through the woods instead?!"

"Yes."

"You—" Owen stuttered over his words, she could sense that once he got them figured out, a tirade was on the horizon.

She stopped him. "You need to relax."

He frowned, putting aside his shock for frustration. "Relax? You want me to relax?! What if something happened to you? You can't take risks now that…" Owen released a breath, running a hand through his hair.

Alanitora sat on her bed, watching Owen pace around her tent. Clearly he wasn't just going to drop that she had gone off on her own, and something told her that yelling at him about the fact that she was perfectly capable wasn't going to work this time around. No, if she wanted to calm him down, she'd have to approach this without sticking her finger in his face.

She stood with a sigh, stopping Owen from his paces with a hand on his arm. He turned to her, and with the fire outside, Alanitora could see a mix of exhaustion, panic, and concern in his eyes. She placed her hand on his chest, and his shoulders untensed slightly. "Owen." She waited until she was sure he was listening to her. "I know you are concerned after today, and I'm grateful for that, but I really am okay."

The redheaded soldier raised his eyebrows, unconvinced. His fingers tapped at the biceps of his crossed arms as he turned away from her, unwilling to yield. So he was deciding to be just as stubborn as her, it seemed.

"Listen to me." He looked up, his eyes focused on hers. "I'm sorry. To have left, to have worried you… You're just trying your best to protect me, and that's alright." She stood there for a silent pause, before bringing her hand to his cheek. "And I thank you for that."

Owen's gaze softened, and she let hers mirror this. After a moment there was a flicker of change, a change she feared to release herself. The princess smiled slightly, as though to ask for forgiveness before removing her hands.

Before she could completely withdraw, the soldier clasped his fingers around hers. Though tension had completely released from his shoulders, the grip he held on her was strong and unyielding. "I—" He turned his head away for a second, as though it nearly pained him to say the words. "I understand. I just need you to be more careful."

So they had come to an agreement. She nodded, ready to put the conversation and conflict to rest before his eyes returned to her. Something new had blossomed in that gaze. Something she had sensed the change of and knew she did not wish to get caught up in it. But the princess had already made her mistake in looking into those icy blue irises again.

It was similar to sadness, but with compassion beneath. Both somber with regret and erupting with happiness. So much emotion was compressed in the look he gave her. She had perhaps seen it before in glances between strangers, but this was the first time it was presented to her in full.

Her chest pulsated in response. Her stomach caved in. Her mind flooded with an ocean of thoughts moving too fast for her to recall.

This terrified Alanitora.

She averted her eyes, slipping her hands from his. "I think my sleep is catching up to me. I'd like to rest if that's alright with you."

"Of course." Owen gave one last nod of his head before turning to leave.

She tried her best to ease whatever had come over her at that moment, pressing her thoughts elsewhere.

In the early dawn of the next morning, Gwendolyn awoke Alanitora with a smile and a cup of tea she said to have made herself. The lady-in-waiting keenly watched her drink it while she lit the torches of the tent before helping her get dressed.

Alanitora watched the sky turn from pink to blue over the dying embers of the campfire as Gwendolyn brushed out her hair. At first, the silence was nice, but it wasn't long before it gnawed at her, replacing serenity with curiosity.

"All set." Gwendolyn smoothed out the remaining wisps in Alanitora's face.

"Thank you... If I may ask, do you know where Korena is?" She checked herself in the mirror, pleased with the loops of soft hair and a set of braids that gathered in the back of her head.

Gwendolyn shrugged. "She said she needed to do something on her own."

"Oh? It isn't like her to run off by herself."

"No, it isn't. I was going to look for her after this, but Uldin asked if I could assist with the horses."

"How is that boy?" Alanitora ventured into the conversation.

"He's yet to treat me with disrespect. I'm beginning to think Korena's connection to him may be in our favor."

Alanitora laughed. "Well, if he does give you any trouble I'll be sure to handle it for you."

Gwendolyn, who was not one for violence and well aware Alanitora wasn't joking, simply chuckled in return.

It wasn't until after her lady-in-waiting left that she remembered the wolf carcass on the floor in the corner of her tent. The idea that Gwendolyn surely saw it and didn't say anything was humorous to the princess, but it did make her consider what she was to do with the corpse. Perhaps hunting last night wasn't the best plan, especially if she was not going to eat the creature. The soldiers wouldn't, would they? She wasn't sure if people from different classes ate such meat.

Aware there would need to be a conclusion regarding what to do with the corpse before they left, Alanitora decided it might be best if someone else was made aware of it.

With this and Korena in mind, she equipped her weapons and "left her tent to head to find where they prepared food in the camp.

It seemed not much of the entourage had awoken yet, as only a few men were walking around camp and those that were looked like they were ready to fall back asleep on their feet. She watched as one man, who was packing things up early, ran into the post of another tent while carrying a pile of blankets. The blankets, of course, prevented him from getting hurt, but it was still quite enjoyable to see him scramble to get his things back together.

If the rising smoke next to the long set of tables was any indication, the tent furthest from her was where they prepared meals. If they were still in a castle with doors, she'd likely knock, but instead, the princess stood patiently outside of the entrance.

"We've been over this lad." A large burly man turned from the table and tossed a fairly large piece of meat into the pot at the center. "You aren't eatin' early. None of you are. Not until Her Highness has her rations."

The man he was talking to groaned before turning and walking past her out the entrance. The chef's eyes followed him out, where he was met with Alanitora "Ah! Your Highness! Your breakfast should be ready in no time, I promise."

"Thank you." She paused, examining the chef. He did not seem to be of the build or posture that suggested he was a soldier, and his age was too old to have just joined the ranks. His sole purpose must have been the meal preparation. "I was actually wondering—do you have any use for wolf meat?"

"Wolf… meat?" The two other men in the tent turned out of curiosity, a different degree of puzzlement on each of their faces.

"Yes," she affirmed. After no one made claims to it, she continued, "I have a dead wolf in my tent, I thought it might be of use for soldier rations. Feel free to take it. If not, I'm sure you'll find another use for it."

The main chef looked speechlessly between her and the others, before turning back with a polite smile. "Yes— yes, of course, thank you very much, Your Highness."

She smiled in return. That was one thing dealt with, now to find Korena.

Alanitora paused at the center of the camp, looking around for any sign of the blonde. There was nothing of her in sight; however, her eyes did

116

catch on the bright hair of her other female friend.

Diane sat on the grass not too far away, her hands fiddling with fabric and needles. When she noticed the princess, she took a moment to scan her. "Good morning to you. Are you alright?"

The intrusive question caught Alanitora off guard, and while she knew Diane would be a good person to talk to regarding yesterday's events, consolation wasn't what she was looking for. "Have you seen Korena?"

Diane tilted her head slightly. "I believe I saw her by the road earlier. Why? Is everything okay?"

"Yes, quite. I just wanted to check on her."

With this information in mind, Alanitora made her way to the train of wagons. She stopped by the wagon that held her clothes first, as it was both on the way to the carriage and the only other likely spot. Considering it had been an hour since her rise and there was no need for a change of clothes, it was no surprise when Korena was not there.

She checked the other wagons on the way for no particular reason before stopping at the carriage and pressing her ear to the door.

Muffled sobs and sniffs could be heard. A small pang of guilt resided in Alanitora's heart. Not wanting to waste time eavesdropping on a private moment, she knocked and opened the door.

"I was just—!" Korena rushed to gather the papers strewn around her. Her eyes were red. Her face was tear-stained. She was a mess. When she realized who had opened the door, her shoulders relaxed. "Oh, it's you, Tora. I'm sorry," she sniffed, wiping away her tears. "Do you need something?"

She wasn't sure why the blonde was less frantic about her presence than anyone else's, but Alanitora decided it was a good thing. "May I sit with you?"

Korena's eyebrows shot up in question, as though she wasn't sure to have heard Alanitora right before shaking her head lightly and continuing to pick up the flurry of parchments. "Of course, yes, please."

Alanitora stepped into the carriage, closing the door behind her. She sat across from Korena, picking up a few of the papers at her feet and handing them to her. They were letters, the subject of which she didn't spend time trying to decipher.

After her lady-in-waiting had her things organized, she smiled softly. "Are you alright?"

"Hmm?" Korena stared up at her blankly for a few moments. "Yes, I suppose— well, I don't know. Might I inquire why you're asking?"

She chuckled. "I suppose yesterday's events have put some things into perspective. It's just—" She paused, looking for the right words. Alanitora wasn't used to sentiments. Nevertheless, her mind reminded her that she spoke the truth. "With everything that has happened, I think it's important I spend what time I have with you and Gwendolyn. Who knows if someone will ever succeed in spilling my blood."

"Don't say that!" Korena's outburst took her back as she felt her lady's hands enclose over hers. "Your Highness, please don't make me more worried than I already am!" Tears flowed freely out of her eyes again, and she pulled her hands away to wipe them. "Goodness, I'm such a mess. It's improper for you to see me like this."

Alanitora sighed. "No, it's alright. Would you like to talk about it?"

"Can I?"

She pressed her lips into a more compassionate smile. It was new, but it was what would make Korena comfortable.

"It's uh, it's my beau."

"The man courting you?"

"Yes, my beloved William. I believe I have mentioned him before—He's wonderful, more wonderful than any other man I've met, and brave too!" She gleamed, but her face soon turned down. "Well you see, these letters are from him. We began exchanging such a few years back… The night we left—the night of the fire—was the last time I saw him. He was on his way to extinguish the flames in the village, and I don't know if he—" Her voice cracked, causing Korena to stop herself.

Alanitora reached out, placing her hand lightly on Korena's knee. It wasn't something she had done before. In fact, she couldn't recall a time when she saw Korena cry so much, and never had she comforted her so.

That was what Gwendolyn did in moments like these, not her.

"You're scared he may have perished?" Alanitora asked. Korena's face said it all as it morphed into a distraught frown, her breaths becoming rapid. "Korena, my dear, it's alright to be nervous about that. I understand."

Before collecting herself to continue, Korena patted her hand lightly as thanks. "I know it's not logical for me to assume he's gone, but I can't help it. I'm terrified, Tora! Everything we had—the future we set up—could be gone. That could have been the last time I saw him! I hadn't thought about it at the time but now I know it might be true. And there is no way for me to know if he's okay—"

"Korena, take a deep breath." She hadn't wanted to interrupt, but Korena was going far too fast for her and Alanitora wasn't used to handling these things.

"Right." She paused, doing as instructed. Gwendolyn often did this with her. "It's just, I never saw him come back, and we've received no word… I think I may be right to assume the worst." She drifted into a somber silence.

The princess smiled in return, the least she could do was reassure her. "I'm sure he's alright."

"You think?"

She nodded. "The castle may not know the path of our travel. A word from him could reach you when you least expect it. Until then it's important to stay hopeful. The way you've talked of him says that the two of you are close. A bond such as that can't easily be broken. If you are meant to be with him then your fates will cross again someday."

Alanitora didn't necessarily believe in fate, she believed there was a certain way things should be, but not that it was set in the stars.

"I suppose you're right," Korena sighed. "You would be one to know after all."

"I'm sorry?"

Korena's eyebrows jumped up, before settling into a confused frown. "Why, you and Owen are on the same path, are you not?"

The statement, and especially the bluntness of it, let out a chuckle from

Alanitora. "I don't think I see what you mean..."

"Oh, apologies I thought—" She paused. "Well, the way you had talked of him those first few years... If I'm not mistaken, I see a similarity to what you've experienced and what you present for William and me."

Her smile faded slowly. "I suppose I understand what you're saying, but no. Whatever it was that I claimed to have felt about Owen and I is now long gone, and I have no intention of pursuing it."

"I see," Korena looked unconvinced, but she thankfully dropped it. "If it's alright with you, I'd like to request some time with my sadness. You can stay if you like."

"Would you like me to?"

Korena met her eyes with a smile. "I wouldn't be against it."

"Then I am here."

10

Path of Destruction

Alanitora left Korena and the carriage not long after, heading back towards the campsite.

She found Gwendolyn in her own tent, packing up her things with the help of Diane.

"Good to see you again, Your Highness," Diane greeted cheerfully. "I had a question for you earlier—"

"Diane, could you give Gwendolyn and me a moment alone?"

The redhead looked between the two, exchanging a look with Gwendolyn to see if the lady was alright with such. When the brunette gave a nod of acceptance she left the tent.

"Where is Korena? Is she alright?" Hidden worries burst from her mouth.

"She's quite fine," Alanitora assuaged. "She seems to be having some issues regarding what was left behind at home."

"So it was about William, was it? Poor girl has been worried sick about him." Gwendolyn let out a breath of relief. "I suppose I'm not used to her handling things without support, but I should be grateful she's growing... Thank you for letting me know. I should be done here soon."

Alanitora placed her hand on Gwendolyn's arm to stop her from leaving. "Korena is not why I wanted to talk to you." There was a flash of panic across Gwendolyn's face that the princess wished she hadn't been the cause of. "I wanted to talk about... you."

Twice in that day confusion of her concern for her friends arose. This time it was more present, and Gwendolyn didn't hide it.

"Korena wasn't the only one who was forced to leave something behind the night of the fire, was she?"

Gwendolyn's eyes flicked up. Solid and cold like ice, but melting away into a puddle at the edges. She was holding her ground, and quite strongly, against Alanitora. A wall stood between them and the princess could see that she so desperately wanted to take it down, but feared doing so.

The night of the fire, She had been stolid, unresponsive. Unconnected to the world besides the burnt doll she clutched ever so tightly in her hand. Now, only a few days later, Gwendolyn was back to normal, but she was missing something in her core, and Alanitora could tell. "You lost something too, didn't you?"

"Yes," Gwendolyn stated. At first, Alanitora thought that was all she'd say. "A chest of my belongings was lost in the fire."

She took a silent moment of condolence and contemplation. "I thought all the chests were already packed up and ready to go?"

"No, they weren't. I was the one in charge of inventory. I made sure everything of yours and Korena's was packed first. It's quite funny, the one chest of mine that was most important was the one left behind. Surely, I thought fate couldn't be so cruel, but the man who was crushed by the beam was holding that very chest when the contents spilled out."

"The doll."

Gwendolyn nodded. "It fell from the top of the staircase, that's when I knew."

"What was in the chest?"

"Memorabilia from home. Drawings, letters, toys all made by my brother."

Alanitora's heart sank. The contents of the chest were from Gwendolyn's sick sibling, the one who was so weak that her lady-in-waiting near expected notice of his passing each month. It made sense that it was most important to her. It held a connection that might be lost at any moment. "I'm sorry," was all she could say.

122

"It's alright." Gwendolyn gave her a sheepish smile. "There are lots else to hold close, and I'm one to look forward to the future."

"You don't have to do that, you know."

"I'm sorry?"

"Pretend like everything is alright just because you're around me."

Gwendolyn frowned. "It's what I've always done, I find it important to make sure others' needs are met. I see no reason to change that now."

Alanitora nearly laughed. The brunette had always been a natural caretaker, but she never knew when to turn that care back around to herself. "Our lives have been turned upside-down, Gwendolyn! If there's anything we can understand about each other, it's the situation we are in. You've followed me this far, I'm grateful for that."

It was true. The events of the previous night had made Alanitora think about how much she valued the life she had. Perhaps connecting with Korena and Gwendolyn was something to help the transition. She could tell that the lengths they'd go to follow her were coming closer to an end.

"Very well."

So both her ladies were struggling with the losses of the fire. They were filled with uncertainty. On one hand, it was relieving to know that chaos was in the air for more people than just her, that they could share their grief. However, on the other hand, this made things more complex. Alanitora was never used to carrying the burden of others. And now, for some reason, it felt as though she was obligated to. It was Korena and Gwendolyn's job as ladies-in-waiting to take care of her, not the other way around.

At least it was nice to see a genuine smile in their eyes.

There was a certain bittersweetness to that morning. For the first time, Alanitora opted to eat with the rest of the entourage. The meal started with a thick awkward silence, as the men had no idea how to properly behave around her. They waited until she took a bite to take theirs, and stayed quiet unless she asked a question to the whole group.

When Corwyn realized this, he proposed a toast in her good health, causing a number of men to join in with their drinks. After that, a certain casual behavior seemed acceptable and conversations began to ensue. She got to join a few, though there were still high nerves when she did. Men directed several glances towards Corwyn before they answered.

Something told her Corwyn had given them a stern talking-to about respect. It was probably part of the reason even Uldin was respectful. She was grateful for that.

After eating, Alanitora helped some of them pack the wagons to pass time. One young man, in particular, made a comment to her about how she was incredibly strong for her size, which was surprisingly not patronizing, like what she was used to.

It had to be around eight in the morning when they were all ready to roll out. The princess joined her close companions in the small carriage, the five of them conversing about more mundane subjects while they waited.

But when the carriage didn't roll forward after the announcement, they went silent.

"What's going on?" Korena asked.

Diane shushed her so they could listen.

Shouts could be heard not too far away but were too inaudible to understand. Something in Alanitora's stomach twisted, pulling her to investigate. Whatever was happening, it wasn't insignificant. She opened the door, ignoring Owen's protests.

"Just shoot it!" a voice cried out. "Or at least scare it away."

"How am I supposed to scare it away?" another voice responded. "It's a damn wolf!"

No, it couldn't be... could it? Alanitora stepped down from the carriage, craning her neck to see ahead of the road. Without success, she began to pace towards the commotion, her steps turning into a jog to get there sooner.

The sight in front of her was exactly what she had expected. A number of her men were gathered on the side of the road, staring at the animal that blocked their path. A wolf. With a coat of fur that glimmered silver in the sunlight and eyes so kind they were almost human. It crouched defensively in the middle of the road, a snarl on its face.

"Silver Moon!" Alanitora called out. She hadn't realized her attachment to the name until his eyes snapped to hers and his snarl softened.

"Shoot it!" a man repeated.

The princess looked around the scene, locating the bow aimed at her midnight friend before moving herself in front of it. "Don't," she stated, shielding the wolf.

"Your Highness—"

"That wasn't a means for negotiation, it was an order. He's friendly."

The soldier slowly lowered his bow.

She whispered a thank you and turned around. Alanitora knelt to the ground, reaching her arms out and beckoning Silver Moon forward. He complied, sniffing her fingers like he did the night before. His tail began to wag and he rubbed his entire body against her while spinning in a circle. His weight nearly knocked her over.

After a few affectionate pats were given, she stood again, turning to the now disarmed collection of men. "This wolf is under my protection, any attempt to hurt him will result in your release." With a satisfied nod, she began to walk back to the carriage, the crowd of people splitting as she and the wolf made their way through.

She was aware people were staring after them, likely with a million questions. In full honesty, she had many questions and curiosities herself.

She looked down at the wolf.

"Thank you, you may go home now." He only stared at her. She pushed him with her foot. "Go on."

But the wolf didn't budge.

"You're wanting to come with, aren't you?" Silver Moon's tail wagged at her words and Alanitora assumed she must be mad if she thought he could understand her plainly. She sighed. "Very well."

He followed her gleefully to the carriage, where she opened the door to let him in. This, of course, wasn't something the rest of her companions expected. Korena screamed out at the sight and shot back. Silent shocked expressions of different degrees were on everyone else's face. She climbed in, the wolf following.

"Is that?—" Diane asked.

"Yes, I believe so," Gwendolyn replied.

"And you're—"

"Yes, I believe she is."

Diane and Gwendolyn seemed to come to the conclusion of their new companion quite nicely. Meanwhile, Owen looked like he was ready to have stern words with her.

"This is Silver Moon, everyone." Alanitora smiled. "He'll be joining us for now."

"Tora, you introduce him like he's a person, are you aware that that is indeed a wolf? The kind of bloodthirsty animal that hunts deer and squirrels?" asked Gwendolyn.

She was aware of this. "I'd say he's quite civilized."

They seemed to finally get the hint that this was not something to discuss or debate about. That, of course, didn't mean there still weren't a number of questions that she didn't feel like answering. If it were but a domesticated dog they'd likely have no issue with it.

Silver Moon spun in the little space and laid down at her feet. He panted happily, a human-like smile on his face when she gave him some scratches. Gwendolyn joined Alanitora in giving him a cautious pet.

Perhaps the addition of a wolf to the traveling party was a bit much, but she didn't care. Silver Moon wasn't just any wolf, she had a feeling. Besides, the look in his eyes told her he wasn't going to go back into the woods. Persistent. Stubborn. She liked that about him.

The carriage began moving as everything else had returned to normal.

It was certainly more heated in the carriage because of the extra body. Not only that, but Silver Moon gave off a strange odor, one that took quite a while to get used to. She didn't necessarily enjoy it, but it was better than the smell some people tended to give off.

"So..." Owen began after a stretch of silence. "What's with Silver...

126

Moon?"

Alanitora sighed. His queries made sense. "I encountered him last night while I was hunting. Must have followed my scent back to camp to find me."

"You went hunting last night?" Korena asked.

Right. She forgot only Owen had known about that. "Yes."

"What? What if you had gotten hurt, or attacked by a jaguar?!"

"Korena, dear, you know there are no jaguars this far south. If you want one, travel to Jabade," Gwendolyn informed.

"Still!" Korena extended her hands dramatically.

"It's okay, Korena, I scolded her for it last night," Owen added.

"Well, it's good someone is looking after her."

Alanitora raised her eyebrows. "I don't believe it to be an accomplishment to claim a scolding over me." She was perfectly capable of taking care of herself, most—if not all—of the people in the carriage couldn't do a better job.

Korena folded her hands in her lap as submission to the statement, and Owen avoided her eyes, only proving her point.

"I'm not sure having him here is such a wise idea. Surely such a prestigious and luxurious kingdom like Donasela wouldn't let a wild animal roam the castle grounds," Diane said matter-of-factly, and a frown pressed into Alanitora's brow. Even if Diane wasn't used to being in her presence, that didn't give the excuse of questioning her, especially with such a tone.

"I suppose they'll have to deal. The prince asked for my hand in marriage did he not? If I were—"

Before she could continue into a more aggressive ground, Korena practically jumped out of her seat. "Oh! Speaking of, we're scheduled to arrive at the capital of Kreaha by tomorrow evening! I've heard they are most luxurious themselves, their prince included. Handsome *and* he's looking for a bride!"

"If we're lucky, we should be able to see the festivities of the event." Gwendolyn looked up. "If I'm correct it started on the equinox."

Gwendolyn was right. Alanitora didn't know much about Kreaha or any kingdom for that matter, but she did know they held festivals at the beginning of each season. It was possible that if the prince was looking for a bride, that they were using this season to do so.

"Perhaps we'll even be able to participate!" Korena clasped her hands together.

Owen crossed his arms. "Might I remind you that you are currently being courted by another?"

Diane hit her brother in the arm. "Oh shush you, let her fantasize. Many dream of marrying into royalty, you of all people should know."

In that moment, Owen's face shifted five shades redder as he scrambled for a response. The girls of the carriage erupted into laughter, Alanitora joining in with them. It was quite fun to see him flustered, and even better since it reminded her of the times where she'd proven herself better and embarrassed him when they were much younger.

Silver Moon, too, got excited about the commotion and stood to lick Alanitora's face violently. She pushed him away, her cheeks beginning to hurt from such a wide smile.

Alanitora looked out the window as the scenery changed, trees becoming more sparse as they happened upon a lake. Kreaha's land wasn't much different from Trenvern's. There were perhaps a larger variety of trees, but just like her home, much of the scenery consisted of green fields and thick forests. She knew the northern part of Kreaha, which was the start of a mountain range, had multiple mining sites rich with amethysts, emeralds, and other gemstones. If you came across a royal jewel anywhere in Mordenla, there was a high chance it originated from Kreaha. It's what made them one of the richest of all kingdoms, and what prompted their colors of green and purple.

Their choice of animal was something to question though, as a raven seemed to be one of the last creatures she would associate with wealth. The black bird had always been, in her eyes, a scavenger. Clever and cunning, but never rich. Of course, her prejudices towards ravens were mainly due to the nursery rhymes and poems Queen Elena told her as a child. In them, the raven was only there to pick up scraps and unattended goods, taking from others' hard-earned values or repurposing what once was nothing into something useful.

Alanitora reached out to stroke Silver Moon's back. The fur was thick and warm and felt fine under her fingertips. She understood why one might want a blanket made of such, but now the mere idea disgusted her, especially since having a creature curl up next to you was much better than any dead blanket.

She let herself relax with the comfort of a warm carriage and the feeling of safety. The sleep she hadn't gotten last night finally took hold of her and she let herself slip into its embrace.

The dreams that came to her in that sleep were more fantastical than what she normally dreamt of. She was in the middle of a vast ocean, the likes of which she only ever saw depicted in paintings. There was a boat far away and in the sloshing waves, her voice was hoarse when Alanitora called out to it.

Calamity threw her this way and that, and the princess struggled to gain control of her surroundings. Her arms thrashed about the water as she looked up at the storm clouds above. Gray and blue, blurry and clear.

"Stop." The voice was her own but it did not come from her lips. She looked left and right but found no source. "Breathe," it said again.

Alanitora closed her eyes to the blackness and opened them to find herself underneath the surface of the water. She took in a deep breath, clarity and light surrounding her vision of the water. Suspended without motion, she looked up at the thrashing waves that were once above and found peace.

"Now focus."

A jolt awoke her from her slumber. She looked around at her companions. A few of them had also been awoken by it themselves, and the others who weren't must have already been awake.

The collective idea might have been to ignore it, had there not been another jolt after. This one a loud thump.

"What was that?" Gwendolyn asked, putting down her book.

Owen shrugged. "We might be rolling over some twigs at the moment."

"Yeah, because twigs are thick and make that noise when you roll over them," Diane said sardonically.

"Okay then, branches!"

There was a snapping sound and then a more aggressive jolt that shot Alanitora forward from her seat.

"Are you alright?" Owen asked, stabilizing her arms.

She nodded, but before she could answer, there was another snap and jolt, sending her back towards her seat.

Gwendolyn placed her hands on the walls of the corner, anchoring herself.

"What's going on?!" Korena yelled frantically.

The carriage no longer swayed left and right but whatever they were riding over was bumpy enough to send them up and down in their seats. Alanitora took a step towards the window opposite of her and opened up the curtain. The carriage flooded with daylight and in the distance, she could see the rest of the wagons getting further and further away.

They had broken off of the main path and were riding at high speed.

"Something must've spooked the horses. The coachman should get them under control soon," Owen said reassuringly, though there was still panic in his voice.

The entire carriage jerked to the right. "Are you sure about that?!" Gwendolyn yelled out.

"Uh... folks?" Korena began.

Silver Moon yelped, bringing Alanitora's attention to the door side of the carriage, where their lantern had fallen off the hook and landed onto the curtain, the entire drapery setting on fire.

"Put it out!" Alanitora couldn't tell who was saying what at this point, her eyes were glued to the flames, the flickers reminding her of the last tragedy that involved fire.

Diane rushed to put them out with her skirts, patting the layers down onto the area, only for her dress to catch on fire. She jumped back.

"We need to get out of here!" Alanitora yelled over the crackling of wood. The fire was beginning to eat at the structure of the carriage. They'd burn with it too if they didn't hurry up.

Owen nodded at her, turning to face the door and extending his arms out to guard all of them from the flames. With a swift kick, he was able to fling the door open. The landscape outside became visible, speeding past with every second.

Sparse sections of forest lined the road, only giving them little gaps to a clearing. She tore her eyes away from the speeding ground. "Silver Moon, go!"

She gave the wolf a small push, but he didn't move. Either out of fear or obligation not to leave her. Regardless, Alanitora knew he could understand her.

"Why does the wolf get to go first?!" Korena asked, having backed up to the non-burning part.

"Because." Diane ripped off the rest of her burnt skirt, the edges still aflame. "Animals are unpredictable, it's better to get the thing out of the way."

Alanitora knew this to be partially true to her motives. With another, more assertive push from her, Silver Moon finally leaped out, narrowly avoiding the flames that glowed like a halo around the door.

"Diane, you go next," Owen ordered, reaching out for his sister. She squeezed his hand, nodding.

Good, the bravery of the girl would no doubt help to motivate Korena and Gwendolyn to follow. She assumed this was not the thinking of Owen, but was grateful for it anyway.

Diane backed up, shaking her hands out and bouncing slightly on her feet as she waited for the next clearing. Alanitora could see her calculating the jump in her head before charging toward the door and diving through. She tucked her knees in to brace for the impact.

For a moment her hair became one with the fire. Red upon red, as though the flames extended from her.

The carriage was beginning to smoke, and her eyes watered more and more. Burning. Stinging. Alanitora struggled to keep them open after blinking away the tears.

Owen reached out for her next, placing his hand on her waist to steady her. "Do you think you can jump on your own?"

It took much effort to force her eyes from the flames. "I think, yes." She bit her lip, squeezing his arm before backing up herself and trying to remember what Diane had done. She could hear her breaths, her heart, her fear.

The clearing came, and Owen nodded at her to count down. "Three, two... one!"

She ran and jumped through the door, tucking her knees and turning to one side. Her back hit the ground first, pain shooting into her shoulder before she rolled into the grass and down the hill to the clearing.

Alanitora's head spun, and in her dizziness, she felt pain. But there was relief in the clean air as she took a deep inhale. Only letting herself rest for a moment, the princess scrambled to her feet and looked after the carriage just as Gwendolyn jumped out and then Korena, both of them unable to land properly, which must have hurt.

Silver Moon was the first to run up to her, and soon after Diane followed, the three of them waiting no longer to run and check on her ladies.

She couldn't remove her eyes from the carriage though. It was nearing the end of the clearing, and as far as she could see the forest was thick. Owen didn't have much time. Her heart was nearly jumping out of her throat when she saw him jump out as well, unharmed.

Both she and Diane were out of breath when they reached the ladies-in-waiting.

"Is everyone alright?" Gwendolyn asked, getting up with a groan and brushing the grass from her.

"Yes, it seems so," Alanitora said between breaths.

Diane nodded. "A little sore."

Owen had nearly reached them as Gwendolyn turned to her blonde friend. "Korena? You alright?"

But Korena's eyes were wide. Her hands were shaking and she looked around frantically, patting at herself. "No... no no no no no." Her breathing began to speed up as panic overtook all of her. "The— the letters! My letters, they're—"

"Is everyone okay?!" Alanitora moved her sight from Korena to the road, where Corwyn pulled tightly at the reins of his horse. When he counted everyone present, he let out a relieved breath.

Alanitora looked between him and back to Korena. Her eyes had welled up completely and were flowing freely as she fought to focus on anything else. She screamed out in a series of cries. Her loss was heavy enough to fill the air.

The princess shot back up, rushing to Corwyn. "I need to borrow your horse."

"I'm sorry?" The elder man asked.

"I need your horse," she repeated.

Confused, Corwyn dismounted, handing her the reins.

"Alanitora, what are you doing…" Owen began to pace towards her.

She ignored him, making quick work to mount the sleek mare.

"Nitora—"

She had a hold of the reins, adjusting herself in her seat, and was ready to go before Owen grabbed the reins himself.

"Get out of my way."

"Whatever you're thinking of doing, don't."

She shot him a look. There wasn't an option. If he wasn't going to let go, he wasn't going to let go, but she didn't have time to argue this.

Alanitora whipped the reins, giving the horse a starting kick and sending it forward. She could hear voices calling after her, but the princess paid no mind, focusing on the road ahead and the glowing flame in the distance.

She wasn't going to let her ladies lose another thing they held precious. Not after what they had all been through. Everything else be damned. She could handle the loss, the pain. Korena could not. Korena would not.

Determination pressed her forward. When the horse reached its fastest, she pushed it forward. The gap between her horse and the carriage began to close. The fire had devoured the entire right half of it by this point and as she got closer the crackling of wood was nearly as loud as the beating horse hooves.

She veered her horse to the edge of the road, pulling back a little as they began to pass the carriage. Heat radiated her cheeks despite being a body length away from the door. They raised into the sky nearly two times her height, gripping at the open air.

She rode her horse up next to the one of the carriage, surprised to see there was only the right one, and that the attachment for the left one had been completely torn off. In fact, the coach bench had also been obliterated. There was a bit of blood on the outside wall of the carriage. She scanned everything again. It was horrendous. What the hell had happened?

Alanitora's frown deepened. She could deduce what took place later. There were more important things to focus on.

Maintaining the same speed as the other horse, her mind raced around the possibilities. She could somehow stop the carriage horse, therefore making entrance in and out much easier, but that seemed unlikely, as the steed was likely running in fear of the heat behind it.

Cutting it off from the front was too unpredictable, and she had no means to separate the horse from the blazing carriage. No, she would have to do this with it still moving.

Alanitora gave the reins one last whip, letting her horse speed up as she swung her leg over to the left side. Her horse would naturally slow down, leaving a small window for her to get into the carriage. The door swung open and closed repeatedly. It was risky, but there was no other way.

She took a deep breath counting out the second with her fingertips and preparing herself to go back into what she had just escaped.

And then it was time. She kicked off from the horse, closing her eyes and ducking her head as she plummeted into the carriage. She was terrified that opening her eyes might result in the realization of her unchangeable doom, but alas, there was no sign of it. Only the thick black smoke that blurred her vision and the searing heat that brought perspiration to her back.

Alanitora pushed herself up from the floor, her shoulder still hurting from the tumble out. She took in a deep breath but all that entered her throat were the thick particles of smoke that took away all of her oxygen, filling her lungs with a cloud of death.

Her eyes were watering beyond belief, but the tears came and flowed fast enough for her to see through them.

She was hot, she was tired, she was in pain. She couldn't breathe. Her head spun wildly.

A sudden, sharp pain bubbled at her ankles, a burning sensation so hot that it felt like ice. She jumped up, looking down at her feet to see if her skin was aflame. It wasn't, but the pain stayed. Alanitora reached down, tentatively putting her fingers over a curled bit of skin before moving to the exposed flesh beneath it, wet and tender, searing at the touch.

She took in a few shallow breaths, putting aside the pain. She was here for one reason: find the letters.

Alanitora blindly felt around the seats, the smoke too thick to even see her hand in front of her as she examined every inch of the cushions. Where were they? She closed her eyes momentarily, trying to take her mind away from the moment, from the pain and the heat to earlier in that day.

Korena sat on the far side of the door, opposite of her. She hadn't seen the papers after then. They must have been hidden.

She ran her hands between the space between the wall and the seat, pushing her hand into the small space, but with no success at finding the leaflets. Had they already burned?

Alanitora put her other hand on the cushion, only to find the familiar touch of parchment at her fingertips. Exultation surrounded her as she brought the papers out from under the cushion, hugging them to her chest to keep them safe from the fire.

Violent coughs erupted in her throat as she gasped for air. It felt like she was inhaling nothing but shards of black. She turned weakly, her head continuing to spin and fade from reality.

She had to get out. She had to leave. The flames surrounded her at this point, closing in like they wished to hug her tightly and not let go. The princess looked at the door. It was closed. A wall of fire replacing it instead.

She was tired, she was weak. She wanted to sleep.

Perhaps sleep would stop her from being set ablaze. Perhaps the pain would not reach her if she let go now. Alanitora sat back down, slamming her back against the wall untouched by flames. She tucked her knees to her chest, holding the papers close as the last of her breath was sucked out

And in that moment, the door opened, and Alanitora saw a tall dark figure through the flames.

Death received her with open arms.

11

Amethyst Gardens

L ight. Not of a fire, but of the heavens. Hazy clouds and a clear blue with a hue of pink. It was the first thing she saw when she opened her eyes.

A small gust of wind brushed her hair across her face. Cool against her cheeks, the air around her prickled at the perspiration on her brow. She drew in a deep breath, the fresh air filling her lungs.

The last of her tears dripped down the side of her face and everything was clear.

Everything was clear.

Alanitora shot up, a sharp pain pressing into her skull. She was still here. She was still alive. A series of coughs that clawed at her throat confirmed such.

The princess examined her surroundings. A clearing. Trees on either side. A field of grass. And Owen to her left, who let out a soft grunt. She relaxed at the sight of him. So he had been the one to carry her out.

The letters were still clutched to her chest, charred at the edges but nonetheless intact.

Alanitora rolled herself over, pressing her hand to the moist grass to help herself up.

Owen's consciousness came back to him, and as soon as awareness reached him, he flicked his head towards her. "Nitora!" Relief washed across his face when he saw she was breathing. The soldier scrambled to close the distance between them, his arms quick to support her. "Are you alright? Are you hurt?" He lifted her chin lightly with his hand.

She shook her head. "I'm fine." She leaned away from his touch, bringing her knees up to stand, but the soldier was already helping her up by her elbows. She grimaced as weight pressed to her left ankle.

"What's wrong?"

"Nothing."

Owen raised his eyebrows scanning his eyes over her posture until he settled on the leg in question.

"Owen, it's nothing—"

But he had already lifted the edges of her skirt, brushing the fabric across the bubbled burn. She released a sharp hiss.

He looked up at her in disappointment. "Don't lie to me about these things."

"So you can hover over me?" Alanitora crossed her arms. "I'm quite content with handling things myself, thank you."

Owen rose back up to face her. "I'm serious, Nitora. You can't just take these risks without thinking of the consequences!"

"I'm fine," she repeated.

He let out a heavy sigh between his clenched teeth. Owen ran a hand through his hair, frustration seething. "What the hell were you thinking?! Do you have any idea what would happen if I— if we lost you?!"

He might be stubborn, but she was too. She wasn't going to let him win this one. She wouldn't. Not when her motives were to help someone besides herself. "That's not your decision to make."

"Not my— Listen to yourself!" Owen's voice raised. "You think it's *your* decision? There's more at stake here! You are too important to lose. Why don't you see that?!"

He turned away from her, kicking at a stone on the ground, flinging it across the field. Alanitora gripped the letters tighter as Owen held back the rest of his anger. She saw how deeply it affected him. She saw how worried he was and how there was a reason for it. She saw how he balanced both

138

the logical and emotional rationale. She understood.

"I'm sorry," said Alanitora quietly. Perhaps she would let him win. Perhaps he was right.

He turned to her again, his gaze softening in response. Owen took a few deep breaths before he began, his tone more demure than before. "I understand that you can take care of yourself, alright? I don't doubt your strength." He stepped toward her, his gaze unyielding. Owen reached out, taking her hands into his.

She looked him in the eyes. They were filled with so much. Fear. Anxiety. Anger.

So many feelings spurred out of them at once. Yet at their core, it was caring, it was sweet, and it was soft.

"But you have to stop with the recklessness. You could have gotten yourself killed." He let out a huff of laughter. "You are so analytical and yet you never think before you do things. What is possibly worth risking your life for?" Owen scanned her face.

She let out her breath, not realizing how staggered it had been. Alanitora raised the set of parchment. "This is all Korena has of what she left behind. They are all she has right now. She's lost the one she loves and this is all she can remember him by in the uncertainty that she may never see him again." Her own eyes were welling up with tears, part of her speaking from something hidden within her that was rising to the surface. "That love, the love you share with someone when you're so far apart is something you can never, ever let go of. You have to keep it close. Losing this would break that for Korena. It's worth taking a risk for a love that strong."

Owen tilted his head, his eyes brightening ever so slightly. His lips separated, but it took a moment before he could speak. "While I do not condone your actions, I must admit that you are right, for there is more truth in your words than I have ever heard spoken."

She swallowed. That same unfamiliar look lay in his eyes. The one she had seen last night, the one that there was only a sliver of when they were reunited. In time it waxed into something larger, and now, it was full.

He continued, "If you love someone, despite the separation, despite the boundaries, then it's worth it."

Alanitora saw the change in his eyes. She saw it bloom like a flower in the morning sun, and it was captivating. "Owen—"

"I love you, Alanitora."

Her mind raced to interpret the words in any other way. The way her mother would say it as a way to tell her how proud she was. The way Gwendolyn would say it to Korena and her when she wanted to express how much their friendship meant. Hell, she even hoped for the way one might say they love a color simply because it brings them joy.

But she knew more than she wished, and suddenly her breath was gone, her throat was dry, and her heart stood still. She parted her lips to speak, but Owen's warm hand had been raised to her cheek, pushing away her hair and landing his fingertips at the nape of her neck.

She couldn't move, entranced by the gaze they held until he closed his eyes and stepped closer, leaning into her.

Their foreheads were first to touch, and soon after she felt his nose upon her cheek. It was then that their lips met.

He kissed her. And Alanitora, closing her eyes as well, could feel herself melting into him. It was soft, and a sensation swirled through her. Her cheek warmed where his nose rested against it, her neck craned to parallel his. Her hands raised ever so slightly to catch herself on his chest before she could fall over. Her stomach twisted like a ribbon as she felt herself falling into his embrace. Her shields melted and her walls crumbled. Her heart opened and soared in a new light. She sank, slowly drowning as his lapping waters held her close, carrying her to the bottom of the sea.

But she would not drown today.

Her eyes shot open, and with one swift motion, Alanitora pushed Owen away. Wiping at her lips to rid herself of the magnetism she felt pulling her towards him. Her breaths quickened. "What the hell do you think you're doing?"

"I—"

She shot her hand up "Don't. Answer that." Alanitora rubbed her temples. "Are you completely mad?! Has it left your mind that I am to be wed within a week from now?" Her mind was still reeling, and formulating words held a challenge. "I can't have any distractions from what I have to do."

"What you *have* to do. That's the thing, it's not what you *want* to do and you know it. You've always chosen your own fate, why is this any different?"

She gawked at him, gesturing around at where they were. "Because this isn't just about me! It's about so much more than me. Is that not exactly what you were saying?"

"So, what? You're willing to take risks with your life even though it affects others closest to you? You're okay with fighting for the love of others but not the love of yourself? Forgive me, but you aren't making any sense. You said mere seconds ago that love is worth taking risks for. So take them!"

"That was different. I wasn't talking about you. I was—" She growled in frustration. She had been talking about her mother, her family. But now the thought of it only agitated Alanitora more. Stop. Calm down. Focus. Control yourself. "I can't just run away from what is necessary. I'm not doing this to avoid my feelings as you suggest, I'm doing this for the future of my people, Owen. You of all people should approve of it, seeing you're so closely dedicated to the crown."

"I'm not dedicated to the crown, I'm dedicated to you!" His eyes were pleading for her to keep the connection she was trying to sever. Her heart crumbled at the sight of it.

"You can't possibly believe you can spit out all of this nonsense and expect me to follow you blindly and run from what I have to do. Trenvern needs me."

"You don't even know if Trenvern exists anymore!"

This sent her back physically, as though he had pushed her. Her voice lost its volume. "Just as you don't know whether or not my feelings for you exist anymore."

His shoulders dropped. "You and I both know the answer to that."

Alanitora was tired. She was exhausted and she hated that he could see through her. She hated what he knew, and she hated the part of her that wanted to agree with him. But she pressed the coldness everyone accused her of into her heart. "I do not love you."

It was as though that coldness had formed an icicle and stabbed Owen in the heart. She saw his hopes crush into nothing and pushed away the guilt that was rising in her chest.

Alanitora turned to leave, but Owen's hand reached out, grasping desperately at her wrist. "Please, just this once, do something selfish for yourself and for us."

"Let go of me."

"I don't think I can."

"Then I suppose I'll have to cut your arm off. "

"I wasn't talking about my hand."

"Then let go of both." She met him with her eyes. Eyes that stood their ground and still asked him to please yield. It would hurt less if he did.

Slowly, he loosened his grip, fingers gliding across the inside of her wrist as she moved away as well. "I'll make sure any of your possessions and a week's worth of rations are left with you, as well as a blanket. Should you need anything else, let someone know. Consider yourself relieved of your duties." She gave him one last nod, this one of pity, and of good luck. "Goodbye, Owen."

She turned away, pulling her feet forwards with as much force as she could. How much she wanted to run, to scream, to cry. But she crushed those urges together, burying them deep within her. Now was not the time.

When she reached the road, she saw nothing but a bare expanse of tracks left in the wake of the flaming carriage. She walked along it, keeping herself from looking back by scanning each of the tracks at her feet. She continued in silence until Corwyn rode up to meet her, having found another horse for himself.

"Where is Mister Conlan?" he asked first, pulling to a halt.

"Disbanded from this journey. I'll ask one of your men to retrieve resources for him. I'm sorry about your horse." Her words came out sharp, emotionless. Perhaps she'd been a little too successful at suppressing her feelings.

Corwyn closed his eyes in relief, though not all of his stress released with his breath. Alanitora could tell the man was both relieved his soldier was alive and disheartened that something had happened for him to be taken off the force.

When they reached the clearing she left the rest of her companions at, she saw that a majority of the retinue had regrouped. Each of her ladies were being checked on.

"Tora!" Korena yelled out, her eyes brightening when she saw what was clutched in the princess' hands. She rushed over. It appeared her tears had ceased while Alanitora was gone, but resumed as soon as the letters were handed over. "Thank you, thank you more than anything! I'd hug you... but you're all covered in ash." Alanitora looked down. She was right. Her dress, which had been a light teal, was now charred with spots of black. The same must have been smudged on her face too. "Oh, maybe just this once!"

Korena flung her arms around the princess, nearly making her lose balance. Alanitora wrapped an arm around Korena as well, giving her a small pat on the back.

Silver Moon bounded over, stopping to sniff one particularly scorched spot of Alanitora's dress. Gwendolyn and Diane came running up behind him.

"You nearly scared us to death!" Gwendolyn said.

"Yeah, but I will admit, it was pretty cool that you did that. I don't think I've seen someone ride a horse so fast." Diane paused to look around in confusion before turning back and scanning her features. She didn't seem to find her answer there either, as her face only contorted further.

"Well, the carriage is gone," Alanitora began, releasing herself from Korena's tight grip. "It looks like all of us will be riding a horse unless any of you would like to ride in the back of one of the wagons."

"Either is alright with me." Gwendolyn smiled, signaling them towards the road.

Alanitora followed but stopped when Diane didn't move in front of her.

The redhead turned to look directly into her eyes. They were beginning to water. "Where's Owen?"

Alanitora mentally kicked herself for not instantly telling Diane he was okay. She likely thought he was dead. "He's fine, he just won't be coming with us anymore." With that settled, the princess began walking again.

The girl's expression changed instantly from terrified to a fiery anger that matched her hair. "What? Why?" She ran to keep up with Alanitora.

Korena and Gwendolyn had slowed down to hear what she had to say. Alanitora wasn't sure if they hadn't noticed or had chosen not to mention it. "We had a... conflict of interests. When he didn't back down it became apparent that things would be much easier if we deviated paths."

"If you *deviated paths*? That applies to when people have a disagreement about what to eat for supper, not when one is to be left to their own devices in the middle of the wilderness!"

Alanitora stopped, turning to the girl. She could understand why Diane was upset by her brother, but that didn't mean she could disrespect her like such. "He won't be left to his own devices, I've supplied him with enough to survive. We've lost enough time so if you'd like to join him, I won't stop you."

Diane clenched her jaw, raising her chin. So it seemed she would yield.

Alanitora nodded. "We'll skip setting up camp tonight and ride straight to Kreaha instead," she announced once a majority of the men were in earshot.

Letting what was now the past to rest, Alanitora mounted her horse, prepared to go before anything else could change her mind.

By the time they started up again, the sun was nearly touching the horizon. Alanitora was riding the horse that carried a wagon of riches. Corwyn, who was worried for her safety, had her up front, resulting in her setting the speed for the rest of the train.

Her ladies had ended up riding in the back garment wagon. She was certain they were discussing what could have happened with Owen, and she was grateful to not be a part of the conversation.

What was he thinking, kissing her? What was he expecting? For her to give up everything and dance around in the fields with him? She had a duty to do. Marrying Prince Daruthel was the only thing that was holding Trenvern together. Even if she didn't want to, it was the protection of her people at stake.

Besides, she hadn't seen him in a whole seven years. It was futile of him to think that her feelings would be so strong for him. They were ten, for goodness' sake! It might have been an age where you could form a lifelong bond, but it was far from old enough to fall in love with someone, let alone even know what love was.

She sighed. And then there was the fact that she had escaped from a burning carriage... twice. All of it was too much. Her life had been threatened so often in the last few days, that at this rate, she wouldn't make it to Donasela before someone spilled her guts out.

Alanitora shook her head. She couldn't think that way, that was how you lost to an opponent. Even if there were more threats to come, she shouldn't doubt herself. Ever. She was strong, skilled, and clever.

She would keep going. Keep fighting.

The forest became sparse up ahead, and Alanitora could see the vastness that was the land of Kreaha. Night had fallen, but the silhouettes of the land were clear. She could see mountains northeast, speckles of light here and there between, marking the villages of the valleys. The air smelled of pine, which wafted from the east, where trees were poking up in the distance. Pointed and arrow-like.

Evergreen trees were common in Trenvern, but the forests were made up mostly of deciduous trees. Seeing a collection of pines felt unfamiliar.

They pressed forward, and it took much effort for Alanitora to stay awake. Her legs were sore from gripping the sides of the horse, and its movements did a great deal to lull her. She was exhausted, but falling asleep in such a position did not seem like the best idea, especially with what happened the last time she let herself drift off.

Alanitora supposed she could have someone else take over the horse while she slept in a wagon, but she decided against it. She could make it to the capital.

Alas, Alanitora was correct. After a few hours of steady riding, a large stone structure peeked over the trees in the distance. Within it, the tall white towers of Kreaha's capital looked over the entire forest, calling them closer like a beacon. Unlike Trenvern, the capital town was inside the castle walls instead of outside of them. It was still sectioned off from the palace, but the protection said much about the people's place in Kreaha.

The entourage turned onto a wide path that led to the large ornate iron gates that allowed entry into the castle walls. Some hedges lined the path, conifer trees standing like guards.

So the kingdom's trees stayed true to the shade of green that fit with their royal colors, just as the green of Trenvern held the same shade as spring oaks.

Corwyn rode ahead of her, holding his hand up to pull the rest of their train to a halt. She watched as he dismounted his horse and handed the reins to a walking soldier before stepping up to the Kreahan guard that stood in front of the gates. The knight handed him a parchment. Alanitora could see the seal of Trenvern on the back of it.

The guard nodded to let them through. As the gates were opened, Alanitora paused to look over her shoulder. Korena, Gwendolyn, and Silver Moon were sleeping soundly curled up in the wagon behind her, and Diane was intensely focused on whatever she might be writing in her notebook.

A magical air settled around her as they passed into the castle walls. Lanterns were strewn across a beautiful hedge garden. Flowers twisted in each bush like paint splotches on a palette, the pristine blooms of every color bursting across her vision. A large fountain rested up ahead on a smaller path, behind it the glorious palace rose into the sky. It was as though she had entered the landscape of a romantic painting.

She looked up in awe of her surroundings, letting her horse slow to a stop as she tried her best to imprint the image into her mind's eye.

"Your Highness?" Corwyn held his hand out to her left. "Might I have the honor of accompanying you to meet the king and queen?"

She smiled. "Of course." Alanitora dismounted, giving the mare one last pat before her reins were taken as well. She watched the rest of the entourage veer onto the left path, making their way along the castle walls on the other side of the garden. The princess turned back. "Though… is it not too late in the night for introductions? Surely Their Majesties have already retired. I wouldn't wish to disturb their peace. That seems like an awful first impression."

He let out a burst of hearty laughter. "When we sent ahead word of our arrival, it seems the crown was quite adamant about extending the gate curfew, and even more so about the chance to meet Your Highness." Her hand now upon his arm, Corwyn leaned towards her. "You'll find Kreaha likes to put propriety before anything else."

She walked with the knight, her eyes wandering the scenery around them as the two made their way through the rose archways and towards the fountain. "I presume you are speaking from some sort of experience?" She was curious to know more about his past. Alanitora was sure he was not a part of her father's court, yet there were few other ways to achieve lordship and knighthood.

He hummed an affirmative, turning her to the path right of the glimmering fountain. "I supervise a number of cross-kingdom trips for other Trenvern officials and nobles. I like to think I've become somewhat of a diplomat myself. My station in Hearthshire early on called for regular correspondence with Kreahan representatives."

"You must know the border officers well, then."

"Not as much as I used to. I've been stationed near the capitol to train recruits for several years now."

Alanitora examined him for a moment. He talked about this all too casually to have been involved in the attempt at the border. And judging by the fact that he was in no way defensive, it was safe to assume he may not even know what had happened there. She wanted to trust Corwyn desperately, but until she was sure of his loyalties, Alanitora would have to keep him at an arm's length.

They reached their destination not long after.

The rightmost section of the palace stretched out from the rest, the rectangular base rising high into the sky before veering inwards at the top. A tall tower stood behind it, attaching the building to the rest of the outermost wall.

Corwyn removed his arms from hers lightly, stepping forward to speak with the vigilant guards for a few moments before turning and signaling for her to follow.

The princess smiled politely at the guards before quickening her steps toward Corwyn as the doors were opened to the bright interior of Kreaha's Throne Room.

12

Raven Crown

The inside of the Throne Room was unlike anything she could have imagined. The walls were smooth, with silver accents etched onto the edges and corners. Two large chandeliers dangled from the ceiling, their light setting the whole room in a warm glow.

The front half of the left side held stained glass windows, allowing light to enter without a clear view of the room's contents. Meanwhile, the entirety of the right side was adorned with glass panes that allowed a view of the garden and the stone wall beyond. The dark green curtains around each window held an uncanny match to the ivy that crawled its way across the outer stone wall.

The floor was a dark polished wood, purple carpet rolled out to the front of the room. Empty raised seats for the court lined the walls. At the end of the room, two tall thrones sat, its occupants just as pristine and poised as the room itself. Beside each of them sat a vacant, lesser throne.

The scene presented in front of her could be yet another painting, as the king and queen were a staple of decorum. Their posture, dress, and gaze from halfway across the room brought more attention to them than their surroundings.

Corwyn led her closer, his arms clasped behind his back. He bowed in front of the royals. "Presenting Alanitora Nayana Leland of Trenvern," he said before stepping aside.

Alanitora made her way to them, engaging in a low curtsy when she got closer. Her mother had always said to treat other royalty on foreign lands the way you might wish for nobles to treat you. The princess had no issue doing this, but as she looked back up to see their faces, she was met with expressions of concern and disturbance.

Her mind was racing to all the things she could have done wrong before the queen spoke up. "My goodness, are you alright, dear? What happened?"

Alanitora looked down at herself, her condition becoming apparent when she saw the smear of ashes on her dress and palms. She'd forgotten completely that the fire left her desperately in need of a bath, and her inability to take one on the road contributed to the tangled mess her hair was. She thought it quite humorous that Corwyn had not said anything. The man must not have minded it himself.

"Ah, apologies, Your Majesty, we ran into some… trouble on the road. There was a fire in one of our carriages."

The king, who seemed not much older than his wife, frowned at the idea, his bushy black eyebrows following the creases of his face. His eyes were sleek and intelligent when they met hers. "Was anyone hurt?"

She thought of how distraught Owen had been momentarily before the physical pain of her ankle reminded the princess the rest of her entourage had been unharmed in the way the king meant. "No, fortunately."

"That's a relief." The queen sighed, her long, straight dark hair cascading over her shoulders like a veil. Her eyes, in contrast to her husband's, were a wider almond shape, similar to that of Alanitora's own mother. Her face was finely sculpted, with high cheekbones, an oval face shape, and perfectly rounded nostrils.

"Well, if you need anything resupplied, we'd be happy to help." The king smiled.

"Thank you."

"Oh!" The queen's eyebrows shot up, and she reached out to grasp the king's arm. "I do apologize, we didn't even introduce ourselves. I am Queen Myrlene and this is my husband, King Barthram."

"It's a pleasure to meet you."

"And you're to be married to Prince Daruthel of Donasela?"

"Yes, Your Majesty."

"Wonderful!" Myrlene clasped her hands together. "It seems so many of the heirs are getting married these days… Though I suppose our son is no different."

"At least, we hope he isn't," Barthram grumbled, an amused smile on his face.

The king and queen had a light banter between them. Things felt more conversational and open to entertainment in their presence than her parents'. Alanitora quite liked it. It was a good break from all the tensions she was feeling from her trip. She felt her shoulders relax a little.

Barthram looked as though he was about to say something else when he looked over Alanitora's shoulder. "Aiden, if you wish to tell me something, you are welcome to do so." She followed his gaze to a young man—perhaps even younger than herself—as he approached the king. "Please excuse the interruption," Barthram said to her before conversing in low tones with the boy.

A frown settled on his face.

"What is it, dear?" Myrlene asked.

"I fear I must apologize, Your Highness, it seems we have no more guest rooms available for you to stay in. Of course, the village is hosting their spaces, but it seems improper to let you stay in such a place." His brow furrowed further as he finished his sentence.

Alanitora held herself together. She really needed a good night's rest, and village beds wouldn't provide such. Regardless, their hospitality towards her was incredibly generous. "That's quite alright—"

"Now now, Mother, Father," A new voice had her turning her head in the opposite direction. A tall young man had pushed himself off of a wall from the corner of the room, walking closer. When he came into focus, she could see his features were just as handsome as the king and queen. So this was the son they were talking about. The one who was looking for a wife. "That's no way to treat a guest with a title such as hers."

Despite much of his face resembling his mother, the prince's eyes were just as, if not more intense than his father's. He approached her with a steady gaze, unyielding when she stared back.

Before she could do anything, the prince bowed before her. "Prince Regenfrithu."

"A pleasure," she replied. When Regenfrithu straightened himself, she stepped her foot forward to trade obeisances. He placed a hand on her elbow, staring into her eyes with such a strong will of passion that she nearly had to catch herself from stepping back. They were green. Not the kind of mossy green that swirled in her own irises, but a green so strong and bright that if she did not know better, she'd think they were made purely of emeralds.

"There's no need to do that, you're our guest, not a subject." Regenfrithu turned to his parents, breaking their gaze. "Which is why she should sleep in my tower if there truly are no more guest rooms."

The king and queen looked at one another. Alanitora shared their surprise, but more out of confusion than any sort of shock.

"Raven, my love," Queen Myrlene began. "You yourself said you wanted to be sure not a single soul stay in your tower during the festivities. To be sure every lady had a fair chance."

"Exceptions can be made, can they not?" the prince asked. "She is, after all, sworn to another. And in any case, I'm sure Her Highness is beyond exhausted."

Myrlene looked at her husband for guidance, who in turn shrugged. "I see no issue with it."

"Very well, I'll accompany her myself. Aiden, can you send some maids to prepare our guest a bath?"

The boy nodded, before walking off to do as requested. Regenfrithu turned back to her.

She had no idea where his kindness was from. Much of her logic was telling her that it was far too good to be true. That, like Devante, there was some other motive that she was ignorant of, but when she joined eyes with him and looked as deeply as she could, she found nothing malicious.

"Shall we?" He outstretched his hand to hers.

Alanitora looked around the room one last time, her eyes stopping at Corwyn, who gave her an affirming nod. She smiled and placed her hand on his. Regenfrithu guided her towards the door right of the thrones.

Alanitora had never walked beside a male of her same class or higher. It was incredibly unnerving. She found herself checking her posture, speeding or slowing her steps in accordance with his, and even reviewing proper conversation subjects despite her usual ability to naturally follow them.

He held doors open for her to stairwells and hallways as if to signify there was no need for such civility, but it only made her feel smaller. It wasn't like her to want to impress someone, especially a boy of her age.

After a long while of contemplation, she turned to him. "You're looking for a wife, I hear." Regenfrithu laughed, looking down at the floor. "What?" Alanitora asked. She hadn't said something wrong, had she?

"Nothing, it's just that despite that being my entire life these past few days, I'm not used to people asking about it. It's a known subject to most, and many are here because of it."

"Oh, I'm sorry. I wouldn't mind talking about something else."

"No no, it's ironically refreshing. It's customary for heirs of Kreaha to get married before they turn twenty. Does Trenvern have a similar custom?"

She shook her head lightly, her eyes scanning over his wavy black hair. "No, we don't have many traditions in that regard."

"Ah, well would you be alright if I shared the details of our events with you? Since you'll be staying with us long enough to enjoy the festivities yourself."

"Of course!" Her voice had perhaps been a little too eager, and when he looked at her with a grin, she averted her own eyes.

They started up a large staircase of white marble that rose into the heights of the castle. She found it arduous, as the design was intended for appearance rather than function. The dimensions were increasingly frustrating against her calves. But it was a sight she could focus on along with the unique tapestries and decorative pieces on the wall while Regenfrithu spoke.

"Kreaha has always prioritized the idea of choice over obligation. That being said, for numerous generations, love has been the focus of our marriages. Tradition calls for heirs to choose their own spouse without the base of political standpoints. There is no prejudice based on class or kingdom. That's why, when a son or daughter of the crown comes of age, we replace our seasonal festivities with an event to find such a spouse. Women from all around Mordenla have come to try at my hand, though the purpose has changed quite a bit, as now it is ironically more a chance for diplomats and representatives to meet up and discuss possible treaties and trades between kingdoms."

"Does such bother you?"

"Not really, even if it were just to find a bride, there would still be different motives for people to be here. I'm no stranger to a flurry of ladies who just try for it in hopes of a class advancement." Alanitora smiled at the idea. She recalled a conversation about this happening when Korena brought up the event. "And while I find myself increasingly tired, it's a way to meet wonderful new people even if they aren't the future love of my life. The idea, in general, is freeing."

Alanitora hummed an understanding of this, contemplating before speaking. "Seems to be the opposite of my situation. Though I'm not sure I'd enjoy the Kreahan way."

"Oh?" Regenfrithu raised an eyebrow. "Please, elaborate."

"I find that no matter how much you wish for it to be untrue, people always have ulterior motives when they profess the idea of a potential romance. Had we done the same, I'm not sure I could trust any of the men who offered to marry me and love me for life. Besides, ruling a kingdom has a lot of business tied to it. Love affairs could get in the way."

"Or make it stronger."

"True." She couldn't deny he had a point.

They paused at the top of the staircase just before a long hallway, Regenfrithu turning to her. "You aren't winded," he stated.

"I'm sorry?"

"By the stairs, you aren't winded."

She frowned momentarily, an amused smile creeping to her cheeks. "No, I'm not."

"Most would be after all those."

"Then I suppose I'm not most." Alanitora smiled and continued walking. He seemed more out of breath than her, and the prince had to walk these steps daily. Of course, this might be due to her constant activity, although she was still feeling the effects of the smoke that resided in her throat.

He chuckled lightly. "Your room is the first door on the left. The bath should already be set, and if you need any assistance, there are servants there now to help. I do hope you enjoy your stay with us, and if you need anything, don't be afraid to call."

"Thank you kindly for letting me stay in your quarters."

"Of course, though I must ask one thing of you."

She tilted her head slightly in question.

Regenfrithu flashed her a bright smile. "When you're done—if you aren't too tired—I'd like you to visit my room. I'd love to continue this conversation, even if it's only for a few minutes."

"That sounds fine to me," Alanitora said.

"Glad to hear it." Regenfrithu reached his hand out, placing it on her lower back and turning her towards the hallway lightly. "You see the door at the end of the hall?" he asked, leaning in closer to her ear. "If you go through there, you'll find another corridor. My room is the second on the left."

With that he released his hand from her, bowing his head slightly before turning to retire to his room.

Alanitora's back tingled slightly where the feel of his touch lingered. The princess watched as the prince left. Something about him was alluring to her, and she was more alright with it than she cared to admit.

After a moment, she pressed her hand to the door, twisting the knob with her other. The first thing she saw was a beautiful circular table, a vase of assorted roses in the center of it.

The rest of the room was just as colorful. A bright fire burned to her left, and on each wall, there were at least two candelabras. Alanitora moved around the table, taking in the room. The bed was huge, and fresh white sheets laid upon it. There were bedside desks on either side of it, the three items taking up the entire far wall. The side of the room opposite from her held two windows with heavy black curtains, and a desk in the middle. Alas, the wall to her right held a dresser and wardrobe in the center and a door on either side. Through the left, she could see her bath.

A young girl was standing next to the door, a pitcher in her hands. She bowed when she saw the princess.

"Welcome, Your Highness. Thank you for staying with us this lovely evening," the young girl said, a bright smile on her face. She wore a predominantly black uniform, a purple necktie at the front, and a long skirt that wrapped around her ankles. "Your bath is ready, would you like me to assist you during your wash?"

Alanitora thought for a moment. She was used to Korena and Gwendolyn assisting her but was slightly uneasy with a stranger doing so. Besides, she wasn't incapable of such, and under the girl's smile, she could tell she was drained. "No, thank you. Just leave my things on the side."

"Of course, Your Highness." She nodded and passed in front of Alanitora to the other door, where she retrieved a set of towels. Her energy was refreshing to the princess, who was more accustomed to unknown servants either cowering from her, being the dullest of folks, or holding minimal respect. Instead, this girl was polite without reservations. She seemed to be satisfied with her employment. Alanitora was especially grateful for her service this late in the night when others might hope to rest.

"Thank you," called out Alanitora. The girl gave one more bow before leaving the room and closing the door behind her.

With a sigh of relief of the final moment alone, Alanitora made her way into the bathroom, looking over the ornate features of both the tub and the furniture that accompanied it.

The towels had been folded neatly on the side, along with cleaning instruments, solutions, and a small mirror. The princess looked down at the water, illuminated by the collection of candles around her. She reached her finger out, grazing the tip across the steaming clear liquid. It was profoundly warm. So warm that Alanitora wondered how they had heated it so fast, and where.

The ripples that lapped out from her fingertips and across the surface were calmer than anything else had been in that day, perhaps even in that week.

Alanitora shed herself of her clothes carefully, the bruises and sores from jumping out of the carriage aching twice as much as she maneuvered her way from the layers. Then, she put her hands on the edge of the tub and stepped in with her right foot, lowering herself in while trying to avoid any contact with her left ankle.

First, her core descended into the warmth, then her head. The swirling muffled sound of everything else being drowned out surrounded her ears. She felt her hair drift against her cheeks under the water as she lay weightlessly in its depth. The water soothed her, and she felt every muscle in her body relax after hours, and in some perspective, days of restlessness. Every worry dissipated out from her into the water.

She didn't emerge until it was needed for her to breathe. Alanitora wiped the water from her face, opening her eyes as it trickled down her features. She looked down into the water, which was now murky with a gray ribbon of ash that had come from her body. A clouded abyss.

Grabbing the mirror on the side, she brought it up to her face. There was still some on her forehead, but it was nothing a bit of scrubbing couldn't remove. She sunk back under the water, letting it take her over once again.

After half an hour of bathing in bliss, Alanitora removed herself from the fantasy. She re-dressed into her undergarments and put on the soft silk robe left on the side for her. By the time she was done with everything, the water had changed from lukewarm to cool, and Alanitora took the opportunity to soak her left foot, grimacing once again at the bubbled burn.

She stopped at the linen closet the maid had gotten her towels from to retrieve a cloth to wrap her ankle before putting her shoes back on. The princess then sat in front of the fire for some time to let her long hair dry enough to manage.

Brushing out her hair and checking that she was decent, Alanitora slipped from her room quietly, intending to speak with the prince as he had suggested.

She made her way down the hall and opened the door to the next corridor. It was as though she had entered an entirely different building. Regenfrithu's hall was far more luxurious than her own. Even the candelabras had ornate engravings. Just as there had been roses on her center table, multiple bouquets lined the walls.

As instructed, she stopped in front of the second door on the right. Alanitora knocked, but the door simply pushed open at her touch.

"Oh, my prince, you needn't worry about it." A maid, different from the one that had served Alanitora, stood in front of Regenfrithu, giggles erupting from her throat as she patted at his arm.

At this moment, the ajar door caught Regenfrithu's attention, and he looked up to meet Alanitora's eyes. "Ah, Your Highness, I do hope your bath was alright?"

"Yes, it was. Thank you," she replied hesitantly, unsure if she should be interrupting whatever moment was taking place in front of her, intimate or not.

The maid turned only momentarily, as though Alanitora's presence was just the sound of the wind. She seemed quite eager to ignore her and continue conversing with the prince.

Regenfrithu's eyes flicked back and forth between the two girls. "I apologize. Mira, this is Her Highness Alanitora of Trenvern."

The maid turned again, no longer ignoring her. "Pleasure." Her voice was far too high to be natural as she plastered a fake smile on her face, giving a small curtsy.

"And you." Alanitora nodded.

Regenfrithu stepped forward. "Thank you, Mira. You are dismissed."

The maid hummed in understanding, a scowl on her face momentarily appeared when she turned. Alanitora met her eyes. The girl was planning something, and it wasn't well-intentioned. She didn't like it, the cunning look that stared back at her even through a sweet smile.

Mira grabbed the pitcher of water from Regenfrithu's table and a few towels before making her way towards the door. The prince followed. She had nearly reached the princess when her feet stumbled against each other. Mira's hands shot out, the contents of the pitcher shooting forward and towards Alanitora.

The princess stepped out of the way in just enough time that only a small amount of water splashed against her robes.

Regenfrithu reached forward, catching Mira's elbows to help stabilize her on her feet.

"Oh my, pardon me, Your Highness, I'm so awfully clumsy."

Alanitora narrowed her eyes slightly. Clumsiness didn't seem to be the source of the mishap; nevertheless, she brushed the concern aside, watching silently as Mira bent down in front of Regenfrithu to clean up the excess water.

But the prince simply kneeled with her, taking the towels from her elbows and resting his hand on her back. "No need Mira, I can clear it up from here. You should retire for the night, get some rest."

"Why of course!" The maid perked up. "I do apologize again, I can only hope my feet aren't so twisted tomorrow during our dance... You will be saving one for me, right?"

"Of course," Regenfrithu responded.

With a satisfied smile that suggested her goal had been accomplished, Mira left the room, ignoring Alanitora's presence as she passed by her.

She waited until the maid was well down the hall before speaking up. "Dance?"

Regenfrithu gathered up the rest of the liquid, setting the towel aside on his dresser before turning to face her. "Why yes, tomorrow we are hosting a ball for the festivities. I'm sure you'll love it. We throw the most wonderful events. There is so much to do, after all. During the day, there are peddlers, games, and competitions. It's all fun and elation. And as night approaches, the ballroom becomes the most elegant area. Imagine dozens of couples dancing in unison, smiles upon every face." He looked in her eyes, his own sparkling. "It would mean a lot to me if you came."

She smiled at the thought. It had been ages since she attended a ball. Trenvern rarely had any nowadays. "I hadn't considered it."

"You should." He flashed her a grin, and she couldn't help but return a smile. "Besides, if you look even more gorgeous cleaned up, I can't imagine how radiant you might be in such an extravagant setting. What do you say?"

"Are you always this flirtatious with everyone?"

"Not necessarily. Is that a yes?"

She let her mouth open slightly, pulling him in with the suspense. "Alright."

What had perhaps been a smirk erupted into a grin. Satisfied, Regenfrithu stepped back from the princess. He opened his mouth to say something else when the distant chimes of a bell tower echoed into the room.

"It appears to be getting later and later… I should let you rest. I'm sure you are tired after a long journey, and if you keep your promise, I'll be promising *you* quite the adventurous day tomorrow. You'll need whatever rest you can get."

It was true that Alanitora would need sleep, but her short time with Regenfrithu was something that she felt would keep her awake. Her eyes widened with intrigue to know more of this man she had such brief interactions with. Regardless of the fire within her that sparked whenever they made eye contact, she did indeed feel the looming cloud of fatigue coming upon the horizon, ready to cover her at any moment.

"I believe I am quite exhausted," she noted, stepping back into the door frame, preparing herself to depart the room.

"Oh, I nearly forgot. Someone came by to tell you that your friends have sleeping arrangements in the village. They mentioned names. Korena and Guinevere, I believe."

"Gwendolyn," she corrected. Good, so they were settled as well. That was one thing she didn't need to worry about.

He chuckled. "I made sure to ask that you be woken up later than usual tomorrow, so you can get whatever rest suits you."

"Thank you, that is quite considerate." Alanitora stepped back into the hallway, aware that the closer she was to him, the more she would wish to stay and talk for hours. "I bid you goodnight, Prince Regenfrithu."

"Raven."

"I'm sorry?"

"My friends call me Raven."

"Raven, then." The name slid off her tongue with ease and tasted sweet as a summer berry.

13

The Maiden

The next morning, Alanitora found she had rested quite well, despite thoughts of her new acquaintance having swirled in her mind for what felt like hours after they spoke. She felt refreshed enough to greet the morning light that seeped into her window, and found a smile on her face when she noticed the small note left on her nightstand.

'Dear Your Highness,' it read, 'Upon receiving the location of your stay this morning, we decided to let you sleep and leave an outfit for you to wear on our outing today. Knowing you, you'll be fine to dress yourself, but if you need help, we've made sure to let the maids of that area know to assist you at your calling. Take whatever time you need and meet us at the front courtyard fountain. Cheers, Gwendolyn.' Just below her name was 'And Korena!' in a different, more loopily scrawled handwriting.

She looked up past the note to the deep maroon dress that rested on the back of a chair, a pair of shoes sitting squarely beneath. Alanitora pushed the covers off her legs and swung her feet to the marble floor, its cool surface exhilarating.

Dressing and equipping was easy enough that she was able to leave her room only a quarter of an hour later. Her shoulders dropped upon seeing that the only occupant of the hall was a scullery maid, who smiled and adjusted the woven basket at her hip.

The princess made her way down the series of familiar stairwells, only to stop short at the bottom.

She had no idea where she was going.

Sure, she retained the memory of her path last night, but that meant taking a trip through the Throne Room, and something told Alanitora that wouldn't be the best course of action.

Opening the door to a different corridor, she looked around for any indication of her destination. Being lost in such a large structure was not something she was used to, for she knew Trenvern's castle like the back of her hand in contrast.

"Excuse me." Alanitora cleared her throat, approaching a young man dressed in servant's attire.

He turned to her with a helpful smile. "Good morning, miss, can I assist you with anything?" The words rolled out of his mouth so smoothly that she was certain he was used to being helpful.

She smiled. "Yes, I was wondering how to get to the fountain. It seems I've gotten myself a little mixed up with my directions."

"Ah, of course." He folded his hands together and bowed lightly. "Don't fret, it's a common issue here. So common that we've even implemented a system to help guests such as yourself."

She tilted her head in question. "Oh?"

The man waved his hands to the walls of the hallway. "Yes, if you look close, there are small gemstones in the walls indicating the path to different directions." She looked where he was referring to, and indeed, there were amethysts and emeralds lining the walls. The purple gems were populous on the right end while the green ones were heavier on the left. "It's used by servants and guards in case there is some sort of emergency in the castle. Purple leads further into the castle where our royalty resides, and the green leads outside to the nearest exit."

"How curious." She couldn't hold back her interest in the decorations. "So If I follow the green—"

"—then you'll find yourself outside, yes. And if you're looking for the large fountain, that one is fairly easy to find."

She smiled at his bright energy. It was a nice deviance from servants at home, who were either haughty or timid and nowhere between. "Thank you very much, sir."

"Of course, miss. If you ever need more assistance, never be afraid to ask."

Alanitora turned away, her path following the green gems but her mind wrapped up in curiosities and questions. Emeralds and amethysts were certainly valuable, so why take the risk of adorning them in a place where they could be easily stolen? Was Kreaha not worried about the theft of them? Or perhaps their opulence was grand enough that losing all the stones in the castle would do nothing to hurt their pride.

The man's directions, she found, were quite perfect, as she exited the palace directly into the garden, the fountain in sight to her right.

The garden was even more beautiful in the daylight, drops of dew settled on the leaves and petals, sunlight reflecting off them with a sparkle. The colors of the different roses stood bright against the green hedges, every petal pristine.

Gwendolyn and Korena sat side by side at the edge of the fountain, the blonde skimming her hand across the surface of the water while the brunette read her book.

When the two saw her approach, they rose from their seats to greet her.

"Tora, you should have seen it! There was a small parade of musicians that awoke us this morning. You would have loved it." Gwendolyn joined hands with her, lifting up her arms in a swing.

"I'm sure I would have."

"And we stopped by one of the bakeries too. There was this really good blueberry tart covered with a sweet creamy sauce," Korena added.

Gwendolyn nodded in excitement. "As well as a—"

A shriek sounded in the distance and Alanitora swiveled her head towards it to see frantic groups of people separating to the sides of the pathways. She drew a dagger from her left side, placing herself between her ladies and the commotion.

A massive gray figure sped through the courtyard and right towards them. Bystanders jumped out of the way to avoid it. The urgency of the creature's speed made it hard to see, but Alanitora knew very well what was approaching.

The creature bounded into the fountain, making the water splash out and over the surface of the rim. Alanitora covered her face momentarily to prevent it from getting wet, but after she cleared her view there was only a wagging tail in motion on Silver Moon's figure.

He jumped out from the fountain in front of her and her ladies, shaking off the water that stuck to his coat. There were a few gasps as a crowd of eyes observed the scene with curiosity. Those who realized there was no longer an imminent threat relaxed their shoulders.

"Momma, how come so many visiting people have wolves as pets?" a young girl asked. The mother in question tugged her away from the scene.

Alanitora looked around at their onlookers, clearing her throat. "My apologies, everyone. My friend here hasn't quite grasped the importance of manners."

While a few continued to glower in disapproval, there were enough chuckles for Alanitora to conclude Silver Moon's intervention was good-humored. For the most part, everyone went on their way.

She kneeled to the wolf, scratching the top of his head—which was significantly less wet than the rest of him. "What did you get yourself into, hmm?" she asked. He panted in reply, turning to drink from the same water he'd just splashed around in. She turned to her ladies. "Now that we have a majority of the party here, let's see what you all are so excited about."

Gwendolyn's smile brightened. "There's a wonderful marketplace in the second courtyard. We didn't spend much time there since we didn't want you to miss it, but from what we saw, it'll surely be a treat."

"Yes! And we explored the town this morning too. It's absolutely giant! Bigger than Trenvern's capital certainly, and more lively." Korena waved her arms enthusiastically, skipping ahead of the two of them and ducking under an archway's hanging blush rose.

Though she had seen its glory the night before, the morning sun allowed Alanitora to take in the full grandeur of Kreaha's palace. It was beautifully built, with tall white walls and flourished ornate windows. A variety of details were embedded into the architecture: from spiraling turrets and engraved columns to bay windows and balconies. Its asymmetry made it ever more beautiful.

They walked through a path that led under an archway and into the first courtyard, which was filled with tables and benches. Servants stood along the perimeter to assist anyone in need while a plethora of guests chatted near the stairways that led to a building on either side. This left the center open for people to walk from one archway to the next.

The second courtyard was where diverse vendors presented their goods. Rows and rows of booths selling any number of things from pastries to jewelry attracted people left and right.

Though Gwendolyn had expressed interest in this area, they went ahead towards the back corner of the second courtyard, where the building split off into the town. Alanitora eagerly followed the large flow of people. As the crowd separated, she could see the tall buildings and bustling events they spoke of.

Ahead of her were three stages set around the center of town, each one collecting its own audience. To her left, there was a large wooden bucket filled with apples, where people bent forward to grip them between their teeth. And on her right a jester danced around, throwing and catching various colored balls.

Everywhere she looked there were new sights, new activities, new people just as eager as her to explore what the raven kingdom had to offer

Excitement bubbled within her, and Alanitora couldn't help but feel lost at where to start. So many things were happening all at once. While she was not necessarily overwhelmed, a plethora of items ventured to grab her attention.

The princess shook her head, looking at the wolf, who stood patiently at her hip. "Where do you think we should go?" she asked, combing her fingers through the fur at his neck.

But the wolf just tilted his head to rub against her leg. So much for communication.

They ended up weaving their way around the layout of the town, pointing out anything that piqued their interest from the dress of foreigners to the architecture of buildings.

It was all wonderful, but nothing in particular caught Alanitora's eye. Save for perhaps the second stage's event, in which men of different ages ran across the stage while swords thrusted up from holes in the floorboards.

There was no real danger to it, of course, as the edges were blunt and the strength low. Regardless, it was comedic to watch some hop around quickly on their feet while others strategized like snakes. Anyone who made their way to the end of the stage was offered a bouquet of roses to give to a lady of their choosing. Alanitora overheard one servant explain to an onlooker that giving a flower to someone was a way to ask them to dance at the ball. A bouquet promised more than a few.

This became especially amusing when a young man approached them, outstretching a single orange rose to Gwendolyn. The brunette politely declined, to which the man looked distraught, but insisted she take the rose as a gift instead.

After making their way through the events of the town and talking with a few strangers about the numerous entertainers, the trio—along with their very exhilarated wolf who got more attention than *said* entertainers—began a trip around the second courtyard's marketplace.

Aware that her ladies' salaries were much too low to provide adequate spending money, Alanitora had no qualms giving them each a sumptuous amount to enjoy themselves. While it took a lot of persuasion to get Gwendolyn to take it from her in the first place, it took even more persuasion to keep Korena from buying every other thing she saw. Gwendolyn had to restrain her when they passed one jewelry stand in particular. It seemed she had a certain attraction to sparkling colors.

On the reverse side, the ladies-in-waiting were able to convince Alanitora to buy her own share of items, including a bronze engraved compass and a pair of shoes embroidered with a design that resembled the branches of a weeping willow.

Perhaps the most hectic part for all three of them was in choosing what to eat. Given the commercial success of the festivities Kreaha usually threw, it was no surprise that vendors came from all around Mordenla, bringing their culture—and by extension, their food—to the stalls. They stuffed themselves with samples alone, only to buy more food for later.

By the time they started heading back, Alanitora wasn't sure there was any energy in her left. She hardly managed to get up all of the stairs before she staggered into her room, Korena and Gwendolyn following promptly.

Silver Moon jumped up onto her bed and curled up at the end of it, falling fast asleep in little time. She envied his ability to rest.

Korena shut the door. "What a day," she sighed. "Thanks for the money, Tora."

"Anytime." Alanitora collapsed into the vanity chair, waving away her worries.

"We have four hours before the ball starts. How about you take a rest, Your Highness? I understand how tiresome these kinds of events can be for you." Gwendolyn set down the basket of their goods.

"I thought the ball started at eight?"

"Korena dear, you and I both know it takes longer for us to get ready. If we pretend the time to leave is earlier, we are more likely to be on time."

"I agree with Gwendolyn," Alanitora said. "About an afternoon nap and our general tardiness."

Korena glanced at her friend. "We will leave you to it then. Enjoy your rest. We will wake you up in a few hours to get ready."

Alanitora smiled and guided herself to the bed, which had been remade since the morning. She watched her ladies gather their belongings as she sunk into the tight blankets. Silver Moon readjusted his position so that his head rested atop her legs.

While she wasn't the lightest of sleepers, Alanitora was grateful that Gwendolyn's call was enough to wake her up. Naps weren't something she enjoyed all that much. A midday slumber held bizarre dreams and if too long, the occasional headache when she woke. This day's nap was just long enough for her to have a dream, but absolutely no recollection of its events.

Regardless, it had rejuvenated her enough to welcome Gwendolyn's familiar face of glee when the lady pulled her out of the warm covers. Before she could say anything, Gwendolyn was bouncing and squeaking, spinning the princess with her.

Silver Moon bounded from the bed to the floor in the fuss, circling the two with curiosity.

"What? What is it?" Alanitora couldn't help an amused smile

"Oh!" the brunette interluded. "Cover your eyes!" She pressed her fingers atop Alanitora's eyes, struggling to stabilize from the momentum of spinning.

The princess chuckled, placing her hands over Gwendolyn's.

She could hear another person enter the room, a struggling grunt revealing it was the last of their trio. There was then a thud on the ground, then silence for a few moments.

"Okay… Open!" Gwendolyn said, removing her hands from Alanitora's vision.

The amount of commotion following her wake perplexed Alanitora as she adjusted her eyesight to see what all the excitement was about. Nonetheless, as she regained her senses, she could see a wondrous color before her next to Korena.

A long, large teal ball gown stood upon its dress form in front of her. The neckline hung near the edge of the shoulders, long bell sleeves descending from them. Embroidery lined the hems of the fabric, small sparkling silver beads sewn into a design that reminded her of lilies of the valley. The needlepoint of the bodice was especially elaborate though, a darker teal adorning the leaf-like designs

She couldn't help the gasp that escaped her throat. "Where did you find this? It's beautiful!" Alanitora took the fabric of the sleeve into her hands, smoothing her fingers over the embroidery. The small beads rolled under her thumb.

Korena's grin widened, a giggle escaping her throat.

Gwendolyn looked over to her friend. "Korena made it forever ago. Took her a long time."

"Oh, I've been waiting for the opportunity to present it to you! It's been a year or two since I finished it, but ultimately I didn't think the time would come that you'd wear it." Korena gave her a wink. "Patience helped it seems… Though I am not sure how well it will fit. You may have been a bit smaller when I drafted the measurements."

Her rambling was endearing, and Alanitora took the time to examine the dress herself. It indeed was beautiful, perhaps the best work she had ever seen from Korena. She guided her hand across the skirt. It was silky, shiny, but not delicate like other materials she'd worn before for occasions such as this.

"Shall we?" Alanitora stood up straight, looking between her ladies.

Their eyes practically sparkled in excitement. "Korena, get the gown ready. I'll prep the undergarments."

Gwendolyn assisted the princess in removing her dress, which was ruffled from her nap. As well as replacing her undergarments with ones that would better suit the ballgown's shape. After the hoop skirt was properly adjusted, various layers of petticoats were placed over the boning for support under her main skirt.

At last, the dress itself was removed from its form and carefully brought down over Alanitora's head. Korena fluffed the skirt to its full, being sure to leave none of the edges tucked so that her handiwork was visible. Then, the seamstress brought herself back up and readjusted the bust and waist, pulling the fabrics back for Gwendolyn to lace and tie up.

Korena had been right about the size. As the tightening began, Alanitora could feel her sides constricting with each pull. The dress was a little small around her core, but the sleeves and height were just fine.

Upon the last lacing, Alanitora took in a deep breath. It squeezed the bottom of her ribs towards each other, and while constricting, one look in the mirror took away any doubts.

The dress was gorgeous on her. The sleeves fit her arms perfectly up until the elbows, where they began to become wide, eventually fanning out into the bell sleeve shape. The bodice embroidery only made her features more bold, and the color complimented her hair and complexion.

Alanitora smiled. "It's beyond gorgeous, Korena." she looked over to her friend, who was blushing with glee.

The satin fabric was smooth to rest her hands on comfortably, as she pressed her palms onto her stomach. Alanitora turned. The skirt's bustle went out slightly, ruffles leading to the back end that looked like a collection of roses.

She looked around the skirt again. There were no folds to hide her weapons in.

Korena must have read the look on her face, for she sighed. "I apologize, Your Highness… You see, when I first began making it, you didn't carry as many weapons on you. Besides, it is a ball gown, I doubt it would be very flattering to have pockets here and there."

Alanitora nodded. She could see Korena's point, but she still felt a little uneasy. She turned to Gwendolyn. "The wrap-around?"

"Mmm," Gwendolyn nodded. "I'll retrieve it along with our dresses."

The maiden returned soon after with another chest and a girdle-like belt with multiple slots and pockets that held daggers and knives with flat hilts. The wrap-around was a piece of alternative equipment for Alanitora's weapons that Gwendolyn made up when they encountered dresses that couldn't be converted to her standard hidden pockets. It was placed a layer or two under the main skirt and hung around the end of her hips.

Sure, it wasn't easily accessible, but it was security nonetheless. Additionally, the blades weren't visible, the only indication of their presence was when she pressed her hand against them.

As the time for the ball approached, Alanitora sat in her vanity chair, arranging her hair while looking over her shoulder every once in a while to watch Korena and Gwendolyn's progress on their own dresses.

Korena's was loose on the top, lilac fabric hanging on her figure and joining at the waist, then flowing out in ruffled ripples to the side and around the back to reveal a long white skirt underneath. Her sleeves were elbow-length, puffing out and joining together at the end. It wasn't often that Alanitora saw Korena in purple, but she liked it on her.

Gwendolyn, on the other hand, wore a more complex dress. The top hugged both core and arms down to her wrists. A v-shaped section rose from her pelvis up to the scoop neck, with tight golden laces atop a cream base. Rumpled edges introduced a deep blue that covered the rest of the dress, including that of the skirt, which had a bunched-up bustle at the back of extra layered blue fabric.

"Everyone ready?" Korena gave her friends another examination for any faults or fixes.

Alanitora smiled. She was as ready as she'd ever been. This was the most excitement she'd had in ages—well, most *positive* excitement, that was. Giving Silver Moon one last pat, she departed with her companions.

Similar to the previous night, the pathways were lined with lanterns, though this time they held many more than before, illuminating the gardens with benevolent and awe-inspiring light.

They were nearly at the fountain when a quick exclamation came from Gwendolyn, and she picked up her skirts and leaped over the ground lanterns into the garden.

Korena looked at Alanitora. "What in the world is that about? You'd think a mad person took over her."

"Something along those lines..." Alanitora watched the darkness as Gwendolyn came rushing back, a mass in her arms.

Gwendolyn grinned. "Can I get one of your daggers, please?"

Alanitora pulled her skirt up, taking out one of the smaller knives and handing it to her.

What did Gwendolyn want this for? What was she holding? It was this white and black speckled mass, with a long silhouetted cloth of a blue and green design hanging over it and down over Gwendolyn's elbow.

Suddenly, the mass moved, and a long blue neck pointed out, the small head of a bird at the end of it. The top of its head held a fan-like structure that waved at Gwendolyn's chin.

"Gwennie!" Korena screeched. "It's a peacock!" A high gasp came from the blonde's mouth as she stepped forward to pet it. "Oh, I never thought I'd see one in my life! It's so pretty."

"Yes, he is," Gwendolyn cooed, flipping the knife in her hand.

Korena jumped back with a shout.

Oh goodness. Alanitora stepped back as well. This was violent, especially for Gwendolyn. "I don't advise that you—"

But the lady-in-waiting had already slashed the knife down. Alanitora shut her eyes at the sound of the bird's squawking, yet when she opened them, she was relieved to see that there was no blood upon the path or their dresses.

"There you are, lovely." Gwendolyn placed the peacock back on the ground, watching as it ran back into the gardens. She then stepped up to Alanitora, turning the princess' head to the side and inserting an eye-shaped feather to the side of her hair. Tucking the edges along the path of a braid.

"Well that was quite dramatic," Korena said as the ladies began walking again, ready to join the crowd ahead.

"Please," Gwendolyn giggled. "It was only dramatic because you made assumptions about what I was going to do. Besides, you're one to talk about dramatics."

"What's that supposed to mean?!" Korena stomped.

Alanitora stifled a laugh. She lifted her skirts and inserted the dagger back to its place while the two followed her close behind.

The left side of the inner courtyard plaza held a grand staircase leading up to the doors that the Ballroom was behind. A line of noble folk led up either side of the stairs, moving forward every few seconds.

They made their way to the left line. Delighted conversation filled the area, different people's excitement buzzing around so loud that Alanitora couldn't hear or see Diane approaching until she was only a few strides away.

Her dress was magnificent as well. It was rather flat for an event like this, but the color, cut, and flow made up for such. It was a medium pink around the formed bodice, and a light pink across the skirt. The sleeves were strange, as there was only a thin strand connecting it to the shoulders as a long fabric hung down, joining again at the bicep only to separate before joining once again at the elbow with fabric flowing down around to the length of her fingertips.

"I wasn't sure when you all would get here, so I've been waiting for a bit," the redhead announced, joining her hands in front of her.

Poor Diane had a slight shiver to her posture. How long had she been waiting? "Well, you are welcome to go in, I'm sure this line is more for those who want to be announced." Alanitora smiled softly.

But the girl shook her head. "No, I'll go in with you all."

As they slowly made their way up to the top of the staircase, a girl not too much younger than Alanitora stopped them. She was wearing a dark, defined purple dress, one with many elaborate details and embroideries that Alanitora could tell she was of higher social status than most of the crowd.

"Good evening ladies," the girl said. The top half of her straight dark hair was pulled back in an eloquent bun, the bottom freely relaxing behind her shoulders. "Thank you for attending our lavish seasonal event. We just have a few questions for you before you enter."

Her eyes wandered over the four girls, landing on Alanitora as an assumption that she would be speaking for the group. The princess nodded in response.

"I am Princess Lorenalia Rangsford of Kreaha, I am delighted to make your acquaintance. My first question regards whether or not you will be participating for the prince's hand tonight, and the second regards what kingdom you are here on behalf of."

The questions she was asking certainly made sense. "My ladies and I are just here for leisure, and the kingdom we represent is that of Trenvern."

"Oh!" Lorenalia exclaimed, her face shifting from formality to excitement. "You must be Her Highness Alanitora! Well, we are quite happy to be within your presence."

"As I am happy to be here, Princess Lorenalia," Alanitora replied.

"Well, follow me right this way. You will be announced soon."

Alanitora nodded, looking back to her companions. They followed her cue as Lorenalia led them up to the opening doors.

A golden glow emanated from the Ballroom, welcoming her in from the cold night. From where she stood she could see there was yet another grand staircase, this one descending to the dancers while the level they were on lined the walls as a balcony to look over the people. A green carpet flowed along the left staircase, while a purple one lined the right.

Lorenalia nodded them forward, where the young chamberlain from the day before stood in the center. The Kreahan princess whispered something in his ear, before stepping back.

Alanitora raised her chin, gazing over the crowd before her. About a third had their attention focused on the announcer, while others were either talking amongst themselves or paying attention to the dancing. She raised her lips into her best smile.

The chamberlain cleared his throat, speaking loud and clear across the entire ballroom."Presenting Queen Alanitora of Trenvern and her ladies."

Alanitora froze, the words reverberating in her ears. One word in particular stood out

Her smile faded as she looked between her ladies. "Queen?" she asked. Surely she hadn't heard that right.

14

Question of Love

Owen threw down the pile of wood next to the remains of a long-extinguished fire. Sure, he'd been successful in finding something to warm his night, but like the previous evening, he was unable to find anything to eat within the vast woods on the side of the road.

The rations they left him with were sufficient, but Owen feared that he may risk running out before he decided what to do with himself.

What exactly was he supposed to do? The first option that came to mind was to return home, but that wasn't much of an option after all. There was a slight chance Owen would be persecuted for failure to follow through with his duties to the crown, and even if that wasn't the case, the boy wasn't sure if Trenvern was still... Trenvern.

That left him with two other options. Either he could leave the knighthood life behind him and find a place to work, maybe settle down in a Kreahan town and start a stable life, or he could do what his heart desired: follow Alanitora.

It was a known fact by this point that people were trying to kill her. It wasn't that he didn't think she could take care of herself—hell, she'd probably murder him just for suggesting such a thing—it was that he was terrified. Terrified of her life being cut short before she could pursue the ambitions he was well aware she was capable of. Terrified of what her death might mean. Terrified of what her absence from this world would do to him.

He was an idiot, letting his feelings lead him like that. What in his mind suggested that she'd share the same sentiment? Alanitora had always been devoid of emotion, even if he did see a sliver of it every once in a while.

Owen vigorously worked at his fire, his thoughts pressing as he watched the flames slowly appear and then evaporate in the next second. He sighed, steadying his hands to start again.

The young soldier supposed that all his problems were sourced from Alanitora. He'd spent the first ten years of his life admiring her, and another seven after that thinking of her constantly.

She had been right when she said she'd changed. He didn't want to believe it. After all, she was the reason he did all of this. She was the reason he kept going.

It was true she was odd for a girl. He remembered that she was interested in fighting at a young age, but never touched a real weapon. She would insist that he was hidden away in a tower by a dragon, and she would have to fight to save him. Then, when she finally defeated said dragon, she'd run up to him and simply claim that he was dead. That he had died trying to escape when he was complaining. Their pretend games always ended in tragedy, and her investment in the more ambiguous things was what Owen believed prompted his continual interest.

Life by her was an adventure. It was taking risks and discovering something new every day. It was stumbling across surprises around each corner. And life without her was cold and bland, as though the colors of small things—flowers, bees, the blue sky—were all sucked away into a world of gray clouds.

Owen was about to put his food upon the growing flames when he heard a small rustle in the bushes.

He sat still, drowning out the sound of a crackling fire to call attention to whatever creature moved behind him.

Another rustle sounded, this time a bit closer. Either it was a medium-sized rodent, or something big trying to hide its mass.

Owen gripped his sword, sliding it out of the sheath as quietly as possible, not to disturb the creature. But it must have seen such, as silence held the night once again. It was still there. It had to be.

He turned his head slowly, calculating the exact position of his prey, then lunging toward it.

The figure stood tall, jumping out of the way of his rampage and into the light. With haste, Owen turned back towards it.

It was a person. Of similar height, but a much smaller build. The fire illuminated their long dark cloak. Which, despite being torn at the edges, was a luxurious fabric.

"Goodness, if someone said my week would consist of my children trying to kill me, I'd think them mad." The captivating voice was that of a woman.

Owen narrowed his eyes. What did she mean by her children? She wasn't his mother. His mother sounded nothing like that.

The woman brought her delicate hands up to her hood, bringing it down to lay across her shoulders. It was hard to recognize her with the shadows the fire below cast upon her face, along with the fact he hadn't seen her for years.

But her facial structure, the long brown hair, and the similar features the woman of his memory held to her... It was unmistakable.

"Queen Elena!" Owen exclaimed.

She chuckled. "You and I both know that I am no longer queen... At least, in Trenvern."

"Traitor!"

"That is something I also am not."

But anger boiled in Owen. This woman had put her life, her kingdom, her daughter at risk. And for what? What was so important that she had to betray the people who loved her?

Owen gripped his sword tighter and ran towards the woman. He watched as her face shifted from surprise to annoyance, and the next thing he knew, Queen Elena had maneuvered herself around him, digging her elbow into his back and stepping down at the hilt of his sword, knocking it out of his hands. She then grasped his forearm and twisted it upwards, forcing his chest to the ground and kicking him down to a kneeling position.

"Listen to me. I don't have time for your childish manners. I have spent days tracing the path of my daughter and I don't intend to stop now. Where is the camp?" Elena growled into his ear.

Owen spat at the ground, immobilized by the woman. "Like I'd tell you."

She sighed, twisting his arm a little further.

He held back a yelp. "You'll never win! You are too late, they are far ahead by now."

Elena took her arm off his back and knocked him with her palm on the back of his head, prompting an exclamation from him. "You absolute dunce. I raised you better than this. Alanitora cannot go through with the wedding, it'll absolutely destroy not just her reputation, but her resolve!"

"What are you talking about?" he grunted.

"I'll explain if you surrender."

Owen looked down at the grass. He had no idea what she was talking about, but one thing was for certain: Queen Elena helped raise both him and Alanitora as children. The woman he'd known then as a second mother was kind and selfless. He couldn't say the same for most others. That fact alone should say something about trust, or a chance of it at least.

He considered the options. If the woman of his memory held, she would do him no harm. Nonetheless, even if her current reputation preceded her, she was the one who needed information from him. Hearing her out—whether they be lies or not—meant he had time to strategize. Either way, he had the invisible upper hand.

The soldier relaxed his arm. "Alright."

But there were no signs of hostility, no signs of manipulation, no signs of malice. Elena loosened her grip, wrapping her cloak back around her to escape the cold of the night. She made her way around the flames, beginning her narrative.

Owen didn't interrupt her, not even when her words contradicted all that he knew. The soldier instead stayed silent, cursing himself for the immediate desire to believe her. But even when those feelings were pushed aside, he found only truth in her words.

It was convoluted and messy, but she told it without a single falter of her voice.

When she finished, the only sound that followed was the crackles of a dying fire. Owen stared at the embers between them, running her words through his head twice over before speaking. "But that means…"

She nodded, a grim look on her face. "I fear it does."

"And you didn't tell anyone about this?" His eyebrows furrowed. Anger bubbled.

"Please, Owen, if I could I would have."

The soldier clenched his jaw, contemplating all of the possibilities. An overwhelming amount of ill fate forced him up off the ground. He grabbed his things with haste, stuffing his sack.

"What are you doing?" Elena asked.

"If what you say is true—I mean, assuming I believe you—We have to get to her now, before it's too late. She has to know!"

Elena got up from her spot, rushing to put a hand on his arm to stop him. "Give me one reason why you should come along."

He raised his chin. "I know where they are. Besides, you're a known fugitive in the eyes of Trenvern. Others will not have the same hesitance as I. You need someone to do the talking.

She considered this for a few moments before nodding her head. "Very well, but save your breath and energy, you will need it later. Right now, focus on getting a good enough rest for us to even have a chance of catching up to her."

"But—" Owen bit his tongue. He wasn't comfortable with the risk, but with his lack of sleep the last few nights, the soldier wasn't sure he was in the best condition to help Alanitora. He relaxed his shoulders.

"Good. Get some sleep, I'll watch over the camp and wake you at dawn." She looked at him, giving the boy a soft smile.

He still wanted to protest, proclaim that she would only leave him as soon as he fell asleep. Or perhaps that there was hypocrisy in the fact she would not be sleeping herself. But her kind eyes only showed him trust. For what reason she allowed his help, he did not know. What Owen did know was that her decision to tell him had to mean something.

He lay next to the fire, wrapped in a warm blanket against the cool ground below him. His eyes drifted up to the night sky, so clear and far, so dark and mysterious.

Owen couldn't remember the last time he looked at the stars. They were strangers to him, foreign things he didn't recognize. But he let himself scan the points anyway. One. Two. Three. Those three in a line, a small cluster below, a bright star far above. That one he recognized.

Orion the Hunter. His mother had told him and Alanitora the story of such a constellation. The same constellation that dawned on the cards Gwendolyn read for him. Orion was a great hunter. One unlike many other mortals. And he fell in love with the virgin goddess Artemis, a deity of both the hunt and the moon.

It was just another story to Alanitora, but to him, it was something more. The story didn't end well for Orion, resulting in his death, but ultimately Artemis helped to put him in the stars as a memory. That ending felt right to him, and Owen couldn't help but smile at the thought of something so bittersweet.

She was strong like Artemis, as he adored her in the way Orion did. With everything that was happening, even if it led to his demise, even if he had a bad ending, Owen would protect her with his life. Because Alanitora was the strongest person he knew.

"I promise you," he whispered into the night sky, " I will fight for you. I will always be your Orion."

Lorenalia approached Alanitora, curious about the delay. "Is there an issue?"

The chamberlain looked between them. "I-I announced Her Highness but—"

"What do you mean, *Queen*?" She repeated. Surely this was a mistake, for the only way that title could possibly apply to her was if...

"Oh. I didn't realize, I thought you knew." Lorenalia's sweet composure broke into worry.

"Know what?"

"Well..." The Kreahan princess paused, wary of her words. "A few days before your arrival there was a letter—different from the one we received just yesterday—saying that the capital of Trenvern had been subjected to an attack..." Yes. She knew this already. Alanitora leaned forward, eager for the fellow princess to continue. "And that the king, your father, perished with it," Lorenalia spoke her words delicately, aware of the gravity.

Despite how softly the words were delivered, she could feel her stomach drop, her hands begin to shake. A million thoughts raced through her mind, and all that rose was anger. "Did either of you know about this?" Alanitora spat, looking between Korena and Gwendolyn.

They looked at one another, and she could see they held an equal amount of confusion as she did.

Gwendolyn shook her head.

"No," Korena whispered softly.

She searched around the room for answers where there weren't any before her eyes settled on Diane, whose head was hung to the ground. Her posture lacked the pride it so often held.

"Diane?"

The redhead looked up at her, somber guilt in her eyes. She opened her mouth to speak, before shutting it again.

"What aren't you telling me?" Alanitora pressed.

"That night I—" Diane swallowed, her voice rasped and broken. "I knew."

"Knew what?" She wanted to hear her say it.

"I knew that your father was dead. I suspected it at least. The night of the fire, he—" She took a deep breath. Alanitora could see tears forming at

182

the sides of Diane's eyes. "I saw him up in the tower, looking down upon us. The room was completely engulfed in flames and— and then there was someone behind him. I tried to call out but I was too late."

So that was who Diane had yelled out to. It wasn't her; it was her father. All this time, from that moment to this one, she had known. She had suspected the fall of Alanitora's bloodline and had kept it from her. There had always been a possibility that he didn't make it out, but this confirmed it.

Alanitora sighed, pressing down the rising magma in her chest. Now was not the time. She looked around the ball. Their hesitancy to descend the stairs was drawing the attention of more than just a few onlookers. "We will talk about this later," the princess said firmly, nodding at the chamberlain with as much of a smile as she could give before leading herself down to the Ballroom floor.

"Tora, maybe we should—" Gwendolyn began, quickening her step to keep up with her.

"Not now," was her only reply. Firm and unyielding. She didn't want to go back to her room. She didn't want to yield to a night that had collected so much promise. She didn't want to be alone with the thoughts banging at her barriers.

Yet inside, she could feel herself crumble. This wasn't good. And it certainly wasn't supposed to happen. Not today. Not when everything was fine for once. She took a deep breath. Everything could be dealt with later.

But no, it couldn't. Her father was dead. Her mother was banished. She was the only royal left of Trenvern. And yet, she was getting married within a week. How did this work? How was it supposed to work? Was she supposed to go back and rule Trenvern, or go forward and marry into the line of Donasela? These weren't things she knew, they weren't things she learned. No one told her what to do if this happened. No one—

"Are you alright?"

Alanitora looked up to see deep green eyes staring into hers. Prince Regenfrithu was standing in front of her at the end of the staircase, concern clear on his face. His voice was low—a whisper almost—meant for just her to hear.

And it felt as though she was the only one to hear it, as his eyes seemed to entrap her within their own small bubble, blocking the rest of the world, the rest of her thoughts, away.

She swallowed the lump in her throat. "No, not necessarily." Honesty was important to her, but it wasn't often she shared her feelings so openly. It took her by surprise. "But I will be."

That was something she was sure of now.

A warm smile covered his face. "Excellent, I'd like you to be in a good mood for our dance later." Raven gave her a small bow and turned, walking through a separated crowd of people back to the dance floor.

If people weren't staring at her earlier, they were now. Alanitora couldn't look anywhere without meeting someone's eyes. It certainly made things uncomfortable.

"You didn't tell us the prince had a thing for you," Korena grumbled as they walked to the side, hoping to evade the current attention.

"Hmm? What do you mean?"

Gwendolyn laughed, sensing the shift in the atmosphere. "Are you serious? You're good at reading people, are you telling me you don't see the desire for you in his eyes?"

Alanitora shook her head. She knew her ladies were those for the romantics, but this was a stretch. It had been established that Prince Regenfrithu was a charming lad.

"You certainly don't stop dancing with a possible suitor and make a path to ask a near stranger if they are okay if you aren't interested in them," Diane noted.

Alanitora gave a small grumble of agreement. She may not have been very happy with Diane for hiding things from her, but she would at least acknowledge her point. "Okay, okay, perhaps that is the case, but must I remind you all that I am to be wed soon?"

Gwendolyn smirked. "Ah, but you aren't yet. Surely you are welcome to have a little fun before you swear yourself to one man for eternity?"

She gave her companions an amused huff. "Alright you all, go have fun. Enjoy the festivities while you can." Alanitora was sure they knew this was her attempt to change the subject, and luckily, they dispersed, letting her be.

Now that there was a minimal amount of attention on her, Alanitora slipped through the crowd of people, glad to be somewhat invisible for once.

That is, if wearing a glorious dress and having been visited by the focus of the party was invisible. A few still stared at her, perhaps pointed, but it was much better than being stopped every few seconds.

The Ballroom was wonderful. Sleek, shiny, cream floors made her feel like she was floating across ice. The hundreds of candles upon both the chandelier and the walls illuminated the room like a golden sun. Windows peering into both the front and back side of the grand room allowed for a beautiful vision of the tree canopy and the sunset behind, which was slowly turning the sky to a glittering dark.

The area was spacious enough for a few thousand people to stand comfortably. Luckily, there was less than that, so traversing through groups of people was easy. Across the room on the left was a long table of small delicacies for those in need of nourishment, and the sides of it held a plethora of comfortable seats and tables. At the very end of the Ballroom, thrones for the king and queen were in place, where they sat over everyone, including the orchestra and a collection of musicians just below.

A lively tune—though more formal than that from Hearthshire—played across the area, the sound bouncing off the walls in a way that made Alanitora feel as though she might be in a giant instrument herself.

A large middle section held a group of dancers, gracefully gliding around the floor in a postured waltz. Most eyes, including her own, followed that of Prince Regenfrithu and whatever partner he held at that moment as they shifted around the other dancers. Their faces moved in casual conversation for a minute or so before he switched out partners and continued the cycle.

Even from where Alanitora was standing, Raven's smile was overwhelmingly beautiful. It made sense why people were so enthralled by him. She

185

was hesitant to admit it affected her too.

Alanitora forced her eyes from following him, choosing instead to examine others around her. It seemed everyone had their place, as those who weren't watching the dancers or dancing themselves were speaking with others to the side, a distinct sound of chatter surrounding the edges.

Her eyes caught on a sway of red. It was small, and something about it was unusual.

Alanitora retraced her scan of the room, focusing on what caught her attention.

It was a young woman, her hair the subject of matter. It stretched down to her low back and while the roots were a beautiful medium brown, the tips were a bright red. Like a fresh raspberry. It was especially odd, as her hair was so informal for such a party. Not only was it down in a natural state but was also incredibly tangled and in disarray.

That wasn't the only odd thing about her though, as unlike all other party attendants, this particular woman wore a masquerade mask over her eyes. Her dress seemed nice at first, but upon another look, it appeared that the edges were fraying and laden with dirt.

Before she could make any more observations, the woman turned, moving further away from Alanitora's sight. She was just about to weave through a group of bystanders when Alanitora noticed the odd shape of her skirt. It was lumpy in a way, as though there was something underneath it, poking out on either side. The outline almost looked like a—

"Sorry to interrupt." Alanitora turned to her left, where a girl stood, her coiled hair short upon her head in a way that almost looked boyish. "I just wanted to let you know that you look incredibly beautiful tonight," she said, gesturing towards Alanitora's general figure.

"Oh." Alanitora paused to look for the strange woman before turning back when her eyes didn't catch her colored hair. "Thank you."

"I'm Princess Tathra, by the way. I'm from Redanor."

Alanitora hummed a polite acknowledgment, examining the girl. They were about the same height, though Tathra's slumped figure made her appear shorter. Her dress had a simple design. The color was a dull yellowish cream luminescent in contrast to her ebony skin. It was a little strange of a dress, knowing that she was from Redanor. From what Alanitora knew, Redanor wasn't necessarily a poor kingdom. In fact, their fur exports should have made them considerably wealthy.

Realizing she hadn't said anything, Alanitora cleared her throat. "I'm Pr—" Right, she was supposedly *Queen* now. "I'm... Alanitora of Trenvern."

"I know. I watched your introduction."

She nodded. The air held an awkward tension. It wasn't anyone's fault, but the volume of the music and Tathra's voice made it hard to hear her. "Are you here to offer your hand to the prince?" Alanitora queried.

Tathra stepped back, her mouth agape. "Oh goodness no! That's not my thing..." The song ended, leading the music to fade out for the musicians to have a small break. Tathra adjusted her voice accordingly. "I'm here to support my cousin, she's trying for his hand."

"That's nice."

"What about you? Are you here to win his heart?"

Alanitora chuckled. "No, I have no intention of doing so. My entourage and I were just stopping by on our way to... And I, well, *we* thought it would be nice to join the festivities for a little." Was she rambling? Why was her composure faltering? She scolded herself for tripping over her words. Perhaps her ballroom decorum was out of practice, but it shouldn't be this bad. Something was nipping at her skin.

"Are you sure about that?" Tathra met her eyes with a satisfied smirk.

Alanitora cocked her head to the side, but Tathra simply nodded her head in the other direction, and she followed her gaze to see Prince Regenfrithu approaching. His eyes were set straight on Alanitora. She felt her heart leap at the sight of him, and she convinced herself that she was startled rather than anything else.

His hands were grasped behind his back when he reached the two. "Ladies..." Raven gave a small nod, then turned to Alanitora, extending his hand to her. "Your Highness."

His smile was infectious. It was one of those smiles that forced Alanitora to smile herself, as she felt such an instant response to it. It lit his entire face, each and every feature highlighted by his delight.

"Good evening," she responded cordially, keeping her tone balanced.

He released a small huff of amusement. "If I may be so bold, will you be the next to dance with me?"

She hadn't noticed until that moment the number of eyes that gazed upon their bubble. Conversations nearby hushed, laughs turned to speculative whispers.

Regenfrithu had approached her. One of the only maidens in the room that wasn't there to try for his hand. He had approached her when every other girl was lined up to dance with him. But he had asked her.

After taking a moment to consider and calculate the possibilities that her heart was pushing aside, Alanitora raised her hand to his, pressing against his warm fingers as he enclosed his thumb atop hers.

She could hear her heart, and wouldn't be surprised if others did too as they made their way toward the center of the Ballroom. Her hands were sweating, her skin prickled. She was nervous. Alanitora didn't get nervous. But here she was, joining hands with a beautiful man while her stomach twisted like vines within her. Part of her wanted to believe this was some sort of elaborate trick. It would certainly explain the attention of the most handsome man in the room.

They made their way past the active dancers, who slowed their rhythm to watch. Most of the couples were older, with no need for conquest if their suitor stood before them. They took their place in the center. Regenfrithu rested a hand on her waist.

"Are you sure this is a good idea?" Alanitora asked.

Regenfrithu smiled. "I know it is." But his words didn't help as she peered around them. "Look at me."

Her eyes flicked up to his, that sparkling emerald green, and once again, there was a bubble around them. Everyone else blurred into the background, and her stomach slowly relaxed, like a feather swiftly settling on the floor. Alanitora took a deep breath.

"You look absolutely wonderful." His words sealed it, and instead of pattering like rain, her heart was light and full.

"I could say the same for you." She raised an eyebrow, glad her anxieties were passing as fast as they had come.

He gave a small laugh. "No, not like that, I mean— You look... beautiful."

Her lips curved into what felt like the brightest smile.

The music began. It was bright, cheerful. The plucking of strings, the melody of the piano, the soaring cello, the serene flute...

And then they began to dance. Three beats, light feet. It's what her mother had taught her, and yet following Raven was smooth, as though each spin was a vast hill, descending into a beautiful meadow.

He held her so lightly, and his emotions were strong. He led her, yet she was free at the same time. And as he looked into her eyes with such deep emotions, she felt they were delicate.

"You're good," he mused.

"I have a good partner."

This brought another light laugh. "If that were the case, my feet wouldn't have been stepped on by the other maidens of tonight."

"Do any of them make a positive impression?" she asked as their steps speed up with the music, then settled with it like an ebbing tide.

"A few, maybe one in particular."

"Ah, lucky girl." Alanitora moved her eyes from his, looking around the room, her gaze settling on a certain maid from the night before. Mira, was it? Regardless, it wasn't her name that made an impact. It was the scowl on her face, directed straight at her. She seemed slightly scary, but the jealousy of another woman was not something that bothered Alanitora. "Do you think it's time we part ways? Let the others have a chance at you?"

He gave a small laugh, and her heartfelt jovial in response, but there was a foreboding feeling underneath, something telling her to be alert.

Alanitora scanned the crowd again. Her eyes swept across dozens of people, looking for the needle of the haystack.

And there it was. Above, upon the bare balcony, looking down upon the dancers, the tip of an arrow was pointing at her.

No, not her. Her partner.

And as though on cue with a crescendo of the music, the arrow was released.

15

The Archer

Her actions moved faster than her thoughts as Alanitora lunged forward, pushing Prince Regenfrithu out of the way as the arrow grazed past, right to the floor before clattering off of the marble and sliding a meter away.

Alanitora followed the arrow's path back to its origin, a snarl forming when she saw the adversary behind the bow. It was the masked girl with the red hair, a smile across her half-covered face. A clump of fabric—presumably her skirt—lay on the ground, her legs fitted with a pair of tight pants beneath a complimentary bodice.

"Now that I have your attention," the girl announced, lowering her bow.

"It's Sagittarius!" Alanitora traced the voice to Princess Lorenalia, who was on a staggered level of the staircase.

The masked girl, supposedly Sagittarius, rolled her eyes. "Don't interrupt. It's rude."

Alanitora took the moment of banter to turn to Regenfrithu, stabilizing herself by holding the ends of his elbows. "Are you okay?" she asked, looking over his face.

He nodded. "Are you?" He was looking down at her arm. She followed his vision.

There was a gash across the front part of her right bicep, blood seeping into her torn sleeve... Shit, the arrow must have grazed her. She hadn't even noticed. "I'll be fine," she growled in response. "But *she* won't be."

Alanitora moved past Regenfrithu, running through the crowd and to the stairs where Lorenalia stood to get a better vantage of both the archer and the crowd.

"Here's the deal," Sagittarius announced, her arms wide, "tonight you all dine lavishly and discuss your riches. You put such faith in your romantics and your parties, while others suffer in the dark. While citizens across the land perish in squalor."

"Who is she?" Alanitora moved closer to Princess Lorenalia.

Lorenalia looked at her wearily before responding. "Her name is Sagittarius, she's a bandit of the area. Claims her profits from stealing go towards those less fortunate. Meli!" The girl switched her attention to a particular guard beside them. "Notify the royal guards of the situation, we don't want this escalating to anything violent. I'll get the resources."

As the two parted to different paths, Alanitora looked up at the bandit. It didn't look like she was ready to attack at any moment, perhaps lecture instead. This Sagittarius looked invested in such theatrics, what a silly tactic that was.

Alanitora ran up the steps, pushing past those frozen in place. Weaving her way through the crowd cultivated at the landing, she rounded the corner, rushing onto the right balcony. She hid momentarily behind one of the pillars. If she was going to take this thief down, she'd need more stealth than her. Especially with a ranged weapon and an aim like that.

"Now," Alanitora peered from behind the pillar as Sagittarius addressed the crowd. "This," she said, holding up a brown sack, "is what you all are going to put some of your riches in. Pass it around, fill it with your jewels and values, whatever worth you have. I don't care how much each of you put in, as long as it fills up the bag. Hesitate or try anything and I'll shoot someone."

"But—" a lady from the crowd began, but she was cut off by the arrival of the bag next to her feet, an arrow pointing straight through it.

"Taxation is cruel, dear, it's time you understand that."

Good, while the bandit was distracted by monitoring her victims,

Alanitora could lunge. It just took a bit of patience. But why was she the only one who thought to stand against her? Where were the guards? The soldiers?

Lorenalia had said something about minimal violence, but that didn't mean they shouldn't try to at least stop her.

Alanitora scanned the crowd for familiar faces. There were a few people that looked up at her, among them both the worried face of Regenfrithu and that of Gwendolyn. She gave her lady a small nod as if to signal that everything was okay.

"You don't have to hide, you know, you are welcome to face me." Sagittarius' voice was quieter, more intimate.

Alanitora froze. Deep breaths. She slowly stood, stepping away from the pillar.

"There she is." The bandit put her hands on her hips, smiling at the princess. "Your skirt is too big and far too pretty for you to hide anywhere."

Damn.

"Stop this." Alanitora stood her ground, staring straight into Sagittarius' eyes, which proved difficult with a mask on. "You don't have to hurt anyone."

She shrugged, her long hair shifting across her shoulders. "I don't plan to, nor have I."

Alanitora raised her eyebrows. "You tried to kill the prince."

Sagittarius' mouth was mockingly agape as she stepped back. "I certainly did not. If I wanted to kill the prince, he would be dead by now. I don't miss." A smirk spread across her lips as she gazed down at Alanitora's arm. "You're the one that got in the way. That's on you."

Alanitora gathered her skirts in her hand with a small grunt. This girl had too much pride. She was willing to crush it. In a quick motion, she reached under her skirt, pulling a throwing knife from the belt and swiftly sending it Sagittarius' way.

The archer, with visible surprise, jumped aside to evade it. "Knives it is." She dropped her bow to the floor and reached behind her waist to pull a pair of blades out.

Alanitora took this chance to pull out her own dagger, flipping it into an offensive position. Based on the way she carried herself, it was apparent to the princess that Sagittarius was used to being on the offense.

She charged at her, staying as low as her large skirt would allow her, then swung the first blow. It was sloppy, but Sagittarius had to lean back to escape the blade.

"Well, aren't you special? Feminine royalty with a kick. Taking the fighting into your own hands. I respect that." She blocked another of Alanitora's strikes by interjecting her blades in the path of Alanitora's dagger before pushing off and turning to the offense.

"You are skilled yourself," Alanitora commented. "Clever too, so I suggest you respect my wishes of leaving these people alone." Now that they were closer, she was able to meet the bandit's eyes with a piercing glare. Strong and debilitating.

But Sagittarius didn't yield as most would, she just stared back, intrigue glistening in her eyes. "Sharp glare you got there. Possibly more so than the weapons you wield. Almost like you have... Dagger eyes. Your dress brings out the little swirls of green in them."

A guttural noise of frustration escaped Alanitora's throat as she swung her dagger at Sagittarius' head. When her opponent ducked, she shifted her weight and reached over to grasp an arrow within Sagittarius' quiver, sliding it out before the bandit could lift her head. Alanitora then swept forward with the dagger again, distracting Sagittarius long enough for her to thrust the arrow towards the other's torso.

Sagittarius yelped as she staggered back, looking down at the damage. The arrow had sliced through the left side of her abdomen, a clear cut across her bodice.

"Well that's unfortunate, I just got this shirt," she scoffed.

"Sagittarius!" A yell from below interrupted their bout. Alanitora looked down. Lorenalia stood in the center of the Ballroom, waiting for the bandit's attention before dropping a different, finer sack on the floor, the contents clattering as it impacted with the marble.

Inside were jewels, predominantly those of Kreaha's pride, though different colored stones of similar size and brilliance lay among them. The sack was full, some of its riches spilling out onto the floor.

"Excellent." Alanitora's head whipped back to Sagittarius, who in turn gave her a smirk before stepping up to the balcony rail with her bow in her hand. She gave her a mockery of a salute. "Good day to you, Dagger Eyes, you made a worthy opponent."

"Don't call me that," she heard herself growl, watching as Sagittarius jumped from the balcony and to the floor, stabilizing herself with a roll.

She lifted the bag. "Seems one of you understands the injustices outside of the world you hide in." Her attention had turned to Lorenalia before the bandit ran off towards the nearest window, kicking it open and leaping into the dark folds of the night with her riches.

The crowd stayed still. Some craned their necks to look out the window while others examined what remained of the spectacle. The collected jewelry in the sack Sagittarius left, the arrows lying idle and forgotten, the small drops of blood on the floor from the wound Alanitora inflicted. Even a few members looked up to her, where she stuffed her weapons back into their home.

No one moved, save for two delayed soldiers that rushed to the window. Upon their commands to send troops around the area, the silence ceased. Murmurs and hushed tones returned to the crowd, yet no one dared to say anything above a whisper.

That was, until a solid voice echoed through. "Lorenalia Audris Rangsford!" King Barthram had stood from his throne at the end of the room, his fists like stones at his sides.

The princess in question turned to the king, the separation of the crowd allowing for a clear path of sight. Lorenalia raised her head, the same way Alanitora would when she faced her own father. Though this was different. Her composure suggested that, unlike the strong bravado that Alanitora would exhibit in such a situation, Lorenalia was confident. She wasn't scared or torn. She had no doubts or regrets.

"What have you done?" There was more concern in Barthram's voice than anger.

"Isn't it obvious, Father? I gave Sagittarius what she wanted."

Though the entire crowd of people had witnessed the events that took place, a collective gasp filled the room. It marked Lorenalia's actions like those of treason.

Queen Myrlene stood at this moment, stepping in front of her husband. "My child, you have severely betrayed the name of our family. Why would you take from our arduously gained wealth to give to such a manipulative and grotesque person?" The way she spoke was not of a mother scolding her child, but of a queen trying to keep up appearances.

Lorenalia's composure broke, a frown visible on her brow. "Why should we put our own interests above the livelihood of not only our guests but the nation that we represent?"

A collective silence formed. Pensive, it seemed.

Upon Barthram's step towards a rebuttal, Myrlene put a hand on her husband's arm. "Very well, Lorenalia. We will have this discussion later. Now is not the time to concern the people who have traveled so far to celebrate your brother's transition into adulthood." Her voice was tight with discontent, but she forced a smile and nodded to others in the room to continue the festivities. The servants were the first to proceed.

Lorenalia sneered, turning and rushing up the staircase and leaving the Ballroom. The shut of the door caused chatter to resume.

Slowly, a few faces turned back up to Alanitora, as though they looked for some sort of explanation from her about the events that took place. She tried her best to ignore their scrutiny, perhaps join the festivities again.

But her day of serenity had ended the moment Sagittarius' arrow was shot. No longer did Alanitora feel the motivation to dance or converse. Perhaps it was the attention, the end of her invisibility that ruined such a moment. Or maybe it was the snap of a battle.

Regardless, Alanitora brushed down her skirts, moving across the balcony back toward the entrance as the music began to play again. Just before she slipped into the blanket of the outdoors, Alanitora looked over her shoulder at Prince Regenfrithu. It appeared Mira had gotten her dance after all.

She made brief eye contact with Raven, before turning her attention and heading back to her rooms.

Silver Moon greeted her with such excitement when the princess entered the beautifully adorned room. She felt tired once again, but it was hard not to smile at the wolf's nudges for her attention.

Alanitora didn't bother to change her clothes, instead only wrapping her wound before collapsing onto the bed. Silver Moon took this chance to jump up with her, curling himself at the end and putting his weight against her legs.

Her mind was blank, and yet she didn't fall fast asleep. It frustrated her more than she liked to admit as she stared at the ceiling above. Her legs began to twitch. How could she be so tired but so restless at the same time?

She sat up, resting one hand behind her and the other to pet Silver Moon. The wolf was a good companion, as he laid without drifting off as well.

Giving him the last few pats, Alanitora raised herself from the bed, plopping her feet to the ground below and stretching her legs out. She hitched up her skirts and took off the girdle, laying it on the table in the center of the room.

She took out each blade carefully, collecting them in her arms before walking toward the vanity and laying them across the table. The princess had just used a dagger, and barely, so there was no need for a thorough cleaning. Regardless, she brought out her polishing and sharpening materials. It helped pass the time and was a relaxing release for any compacted emotions she might be feeling.

After a long while, Alanitora set down her materials and looked up at the mirror. Olive skin, bronze-colored hair with golden tones, brown eyes with a few slices of green… She didn't make a habit of staring into her own eyes. She could read into them as she did with other people, but it was different. Whether it was because they were hers, or because she only saw them through a mirror she didn't know, but they were always so bare. Sure, they were sharp, a beautiful color too, but they weren't deep. Sort of like a ghost.

There was a knock at the door. The ball was over by now. Her ladies must be returning.

"Come in," she rang, beginning to wrap the weapons.

"Hey." At the sound of a deep voice, Alanitora sprang her eyes up to the mirror, her viewpoint only showing the bottom part of the figure's torso in the reflection. She recognized the embroidered waistcoat, even if she'd been more focused on his smile that night.

She turned her shoulder to see Prince Regenfrithu. "Ah, hello!" Alanitora stood from her chair, patting down her skirts.

"How is it?" Regenfrithu raised his eyebrows, signaling towards her arm.

Alanitora looked down at the wound. She had forgotten about it completely. The sleeve of her dress was torn with it, blood-seeped edges. Poor Korena would no doubt be upset about the destruction of something she worked so hard on. Then again, she always protested to Alanitora that the princess could only wear dresses once when it came to the fancier ones. Regardless, it didn't sit right to have such a gorgeous garment destroyed. "It's alright."

He stepped closer, extending his hand tentatively. "May I?"

She nodded.

Raven carefully unwrapped her bandage. His fingers were cold as he felt around the edges of the wound. "Let me know if I hurt you," he whispered, peering closer.

He separated the ends slowly, examining how deep the cut was before pulling his hand away and reaching into his inner breast pocket, bringing out a white handkerchief. Regenfrithu then dampened the edge with his tongue and pressed at the bottom part of the wound, wiping away the dried blood.

"Will you need to sew it together?" Regenfrithu asked after a moment.

She shook her head, a small chuckle escaping her mouth. "It isn't too deep, I'll just wrap it to keep from infection while it heals."

"You fought her." His green eyes met hers for a moment. "You fought Sagittarius."

Alanitora gave him a small smile. "I did."

"That was incredibly brave of you, you know. I had no idea you were skilled at fighting."

"As you might be able to understand, it isn't necessarily something I mention upon meeting someone." Well, and the fact that her infamous abilities were common knowledge within her own kingdom.

As silence fell around them, Alanitora looked down. Raven too stood quietly. After a moment, he extended his hand out to her. "Come with me, I have something to give you."

Her heart jumped as she put her palm in his, his fingers enclosing around her knuckles. Raven pulled her lightly through the door to the hallway, leading her into his chambers, before releasing her hand in the center of his room.

She had been so focused on him and Mira the night before that Alanitora hadn't had the time to examine his room in detail. The area was twice as big as her own down the hall. The walls were adorned with decor, along with a lavishly furnished layout. It was neat if not slightly cluttered, but comforting in a way. It held the characteristics of both Regenfrithu and Kreaha.

She looked up to see the prince beckoning her toward the balcony door. He held it open as she walked through onto a white limestone balcony. An ornate railing lined its sides, and the height held a wonderful view of the night sky.

Alanitora leaned her elbows against the railing as Regenfrithu followed her.

"You left the party quite early," he remarked.

"I did... Something told me that sticking around was going to be less interesting than the previous events." And the fact that people would probably stare at her for the rest of the night if she stayed.

"You were certainly right about that."

Regenfrithu excused himself for a moment, leaving Alanitora to take in the view. Below was a hedged garden. There was a patio with benches alone in the middle, the rest of it green with groomed grass and patches of bright flowers. A tall hedge grass lined the edges, only allowing entry from the castle itself. A few peacocks roamed the sides, but the movement of bushes suggested they weren't the only ones living in the garden.

"It's the private royal garden. Special in that it holds rare flora and fauna across the land," Regenfrithu said as he reappeared beside her.

"Like the peacocks?" Alanitora asked.

"Yes, like the peacocks."

"One must have found its way out, then." She lightly brushed the feather that lay in her hair.

He snarled jokingly. "Damn birds. I suppose I could understand though, beauty can't just be contained." With that, the prince turned to Alanitora, pulling something from behind his back, presenting it to her.

It was a lone crimson rose, the perimeter of its petals curling in a swirling color of deeper red. The edges were black, almost like they had been burnt off or touched lightly with black ink.

"This," Regenfrithu began, "is a rare rose from the gardens. One of the most beautiful far and wide. It took generations of work to perfect its naturally dark color."

"It's gorgeous."

"It's yours."

She smiled as a thank you. Alanitora twirled the stem between her fingers, careful not to have the thorns snag her dress. She examined the beautiful sight as the rose's aroma found its way to her senses.

The princess looked past the palace walls to the forest. Far beyond the conifers, she could see fields, landscapes, and hills. That was where she was going. She would pass those very hills to save her kingdom. Her eyes flicked left towards the mountains in the near distance of her new home. Rocky. Cold. Those were the words that came to her mind. She could feel it scratching at her insides, trying desperately to get out.

"So," Alanitora cleared her throat. "How *was* the rest of the night?"

"Relatively boring." She looked up at him as he peered across a blank sky.

"Did you get your toes stepped on more?" She teased, nudging him slightly.

He smiled back. "Yes, they did. There was a dancer from Crosa that was really good though."

Yes, that made sense to Alanitora. Crosa was a powerful kingdom on the west coast. They valued sophistication and perfection in their culture, so it would only make sense for one of their delegates to uphold etiquette. She hummed in agreement. "Hopefully the next couple of days will have better dancers."

"About that," he said, turning to face her. "I think I've already found the person I'd like to choose."

"How exciting," Alanitora gasped. "Is she local or far?"

"She's from a nearby kingdom."

"Lucky girl." At her words, Regenfrithu began to laugh. "What?" she pressed, barely suppressing a smile herself.

"It's just—" He paused, continuing his fit of amusement.

"*What?*"

"For someone so incredibly smart, you certainly have an... interesting viewpoint towards life."

She cocked her head to the side. "What exactly does that mean?"

Regenfrithu's laughs died down as he stepped toward her, putting a gentle hand on her arm and turning her to face him. "You are different from everyone I've ever met," he said in a low, intimate voice.

Alanitora looked back and forth between his two eyes, trying to process the impact of his words on her. And before she could stop herself, her arms were wrapped around his neck, as the princess pulled him down to her height. He came willingly, closing his mouth around hers while holding her firmly by the small of her back.

They stayed there in a moment slowed down by time.

She parted from his lips gently, pressing her forehead to his as she took in a breath. Their noses brushed past each other to switch sides and they came close again, both his lips closing around her bottom one. There was a sweet aftertaste to his mouth, like one you'd feel after swallowing a summer blackberry.

As though in perfect communication, Alanitora and Regenfrithu separated from each other, stepping back slightly. Her eyes fluttered open as she looked up at him. It was taking so much not to spurt out an exclamation of awe. He met her with a smile, pressing his hand to her hair and leaning down to kiss her again.

She let him take the lead, just as she had done with their dance earlier that night. She nearly felt surreal as her mind drifted into a different world. Alanitora felt something pulling at her. Something reverberating in her ears.

She opened her eyes, glancing to her right, her eyes drawn to the sky. Three stars. Those three stars.

The constellation of Orion. She could hear it. She could hear him.

Regenfrithu let go of her, seeming to sense her withdrawal. "Are you alright?"

"Owen," Alanitora whispered.

Regenfrithu frowned at her. "Alanitora," he stated, waiting expectantly for her response.

She shook her head, snapping her eyes away from the constellation and turning to the prince, no longer in a trance.

"Who's Owen?"

Alanitora stepped back in consternation, pressing her fingers to her lips. She could remember Owen's kiss. The last time she saw him. "He's... He's my..." she trailed off, looking back at Orion, her eyes softening. Something was pulling her out of the present, beckoning her to lose consciousness in the clouds above.

Regenfrithu scoffed, grabbing her attention once again. His expression changed almost instantaneously. His eyes lined with frustration. The prince stepped back from her, raising his hands. "I should have guessed. It was foolish of me to think that something so perfect was without its flaws."

Realization of his insinuation struck her. What was this trance she was under? What sort of bewitchment had overtaken her? "Raven, that isn't

202

what it is, it's—"

"It's what? Tell me, who is this Owen to you?" he sneered.

"He's just my—" She froze. What was he to her? Owen wasn't a friend, but he certainly wasn't less than that. Perhaps he was something else.

But before she could attempt an answer, Regenfrithu spoke. "Forget it."

"Regenfrithu—"

He raised a hand to stop her from finishing, turning his head away. "Please leave." His voice was cold, his eyes unreadable.

After a moment, Alanitora cast a small sigh, moving her lead-like feet cautiously through the balcony entrance and toward the door out of his chambers. She looked back at him before opening it. When he gave no response, she stepped through, closing the door softly behind her and releasing a small, shaking breath.

Her mind was reeling, buzzing, and dazed in a contorted mess. She felt her consciousness float away from her body. Time had fluctuated. One moment she had been on that balcony, where the passage of time didn't exist, and the next moment she was in the hallway, with little recollection of even walking there.

There was a growl from inside the room, followed by a crash, causing the princess to jump out of her stupor. She pressed her eyes closed until there was silence, gripping the rose in her hand as she descended the hall to her room. Shaking away the possession that followed her like a shadow.

Alanitora wasn't sure of much in those minutes. All she could say for certain was that she had messed up. Badly. She wanted to believe her mistake was in getting distracted, but deep down, she knew her guilt was sourced from something else entirely.

Something that went against everything she had been telling herself in these past few days.

16

Priorities

lanitora didn't like the way dawn greeted her the next morning. Her neck ached and the sun was far too bright for comfort. The smell of smoke wafted over from the dying embers of her fire, and it only reminded her of the fire just a couple days before.

There was a light knock on the door before she was even able to raise her head. Right as the door was opened, Silver Moon jumped from the bed and rushed out, a squeal of panic escaping what the princess knew to be her ladies.

"Morning." Korena gave a small bow, setting a folded dress on the vanity. "Bath first, then a light breakfast."

Alanitora nodded, pulling her covers off of her and folding them back over. After the outburst with Regenfrithu, she had taken off her dress and crawled straight into bed. She now stood still, only her undergarments upon her.

As instructed, she began to get ready for her bath. Gwendolyn placed down a bowl of porridge before looking around the room. She stopped at the center vase on the table.

"This is beautiful," she said in awe. Alanitora turned her attention to the curly-haired brunette. She was touching the petals of her black and red rose delicately. "So perfectly crafted too."

"Yes, it was a gift from Regenfrithu last night," Alanitora replied, brushing out her hair.

"Oh?" Gwendolyn mused. "And *how* did that go?"

"It was nice, at first. However, things did not end as I might have hoped they would." She could still hear his cutting tone echoing in her mind.

"Perhaps it's for the best." Korena approached from the bathroom.

Both Alanitora and Gwendolyn turned their attention to the girl, looking for an elaboration.

"I just mean—" Korena said, looking between the two. "Despite the obvious attraction between the two of you, your interests and ambitions seem distant."

Deciding this wasn't quite the conversation she wanted to go deeper into, Alanitora made her way to the bath, removing her undergarments to step in.

The conversation, however, followed the ladies right in.

"Well, that's hardly important, especially in the early stages. It's more about the bond," Gwendolyn argued.

Alanitora stepped into the water, which was much warmer than she had anticipated. Slowly, she submerged herself.

"Well," Korena said, placing Alanitora's fresh clothes on the side. "A stronger, longer bond is arguably more valuable."

The princess really didn't want to hear this. She sank into the seeping warmth of lapping water, letting her chin under the water, then the rest of her head. Her ladies' voices clarity were slowly blocked by the fold of water as she sank. She could feel her long hair flowing ever so delicately around her shoulders.

Yes, this felt nice. She let her arms drop to her sides. A sudden, sharp pain twinged in her right arm. Alanitora gasped at the sudden feeling, nearly choking as she emerged her head above the water. She coughed out the liquid that found its way to her lungs.

The splashing soon settled as she brought her hands to her face, wiping away the water from her eyes and looking over at her startled ladies apologetically.

Korena rushed out to grab something to collect the water upon the floor as Gwendolyn kneeled in front of the tub. "Are you alright?" she asked, pushing back the wet locks of hair from Alanitora's vision.

"Yeah." She gave a reassuring smile. "I just forgot about this little pain." Nodding towards the arrow wound, Alanitora slowly removed the soaked wrap. The edges around it were puffy and pink, the wound itself looking quite gruesome now that it was moist.

"Let me see it," Gwendolyn said. The lady's fingers brushed delicately over the sides of the wound. She turned her arm either way, then took a small cloth and dabbed the opening lightly. "You didn't clean it last night, did you?" Alanitora didn't have to answer that. "Well, she got you pretty good."

"Yes. It appears so." For the first time, thoughts of the previous night that didn't pertain to Regenfrithu entered Alanitora's mind.

Sagittarius had indeed been a strange character, and the princess couldn't help but feel a sense of envy toward her for a reason she couldn't decipher. But also… respect, perhaps. It was hard to explain. The archer didn't try to triumph over her: instead, her fighting skills reflected some semblance of honor. This of course contradicted her appearance and language when facing the rest of the attendees. Was it wrong for her to say she enjoyed the fight?

"She was good," Alanitora said after a long moment. "At fighting, that is."

Gwendolyn paused the scrubbing of her arms. "You, praising an opponent's skills?"

Alanitora shrugged, "It's true. I may not necessarily condone her actions, but she fought well. Reputably."

"My, but did you see what the princess did in response?"

Yes, Lorenalia had given the bandit an entire sack of the kingdom's riches in order to prevent carnage. Alanitora saw how it angered her parents, though they didn't seem to have as much rage in them as Ronoleaus would have if she had done the same.

Then again, would Alanitora have even done the same?

She would never be in such a circumstance in the first place. Trenvern didn't have the same riches that Kreaha did. Their main export was not precious metals or glittering gems, it was lumber. Surely no bandit would prey upon their fortune, for what fortune did they have?

In addition, Trenvern was not the type to negotiate or tolerate anyone who threatened the lives of those in power, though that was not the point.

But whatever her kingdom's policies were, the point she was pondering was whether or not she would have given the bandit what they wanted. In the interest of protecting innocent lives and de-escalating the threat, her answer would be yes. But another part of her, one that she felt she listened to more often, said no, that there were other ways to keep everyone safe without giving the enemy what they wanted. Perhaps trying to fight or trick the opponent had a risk, but it was the option that kept her kingdom in balance and her pride intact.

And yet, something else inside Alanitora told her that at the moment, she wouldn't pursue either of these options. That she wouldn't have such a moment of strength projected in both pre-meditated scenarios. She frowned at this notion.

"So what do you say?" Korena's voice pierced through her thoughts

"About what?" Alanitora asked, turning her head and attention back to her ladies.

"Attending the lunch requested by the royal family!"

"I apologize, I wasn't listening."

Gwendolyn raised her eyebrows.

"What?" Alanitora queried.

"Nothing, it's just, even when you drift into your thoughts, you're usually still listening..." She shook her head. "Never mind it. In short, Korena and I were speaking about going to the Great Hall soon. Last night, everyone was invited to attend a meal on the subject of Prince Regenfrithu's decisions."

"Hmm..." Alanitora raised herself from the tub, letting the girls wrap her in a warm towel. "I'm not so sure..." She didn't really want to see Regenfrithu again, but being as they were scheduled to be here for the next few days, it would be hard to avoid someone whose room was just a few doors away from her.

"Oh, pleeease!" Korena whined. "There will be so many people there, many of which we talked to last night. I'm sure it will be fun!" *We*, of course, meant folks her ladies came across after Alanitora left. She recalled only speaking with one attendant.

That girl was incredibly good at making Alanitora feel guilty. "How soon is it?"

"About an hour or two from now?" Gwendolyn said, wrapping the princess' soaked hair.

She sighed. It would give her enough time to prepare, and if there were a lot of people there as her ladies had suggested, she shouldn't have to worry about making direct contact with Prince Regenfrithu anyway. "Alright."

A shrill squeal burst from Korena's mouth as expected, and Gwendolyn smiled brightly.

A while after her ladies left to get ready themselves, Alanitora decided to go to the Great Hall early. She didn't have much else to do cooped up in her room, and going there might give her a chance to talk to the few nice people she didn't get to meet the night before.

She was following the emeralds through the hallways, her mind adrift as she scanned each one when something bumped into her. Alanitora flicked her eyes over to see a girl a little taller than her glaring sternly. Her eyes were an intense black, complimented further by dark curls that framed her face

"Try looking where you are going, *princess*," the girl addressed her with a sharp tongue, one that Alanitora rarely heard directed toward herself.

"Pardon?" Had she heard that right? Alanitora looked past the girl down the hallway. The princess herself was on the far right, and there was plenty of room for the other girl to move aside to the left. If anything, it was her that should be looking where she was going.

The girl's lips were pressed tightly together. Why was there such spite on her face? "Or perhaps you make a habit of thinking the world revolves around you."

Her words, quite frankly, startled Alanitora so much that she couldn't find a response within her before the girl turned and began walking away.

She watched her go in both confusion and silence, and when she finally rounded the corner, Alanitora released her gaze and shook her head. With a sigh, she continued to the gardens.

The princess couldn't help but wonder what such an attitude was for. She couldn't comprehend any reason for such brash behavior, especially in a place so grand with hospitality.

It then crossed her mind how there were girls from various backgrounds trying for Prince Regenfrithu's hand. Just because they were in a place of warmth, it didn't mean everyone here had come from a similar place. His approach to her last night and the fact that their dance lasted much longer than the other suitors didn't help.

Were people really that obsessive about marriage that they would be so rude to someone they had never met? Alanitora suddenly didn't feel as comfortable going to this lunch, where she could encounter a number of such characters.

Nevertheless, her mindless wandering had already led her past the fountain and to the entrance of the courtyard, where people were filtering into the Great Hall. It was much easier to see the mix of nobles and common folk with their daily wear, rather than extravagant suits and dresses.

With a heavy breath, she followed the crowd in. It took some energy to fully grasp the area around her. Rows and rows of tables lined the room, a clear path in the center to the head table, which was empty as of yet. Most attendants were engaged in conversations on the side, some choosing where to sit, while others drifted from table to table.

The hall was much grander than Trenvern's, which was no surprise given the rest of what Alanitora had seen of the Kreahan kingdom. It could hold just as many as the Ballroom and seemed it would have similar attendance as the previous night.

"Alanitora!" Her eyes flicked over when her name was sounded to find the amiable princess from the previous night waving her over.

"Good afternoon, Tathra."

Tathra's face lit up. "You remembered!"

"Why of course, you were one of the only people to talk to me last night."

Tathra's excitement was amusing. The Redanorian princess was wearing a simple white blouse. Furthermore, unlike the usual skirt that would be paired with such, she wore workman's pants. The ensemble was hardly something a royal would wear, regardless of gender. And unless Alanitora's information about Redanor was wrong, she was quite certain it wasn't the standard there either.

She chose to ignore such informality as Tathra gestured to the table. "Why don't you join me? I had saved a seat for my cousin, but it seems she has decided not to come after all."

"If that's alright with you." Alanitora smiled, settling down next to her.

The two conversed for a while, primarily about the confrontation with Sagittarius from the previous night, in which Tathra revealed that she had a large spot in her heart for swordsmanship. They had just begun discussing their opinions of the longsword when Korena and Gwendolyn found their way to the other side of the table, not hesitating to sit down.

"Korena, Gwendolyn, this is Princess Tathra of Redanor." Alanitora gestured between them. "Tathra, these are my ladies-in-waiting."

"Lovely to meet you, Your Highness," Korena chirped, bowing her head.

Tathra gave a small, nervous laugh, "No need for formalities. It is wonderful to meet you."

Gwendolyn smiled as a greeting, and when Tathra's eyes lingered on her, she stuttered to speak up. "I like your hair."

Poor Gwendolyn wasn't always one for a sturdy introduction, especially in a crowded place such as this. Regardless, the princess gave her a small thank you, running her hand across the top of her dark coils.

The doors soon closed and everyone took their seats as servants came around with platters of food. All sorts of dishes flooded the tables, barely giving enough room for the dining plates themselves as people collected a day's worth of food for their servings.

It was at this moment that the royal family strolled through the doors at the front of the room, taking their respective seats at the head table. The two men sat in the center, Regenfrithu on the left.

The prince's eyes did not wander, which was something Alanitora was grateful for, as it prevented a situation that might cause her to freeze in her tracks. He instead seemed reclusive, closed off in a way that restricted her from reading whatever he was feeling.

King Barthram stood, raising his glass, and waited for the room to become silent. It wasn't long until his wishes were fulfilled, a few from the crowd raising their glasses in response.

"Good afternoon, ladies and lords, nobles and common folk alike. Kreaha welcomes your presence this fine day, as we dine together, collectively, regardless of class or kingdom. Let us start with a free feast for all!"

This prompted a collection of cheers and applause as the king sat down in his chair. The dining commenced, a medium chatter settling across the room in between the clattering of silverware. Neighboring guests would take the time to engage in small conversations with Alanitora and her entourage before returning to their own.

The first course began to wrap up, and the conversations gradually died down. It was at this point that King Barthram stood again, raising his glass for the attention of the hall.

"Now, I'm sure many of you have become quite full." A laugh took over the crowd. "But you are all probably eager to hear what we have summoned you for. My son, Prince Regenfrithu, will now have your attention."

There was collective applause as the young man raised from his seat, looking over to his sister on his right before flashing his ever-so-charming smile over the audience. Alanitora peered around the room. The number of young ladies gazing longingly would have convinced her that witchcraft was real, had she not felt the same pull toward him the previous night.

"Thank you, father. My deepest greetings, all of you," Regenfrithu began, his eyes panning over the crowd. "As you all know, last night I came to a decision regarding the lady of my choosing."

Alanitora put down her fork, her eyes unable to move from him. He had? Her mind raced. Regenfrithu had chosen a wife after she left the Ballroom?

She looked over to her ladies, who returned her gaze with a small nod and a shrug respectively.

So that meant... Last night when he visited her, he had already decided who he was to marry? She remembered asking him such, and he confirmed it just before they...

But that was where the princess was lost. Was she, someone who he was well aware was already betrothed, his choice? Or was it another maiden of the evening? And if the latter was the case, what did that mean about what had happened between them last night? It may have ended badly with the mention of Owen, but what was she to him in the moments leading up to that point? A consolation prize? A runner-up? A last-minute thrill of passion?

She had not blamed him for his outburst before, but now, her mind reeled with both denial and frustration. Perhaps he was not the only one who had a right to be angry.

Alanitora forced her attention back to the present, staring up at the prince in question.

"Which is true, I indeed decided on the winner of my affection last night. A young woman of beauty and elegance that I felt would do the upcoming throne justice. A maiden that, upon meeting, had already convinced my heart to cut this event of ours short. However," Regenfrithu paused, and despite not having acknowledged her presence as of yet, locked his eyes directly on Alanitora, pulling her into his green irises from across the room. She felt like she couldn't move. She felt like she was suffocating. His next words were soft but cold and distinct. "Upon further thought, I have found that it is too soon to proclaim such a love with someone I barely know." He looked away from her finally, ripping a string of her heart in the process. "That being said, despite my original intention of this feast to be the end of our festivities, such will continue."

A collection of both cheers and whispers set a blanket of noise on the crowd before Regenfrithu continued his speech, going on about the details of the upcoming events.

"Excuse me, Your Highness?" At the tap of her shoulder, Alanitora tore her eyes away from the prince to see a young servant boy. He held out a sealed letter to her. "I believe this is for you."

Cautious and still dazed from Regenfrithu's ever-present glare, the princess hesitated before taking the letter from his fingers and looking down to examine it as the boy left. The wax seal was bright red, almost orange, and held an elaborate coat of arms, centered with a fox.

It was the seal of Donasela.

She turned to her ladies with a concerned frown on her face, presenting them the envelope before breaking the seal to reveal the contents. The letter was short, simple. Scrawled upon fancy parchment with well-flowed penmanship.

"Dear Princess Alanitora of Trenvern,

News of the ambush upon your home kingdom and your departure from it nights ago has come to our attention, and as a royal court, the kingdom of Donasela sends deepest regards to you and members of your retinue who have lost something.

The revelation of what this news bears has also become apparent to us, and in the best interest of your kingdom and ours, we find it of the utmost importance that the union between our people in matrimony be brought forth to a sooner time. This conclusion is something we heavily encourage in order to support you and your people.

Following the set schedule for your travels, had the ambush not pressed for your leave from your kingdom early, your party would have just reached the kingdom of Kreaha upon receiving this letter. However, it is understood that you may have already been in such a position for a day or so.

We request, with your permission, that you depart from the kingdom of Kreaha as soon as you possibly can and make your way to the capital of Donasela without interruption or hesitation.

We hope that our resources upon arrival will compensate for anything that you or your retinue may have had plans to retrieve from the kingdom of Kreaha.

Nevertheless, you must be swift in your way to Donasela, as we fear that the matrimonial event should not wait in the wake of your kingdom's status. Swift

delivery and safe travels,
    Crown Prince Daruthel of the Donaselan royal family."

She looked up from the letter, a sense of unsettled panic finally finding its way to her core despite her efforts to run from such. A date of doom was catching up to her, weighing her down like a ball and chain secured to the ankle of an ill-fated prisoner.

"What is it?" Korena asked with concern

Alanitora took a deep breath, handing the letter over to her ladies, tapping her fingers as she waited for them to read it. Gwendolyn seemed to skim it quickly, while Korena spent a little longer to process it.

"Well, what are we to do?" Gwendolyn asked.

"I suppose we should get our things in order and leave as instructed." Alanitora saw no other option.

"Awww, but I was going to watch the theater performance this evening!" complained Korena.

Tathra interjected. "If I may ask, what is going on?"

Gwendolyn looked at Alanitora to be sure she could answer, then back at Tathra. "Due to our previous arrangement, it seems our stay in Kreaha is cut short. Alanitora is being requested in Donasela."

"Oh! What a lovely coincidence that Donasela is the destination of your travels. My cousin and I had plans to stop there for a small while before heading back up home." It seemed to Alanitora that the Redanorian princess didn't have a grasp on the gravity of their situation.

It appeared Gwendolyn had put aside her worries as well though, intrigued enough to ask Tathra for details before Alanitora interjected herself. "I'm afraid the main concern at the moment is whether or not the entourage is ready to continue forward, with the incident having destroyed our carriage and all." She looked between her ladies, glad to see Gwendolyn back in focus

Korena raised her hand. "Ah! Why don't you ask the dashing prince for a favor?"

Alanitora looked up at Raven, who was preoccupied answering the questions of the crowd. She was aware that though he might help her out of a gentleman's duty, the prince would not be too eager to, given what happened last night. "No… But you do have a point…"

They would need to ask for assistance, and she knew just the person who had both the ability and inclination to help.

Alanitora set aside the matter for the rest of the feast, letting the predicament untangle in the back of her mind as she and her ladies discussed a matter of triviality with Tathra. She watched keenly as people began to trickle out, keeping her eye on the royal table.

As Lorenalia dismissively separated from the rest of her family and began talking to the same guard who had been at her side last night, Alanitora excused herself, asking that her ladies gather the rest of the entourage to prepare. She made her way over to the princess, weaving through people going the opposite direction and quickening her step when she saw that she was about to go through the side door. She called out to Lorenalia.

It was only a few hours past noon when Alanitora got word that everything was ready to go. This was good. The fact that it was not yet sundown meant they were ahead of schedule.

The princess had yet to run into Silver Moon, but she was not worried. Her intuition told her he would show up soon. Her only grievances were what trouble he might get into without her supervision. Sure, he was gentle with her and surprisingly domestic, but mischievous nonetheless.

As arranged, Alanitora approached the fountain to meet her companions. Korena and Gwendolyn had smiles on their faces as they chatted, and Diane was on the other side focusing on what looked like embroidery.

"Is everything prepared?" Alanitora asked.

Gwendolyn looked up, her grin unwavering. "For the most part, yes. I think we will be able to leave within the hour."

"Then let's go over there!" Korena jumped up, springs in her feet, and began skipping ahead towards the main gates, Gwendolyn following with a mockingly disappointed shake of her head.

With a smile, Alanitora began to follow suit. That was, until Diane's voice rose from behind her.

"Your Highness." She had never heard the girl's voice hold such a formal tone. The redhead was generally cordial, but this time around, her tone was cold and structured.

Alanitora turned, the slight smile on her lips turning neutral as she saw a sliver of rage in Diane's otherwise icy collected eyes.

"Yes, Diane? Is something the matter?" Her thoughts flicked to the attempts on her life, the warnings Diane gave with the same tone that she was holding now. "Is it the Men of the Blood Dragon?" she asked, lowering her voice.

The redhead shook her head. "No, not that. Though... I can understand the confusion, and if you do need to talk about it, I'd give you that much." She shook the subject away with her head, before taking a deep breath. "I think it best I do not continue my travels with you."

Alanitora raised her chin. She did not hide the fact that she was surprised by this. While her eyebrows raised in bewilderment, her voice stayed stable. "...Very well."

The princess would have thought this was the exact response someone might want to such an announcement: acknowledgment and understanding. But Diane's frown only deepened, creasing her freckles together. "That's it?" her tongue was sharp, viper-like.

"I'm sorry?"

She huffed exasperatedly. "Lord, have you no heart?! Have you no consideration for the well-being of others? Do you feign care for them up until they are of no use to you? Actually, never mind feigning. It's likely more malicious and manipulative than that, considering you somehow always end up as the hero!"

"Diane, I—"

"No, Your Highness. I apologize but I ask you to let me speak my mind, for I can no longer keep my resolve in your presence." Alanitora took a moment to look around the fountain. No one had much interest in their conversation. She hoped it stayed that way. Diane continued. "I could understand your hesitance of trust, I could understand your priorities, but I cannot for the life of me understand your disregard for my brother and the ignorance of your allies' feelings."

"So this is about Owen." Alanitora nodded. It made sense that she would be confused about why Alanitora disbanded him. She relaxed her shoulders. Diane simply did not know about her brother's expression of affection, and how much it jeopardized the entire intention of their travels.

"My *entire* life, I have thought of you on the side of good, and while I do not believe that you are in any way evil, your lack of compassion is inhumane. How do you expect people to trust you and put faith in you as a leader if you do not care for them in the least bit? What you seem to consider affection is tolerance at best, and it deteriorates the feelings of anyone around you."

Alanitora swallowed. This was deeper than Owen. These were words she heard whispers of, but never from the mouth of someone she trusted. She could never put a name to the faces of people who said such with their back turned, and now someone she knew was facing her and daring to say so much more than would be appropriate. An unfamiliar heavy feeling clenched her insides, as though the thorns of the lovely roses around her had engulfed her stomach, twisting and turning to scratch and scrape.

"Despite all he had done for you, to keep you safe, to make sure you were okay... You abandoned him. You left him on the side of the road with nothing to fend for himself. I know my brother is strong, but I cannot forgive the mistreatment of him. I apologize, Your Highness. I wish I could help you further, but my family comes before anything else."

"... I understand."

"Do you? I'm not so sure. I wish you could see what your lack of compassion does to others. And if I had the energy to care I would lay it out for you here and now, but my focus can no longer be on you. I have a family to take care of, and you have a wedding to get to."

Somewhere in her tirade, Diane's words struck a chord within the princess. A key had been placed into a part of her that she thought was long ago locked away, and now Alanitora had no say in the turning of its mechanisms. She wanted to feel angry with Diane. She wanted to yell at her, tell her that she was wrong and that she was just a little girl who knew nothing, but Alanitora didn't believe any of that. Never in her life had anyone dared to talk down to her in such a way, and despite her belief that no one ever should, there was something about what Diane said that she knew was true.

Something that she knew she cared about, regardless of her hopes to keep those feelings locked away forever.

Alanitora took a deep breath. Despite what Diane suggested about her heart, she felt pity within her. Her mouth formed the words delicately, not wishing to break her own resolve. "Alright. I wish you the best of luck. I'll have Corwyn provide you with whatever you need for your journey, and pay for any costs." Diane's shoulders seemed to relax—whether out of relief or disappointment, she could not tell. With no intention to agree or disagree with her harsh words, Alanitora stepped away. "And Diane? I'm sorry we had to part like this."

Diane met her eyes one last time, a cool mixture of respect and unearthed resentment aided her glare. "As am I."

17

An Absent Farewell

Alanitora drew a heavy breath, shaking away the lingering guilt that found its way into her chest. She pushed forward, intending to meet with Korena and Gwendolyn up ahead. The ladies were talking to the side of one of two black carriages graciously provided by Kreaha. They, at least, seemed at ease.

Had they known that Diane was making her departure? Likely not, for if they had, they likely would have stayed back to eavesdrop on the conversation.

That meant Alanitora would have to tell them.

It was a shame, really. In their small time together, she could tell her ladies had taken a liking to the girl. They may have been a year older than her, but Diane's maturity kept up with their conversation. It wasn't often that the two got the chance to socialize with others their age, and if they did, it was only in passing. After the bond that brought them together in the past few days, Korena and Gwendolyn would be distraught to know she was leaving.

See, the very thought about that only proved that what Diane was saying wasn't entirely true. She did care about her allies. Just because she didn't actively show it, didn't mean it was non-existent.

Regardless, before she could approach her ladies, a familiar tuft of fur stuck out from the other carriage, grabbing her attention. A grin formed on her features, and Alanitora shifted directions to approach the wolf.

"Now, now, what trouble have you been getting into, mister?" She asked in a light tone. Curious as to Silver Moon's latest hijinks, she stuck her head through the door.

To her surprise, there was not only the body of her beloved companion but another wolf sitting patiently beside him. Slightly smaller in size, its fur held a sandy coloring with a white underbelly and streaks of darker brown along its spine.

"Oh *hell* no." A voice came from within. Alanitora looked past the two wolves to see a girl sitting in the corner of the carriage, her arms crossed and a stern frown on her face. She recognized her features nearly instantly as the same girl who had rudely rammed into her that morning in the hallway.

"Can I ask what you are doing here?"

Instead of replying, the curly-haired brunette let out a short huff before calling out. "Tathra!" Annoyance rang in her voice.

Had she more time to fit two and two together, Alanitora might have gotten an understanding of the situation. However, such a deduction was cut short with the hasty arrival of the Redanorian princess behind her.

"Is everything alright?!" Stopping to take a breath, Tathra looked between the two. "Oh! Introductions—"

"No need," the girl said flatly. "Is *this* really the princess you were gushing about? Her *Royal Highness Alanitora*, entitled princess of the west?'" Her mocking tone brought forth a scowl.

Tathra's mouth dropped open. "Zinaw!"

"There is no way in hell I'm sharing a carriage with her!"

"Fine, you don't have to. We can just go to the carriage up front." Tathra gave Alanitora an apologetic look, to which the princess responded with an understanding smile. So *this* was Tathra's cousin.

She took a longer moment to examine the girl. There was a slight resemblance, but such was held more in the shape of their faces than their coloring. Zinaw's skin was a lighter brown than Tathra's, and the curls of her hair were more defined. She was incredibly beautiful and

220

would be more so if there weren't a permanent scowl on her face.

Zinaw raised her chin. "My wolves and I are quite content where we are now."

Alanitora frowned. "Your wolves?" She reached out to Silver Moon, who had grown quite excited at the commotion, and pressed his head to her hand. "I don't believe you hold ownership of Silver Moon." Normally, the princess might be enraged with a berating from this rash girl, but she instead found it amusing how much she claimed to know. She had to admire the confidence in her eyes, even if she was wrong.

Zinaw's shoulders dropped. "Oh, so he's your wolf? I should have guessed based on his untrained temperament."

"Zinaw. That's enough!" Tathra stepped between the two. "Princess Alanitora has been kind in allowing us to travel alongside her to Donasela, and it is unfit of you to say such vile things. Regardless of how jealous you are."

She scowled. "I am not—"

"It's quite alright," Alanitora intervened. "There is no need for argument. I'm fine to have my companions and I settle in a different carriage." She decided to take the higher ground. Patting her leg to summon Silver Moon, she gave the two one last formal smile before distancing herself from the carriage.

Her wolf came to her side, nudging his wet nose against her hand contentedly. A large rattling sound brought forth the other wolf, who decided to stick itself to the side of Silver Moon.

It seemed that in their time apart, her companion had found quite the friend. She hadn't known Silver Moon was the type to get along with any of his kind, considering the exclusion from his pack. Additionally, Zinaw's wolf carried itself in the manner a domesticated dog would. Despite this, the two seemed to get along quite nicely. She watched the two canines interact before Zinaw's voice rose behind them.

"Bechorath! Come here, girl."

Sensing further conflict was due, Alanitora kneeled to Silver Moon, giving him a good scratch behind his ears to momentarily get his attention away from his new friend. "Go on, my love. I don't intend to separate the two of you." She nudged him slightly, and when Bechorath turned back to her owner, Silver Moon moved towards the carriage as well.

His behavior meant one of two things: either the wolf was surprisingly skilled at understanding the human tongue or his bond with his new lady friend trumped his connection to her. While she would have preferred the former, the latter was amusing enough for her to stand with a smile.

Alanitora approached her ladies, her hands clasped behind her back. They were happily chatting away, and it pained her that she might take away those smiles. Grabbing their attention, she lowered her voice slightly. "I thought I should inform you, Diane has decided not to go any further with us."

Korena's face contorted into a pout. "Wait, why? Did we do something to offend her?" The blonde looked over at Gwendolyn, who shrugged, returning her attention to Alanitora.

The princess was aware that Korena was more worried about if she and Gwendolyn had done something to annoy the girl, and in that context, the answer was no. Regarding the real reason concerning her, however, she had to admit that the answer was closer to yes. Alanitora felt compelled to say no and leave it at that, but with that answer, an indescribable guilt nagged at her stomach. Why, though? Was she afraid of her ladies' judgment, or her own?

"Her heart seemed more set on home. I think her interests wavered with Owen's departure from the entourage." This was not the full truth, but it was not a lie. She could live with the statement.

"Well, I do hope she'll be okay to make whatever journey she needs on her own." Gwendolyn gave her a reassuring smile.

"She's tough, that's for sure. I'm sure she'll be fine, but even so, I've made sure she has access to our resources. Corwyn should provide her with rations and an extra cot." Alanitora relaxed her shoulders. "Either way, it looks like it's going to just be the three of us once again."

"About that…" Gwendolyn tilted her head to the direction of the carriage, an awkward expression not far from a grimace on her face.

222

Alanitora redirected her attention to the carriage behind them, her vision focusing on Regenfrithu's tall figure helping his sister raise a chest onto the back of the vessel. Lorenalia handed him a few bags once he was done and was quick to notice their gaze. She waved them over gleefully.

While her energy was welcoming, a quick shift in glance sent dreadful knots into Alanitora's stomach when her eyes met with Regenfrithu. She hastily pushed down any feelings that were creeping up her spine and moved forward.

"All ready?" Alanitora asked, settling a polite smile on her face. Between everything that was happening, she was beginning to tire of this feigned contentment.

"Yes! We should be good to go very soon." Lorenalia clasped her hands together. Unsure what exactly 'we' meant, Alanitora was about to open her mouth when the Kreahan princess called out instead. "Meli! Do you have the pillows I asked about?"

The same guard from both that morning and the previous night—who Alanitora now assumed to be Lorenalia's personal assistance—emerged from around the corner, a tuft of pillows and blankets in their arms.

It was now, when her attention was not focused on something else, but rather avoiding someone next to her, that Alanitora noticed just how androgynous this Meli was. Though their facial features seemed more feminine, the cut of their hair, clothing, and build of their body were masculine. Their hair was a dark gray, cast over one side of their rounded face and shaved around the other side.

Her observations were cut short as Meli followed Lorenalia into the carriage. Her ladies having disappeared almost magically off somewhere they would later proclaim as preparing for leave, Alanitora was left in solitary with one other being next to her.

Regenfrithu.

She could feel his eyes on her, and she froze, her mind overflowing with words but her throat too dry to say any of them aloud. The bubble that had trapped them away from the rest of the world only the night before was now gone, an aura of uncertainty replaced it.

"This is goodbye, I presume?" he spoke formally, but unlike Diane, there was no anger in his voice.

"It appears so, yes." She gripped her hands firmly in front of her, turning to face him. The last time they had been this close, it had been during an intimate moment and Alanitora, though disappointed in herself for dwelling in such, couldn't help but think back to it.

A few long moments of silence followed, much of which consisted of Alanitora uncharacteristically averting her eyes from his. She did not want to know his thoughts. She did not want to see his truth within them.

"Here." With the movement of his hands, her gaze was brought down to them. To her surprise, within them was the rose he had given her not long before. The ends of the petals were curling without moisture. She dared look up at him as he spoke again "I understand why you had decided to leave it in your room. But if you found any affection towards me in your heart, I'd like you to keep it."

"Thank you," were the only words Alanitora could bring from her throat. She was locked in his gaze, in his brilliant green eyes. Wherever had the anger towards her dissipated to? Alanitora reached for his hands, taking the rose delicately in her own and stepping back slightly.

So many words had been exchanged between the two without either speaking. And though some of her deepest questions were answered, more surfaced, suffocating her with what-ifs and possibilities.

He shifted his attention from her to the carriage in front of them, releasing his debilitating gaze. Regenfrithu called out to his sister, waiting for the princess' head to peek out before he held his hand out to her, helping her down.

As the Kreaha siblings shared a farewell hug, Alanitora turned to greet her ladies instead, who were suspiciously just now reappearing once the exchange between her and the prince came to a close.

Korena peered over her shoulder. "So Princess Lorenalia will be traveling with us after all?"

"Yes, I believe so," Alanitora replied.

"I knew it! We saw her talking to Corwyn earlier, and then there were all

224

these personal effects and the addition of a few extra wagons... I wonder why though. You didn't invite her to the wedding, did you?"

Alanitora smiled. "I did not." It was unexpected that Lorenalia would be traveling with them, but she held no opposition to it. After all, they owed her something for setting the entourage up with the proper resources in the first place. The least they could do was grant her passage with them. Safety in numbers, and that included the small troop she was bringing with her.

It was an added benefit that Alanitora might have the pleasure of learning about her. She was interesting enough of a character to pique her interest, and there hadn't been nearly enough time to get to know her on a personal level in the last few days.

"I believe it may have had something to do with the altercation last night," Gwendolyn noted. When both of the other girls showed intrigue, she continued. "Well, we would have to ask her about it, but I imagine giving away a collection of priceless crown jewels is frowned upon for royalty. Her parents didn't seem too happy with her decision."

"Oh, yes, Gwenie! We should ask her right now!" Korena pulled at her friend's sleeve, directing her towards the carriage. Regenfrithu had since taken his departure from it. Alanitora could see his figure returning through the heavenly rose gardens and towards the palace.

"Actually... about that," Alanitora interjected. "Could I borrow you for a second, Gwendolyn? Korena, you are welcome to go ahead."

Korena's shoulders sank before she continued towards the carriage without them. Gwendolyn looked after her before turning to Alanitora, curiosity and concern in her gaze.

"I need a huge favor from you." The princess paused, weary to continue. She didn't like asking personal requests of her ladies regarding other people, more so now that Diane's comments about her lack of compassion were still spinning around her mind. "Tathra's cousin has a wolf that I believe Silver Moon has come to bond with..."

"Oh?"

She hesitated. "Yes. It seems they have become inseparable."

225

"...And you're worried they'll mate?" Gwendolyn asked. "We nearing winter Your Highness, there is no need to—"

"No, that is not my concern." She chuckled at the implication. "My concern surrounds that of Tathra's cousin herself, Zinaw."

"Ah."

"She seems to have taken a disliking to me. And while it makes me uneasy, to avoid disagreement, I have decided to let Silver Moon travel in their carriage."

"And you would like me to..." Gwendolyn began.

"...Ride with them as well and keep an eye on our wolf friend, yes. I'd do so myself to spare you the trouble, but considering you are good at... defusing conflict, I think it best you be in the presence of Lady Zinaw. It'll only be for the first segment of travel. I'm sure we can switch around at the rest stops."

To her relief, Gwendolyn smiled in response. "I'll gladly do so, Your Highness."

Alanitora smiled in return, resting a comforting hand on Gwendolyn's arm. "Thank you." Her shoulders were finally beginning to relax.

The first few hours of riding went smoothly. Not only were there fewer people per carriage, but Kreahan carriages were much more spacious and luxurious. Feather-stuffed pillows and thick blankets accompanied the seats, there if passengers wished to rest. There was space for storage above their heads and room to stretch their legs beneath. Furthermore, the construction of the carriage's exterior allowed for steady passage over bumps on the road.

As Gwendolyn had predicted, Alanitora found out that Lorenalia was traveling with them due to conflict with her parents. As the princess not only disagreed with their views but also had apparently come to terms with the present possibility that she would never rule over Kreaha, given her brother's unwavering position as Crown Prince.

She confessed how she had an interest in learning the ways of other kingdoms besides her own and was able to convince the king and queen that traveling to Donasela with little planning would be beneficial to her studies and understanding of economic affairs.

All this made sense to Alanitora, save for how few Kreahan soldiers there were traveling with her for protection. Though it was more strange that their other traveling companions, Zinaw and Tathra, had no accompaniment at all. Putting faith in another kingdom's guard felt odd.

Questioning this not only confirmed that Meli was Lorenalia's wait and sole protection, but also that neither 'she' or 'he' were used in reference to them. Such was presented whenever Lorenalia spoke of them. It was a curious subject, but Alanitora didn't ask for fear of intrusion or disrespect.

In other terms, Korena and Lorenalia seemed to get along quite well. They held similar, more feminine interests than both Alanitora and Gwendolyn, giving the blonde lady a chance to speak of her interest in clothing, fine arts, and romance. The latter of which, to Alanitora's relief, was about Korena's love life rather than the supposedly interesting subject of her own.

This didn't bother Alanitora one bit. She felt talking was tiresome anyway and now that the most talkative of her friends was engaged, she could drift off in her own mind… Which wasn't necessarily a good thing.

Her thoughts consistently wandered back to Diane. Specifically the girl's honest and intrusive opinions she had shared before they went their separate ways. She—someone who Alanitora considered an ally and showed hospitality to—had called her heartless.

Sure, she had heard it through whispers and secondhand stories time and time again but never sourced by someone she considered a friend. Alanitora thought the reason was that others did not know her nearly well enough. She had shown Diane parts of her past that surface personality despite this.

The princess wished she felt unmoved by such, or even angry. Instead, her stomach didn't sit right with her, her chest felt tight, like it had when she was poisoned, yet not from a physical source.

Was this truly guilt? Surely not. She had felt guilt before: when she lied to her mother or got caught snooping around the castle with Owen. And even if it was, why was she feeling it? The princess knew to never doubt her actions. She'd been taught that for a long time. To show guilt is to give into vulnerabilities and reveal flaws. So why couldn't she block this feeling out?

Alanitora looked down at her hands. She slid her fingers across her right palm. Her hands were rough and calloused as always, but they looked more delicate. Relaxed. Something had changed. She felt it inside her. But what?

"May I, Queen Alanitora?" Her head shot up to Lorenalia, before following the princess' gaze down to her own lap. She was gesturing at the rose that lay under her hands.

So the conversation ended up switching to her romantic endeavors after all... She nodded. "Of course." Alanitora picked up the rose delicately and handed it to her. "And please, I'd feel much more comfortable if you call me princess rather than queen, the title is not official as of yet."

"My apologies." Lorenalia grasped the slightly wilted rose, twirling it between the tips of her fingers the same way her brother had. "Leave it to Raven to show his affection with one of the most beautiful blooms of the garden... Did he tell you about it?"

"I believe so, yes. He told me it was specially crafted, I think."

"Did he tell you the name it was given?" Alanitora shook her head. *Depths of the Heart's Desire.* I'd say it's a tad dramatic, but then again, what isn't with my brother?" Lorenalia handed the rose back to her, before folding her hands into her lap. "Do either of you have siblings?"

Korena shook her head "No, though Gwendolyn has enough to go around for all three of us."

"Understandable. There has been a low fertility rate across Mordenla for a few generations now. But I suppose I consider you lucky in a sense. The two of you are strangers to typical sibling rivalry. I love my brother,

I do, but sometimes I feel as though he is too over the top. If there is any attention left to be caught, he'll snatch it. Makes sense why he was so intrigued by you, considering how differently you carry yourself—not that his affections weren't true. Just that—" She bit her tongue, shooting Alanitora an apologetic look.

"You're fine. I think I understand what you mean." If Lorenalia was referring to the idea that her brother's interest was based upon the chance to try at something new, she understood her exactly. In hindsight, it was the same reason she was enthralled by the Kreahan prince. There was no denying that he held a certain air to his name. Of course, that didn't mean it was completely sourced by that.

The dark-haired princess relaxed her shoulders. "I've been in his shadow a long time. So much that I'm not sure I know who I am outside of it. It's why I decided to come with you, just so you know. Perhaps his shadow only reaches as far as the capital walls. Perhaps I've just yet to find my place... Though I think my parent's quick acceptance of my request to travel says enough about my importance to them," she grumbled, her eyes momentarily drifting to the side before she snapped her head back up. "I'm sorry, that's beside the point now, isn't it?" Lorenalia held the rose out. "Here. I suggest hanging it upside down to dry. Helps preserve shape and color, and lets out the wonderful aroma."

Alanitora took the rose from her fingertips with a hum of acknowledgment. She turned to her lady. "Korena. Some string please."

The blonde reached into her girdle, bringing out a thin twine with an exclamation before handing it to her. As Alanitora began wrapping it around the stem of the rose, Korena turned to Lorenalia. "What were we talking about?"

"Boys. Men. Gentlemen. The difference between them."

"Ah, yes! Well, I think that out of the three, my beau is a man. Well, he's still pretty much a lad, but he has that seriousness and respect to him that leans towards a gentleman, though I suppose there might be another word for that..."

Alanitora sat back, observing the conversation as it shifted into gifts from admirers, the two of them excitedly listing off each of their adventures in love. A smile tugged at her lips when Korena shot a glance toward her as she told Lorenalia about the letters.

It was only then that she realized the change. Only a week before, Alanitora wouldn't have retrieved those letters from a carriage aflame. Not without hesitation or contemplation of the risks. Instead, she had acted recklessly.

Perhaps that moment of weakness in judgment was where her issues of the past couple of days stemmed. It was not the same embers that burned her home, but the rising flames had been a pressing reminder of the castle set ablaze. The possessions lost. That had been such a strong moment of vulnerability. A vulnerability that resurfaced last night and that morning as well, when the mention of what she lost was brought up.

But she had not had such a visceral reaction to her *own* plight as she did to Korena's. Were the letters a surrogate for everything Alanitora left behind in the capital fire? Or was it the idea of one of her closest friends losing a prized possession that drove her to act carelessly? It was ironic, the prospect of her caring causing her to be careless. Vulnerable.

Though... She had been vulnerable right after that. That was when Owen kissed her.

She let her emotional guard down and let him kiss her. Oh goodness, that's why she was having such a hard time brushing off Diane's comment. And now she was doubting herself.

Had she become weak? Soft?

Those words were different in meaning, but synonymous when applied to her.

Furthermore, there was the comment Diane had made about her ladies-in-waiting. Her eyes flicked over to Korena, who had somehow moved the conversation to a discussion about what colors went with a person's complexion. Did Alanitora, deep within her, truly think she was mistreating them or had she become paranoid? Did they think she didn't care? Her way of showing affection was unconventional, she knew that... But did they?

She *was* beginning to doubt herself. Before these past few days, she had never cared if Korena and Gwendolyn enjoyed her company or feigned it for the pay, but now she was seeking some sort of validation. In the way a fire might turn a fortified castle into ruins, it may have just burned her barren.

"Silence." For the first time, Alanitora heard Meli speak. She looked up and scanned the faces of the others. Korena looked just as, if not more confused, and Lorenalia looked incredibly concerned.

That couldn't be good. "What is it?" Alanitora asked.

"Something is wrong," Meli noted.

Lorenalia looked between Alanitora and Korena. "Meli is a tracker, they tend to know when the environment feels… different."

Korena opened the curtain on her left, peering out into the fir-filled woods. "I mean, it is nighttime now, maybe it just feels colder."

Meli shook their head. "No, I think—"

But the warrior was cut off by a blur of brown passing Alanitora's eyes.

Korena shrieked, grabbing her attention. An arrow stuck between the back cushion of the seats right next to her lady-in-waiting's head. Its angle could be traced back to the exposed window, originating from somewhere up in the tall dark trees.

Alanitora closed the curtains with haste to prevent further field of vision. A frown sharpened on her features as she forced the logic of her mind awake. Analyze. Think. Then act.

Her eyes focused on a small piece of parchment wrapped around the shaft of the arrow. Alanitora dislodged the arrow from the cushion and quickly tore away at the twine holding the parchment in place. Her fingers fumbled to unroll the note.

"The arrow, if I may?" Lorenalia asked frantically, her outstretched hand twitching slightly.

Alanitora held the arrow out without hesitation, her attention focused on the unfurled words before her.

"Draw your weapons, Dagger Eyes, and be ready."

Korena's eyes darted between all of them. "What is it? What's going on?"

231

Dagger Eyes. Only one person had ever called her that. They were the only person it could be.

"Sagittarius." Alanitora and Meli spoke the name in unison, their eyes meeting with the realization.

"It's certainly her arrows," Lorenalia ran her fingers across the grooved details of the shaft. "Has all her custom markings."

"Well, what do we do?" Korena's breath was beginning to quicken.

Alanitora handed the note to Meli and Lorenalia. Using her free hand, she reached under her skirts to retrieve a small binding of throwing knives around her thigh, as well as one of her daggers.

"What are we supposed to do? Is Sagittarius about to attack?" Korena shrunk into her seat anxiously, her eyes darting between the two doors of the carriage.

Lorenalia shook her head. "It's highly unlikely. Sagittarius' entrances never lack in grandiosity. They don't come with a warning, or give anyone time to react before she has the upper hand." A hand came up to her chin pensively. "Though I can't be completely sure. We haven't encountered her on the road before."

"Well, based on the targeted note, she knows it is us and is aware of the fact that we will put up a fight." Meli was getting their weapons ready as well.

"How do we know? Maybe it's just to scare us or something— Oh I hope Gwennie's okay!"

"I'm sure she's fine, Korena." Alanitora put a hand on her lady's arm to console her when a sharp scream sounded from outside. A scream so terrifying that it could only bring an omen of bad fortune.

And then the carriage came to a slow, tumbling halt.

18

The Crooked Flickers

"Ladies," Meli shot them a dark glare. "It is imperative at this moment that you stay inside. I'm going to investigate."

The Kreahan soldier moved towards the door. They were about to get out when a loud bang sounded above their heads. There was barely any time to speculate what could be on top of the carriage when a hand shot through the window, busting past the curtain and grasping Lorenalia's arm firmly. The princess called out as the arm pulled her closer to the window.

The torso of a man hung upside-down from the top of the carriage. Piercing blue eyes peered into the carriage as a wolfish grin spread across his crooked teeth. "Well hello there, little ladies." His accent was thick and improper. The vowels were weighed down and his tone dropped off lazily at the end of his words.

Alanitora took a survey of the situation, looking for where she might be able to use her dagger without hurting the princess in his grasp. She had flipped the dagger into a defensive hold in preparation when Lorenalia yanked her arm inwards to pull the man closer. Before he had the time to react, his captive sank her teeth into the flesh of his bicep with enough force to break the skin. He withdrew his arm out of reflex, yelping out a series of curses. Lorenalia retched at the taste, wiping her mouth with the back of her hand.

"Oi, lads! Looks like we have some feisty little princesses!" she could hear the man announce above them.

So there were more. This was an ambush by a *group* of thieves.

Alanitora's gaze met with Meli's. They had the same intention in their eyes. Sharing a nod, Meli held up their hand, beginning to count down.

It wasn't long before the man looked back down into the window, and when he did, Meli was ready. They kicked the door outwards, the top of it hitting him square in the nose. Alanitora and Meli took the chance to jump out.

Within the thicket of trees, a dozen or so men stood, awaiting their time to attack. Some held weapons in preparation, others stood with torches, the flames illuminating their ghostly faces within the dark covering. A few had already emerged, ready to direct the rest of the crew however they saw fit. The man Lorenalia bit had hopped down from the carriage to join them.

"Bandits!" a Trenvern guard shouted. "Spread out! Protect the valuables!"

Right. Because announcing to protect the valuables wouldn't lead said bandits to them. Not at all. Now the thieving troop knew exactly where their attention should be. Alanitora held back her irritation, channeling it elsewhere. She could at least be thankful for the handful of guards that gathered around the carriage to defend it.

She gave them a stern glare. "Keep Princess Lorenalia and Lady Korena safe. Don't let anyone near them."

Alanitora had hoped her soldiers would know by now that it was unnecessary to question her. Thankfully, those from Trenvern had figured this out and had no hesitation to follow her commands.

The same couldn't be said for one young Kreahan soldier in particular. "But, what if—"

"Do it. I'll get the rest from the other carriage and lead them here." She looked between him and Meli. "I trust you to defend them."

The group of bandits had yet to initiate their attack, and Alanitora took the opportunity to slip past the carriage. Her attention momentarily caught on the bloody body of their coachman, who was clutching his stomach

234

on the ground next to the horses. Based on this and the carriage fire, it appeared being the coachman might be the most dangerous of all jobs in the entourage.

She held back a grimace and continued on, picking up the pace when she saw the other carriage a few wagons ahead. She maneuvered her way through the small crowd of soldiers preparing to guard the wagon with more precious belongings.

Shouts sounded behind her, but Alanitora did not need to stop to know what they were for. Men emerged from the woods, most in clusters. One particular adversary ran towards her, swinging his sword wildly at her. She ducked under it, digging her elbow into his side before she kept going. She had to be sure Gwendolyn and the others were alright before she stopped to fight back.

Upon reaching the second carriage, the princess was surprised to see that rather than waiting within the safety of its doors, Gwendolyn, Tathra, and Zinaw were standing in the shadow behind it.

She slipped to the side of the adjacent carriage, kneeling to catch her breath momentarily. "Come on, we need to stick together. This way."

Tathra straightened. She held a sword tightly in one hand and held onto Gwendolyn's with the other. Turning to the lady next to her, she spoke in a low tone. "You ready?" When she nodded in agreement, the Redanorian princess led her out of the shadows and into the chaos.

"You too," Alanitora said to Zinaw, who responded with a scowl. She raised her eyebrows. "I'll cover for you."

With a grumble, Zinaw peaked her head out of the shadow, looking around for a brief moment before swinging the carriage door open. She let out a quick whistle, which prompted Becorath to jump out at the ready. Silver Moon followed suit.

The four of them bounded across the procession, weaving their way through a collection of small battles between soldiers and bandits on either side.

Besides focusing on staying on her two feet despite her pumping heart, Alanitora was doing her best to survey the landscape. The attacks were unorganized but coordinated in a way that suggested all of the bandits must have been in communication. They had a plan, she just had to figure out what it was, and how Sagittarius was involved.

They caught up with Tathra and Gwendolyn in no time, the blood on the princess' sword suggesting they had had some sort of run-in on the way there. Alanitora moved quickly, ushering the two inside of the carriage.

Korena's eyes were filled to the brim with tears. She rejoiced at the sight of her dear friend, swinging her arms so swiftly around Gwendolyn that it was a surprise the two of them didn't fall out of the carriage.

Alanitora waited until they separated before she spoke. "I need all of you to stay in here." She turned her shoulder to check that there were no adversaries behind her before continuing, "Tathra, keep watch. Protect them if anyone breaks through. Hold your station otherwise, yeah?" Tathra nodded. "Good, I'm going to go help with the fight. Shut the door. Close the curtains. Stay alert."

She stepped back from the carriage, giving her ladies and the two princesses a reassuring smile before readjusting the grip on her blades.

"Alanitora!" Zinaw yelled out.

She looked over to the other girl, who gestured her head to the woods. In the faint light, she could see their adversaries' reinforcements preparing to charge.

Zinaw reached down and grabbed a long stick from the ground.

"You want a blade?" Alanitora asked, shifting her weight from one foot to the other. Her legs, which had been stationary for a few hours, were now aching from her dash between carriages.

"Nah." Zinaw tucked the branch under her arm momentarily, using her free hands to bring her brown curls up out of her face. "I don't do blades, and since my staff is near the back, this'll have to do." A satisfied smile spread across her lips. She looked down at her pet wolf. "Becorath. Get 'em."

Without hesitation, the wolf sprang towards the group of men running out onto the road. Silver Moon caught onto the nature of the situation, following her lead to rush them as well.

236

Only a few of the thieves appeared disturbed by this, stopping in their tracks at the notion of two full-sized wolves bounding towards them with murderous intent. The rest grazed past, their targets set on Zinaw and Alanitora.

Seeing that their princess had joined the fight, two guards stepped forward from their position to help her and Zinaw at the offense. They stood their ground when bandits came tumbling forward, leaving Alanitora enough space to move freely.

In the meantime, she focused on the second layer of thieves in the distance, making use of the range her throwing knives allowed. Only a small percentage missed their targets, most able to catch them at their core or at least slash their arm. Either way, their yelps and hisses of pain did not go unnoticed. Their associates caught onto the advantage of range weapons, shifting their attention to the source: Her.

They must have noticed the initial surplus of foot soldiers among their numbers and assumed there would be confined bounds of battle. Good, as long as a portion of the bandits were focused on neutralizing her, it gave some leeway for those guarding the valuables.

It was overwhelming really, how many there were. How many battles were happening left and right, how many sounds came from every direction. The more that came her way, the more she had to shift her focus. Zinaw was faring well beside her, knocking men down with the branch, jabbing them at weak points. The more they fought, the more dust that rose from the dirt road. Through the puffs of obscurity and particles that clung to her eyes, she tried to twist her way around their attackers.

A piercing scream sounded behind them, and within it, Alanitora heard her name. She whipped around to see the carriage containing the girls veering off past the rest of the procession and to the road ahead. Someone had taken control of the horses and based on the satisfied chortle of a bandit who met her eyes in the area of where the carriage once was, the driver hadn't been one of their own.

Panic bolted through her entire body. No. They had intentionally preoccupied her to get the carriage. That was their plan. Not the resources or riches. The princesses. Of course, that was the truest item of value. Who knew what priceless ransom a kingdom would pay for the safe return of their royalty?

Alanitora scanned the area. She needed to think fast. A majority of their party was likely too preoccupied to notice the carriage, and if they did, there were too many attackers for them to drop everything and run after it. The two guards were fending off their area well.

"Zinaw, with me!" She ran to the empty space in the train of wagons, meeting with Meli in the middle.

"I'm sorry, Your Highness, I didn't see them board it, I was too focused on other attackers." Meli rasped, running a hand through their hair.

"It's not your fault, they had us occupied too." Alanitora gathered up her skirts in her hand. She'd need a free range of motion for her legs. "We can still catch up, those horses have too heavy a load to run fast enough."

The three of them began their sprint past the rest of the procession, dodging oncoming attackers in the interest of saving their friends. But even when they got beyond the wagons and the distance between them and the carriage began to close, their breath became shallow and the carriage had gained traction, growing smaller in the distance.

Alanitora slowed her steps, gasping for air. The other two halted next to her, all three of them coming to a similar conclusion.

"It's no use," Zinaw said, hands upon her knees. Meli narrowed their eyes, scanning the distance as though several calculations were running through their head.

They had to figure something out quickly, but for this singular moment, they needed to catch their breath. As the rhythmic sound of Alanitora's pumping heart in her ears and her heaving breath faded, the sound of hooves approaching from behind rose.

She turned to see a pair of horses approaching with haste. Thank goodness, they could use some strong steeds right about now.

Then the dust settled, and vision of the rider became clear.

"Well, are you all just gonna give up?" The first thing Alanitora saw was a flash of red illuminated by a lantern. Her eyes drifted off to the mask-adorned face of the rider. "Get on, you three, unless you actually want to lose them."

It was Sagittarius, in flesh and bone, mounted on one horse while simultaneously holding a lantern and the reins of the other horse firmly. How she was able to do that, Alanitora didn't know. She may not have been much of an equestrian herself, but the princess had to admit Sagittarius must be one hell of a rider.

Meli didn't even ask questions, rushing to the second horse and swinging their leg over, only waiting for Zinaw to mount before taking the reins from the bandit. Though questions swirled in Alanitora's head, now was not the time to explore them. She kicked herself up onto the seat behind Sagittarius. Prepared to go after the carriage.

"Hold on tight, Dagger Eyes. We'll catch up to your friends in no time." She could practically hear the cocky grin in her voice.

"*Don't* call me Dagger Eyes," Alanitora spat. She wrapped an arm around the bandit's waist, not desiring any form of contact, but aware that she would need to hold onto something if they were going to catch up.

Sagittarius took this as a sign to push the lantern into Alanitora's right hand. "Excellent, hold this." She readjusted her grip on the reins, giving the horse a kick in the side, and lurching them forward.

"I presume you stole these horses?" Meli shouted from ahead, Zinaw similarly holding onto their waist with one arm.

"Borrowed. And are you seriously questioning me while your friends are being attacked by a group of overly-pompous, self-righteous, grotesque men?" The wind from their acceleration threw Sagittarius' hair into Alanitora's face. It smelled of dried raspberries on a hot summer day, which was possibly the only positive of the situation.

Zinaw turned her head, narrowing her eyes. "And how do we know you aren't a part of their little party? Your timing seems awfully convenient."

"I don't know who the hell you are, but your insinuation that I would band with a group of scums is honestly hurtful," Sagittarius feigned an offended tone. "For your information, they call themselves 'The Crooked Flickers', a terrible name if you ask me—"

"—Better than naming yourself after a constellation..." Alanitora said in a hushed tone.

"I didn't name my—" The bandit sighed in annoyance at the princess. It was safe to say the feeling was mutual. "They are a bunch of greedy men who believe their superiority is unmatched. Most of them are a collection of drunkards from the south mutually upset about their inability to get a wife... So they take what they please instead. Not very competent opponents, but there's a lot of them. Our interactions have not been enjoyable."

"Pretty sure that's every interaction with you!" Zinaw shouted back.

"The group is up ahead," Meli announced, giving their horse an extra kick.

The carriage was surrounded by a dozen men, who were hollering with laughter as they grabbed the vehicle and shook it back and forth to terrify the girls within. The closer they came, the better Alanitora could hear the shouts from inside. They primarily consisted of Tathra yelling out vulgar threats, none of which seemed to be working.

As soon as the men noticed their arrival, Meli dismounted, pulling a sword from their scabbard. They had no hesitation in grabbing the attention of their opponents, leading some away from the carriage.

"Go, I'll cover you," Sagittarius ordered, steadying the horse and swinging her bow from over her back.

Alanitora voiced an affirmative and got down from the horse. She withdrew a lighter dagger so she could hold it with one hand and the lantern in the other. She waited until one of the men caught her eye and readied to charge. Hopefully, the men being drawn away for battle would give her ladies and the two princesses a chance to readjust.

But another, larger man came towards her instead, catching her by surprise with the swing of a morning star to her left. He grinned when she jumped back, slowly putting momentum into his weapon.

She braced, and when he raised his arm to attack again, the princess ducked out of the way, flipping her dagger to a defensive position and slashing a large gash through his side.

240

He growled, yelling out a string of profanities that made no sense in the way they were put together. This grabbed the attention of a nearby bandit, who charged towards the two of them with a glint of insanity in his wide eyes.

She turned, taking the lantern in her hand and swinging hard when he got close, hitting him squarely across the head. It forced him aside, and based on his agonizing cry, must have also burned him.

As soon as there was a clear path to the door of the carriage, Alanitora took it, checking the others fighting alongside her. When she was sure enough adversaries were well occupied, she opened the door. Her entry was greeted with the sight of Tathra's blade prepared to slice her head off.

"Alanitora! Thank goodness you are alright," Gwendolyn exclaimed.

Korena rushed to hug the princess, but Lorenalia pulled the girl back by her arm, aware of the risk in their current situation.

"Is everyone okay?" Alanitora asked with haste, barely waiting for the collective nods before she continued. "I think the best tactic would be to get you all out of the carriage. It only takes one man and a moment of distraction in this chaos to run off with you all again. Everyone needs to stay close to a respective fighter so we can keep watch of each other."

"The buddy system!" Korena shouted out.

"Er, yes... the buddy system," Alanitora replied. "Tathra, are you okay to cover me while I get my weapons ready?"

Tathra gave her a quick nod before turning to Gwendolyn, offering a hand to the lady-in-waiting to help her out of the carriage. The two made their way past Alanitora.

She placed the lantern on the ground and hoisted her foot on the carriage. Alanitora rolled up her skirts, wiping her bloody dagger on one of her darker undergarments before replacing it with the pair on either side of her left leg.

Lorenalia maneuvered her way out from the carriage and past the princess as soon as the path to Meli was clear, leaving Korena to stick with Alanitora.

When she was ready, she nodded at Tathra, who had been keeping three adversaries busy at once with Gwendolyn close behind her. Even with a short examination, Alanitora could tell the Redanorian princess was an incredibly skilled fighter, no doubt trained in the same regard as knights, if not better. Though she didn't know Redanor's standard, Tathra had to be the product of their best resources.

Her upper body strength was impeccable, the perfect amount required when blocking multiple blades or parrying them. Such was the case in the present moment, as Tathra blocked the path of two overhead daggers and threw them backward with a quick swing.

Alanitora took this opportunity to take her place. One of the men continued to pursue Tathra, who had backed away to a different area to spread the bandits out.

With the two left, Alanitora swung her right dagger wildly to feign an attempted slash of one's chest, before taking the left dagger and plunging it into his lower torso. The other man noticed her maneuver, and in an understanding that this would be a more difficult fight than anticipated, backed away. He was clearly unconcerned with his collapsed ally.

Momentarily without an opponent, she scanned the crowd for her allies to see if anyone needed assistance. Alanitora's eye caught on the duo that was Lorenalia and Meli, who were back-to-back, each facing their opponents. She watched curiously as Lorenalia took no initiative to attack, but instead showed incredible balance and flexibility when it came to dodging them. After a few attempted strokes from their attackers, Lorenalia and Meli would switch places and allow their opponents' rhythm to automatically be thrown from offense to persistent defense and vice versa. Alanitora had to admit it was an excellent method.

In the midst of clashing swords and battle yells, Tathra's voice rose above the commotion. "Using a damn stick?!" she yelled out.

Alanitora made sure to catch Zinaw's annoyed expression towards her cousin as she poked one of the ends towards a bandit to hold him further away from her. "Oh shush, my staff is with everything else. I didn't think we'd be running into a group of barbarians on the way."

"Tends to happen when you travel in a fancy carriage with a procession of royal goods!" Gwendolyn yelled back. Though the retort was confident, there was worry present in her voice.

Unfortunately for her entertainment, Alanitora's attention was ripped away when another man charged her. He held his saber without the barbaric dramatics the others had, giving him the advantage of stealth. Yet his precision left room for predictability, and Alanitora simply twisted herself out of the way of his blow, gearing up her blades to go on offense.

A small yelp from Korena called the princess' attention behind her to see if she had been struck by the man's blade. Though, just as Alanitora confirmed she was fine, she felt a small tug at her hair and looked back to see that an arrow had picked some strands upon its path into the man's chest. He staggered back from the shot, then was hit again, knocking him to the ground.

Alanitora whipped her head around at Sagittarius. Was the archer *trying* to cut off her ear?

Sagittarius seemed to acknowledge this idea as well, shrugging at the princess' glare. "I told you, I don't miss," she shouted

Alanitora grunted, turning to face her next target. The numbers were far less now, with only a few more men on the Crooked Flickers' side in the way of their victory.

There was a shout to her left, but Alanitora stood her ground, unable to see past the two men fighting Zinaw in front of her. Nevertheless, another feminine shout of struggle was heard, and the princess knew it couldn't be anything good. She moved her perspective to see what was happening. Both Gwendolyn and Tathra were on the ground. Her lady-in-waiting had been knocked aside and was struggling to get up while Tathra was pinned underneath the weight of a large man, a wide smile on his face.

Tathra was struggling to get out of his grasp, grunts of frustration escaping her throat. Everything was happening so fast, and it felt like an eternity until Alanitora was able to tighten her grip and start towards the three of them.

Just as she was ready to lunge at the man, he whispered something low that Alanitora couldn't make out, and Tathra's face morphed into revulsion.

243

"Get your grubby hands off of me, you swine! I'd rather die than kiss any man, especially the likes of you," she growled, getting ahold of her sword and swiping the hilt up and into the man's nose.

He staggered backward and off of the girl, allowing her to squirm out from beneath him, taking her sword back into offensive position and stabbing it right into his core. It was possibly the most fatal blow that had been delivered that evening, a close second at Sagittarius' arrows, which didn't cause instant death but would likely lead to an infection.

His body slumped to the ground, and a few heads turned towards them. Tathra went over to help Gwendolyn up before turning back to the chaos and shouting out. "Hey!" A few kept fighting, but for the most part, the battle died down as she grabbed their attention. "Look around you. Those of you still fighting must be well aware by now that a number of your people have been immobilized. Whatever you are trying to get out of this fight, you won't win. You should give up now while you still have the chance."

No one dared move in those next few moments. Silence fell over the crowd as bandits looked between one another. Alanitora couldn't help the smile that tugged at her lips. They were trying to find a leader in their group, and none was surfacing

Following the confusion, Sagittarius kicked her horse up to the center of the fight, looking around at everyone as she steadied the steed. "Come on now, boys," The bandit began, a merry tone in her voice. "You heard her. Surely you know when to admit defeat. Is it really worth your lives?"

Silence continued.

"To hell with this." A large man with a bald head and unruly beard dropped his knife to the dirt. "I signed up for money, not war. Ichabod! Help me carry your brother."

The man in question moved towards him, putting away his weapons and kneeling down to fetch another who was curled on the ground.

One by one, others disarmed themselves and stepped away from defensive positions to aid their fallen brethren. A loud whistle was blown by a particularly tall man.

This, of course, did not put Alanitora and her companions at ease. They stationed themselves in case a surprise attack was underway. Luckily, this seemed to be unnecessary, as the Flickers' only interest was retreating from the bloody scene.

As the men made their way into the woods, hoisting wounded comrades upon their shoulders, a meek, hunched one turned to them with a scowl on his face. "You better hope you don't cross our paths ever. If we come across any of you again, it'll be your last day alive. The Crooked Flickers don't take vengeance lightly."

Lorenalia stepped forward, her nose in the air. "That's awfully rich coming from the provokers of this fight."

The man scoffed, following the rest of his men into the dark of the woods.

All of their shoulders collectively relaxed, Zinaw going so far as to slumping her entire body against the carriage and throwing her stick to the ground. "What are you, Alanitora? A magnet of violence? I estimate a third of the folks we've just fought are destined for death."

"It's not her fault!" Korena wailed.

"Blondie's right. It's not." Sagittarius jumped down from her horse and approached the group with her hands on her hips. "They wouldn't have attacked you in the first place if your long line of caravans were more *modest*." She shot a look at Princess Lorenalia before turning to Alanitora. "And with that, my work here is done. I'll be taking my leave now." She leaned forward, narrowing her eyes mockingly. "You lot can thank me later."

"Not so fast—" Alanitora interjected, placing her hand on the bandit's elbow. Sagittarius' eyes flicked down to her touch, then back up to meet her gaze. Despite the mask obstructing part of her face, the princess could see that her curiosity was piqued. She smiled. "I'd like you to stick around. At least until we set up camp for the night."

"Why?" Sagittarius narrowed her eyes.

Alanitora pressed the same energy. "Humor me."

"So you can, what? Arrest me for my *crimes*? Forgive me if I'm not one to trust easily. And if you don't off me, they will." She nodded her head towards Meli and Lorenalia.

"I will ensure your freedom, you have my word."

"And I'm supposed to put my faith in that?" Sagittarius let out a laugh.

"Yes, you are. Just as I put my faith in your hands this evening," Alanitora retorted.

She considered the words for a long moment, her face morphing in consideration of different responses before coming to a sound conclusion. "Very well, you've attracted my interest. But—" Sagittarius held up a finger in protest. "No way I'm riding in a carriage. I get my own horse and under no circumstances will I be pestered by your little soldiers."

Alanitora opened her mouth to respond but was cut off by a number of horses speeding towards the stranded carriage. Sir Corwyn rode in the lead, familiar faces behind him. "Oh thank the owl's wings! I thought we'd lost you all. Is everyone alright?"

She turned back to her companions, checking for any injuries. "Yes it seems, and on your end?"

"Valuables were untouched, thanks to our men. However, a few other wagons were rummaged through by the thieves. There are men taking inventory now that the adversaries have retreated."

"They surrendered to you all as well?" Lorenalia queried.

A soldier to the left of Corwyn shook his head. "There was a whistle sounded, we believe by their leader, and they just… retreated into the forest."

"Good," Alanitora intervened. "Round up the rest of our entourage and lead them here. Once everyone has reconvened, we'll ride forth until at least midnight—it's best we get a good start on our journey and past this area."

Corwyn gestured to two of the other soldiers, who turned their horses around to ride back while the remaining two dismounted. She stepped past her allies to join Corwyn in a debrief of the situation.

According to the soldiers, most of those who protected the wagons had come out of the altercation unwounded, and those who had been were in recoverable condition. Despite Alanitora's doubts that their methods would be futile against the bandits, in the end, nothing of importance was stolen. She and the younger of the two soldiers theorized that the intention was indeed to kidnap those in the carriage for ransom. It made sense as to why the battle Alanitora and her companions fought was more arduous.

Within less than five minutes, the rest of their entourage had caught up to the area. Corwyn stepped away from Alanitora momentarily and got straight into instructing different groups. He sternly ordered for some to check in with the ladies and princesses, and others to examine the carriage for needed repairs. It appeared that their party was starting to get a hang of the chaos that surrounded this trip, and a prompt session of work followed.

It had been the familiar face of Uldin who brought Silver Moon and Becorath back to the custody of Zinaw. According to him, the wolves had done the most damage in the fight, given that the wounds they inflicted were the only ones significant enough to require other bandits to drag their allies off the road.

Though it slightly disturbed Alanitora the violence that her wild pet was capable of, Zinaw was quite thrilled about the whole ordeal. She gave both wolves scratches behind the ear and praise.

They had done well. All of them. Not just the wolves, or the princesses with her, but the whole entourage. It was strange. A few days ago, she would have credited them as a group of dimwits—unable to organize themselves in a procedural fashion, doubtful of her abilities—but now? She felt a certain warmth towards them. If the Crooked Flickers' attack indicated anything, it was that these people, while not always perfect, were capable.

Maybe, just maybe, she would be able to sleep easy that night.

19

Wolves & Hares

As soon as everything began moving again, Korena instantly fell
asleep on Alanitora's shoulder while Lorenalia curled up to the
side across from them. Meli was more focused on looking out
the window to actively watch Sagittarius, who rode next to their carriage
upon request.

The silence was not an issue for Alanitora, as she too was exhausted from
the events that had happened. While she found her body relaxed at that
moment, it didn't change the constant buzzing of thoughts in her mind.

Perhaps what prevented those thoughts from settling as well was their
atypical nature. Contemplation had been heavy in the past few days, but
the subject of such tended to focus on things Alanitora had a direct tie
to: her friends, the threats on her life, the mystery of her foes. But now
her reflection surrounded people away from her touch, who she only had
passing instances of viewing. Those who lived their lives much differently
from her own, away from palaces and castles, from the opulence and praise
of royalty.

It wasn't as though this was her first time thinking over things like this,
but the attack of the Crooked Flickers had brought a new light into the
keyhole of an otherwise dark room. The thieves had not attacked solely
for power or strategic advantage, but out of greed and envy.

In a way she pitied them for their selfish desires, but who was she to say anything about desire when she had everything they did not? The prospect did not make her feel guilty in any manner, for the way of the world was far from humbling: it just was what it was.

No, it only made her curious about a life that she had not lived. Alanitora possessed no knowledge of what it would be like to live in even slight destitution. Some might claim to be happier in a position like that, but she saw no correlation to happiness and materialistic value, whether you had less or more.

Her only nearby resources to these wonderings were Korena and Gwendolyn, both of whom grew up in a lower position than her. Korena was born under a lord and Gwendolyn in a household noble only in ancestral ties. Between the two she couldn't say which of them was happier.

Korena may have been more cheerful on a day-to-day basis, but tended to be discontent with the smaller things of life. Contrarily, Gwendolyn was serene and docile, but always took matters as they were, and did not dwell on the misfortunes of life.

Regarding Alanitora herself, she certainly did not feel discontent, but in no way was she completely satisfied. She always thought of herself as more composed than most. However, less liveliness did not mean less happiness.

Hell, even happiness was a difficult word to define within her life. And in such terms, unhappiness was not something she felt she could recall.

It was an odd predicament, and in the end, Alanitora pushed it aside, instead focusing on the present moment, like the colors of the fabrics around her and the lights in the night sky. Her eyes shifted to the window for the remainder of the trip, gaze falling on Sagittarius, who looked straight forward on her horse. She was mesmerized by what might be going through the head of the archer in retrospect of the evening.

As the middle of the night approached, the camp was set up for the soldiers and horses to get their much-needed rest. Tents for her companions to sleep in were quickly formed as well.

Alanitora spent no effort to wake Korena, instead lowering her head onto a pillow in place of her shoulder, aware that any attempt to move the girl would result in a grumpy blonde fussing about her sleeping schedule.

Meli woke Lorenalia lightly, and the three of them took care to quietly exit the carriage.

The camp was much smaller than usual for the convenience of time. It was a quaint and cozy tent circle, an extra change of scenery not only with trees differing from the west but the variety of tent designs added from Kreahan supply for the extra soldiers of Lorenalia's.

To Alanitora's dismay, a smaller campsite meant she would be sharing a tent not only with her ladies but also with Tathra and her particularly snobbish cousin. It may not have been ideal, but she had agreed with the decision to set up on a smaller scale. Fewer tents meant fewer posted guards, which equated to an overall more alert entourage on the road. And of course, if they spent less time setting up and packing down, they could get to Donasela much faster.

The problem of having to share a tent with Zinaw did not end up being an issue, as when the party of the second carriage met up with them, her cynical behavior was replaced with tired grumbles. The brunette moved past her instead, falling straight to sleep curled up on a cot in the corner.

Alanitora was just getting herself ready for bed when Gwendolyn came up from behind, tapping her lightly on the shoulder before enveloping her in an embrace.

The princess couldn't help the smile spreading across her face as she returned it. She pressed her hands to Gwendolyn's back, closing her eyes momentarily. "I'm sorry we didn't get to talk earlier, after the fight. I should have checked in with you." She could have lost her ladies today. Had their response to the attack gone any other way, they could have been seriously hurt.

"Nonsense!" Gwendolyn separated from the hug with a cheerful laugh, resting her hands on Alanitora's elbows. "I was and am all fine, thanks to you... and Tathra." She glanced over at the Redanorian princess, who was rolling out blankets atop her cot. She turned back to Alanitora. "Though I am curious as to how Sagittarius ended up being involved." The lady paused, looking up as though she wished to find the correct words. "Princess Lorenalia told us the situation with the arrow, but I'm still confused as to why you've allowed her to tag along with us further."

"That I am not so sure of." Alanitora smiled at her honestly. "I find myself trusting her for some reason. I think she can be of some use."

"Well," she sighed. "If you trust her, I do too, even if I have my doubts." With one last pat of her arm, Gwendolyn separated from the princess to help Tathra.

Alanitora smiled at the prospect of their blossoming friendship before turning towards the entrance of the tent. In regards to the red-tipped brunette, she should probably have a chat with her before Sagittarius decided to abandon their deal.

To her surprise, as soon as she exited the tent, her eyes locked with the bandit, who was sitting on the opposite side of the campfire. She held one of her arrows in her hand, carving out bits of the shaft with a small knife.

Sagittarius stood when she saw her, meeting the princess halfway before putting the arrow she was engraving back into her quiver. "Dagger Eyes," she greeted.

"Sagittarius," Alanitora responded, too tired to correct the phrase.

"So." The bandit gestured around the camp, her eyebrows raised. "This is what traveling with royalty looks like." She laughed, allowing Alanitora to see the bright crease of her eyes beneath the mask. "I won't waste too much of Your Highness' time. You look quite exhausted after all. I'm sure you'll be needing your beauty rest."

Alanitora released a sigh of annoyance at this remark, which only made the archer's smile grow. She extended her hand out, a piece of folded parchment between her fingers. "Here."

"What's this?"

"It's the location of where I will be sleeping tonight—can't have one of your pointless little guards attempting to murder me in my rest." Alanitora was about to interject, but she cut her off with a raised hand. "I'm willing to hear you out about whatever kind of deal you're wanting to make, but you need rest first. You are welcome to come wake me in the morning, I'd just rather no one else have my location because I don't trust anyone."

"And yet you trust me..." Alanitora ventured.

251

Sagittarius shrugged. "You told me I could. I believe it."

Alanitora, quite amused by the gesture, took the note outstretched in Sagittarius' hand.

"Goodnight then, Dagger Eyes." There was that damn nickname again. Rolled from her lips with such ease. Alanitora would have to set it straight later.

"Goodnight, Sagittarius."

And with that, Alanitora turned into her tent to retire for the rest of the night.

Dawn had not yet risen when a guard awoke Alanitora and her tent to let them know it was time to pack up.

Korena must have migrated to the tent at some point in the night as she was among the others, rubbing her eyes in an attempt to keep herself awake. In silent agreement, everyone respectfully dispersed to their own activities in preparation for the inevitably long road ahead.

It was then that Alanitora fished the note from Sagittarius out of her pocket, half expecting it to read something along the lines of *'Congratulations, by the time you read this I'll be gone. I've stolen all of your loot.'*

Instead, it was a birds-eye drawing of the campsite scrawled in charcoal, reminiscent of one of five-year-old Owen's treasure maps. Regardless of artistic skill, an arrow pointed in between two tents and towards the woods where there was the drawing of a log and then another arrow pointing to a circle of dots.

The princess was able to follow her directions with a certain amount of ease, coming across each of the drawn landmarks like a little scavenger hunt. Part of her logic was telling her to be wary of traveling into the woods alone at the beckoning of a stranger. Despite this, the other part of her, the part based on limited knowledge and gut, said otherwise. It wasn't often that she cast aside logic, but this time around she did so with ease.

Upon reaching a circle of rocks that reminded her of a mushroom ring from tales of the fae, Alanitora paused, looking down at her map and around her. There were no further instructions and no cot nor campfire in sight.

"Mornin'." Sagittarius' voice echoed down from the canopy. Alanitora flicked her eyes up, met with the sight of the bandit slouched across a series of branches. The informality of her nature made a part of Alanitora long hidden in etiquette lessons twitch. She ignored it.

"Good morning to you as well," Alanitora replied cordially.

Sagittarius leaped down from her position, landing in front of Alanitora and kicking the circle of rocks in disarray "So you're taking off?"

"Yes, we are. And you?"

Sagittarius cocked her head to the side. "You say that as though you don't hold the answer to that question."

"I apologize—" Alanitora began.

"No, no. Don't fret about it. I'm teasing. Though I still don't know why you asked me along with you… Unless you don't know yourself and you just made up an excuse to spend more time with me." She raised her eyebrows.

Alanitora gave her a tight smile, ignoring her suggestion. She may have had the patience last night for the bandit's antics, but right now her tolerance was thinning. It didn't help that the first interaction she was having this morning was with an outlaw unconcerned with rules. "I asked you along because I believe I could use your skill in the days coming forth. At least until I reach my destination."

"Is that all?" A smirk curled onto her lips.

"No, it's not. My destination is Donasela. I'm to be wed there."

"So you… want me to officiate your wedding? Seriously, Dagger Eyes, I'm not one of your maids, I can't read your mind." Sagittarius leaned forward, a lopsided grin melting the exterior of procedures between the two of them.

At this point, Alanitora could barely stifle a chuckle, as while it was a rude gesture, she was not used to someone speaking to her with such casualness. "From what little I know about you, you seem to have good intentions. When you ordered for Kreaha to give you their riches, you claimed the purpose was to give it to others." She paused as Sagittarius' amused smirk shifted into one of intrigue. "However, the way you go about it—the thieving, the violence. It is less than honorable."

"So… you want to arrest me?"

Alanitora shook her head. "I want to compensate you in persuasion to set you on a better path."

Sagittarius was silent for a few moments before inhaling sharply. "You know this proposition is awfully strange coming from someone who hides several weapons in her skirts. How *very* self-righteous of you."

"I'm not forcing you. Will you join me or not?"

Sagittarius raised her hands in defense. "Okay, okay. Sure. As long as I'm not ostracized by your men.

"Alright, but if they end up doing anything to insult you, I'd prefer you *not* to shoot them."

"Deal."

Alanitora had just finished speaking to Sir Corwyn in regards to taking breakfast while on the road when Gwendolyn approached her. The lady had a slight worry to her brow, but a lightness in her eyes that suggested nothing serious was amiss.

"Your Highness, if you don't mind… I'd like to ride with Korena for at least the next stretch of time."

"Is there an issue with the previous arrangement?" Alanitora ventured. Perhaps Zinaw got on more than her nerves.

"Ah, no, not at all! The Redanorian-Kindarian company was quite enjoyable, it's—"

"I'm sorry, hold on," Alanitora interjected, raising her hand. "Kindar?"

Gwendolyn blinked in surprise "Oh! Did you not know? Zinaw is from

Kindar."

"Interesting, I hadn't realized we had a representative of yet another kingdom traveling with us." If such was true, it at least made sense why the girl had such an affinity for wolves, as Kindar was, quite amusingly, the kingdom of wolves. She could ponder over the parallels of such later, though. "What were you saying?"

Her face became distressed once again. "It's just... I worry about our friend sometimes." Alanitora cocked her head to the side, prompting Gwendolyn to elaborate. "Well, yesterday during the attack, she was quite frantic about the ordeal. More so than usual. I don't want to claim myself as important, but I believe I may have an impact on maintaining her composure sometimes. I did want to check with you first though— I'm sure you are enjoying your company so if you don't wish to..."

"No, it's quite fine. It would be better to be sure Korena is alright. I'm sure there is not much I could do for her in the event of her unease."

A bit of curiosity rose to Gwendolyn's eyes at this moment. She looked at Alanitora as if there was something she didn't quite understand.

"What is it?" Alanitora asked.

"Nothing—" Gwendolyn shook her head. "Your concern for her..." It seemed her lady was about to say it was unexpected but changed her mind. "I'm grateful for it. Thank you. But if you do feel you need one of us, feel free to summon us at any time."

Alanitora gave a light laugh. "I'm sure I'll be able to manage. I will have Silver Moon with me after all."

Gwendolyn nodded, her smile having reached her eyes. "Have a wonderful day, Tora."

Strange. It was often only Korena who called her Tora, and most of the time it was not directed towards her, but rather in reference to her. Alanitora's eyes lingered on the girl as she walked off in the direction of Tathra to explain the situation.

She continued to stare at them with curiosity. Upon reaching the Redanorian princess, Gwendolyn clasped her hand around Tathra's in the caring manner she often did with her and Korena. Alanitora smiled.

255

It seemed Gwendolyn had made a friend in Tathra—more so than her at least. Tathra looked at her lady-in-waiting with the same regard, her eyes scanning Gwendolyn in a sort of bashful joy. The look between the two was one of a friendship that would last forever.

Not wishing to envy herself by continuing to watch, Alanitora decided to grab her things and head to the new carriage toward the back.

On her way, she noticed Zinaw to the side with a bucket of water, sitting down in the grass next to the two wolves and massaging their thick, damp coat. There was a pile of white berries next to her, which she took in between her fingers every once in a while to squish and lather on one of the canines. Silver Moon looked quite content with what Alanitora believed to be the bath he was getting.

Furthermore, Zinaw seemed merry as well, much more so than her normal pessimistic demeanor. She was cooing at the two with a wide smile, which Alanitora found looked much more appealing on her than the usual scowl.

After watching for a short while, Alanitora decided to step in. It was her wolf after all. "What are you doing?" she asked in a curious, hopefully unthreatening tone.

That didn't matter. As Zinaw looked over to her, her smile dropped slightly and her usual tone of voice came. "Giving them a wash. They had quite a bit of blood on them from yesterday, and Silver Moon's fur is tremendously matted. It's as though you have never bathed him. Not that I'm surprised. You don't seem to have much ability in animal care."

The comment was intended to insult Alanitora, but she was aware what taking offense would do. "Correct. What are those?" She nodded to the white berries.

Zinaw seemed a little peeved that she had brushed over the subject, but answered her anyway. "They're snowberries. Native to this area. They help with dirt and grime."

Alanitora nodded, picking one up between her fingers as she kneeled to give Silver Moon a scratch behind the ears. "Do you have an interest in botany?"

"No. I have an interest in habitats. Completely different, not that you'd know."

"The environment in which certain creatures inhabit along with the plants and animals prone to that climate and location." Zinaw raised her eyebrows at the princess, a sliver of intrigue behind her irises. "A majority of the kingdoms' borders rely on said habitats."

"So you have an education after all."

Alanitora could feel herself doing something she didn't often, especially not in this kind of instance. Nevertheless, Zinaw's persistent confrontational attitude had brought it out, and she was okay with exploring it.

She was taking a passive route in the conversation. She never backed down from a challenge, but this time she strayed from proving authority. It was a new feeling, and it didn't feel like she was herself. But if it meant keeping animosity at bay between her and Zinaw, so be it.

Zinaw seemed like the kind of person who put up defensive and standoffish walls to protect herself from scrutiny, instead scrutinizing others to hide her insecurities. Sure, it got on Alanitora's nerves, and it would be ever so satisfying to put her in her place, but the most effective way to break those walls was to hold such a passive position that Zinaw would have to take them down. Her rising annoyance in the process was an added benefit.

She shrugged. "Just common knowledge, as all should have."

"I can tell you are faking modesty. Being modest isn't going to get you far at all." Zinaw growled.

"As opposed to what?"

"As opposed to the fact that I *know* my worth. And I own up to it. You say you know the common knowledge of kingdoms, whereas I know each and every member of royalty in all of Mordenla."

"And do you think that you are better than others?"

"No. It's not what I think, it's what I know."

"She's just saying that because she's upset about being born out of wedlock."

Alanitora turned to see Tathra, who had a teasing smile on her face. She looked between the cousins. Zinaw seemed annoyed but more amused than upset. "You're—"

"A bastard child? Yes. And Tathra, lovely of you to join us."

Tathra threw back her head in laughter. At least the two of them had a playful attitude with one another. "Believe it or not, dear cousin, I didn't come here to embarrass you. Rather, it was to tell you all it's time for us to depart. The Trenvern commander just told me so."

"Ah. In that case—" Zinaw patted her thighs as she stood. "Let's go, loves."

Bechorath stood immediately, following so close to her owner that it was a surprise that she didn't trip on Zinaw's ankles. Silver Moon, in the meantime, had the sporadic nature of shaking the water from his fur before bounding towards the carriage.

Tathra groaned. "You're making us ride with wet dogs?!"

"Consider it the price of your intrusion… Besides, I let you keep your friends with us."

"Hey! I thought you liked Lady Gwendolyn." Tathra held the door open, offering for Alanitora to go in first, who obliged.

"Yeah, I did until you two started talking my ears off."

Gwendolyn? Talkative? Alanitora watched as Zinaw seated herself in the carriage. Were any of this girl's observations of others accurate?

Tathra climbed in to sit next to Alanitora, as the other spot was quickly taken by Zinaw's wolf, leaving Silver Moon to rest upon the floor. Alanitora assumed this was the exact arrangement as when Gwendolyn was with them.

Once everything was secure, the procession began to move forward, slowly at first but speeding into a steady pace after a little while. Alanitora was the first to speak up. It was unusual for her, as she usually enjoyed the silence, but this time her curiosities were more pressing. "I know Kindar and Redanor have close relations but are the two of you actually cousins?"

The subject still seemed to spark a bitter chord for Zinaw. She averted her eyes, leaving Tathra to answer. "My mother was a princess of Kindar before she married into Redanor royalty. Her older brother, King Ulmar, is Zinaw's father through his mistress."

"It should be noted though," Zinaw began, raising a finger in the air, "That Kindar and Redanor royals always take spouses from the opposing kingdom. I am the only child of our generation to break this cycle. That makes me purely Kindarian. Which also explains my intelligence."

"Wait," Alanitora cut in. "Does each side only come from royal bloodline? Because if that's the case then—"

"Oh goodness no." Tathra looked appalled by even the idea of what the princess was suggesting. "Most of the time the exchanged spouses are nobles rather than the royal family. My parents were the first in many generations to have royal blood on both sides."

Zinaw added on. "Which is a good thing, since having two parents of close enough relation will cause the child to be… unfortunate."

"Yes, I've heard of such. Supposedly the child is cursed with several afflictions."

"It has nothing to do with a curse," the half-princess argued. "There is a much more scientific explanation as to how familial contraception changes the bodily performance of a child."

"And do you hold proof of such an explanation?" Alanitora ventured.

"Not as of yet… Nevertheless, it's good Tathra and her siblings weren't victims of this, as deformities are frowned not only on royals of Redanor but on all of Mordenla, really. It would create political disaster to put a dynasty in the hands of someone so unhealthy. Never mind the social scrutiny of it all."

Alanitora hummed in acknowledgment, changing the subject away from something she knew so little about. "Siblings?"

"Yes, I have seven." Tathra chuckled when Alanitora blinked in shock. "Of course, that doesn't count stillborns and possible bastards. I'm the fourth. Zinaw has two older siblings, you?"

"None. Just me."

"Damn," Zinaw spat. Alanitora turned to her in question. "I was hoping you might have a brother to marry. Turns out you're even more useless to me than originally anticipated."

Alanitora scoffed a small laugh. This girl was self-absorbed and relentless,

259

wasn't she? "I presume it's not because of my appearance that you wish that."

"No." Zinaw rolled her eyes. "I'm not a girl who likes girls, unlike some people."

"What she means to say," Tathra intervened, "is that she would like to climb the ladder of power. She's quite jealous that her brothers have an advantage of status."

"I am not jealous. I simply know that those dimwits would be much worse at ruling anything than me. I'd like to show them that someday. Though a nice looking heir to marry *is* preferred.

"So that's why you were at Kreaha?" Alanitora nodded. It made sense why Zinaw had been so rude to her in the hallway, but never showed any actual romantic interest in Regenfrithu. If his distraction to Alanitora hadn't stopped him from dancing with Zinaw, she might be living out her fantasies. *Might*, of course, being a keyword in the statement.

Zinaw raised her eyebrows, tilting her head in approval of Alanitora's statement. "You wouldn't be willing to let me marry your betrothed would you?" The first hospitable grin Alanitora saw on the half-princess' face appeared then.

She smiled back, settling for the playful tone. "Not if I would like my home kingdom to survive, no."

"Damn."

As their journey continued, the conversations became less forced, tensions dissipating between Zinaw and Alanitora. The both of them were used to holding up walls for the sake of surviving, but time broke them down.

Alanitora found herself learning a great deal not only about the two girls, but also the traditions of Redanor and Kindar, which she found increasingly ironic that their national animals had such opposing meanings. Redanor being a hare to Kindar's wolf.

It became apparent that the kingdom domesticated and bred the canines to help them hunt. Zinaw, who didn't go into royal studies like her elder brothers, spent a majority of her childhood thriving to cultivate this knowledge. She picked up the training of wolves from the kingdom menagerie, and when she wasn't befriending and training dogs, she was busy reading in the library.

Alanitora could relate to this pursuit of knowledge, as she did the same with her combat. When she brought this up, the conversation merely shifted to the discussion of weapons, where all three of them had a fair amount of experience.

Zinaw proclaimed herself a master of the staff, one that Alanitora had limited use with. They debated whether or not it was the best handheld weapon, which concluded with an agreement that the stock of a person changed which one was best used.

From there, things flowed naturally. Something about the discussion of weapons clicked the three of them into a comfortable space. So comfortable that even the wolves were wagging their tails and pushing their heads into palms for pets.

Alanitora smiled. The nature of a blooming friendship, the simplicity of what bonded them. All felt well in that little carriage, for while she had not known Zinaw in a benevolent light, they were no longer strangers.

20

Crossroads

O wen awoke on the forest floor. His eyes scanned the trees to the side of him before the reality of his situation returned to his mind. Alanitora. The carriage incident. Queen Elena.

The soldier rushed to his feet, his head swiveling around the campsite. Smoke was still rising from a recently extinguished campfire, across from it lay a collection of disheveled sheets. So he hadn't dreamed her presence. Then... where was she now?

"Queen Elena?" Owen called out, waiting for a response. When none came, he walked around the campsite, repeating the call over and over. No response came.

Perhaps she was a figment of his imagination, perhaps she abandoned him... or perhaps she was taken by the threat she'd so thoroughly described to him the previous night. His heartbeat began to pump faster, and he ran towards the road, looking left and right for the woman. He yelled out her name across the bare landscape and was ready to run down the path when a harsh shushing noise sounded behind him.

He turned to see Elena, in her cloak, hands on her hips reminiscent of a mother ready to scold her child. The mother she once was.

"Do you have any idea how to keep quiet?!" she whisper-shouted.

"Where were you? Gave me half a fright, I thought—"

"Must I remind you I am more capable than you've been led to believe? I was getting a means of transportation. Now go back to camp and pack up your things. It's time we go. It's bad enough that you're so loud to grab the attention of everyone within a league's radius."

Owen complied to her orders. He could protest against Alanitora, but Elena was not the person to cross if he wished to travel with her. If anything, Alanitora's abandonment of him gave further evidence why he shouldn't stand against the very woman that raised her.

He followed the path back to the campsite, where he collected his things in a hurry. He took the opportunity to put together Elena's things as well before she emerged from the woods, leading a horse behind her.

"Come now." She ushered him towards the steed.

"Where did you— Did you steal this?" Owen was aghast that Queen Elena would do such, and from *who* was another question.

"Whether or not I stole the horse should not be your concern, rather, getting to the capital of Kreaha should be. Let's go."

He mounted the horse, which seemed to protest at first to not only a new rider but to one with limited experience. After all, he only ever rode during training and when otherwise necessary. Owen hated it regardless. It didn't matter how long or how short he rode a horse, they never listened to his commands and his legs were sore the next morning.

When Elena noticed the defiance from the steed, she ordered him off and got on herself to hold the reins. Owen held on from the back of the saddle, accepting of this alternative. Queen Elena was smaller than Alanitora was—apart from her superior pride perhaps—making it relatively easy for Owen to see over her head at the road beyond.

Owen wondered whether or not it would be faster to walk than let the horse carry two grown people, but alas he moved forward without hesitation under Elena's control and began to trot at a steady pace.

Silence surrounded the two of them as they began their journey. It was considerably hot out, the hottest it had been since summer began to near its end. Beads of sweat dripped from Owen's scalp every few minutes, and the proximity to two other warmblooded beings wasn't helping.

Elena seemed fine with the heat. She had wrapped a nice scarf—though not as nice as silk or satin—around her neck and head. It looked like it might make one more heated, but Owen believed the lightness of the fabric helped shield the former queen from the sun. Curious and unable to resist the nipping annoyance of silence, Owen asked her about it.

Elena confirmed his suspicions but told him that it was further a preventative measure to conceal her identity from anyone who might know it. "I may have stayed within the castle walls for much time in the years, but word of my appearance has been discussed, as most royal affairs are. There is no telling what people who have seen me before might remember about my features. I find that facial structure, the bones beneath your cheeks and chin, hold most of your identity.

"My cloak is usually more comfortable for nighttime and for concealing myself, yet I am not asked to look into others' eyes as much as when I wear this. Though I do suppose…" She gestured for Owen to hold the reins as she looked through her bag, pulling out another scarf, this one slightly more sheer and crumpled than her own. She threw it over her shoulder before gripping the reins again. "It'll help with the heat, and help your unruly bright hair from attracting unwanted attention."

Owen felt at the mop his hair had become in the past few days. Unruly was a probable word to describe it. He wrapped the scarf around his head similar to the way an infirmary would a soldier who got kicked in the jaw. Without a mirror to check his appearance, Owen assumed he looked like an old beggar lady. The kind he would always see with a scowl on her face.

As the day went on, he found that the covering helped a lot with his heat issue. The sun no longer shone directly on his scalp, and instead what passed through was a slight breeze every once in a while, which cooled the moisture permeating beneath the cloth. It also helped shadow his forehead, and if he looked down, his eyes as well.

But the rest of him was not as fortunate. Ditching all other upper body clothing but his tunic due to the heat had the consequence of exposing his skin. In comparison to his mother and sister, Owen's skin was tan, but he still adopted the family tendency to burn easily. Red planted across his forearms and upper chest, marks of white holding whenever he pressed a finger to it.

After a few hours of straight riding, which marked a little more than a third of their way, a bridge came into view, signifying the location of freshwater. Owen had passed this same area the day before and was quite familiar with the clear coolness of the water. Elena seemed to have the same thought as him as she pulled the reins back upon reaching the bridge, dismounting the horse, and leading it down to the river.

Owen gulped down the rest of his canister and went down to the shore as well, filling it up as he removed his scarf to splash water on his face. It felt pleasant and cool, a needed relief.

They spent around fifteen minutes there, taking a break in the shade of the dappled sun as the steed rested its legs. The beast wasn't too tired, but Elena, who Owen realized had an affinity for horses, insisted they give him a break.

It was warming to see the woman he had considered his second mother for much of his early years caring for something again. She had such a stern face whenever she talked to him, but with the horse, she was calm. Her features were not tight, the wrinkles that sat at the edges of her eyes softened.

When she acknowledged his attention to her, a jolt of habit made Owen look away, expecting a berating similar to what her daughter would give him, but the queen simply nodded and continued what she was doing.

During this time, Owen also took the chance to eat. He hadn't yet, not since the day before. And his satchel of rations given from his old entourage was still relatively full. Had he not turned around and instead continued his travel towards home, they would have lasted him nearly the entire trip if he ate one or two meals a day, and until Hearthshire if he filled his belly.

But now he was traveling with someone else, who had no rations herself, and Owen feared any overindulgence wouldn't last them. Elena refused to eat with him, for she knew this as well, and was waiting until they were in Kreaha to eat and properly rest. For her stature, she had plenty of energy. Owen admired that.

Between the two of them, they also had little money. Owen hadn't thought to bring his money from home in the hurry from the attack, and any other belongings he might have had were still among the wagons in Alanitora's possession. Fortunately, Elena had a small amount for if they needed it, though her inclinations seemed more frugal than Owen would have wished.

They started up again, the horse's stamina having heavily improved since the start of their break. Elena explained that based on the rate they were traveling, keeping in mind the tiring of their horse, it was likely they would reach the capital of Kreaha just before sunset.

This thought kept Owen's hopes up. In just more than five hours, all of this would be over.

Though the sun shone directly in their faces that afternoon, the air had cooled significantly, allowing smooth travels. Neither the former soldier nor the former queen spoke much, perhaps the occasional verbal thoughts about the scenery, or comments to their beast.

Traveling on the main road proved to have both advantages and disadvantages. The limit to rocky terrain allowed for them to ride more smoothly, but every once in a while they would come across a traveler going the opposite direction. Elena would tilt her head down at these instances in paranoia, while Owen made sure to scan their movements just in case.

Just after the rest at the next third of their travels, Owen noticed the fork in the road from which Alanitora's carriage had split from the rest of the train. He looked across the distance.

He was still not sure what happened that day but had they not traveled that road, Owen would still be with her. Be there to protect her from the secret that was bound to come out soon enough. The secret that Elena held with a heavy heart. But perhaps this was better, being in the know. It allowed him to come up with scenarios of how such a secret might be shared, and how one might deal with it. This way he could be prepared to stand by Alanitora no matter the outcome.

The sun leveled with Owen's eyes, signifying the last quarter of daylight and the nearing of their destination. Owen was exhausted. His legs felt feeble from holding onto the sides of the horse, and the rocking of its trot was lulling him to sleep. He fought such persuasions, his energy drained to a consistent state of relaxed awareness.

A sudden jab of Elena's elbow into his torso snapped him awake.

"Bring your scarf up above your nose and wrap it tighter. Be sure your hair is not showing." She ordered, turning her head slightly.

He complied, unsure of the reason. He couldn't see too well ahead, but he knew they were approaching another stretch of forest. He tried to peer past the rays of cold sunlight, but Elena's sharp voice drew his attention once again.

"Keep your head down. Stay on the horse and no matter what happens. Do not speak or change your position, understood?"

She was asking him to trust her. "Understood," he whispered, hoping to keep his rising heartbeat down.

Elena turned and grasped at the handle of his sword. No. That couldn't mean anything good. Whatever was about to happen, Owen didn't know, but his hands jittered at the thought of it.

But instead of withdrawing the sword, the queen pulled out her cloak, wrapping it around the hilt before turning her posture forward and relaxing her shoulders.

After a few more moments, Owen kept his eyes down despite what his instincts were telling him to do. Elena pulled the reins lightly and dismounted the horse, swinging the ropes over to lead the steed instead.

"Good evening," Elena began. Her voice was rid of its usual formality.

Out the corner of his eye, he could see a figure was approaching, but he paid no mind.

Until she spoke.

"Good evening," replied a voice so recognizable that Owen nearly jolted from his position. Just those two words gave away who it was.

It was Diane. It was his sister.

Everything in him urged to look up at her, to hug her, to hold her and tell her what they were getting into.

Behind her back, Elena closed her fist tightly.

Stay.

He did.

The horse came to a stop. "If I might ask," Elena said casually. "My son and I fear we might be incorrect about our whereabouts. Do you know if the Capital of Kreaha lies ahead of this road?" He wondered if she was not aware of the relationship, or if she was just that good at keeping herself collected.

His head unmoving, Owen's eyes raised slightly, just enough to see through the sheer fabric at his sister.

Diane's head nodded, bright curls moving with it. Her hair looked much more managed than the last time he had seen her. So Kreaha had treated her well. His heart ached too much to smile at the thought.

"Yes, it does." Diane's usual sassy tone was exempt from her voice. Only respect and an indication of curiosity stayed.

"Oh, wonderful. We were hoping so. You see, we wanted to attend the festivities, but there were some complications on the farm. I do hope they are still going on..."

Owen understood what the queen was doing now. He had been confused why Elena spoke to his sister if she didn't want her to recognize him, but it seemed Elena was putting her trust and faith in the girl without Diane knowing it. Of course, she knew she would be a reliable source based upon her closeness to their mother.

Nevertheless, the question of how his sister did not recognize the queen of their own kingdom confounded him. He would have thought his sister would have a better memory. Then again, the amiable and humble act that Elena was putting on would deter him from recognizing it was her, too.

"They are. I believe it'll continue for the next day or so. I can't be too sure, though."

"Hmm? Were you in attendance for them?"

"In a way, yes. I was more... associated with a group of attendees."

Owen straightened his shoulders. Had Alanitora ordered her abandonment as well? What separated her from them? Had something bad happened?

Elena turned, connecting her eyes with his and nodding slightly, another warning to stay put, before turning back to ask Diane as if she heard his thoughts as well. "If I may ask—forgive me for my intrusiveness—but did something go awry? I can't help but notice you have a sullen face."

Diane tilted her head, visually confused as to how Elena would see such. "My party and I had a... disagreement surrounding the well-being of another member."

So she must have gotten into an argument with Alanitora about him... It was comforting, the confirmation that his sister cared.

"Ah, that sounds awfully unfortunate, my dear. What is it you plan to do now?"

"Why do you ask?" The edge of suspicion sent swirls in his stomach.

But Elena simply gave a light, caring laugh. "Forgive me for my motherly instinct. I'm simply worried for your safety, being on your own and all. Traveling alone can be dangerous for a young woman such as you or I... not that I'm very young."

The giggle from Diane suggested Elena had winked at that last part. "That is very kind of you," she began. "I plan on reconnecting with my family. I think it's best to make sure they are alright."

"A good plan indeed," Elena hummed before her voice became smaller, detached. "Family is important." She shook off the distraught tone. "Well then. Felix, do you mind dismounting for me?"

Owen froze. Was she talking to him? He could understand the use of a different name, but she had said not to move no matter what. He watched as she turned, the smile fading from her lips as she nodded an approval at him.

He swallowed, unsure what was to happen. He dismounted on the side opposite of Diane. The soldier fidgeted with his fingers as Elena reached up to the saddle, readjusting it and taking the small sack that hung on the side off and swinging it over her shoulder before turning back to Diane, a warm smile returning.

From behind the horse, Owen peered cautiously at his sister, thankful that she held no interest in him. On her shoulder was a satchel bigger than his. Alanitora had given her rations as well. Such was a relief. It meant that she and the princess had parted without animosity. Even so, he couldn't help but worry that it still might not have been enough for her to make it to Trenvern.

"Here." Queen Elena held out the reins to the girl, whose face showed a degree of surprise at the offering. "He's a fine steed, good temperament, and easily controllable."

Right. Easily controllable for the queen, maybe.

"I-I couldn't take such from you. It's too—"

Elena shook her head. "I insist. I do not know where you are headed, but the more prepared you are for the journey the better. Besides, us ladies must look out for one another." Her tone suggested the accompaniment of another wink.

"Thank you very much! I-I have some coins in my bag that I can give you, it's not much but—"

"No need."

Diane hesitated for a few more moments before taking the reins with a bright smile. She pressed her hand to the side of the horse to greet him.

Owen moved out of the way, reaching into his bag for an extra few rations. He and Elena would be in Kreaha soon where they could buy their own food and furthermore join Alanitora's group. They wouldn't go hungry. Diane might.

But before he could step forward, Elena placed a firm hand on his arm, gripping him in a way that told him a stern no. He made eye contact with her, a frown settling on his brow.

After a few moments, Elena sighed, taking the rations from him and handing them to Diane with a, "Just in case."

Diane clasped the woman's hands in appreciation as Owen watched cautiously from the side. The lower half of the queen's face may not have been revealed, but the longer his sister stared, a slow look of recognition began to rise.

Elena noticed this as well, giving the girl a brief farewell before leading Owen away from her and towards their destination.

Owen stayed quiet for as long as he could while they increased the distance between him and his sister. However, as soon as they were far enough away that she couldn't hear them unless he screamed, Owen tore the covering off his face. "What was that?!"

"I decided it would be nice to help a fellow traveler." Her voice was composed and proper once again.

"You know damn well that's not what I mean," he spat. "That was my sister!"

"I am aware, Owen."

"Traveling alone!"

"I am aware, Owen."

"Then why wouldn't you let me talk to her?!"

Elena turned, looking up at him with the same sharpness that her daughter held in her eyes when she was angry. "You need to calm down."

Owen's frown deepened. "Calm down? Calm down?! She left to look for me! And she'll be damn lost when I don't show up along that road!"

"Then she'll go straight home, hoping to instead meet you there and be reunited with your parents."

Owen was unsure how she could possibly justify keeping him from his sister. "You know more than anyone that Trenvern is the most dangerous place to be right now, you said so yourself. How could you possibly think it's okay to just let her go there? She's a child!"

"And a capable one at that." Her composure was cracking. "What? Would you rather expose yourself and motivate her to travel with us, knowing what is to come from the path we are heading towards?"

"Yes."

"No. No, you don't. You need to realize that your lack of knowledge of the situation clouds your judgment."

"Then tell me the whole situation. I'm getting really tired of your elusiveness," Owen snapped.

"It is not for you to decide what information you know and do not know. Just because I trust you to travel with me, does not mean I trust your judgment. Having the full story would only fuel your unpredictable range of emotions. I cannot have that. I cannot risk it."

Owen released a huff of breath. He wouldn't admit that she was right, not yet, but he would at least acknowledge her point, to prove her otherwise, if not that he believed it.

With the conversation's end, the two began to walk again, which was surprisingly quite a relief after being on a horse all day.

"How come she didn't recognize you?" he asked after his anger had simmered down.

Elena gave a coy smile. "There is a reason I had your mother never bring Diane around the castle when she was born."

"And that is?" Owen pressed, quite exhausted of the continuous secrets.

"Everyone has their role to play, you'll learn hers someday." While this answer frustrated him, he was tired of trying to fight Elena. She looked down at the road momentarily, something clearly on her mind. "She'll be okay, Owen. I can tell you that."

He wrapped the scarf back around his neck. "I know."

The orange of the setting sun peeked its way through the conifer trees when the path to the palace became clear. They did not waver, picking up their pace as they walked through the path of greenery. A groundskeeper stood at the top of a ladder, bringing fire into one of the lanterns a few paces from the closed gates.

Upon seeing the guard, Elena stopped, motioning for Owen to go forward. He did such, clearing his throat to grab the man's attention. "Excuse me, good sir, I was wondering if you might allow my mother and me entry?"

The guard looked towards the former queen, then back to Owen. "I'm sorry sir, I cannot allow you entry."

He bit his lip, looking back at Elena nervously. When she didn't yield, he took a deep breath. "Please, it's very important."

"I do apologize, but there are no exceptions. For the safety of Kreaha, no one is allowed in after seven."

Owen examined the guard for a few seconds. He was genuinely apologetic about not being able to let them in, but he also seemed the type to follow rules above personal feelings. It would be no use. His heart dropped. "Thank— uh, thank you. Have a good night."

Turning on his heel, the boy made his way back to Elena, meeting her grim expression with an apologetic shake of his head.

She inhaled deeply, a dark gleam among the shadows of her face. "So they close at seven. It's nearly half-past."

"You mean—?"

She nodded. "Had we not given our horse to your sister, we would have made it."

Owen cursed, the sinking feeling of disappointment surrounding his chest, suffocating him.

Elena sighed. "We'll set up camp outside the gates, take turns sleeping. If anyone leaves Kreaha, we'll know." She looked up at him, and though he could see that she was just as distraught, Elena kept a brave face. She placed a hand on his shoulder. "Don't worry. We'll get to her as soon as the sun rises. I promise."

He relaxed his shoulders in defeat, nodding solemnly.

Not all promises could be kept.

21

Honor Among Thieves

Morning light had not even touched the edges of the sky when Alanitora and her companions were awoken for their next stretch of travel. Fourteen hours of straight riding had not left a majority of the entourage in good shape, and even though they stopped for a portion of the night, the princess doubted many got the necessary sleep.

Alanitora too was exhausted, but she wasn't going to complain. They did, after all, have a genuine reason for the rush, and Sir Corwyn had explained that this would be the last stretch before the Kreahan-Donaselan border.

Gwendolyn approached her as they waited in the cold on the side of the road, asking if she, Korena, and Alanitora could ride together. Alanitora gladly acquiesced.

Unfortunately, that meant there was only room for one more passenger in each carriage, and Meli was adamant that they not be separated from Lorenalia. She knew the wolves would also not wish to be separated, and Zinaw had an attachment both to them and her cousin, leaving a predicament that was too complicated to figure out two hours before dawn.

Alanitora was about to deny Gwendolyn's request when Sagittarius came barreling into their conversation, shoving the reins of her horse into Meli's hands accompanied by a comment about them "getting to play lookout".

"I'll hitch a ride with Dagger Eyes," she said with a jeering smile.

Too tired to argue, Alanitora agreed to this. Though not without showing a small expression of annoyance on her face.

That was how the four of them came to be: sitting in silence at an ungodly hour of the morning, half-asleep, but not relaxed enough to drift away upon the bumpy road. As soon as they realized there was no going back to sleep, the question of whether or not the silence should continue was collectively raised.

After staring out the window for an hour, Sagittarius pulled out a small knife and began carving at the shafts of her arrows. Gwendolyn didn't seem to mind her presence, but Korena seemed awfully curious and uncomfortable at the same time. Alanitora noticed that she was biting her tongue.

The archer noticed this as well. "You all are welcome to continue your usual conversations as if I'm not here, you realize that, right? I honestly don't care about whatever you care about." Gwendolyn chuckled in response to this, shaking her head lightly as she averted her eyes to the window. Sagittarius made a face back at her. "Unless all you talk about is politics. I could understand why you might not want me to hear about that… Then again, I'm not sure there is a point in hiding it, considering your princess employed me to keep you safe. I'd say that's pretty political."

"You did?" Korena's head raised in question.

Alanitora nodded. "I need people I can trust."

"What about the guards? Isn't that the reason we have them?"

"Korena, you know very well that the guards are the last people we can trust, especially if we don't know them." The princess looked between her ladies and the archer. While she had just made it clear that they could talk about whatever they wanted, the three of them *were* talking about her as though she wasn't there. She didn't seem to mind, oddly enough.

"Don't know them? You have no idea who Sagittarius is either!" Korena's eyes flicked over to the subject of their discussion. "…No offense."

Sagittarius kicked her legs out, leaning back with an amused smile on her face. "None taken."

"Listen, Sagittarius is nowhere near the situation at hand. Every other attack traces back to some degree of inside knowledge, particularly if we consider Devante's role. Her distance from such a position makes her trustworthy. And I can tell she's not ill-intentioned."

Sagittarius gasped. "I'm flattered!"

Alanitora ignored her.

"But that's why you should have kept Owen! He's a good man and a warrior at that."

Alanitora's gaze flicked up to her lady, her eyes darkening. Korena had taken it too far. Even if she hadn't told her ladies why Owen was released, they should have known better than to bring it up. Especially with someone else in the carriage.

She took a moment to compose herself, banishing the sensitivity around Owen's name. When she spoke, it was quiet but distinct, "That has nothing to do with this, and even if it did, it's all the more reason why we need someone not related to Trenvern."

"Oh, there's gotta be some drama behind that. Care to share?" Sagittarius leaned forward expectantly. The three of them stared back at her. She raised her hands in defense. "Hey, you don't have to tell me, I'm just saying it would be a lot easier to help you if I knew what was going on."

"And it would be a lot easier to trust you if we knew anything about you. While I trust Alanitora's judgment, I still wish to form my own opinions," Gwendolyn retorted.

Sagittarius quirked an eyebrow. "Like you did with Miss Tathra?"

Gwendolyn's mouth gaped open. She gawked for a long moment before looking away to fiddle with her fingers. Alanitora looked between the two of them, not quite sure what was being suggested. She didn't have time to question it.

"Okay okay, I get it. I need to develop a filter..." The archer looked around at the hostility in the carriage. "Tell ya what. How about I let you all ask me some questions. I'll answer honestly as long as I don't think them to be too invasive. That way we can all be the best of friends and skip around in circles." Despite her sarcasm, Alanitora could tell this was a genuine offer.

The four of them sat in silence, unsure where to start before Korena took the initiative. "So do you... kill people?"

"I'm sorry?" Sagittarius asked, turning to the blonde who had deliberately placed herself on the opposite side of the carriage.

"Do you kill people? You seem to be morally confused in other aspects so I'm just wondering—"

She laughed out loud, with such joy in her voice that it was clear Korena was amusing to her, if not stupid. "Doesn't your princess?"

The two looked to Alanitora, who raised her eyebrows and peered at Gwendolyn for possible help. The pacifist lady-in-waiting paid no mind, simply continuing to embroider her latest handkerchief.

"I—" Alanitora paused. "I suppose when it is necessary, yes, I do."

"Well still, you kill people when it *isn't* necessary, right, Sagittarius? I mean, that's what you do when you steal, too."

"I find it interesting that you bring up the subject of my morals when I helped save you less than two days ago... To answer your question, I don't kill people unless necessary. I mortally wound them at most, but that's if they are genuinely bad people."

"And do you make that distinction?" Gwendolyn finally spoke, looking up. Her question wasn't necessarily out of curiosity, nor was it loaded like Korena's.

Sagittarius raised her eyebrows above her mask just enough that Alanitora could see that they were a dark brown. "Just because I am a criminal in your eyes, does not make me a bad person. I could in return ask you how you distinguish who should rule your kingdoms."

Korena seemed eager to give her reply. "Well, by being born into it of course, then married into it at most."

"Yes, but who decides if someone is correct to rule?"

It was quiet for a few moments, as none of the other women in the carriage held an answer.

"Well, that's what war is about, isn't it?" Alanitora asked. "The desire of one person to rule instead of another. Either by selfish means or if they think the other person is unfit."

Sagittarius flashed Alanitora an approving smile, one that she did not necessarily want or need from her.

"If you are wondering, I don't think anyone is superior to another," Sagittarius began. "Life or death, ruling or serving, I think we are all at heart, quite human, and that makes us flawed in many ways. The world is a nasty place. Some people see it that way and are saddened by it while others see it and use it to their advantage. If I am being honest, no one person should rule above anyone else. Instead, the representation of the essence a kingdom has should be what's in charge."

"So you support anarchy?" Gwendolyn asked.

"I support equal opportunity."

This sent the carriage into a long stupor of contemplation. As though they all agreed with the statement in theory, but ultimately were confounded with why they might have been against it.

Alanitora hummed an agreement, putting a natural end to the conversation before looking out the window. Sagittarius had a point, but without order, things were bound to corruption, weren't they? Not every monarch was perfect, but it at least offered some consistency.

Gwendolyn cleared her throat. "Okay, I'll pose a lighter question: Do you have any family? Any siblings?"

"I do." Sagittarius hesitated for a moment. "A younger sister, Aqua."

"Is she also named after a constellation, or is it because you live on the coast?" Gwendolyn questioned.

A look of consternation covered Sagittarius' features.

"There are certain plants you can only find south of here. One of which happens to be the wood you make your arrows out of. When you take into consideration the berries you use to dye the ends of your hair, it only makes sense."

"How the hell did you...?"

Gwendolyn shrugged. "I saw them inside of your pouch earlier."

"Clever girl." Sagittarius raised her eyebrows, genuinely impressed.

"Not necessarily. I just know a lot about plants."

"Well, you're right. And in more ways than one. As you first guessed, Aqua is named after a constellation, and yes, I am from a remote village in Mariane."

Korena tilted her head in wonder. "Wow, your parents must really like the stars."

Sagittarius snorted. "It's a little more than just them…"

Gwendolyn quickly moved on to asking Sagittarius her age, not wishing to let the archer's period of transparency be lost. When she explained she was nineteen, Gwendolyn excitedly responded that her older sister was the same age. The two divulged into a tangent discussing the matter of siblings, allowing Korena and Alanitora to move back from the conversation.

Her brunette lady-in-waiting was getting moderately more comfortable with every moment. It may not have been as relaxed as it would be with just her and Korena, but it was an improvement from her demeanor in the previous days.

No longer needing to stay attentive to the conversation, Alanitora looked around the carriage, her eyes laying on the drying rose hanging above her. Quite honestly, she had forgotten about it since she had hung it.

Reaching up, she grasped the stem between her fingers. It kept its complexion quite well, the colors barely fading with the wilt. It still smelled magnificent nevertheless.

"I see you made away with one of Kreaha's less pecuniary values." Sagittarius nodded at the rose.

"Yes, we talked about it the other day with Princess Lorenalia," Alanitora stated, not wanting to repeat the conversation about suitors.

"He must have *really* liked you to go so far as to give you that. I suppose thanks are in order, though. If it weren't for the prince's fascination with you, my heist likely wouldn't have been pulled off."

Alanitora frowned. "And what does that have to do with it?"

"Well, everyone was so captured by the image of you two dancing gleefully—" Alanitora rolled her eyes. Yeah, it wasn't *that* fantastical. "—no one paid attention to me until I sent an arrow at the prince. I sent three more before then, you know."

"You did?" This was news. Alanitora distinctly remembered hearing the faint sound of the bow being pulled, but only once.

"Yeah, of course, I really would have gotten away with it, but I wasn't expecting you to play the hero. I'm sure you and I gave quite the spectacle for the guests. I'd say we were the ladies of the night." That was a stretch. "I had half a mind to steal you from the prince as well."

"That's... a bit far," Gwendolyn intervened.

"Yeah, partially since she doesn't belong to Regenfrithu anyway. Alanitora has another." Oh goodness, somehow the conversation always had to swirl back around to her love life, didn't it?

"You consider a random prince she's betrothed to be this other?" The bandit chuckled.

Alanitora couldn't tell Korena to shut her mouth in time. "Owen, of course! Tora's childhood best friend."

"My my my..." Sagittarius raised her eyebrows. "You've got yourself in a little love triangle, don't you?"

"A love what?" The question slipped out of Alanitora's mouth before she could stop herself.

"Triangle. It means you have two suitors that you must choose between."

She frowned. "I'm not choosing between men in something as trivial as romance."

"Riiiight, because your third choice is a haughty Donaselan prince you've never met."

Alanitora shook her head "What is it with everyone and their constant interest in the affairs of my heart. Do none of you understand that is not what's important in life? Especially when it comes down to matters of life and death, like the situations we've faced this past week."

Repose collected in the carriage as the rest of them came to an understanding of why such might upset her. The princess sighed, hanging the rose back up. She had enough to think about, the idea of a romance between either Owen or Regenfrithu was of no prominence to her.

"But since we're on the topic..." Korena began. Alanitora braced herself, holding in the heavy sigh that was ready to escape her breath. "Do you

280

have a love in your life, Sagittarius?"

The archer smirked. "Not as of yet. I find that men are—"

"Well, I do! I'm surprised I'm the only one here who has a beau, considering we're all such lovely ladies. I've been trying to help Gwendolyn in the art but she's too shy. My William and I met a couple of years back, but he didn't start courting me until more recently. He's really such a gentleman, I wouldn't be surprised if he was granted lordship..."

Alanitora decided to let the girl talk. It made her happy, after all. Besides, letting her get the details of her love life out now prevented her from talking about it at a worse time.

"...Then he would be of the same class as I, which brings a bit of the romance out of it, but I think that's okay since my privileges won't be taken when we marry."

"Interesting," Sagittarius mused sarcastically.

"I know! He really is quite the handsome fellow, though. I like to think that our fates are intertwined. That he and I will be together until death."

"'Til death? That's an extreme way to put it—"

"Not really, quite a few kingdoms require it for consummation. What do you two think?"

Gwendolyn exchanged a look with Alanitora, who didn't feel too keen on answering. "I suppose it makes sense if you feel there is a strong love between two people."

Alanitora simply hummed. She'd never been in love and was doubtful that any of the others had, Korena too despite her protests. Luckily, this lack of answer sufficed in Korena's eyes and she continued her rambling, draining everyone else's energy in the process.

Gwendolyn at least looked at her with intrigue, nodding at certain points and asking follow-up questions. In opposition, Sagittarius looked like she was ready to throw herself out the carriage window.

The rest of their conversations that day remained mundane. Mainly consisting of exchange in gossip between Korena and Gwendolyn while Sagittarius closely examined each of her arrows, leaving a small pile of wood shavings on the seat. It befuddled Alanitora how exactly her ladies never ran out of things to talk about with one another, especially since they had been away from home for the past week and shared all the same experiences. She supposed this might just be a difference from her, as the princess rarely brought up subjects with others, and only went with where the conversation already was.

It was almost procedure how Korena brought up a subject, talked with Gwendolyn about it for a while before the other lady-in-waiting posed a more general question, prompting Alanitora to answer. Then, the three of them would cycle through. Though, Korena's occasional scattered nature must have made it taxing for Gwendolyn to keep up without another person to help her.

Alanitora was at that moment beginning to understand why the two relied on one another, and why there was such comfort in it. She hadn't realized before that the process of talking with them was relieving to her as well.

Perhaps the most confounding part though, was that it made her smile. Not from amusement or entertainment as usual, but as a warm reflection of belonging within her heart.

She let this reside in her for the rest of the day, stepping in and out of conversations comfortably to aid her own queries.

Sagittarius seemed quite bored by the end of the day but would put in her bit here and make a sardonic remark there.

It was late in the afternoon when they slowed their travels, coming to an eventual stop. After riding for so long, it felt a little weird to not be in motion. Corwyn soon knocked on their carriage door to let them know it was a good time to stretch if they needed to before they went through the border. He also told them that he'd be putting extra guards—including himself—near both carriages to ensure their safety. He asked that he accompany Alanitora if she headed anywhere for her safety. It seemed he was being extra cautious, considering the last time they went through a border.

She was glad to be in Sir Corwyn's presence, as he was much more honorable and genuine than many of the men she had previously come across. Alanitora took a mental note to thank him, and perhaps discuss his own upbringing once everything was settled. She didn't know if he would return to Trenvern or not, but it would certainly be in her favor if he stayed in Donasela… Though she wasn't sure if transfers were even allowed.

According to another guard, there were a few carriages and caravans in front of them, but it wouldn't be long before it was their turn.

After Alanitora and her ladies stretched their legs and got out their restless energy, they re-entered the carriage. To the princess' surprise, their fourth companion jumped at their arrival.

"Is everything alright, Sagittarius?" Gwendolyn asked. If the lady was concerned for the archer's wellbeing, it meant she had grown on her to some extent.

"I'm just— I forgot to ask where you all want me to meet you on the other side of the border."

"I'm sorry?" Alanitora asked.

Sagittarius cleared her throat. "I don't have any form of identification on me, there is no way they'll let me in."

"How do you think customs work?" Korena asked.

She frowned. "Whatever do you mean, will they not arrest me for my treason in Kreaha?"

"You say that as if you have a high price on your head."

"… I do."

"Oh," all three women said softly.

Alanitora shook her head. "That doesn't matter. You're fine where you are."

"But—"

"You are traveling with royalty, they'll have no need to question you, and if they try to arrest you, I can claim jurisdiction over you as a prisoner."

"Oh, thanks Dagger Eyes, that's real helpful."

"She's just telling the truth of it. Further, Lorenalia could always vouch for you, they will listen to her." Gwendolyn informed.

"And if she doesn't?"

This was the most anxious Alanitora had seen the cool-headed bandit in the short time of knowing her. "We'll make sure you get through."

The bandit narrowed her eyes for a moment, before mouthing a small "thank you".

Once they had all relaxed again, Korena piped up with questions quite similar to her first round. "Are you wanted for treason then?!"

"If you wanna put it that way, sure."

"How big is your bounty?"

"Depends. What's the maximum price I can say that will result in you *not* turning me in?"

"Well, I suppose—"

"It was rhetorical, buttercups."

"Butter....cups?"

The Kreahan-Donaselan border was vastly different from Trenvern's. Instead of a campsite in front of the border wall, there was a town that was split down the middle by a stone wall, while a larger wall, perhaps twice the size, lay behind it.

The road widened significantly at this point. All the houses faced it, their shop-fronts open to travelers. Stands were set up right at the edge of the border, where bakers and blacksmiths alike waved at the entourage as they rolled on by.

Having pushed back the curtains, Alanitora and Korena watched through the window as a few Trenvern soldiers stopped to buy food from the farm stand, or show their swords to a collection of young boys on the side.

Someone behind them sounded, "Your Highness!" To which Alanitora peered out her window to find that Princess Lorenalia was riding on her own horse and waving at the villagers. She wasn't sure if the princess was naive to the dangers of being out in the open, or if she did not have a threat upon her life in the same way Alanitora did.

Kreaha was always considered a stable kingdom after all, with a limited amount of assassination attempts in their history—to her knowledge at least.

What caught her off guard though, was Lorenalia's trot up next to their carriage, where the princess insisted that Alanitora also get on a horse and ride with her.

She declined, not out of bashfulness, but out of caution. Lorenalia may not be a target, but Alanitora didn't necessarily have a good experience with her last border passage.

"May I, Tora?!" Korena said, her voice high and giddy. It... certainly wasn't what Lorenalia meant, but Alanitora shrugged in agreement. Her lady-in-waiting seemed excited about the idea, and who knew, it might satisfy her need for attention, or at least tire her out.

Korena hopped out, running off in search of her own horse.

A near half-hour later, their carriage finally rolled in through the first wall where two large stone buildings—not unlike the one in Hearthshire—stood on either side of the wide road. They stopped in front of the one on the right, where Corwyn met them to open the door for the princess.

By this time, the two others in the carriage had already become bored or disinterested with their surroundings and returned to their independent tasks. It made Alanitora wish she had taken up embroidery, if only to pass the time.

She descended to the ground, pulling up her skirts, more heavy than normal.

A man around twice her age greeted her with an obeisance and a small pleasantry, introducing himself as Sir Jean Clarke, lord of regional relations between Kreaha and Donasela.

She responded tersely with her name and title, to which he laughed heartily.

"I am well aware, Your Highness. Why don't you join me inside?" He gestured to the door of the fort-like building. A pang of familiarity caused Alanitora to hesitate. Was she to say no and be considered rude? Or fall for the same attempt at foolery as Sir Devante once tried?

"If I may interrupt." Corwyn stepped forward between the two of them. "We'd prefer the princess remain in the protection of her own."

Alanitora froze, her eyes flickering to Corwyn. He knew? How did he know? There was no way he would know such specific details of what happened with Devante. She swallowed, keeping her composure. Surely Corwyn wasn't plotting against her...

She cleared her throat. "Yes, I find it much more comfortable."

"Alright then, we can speak in ear of the public." He paused, looking around before his eyes fell on a boy to the side of him. "Quinn. Fetch your horse, you may start the delivery of your message now."

The boy nodded, rushing towards the Donaselan side with his hands clasped behind his back.

"What is going on, if I might ask?" Alanitora questioned, careful to keep her expressions in check. She'd rather her first impression on people she'd soon be the queen be one of fortitude.

Jean Clarke smiled. "I presume you received your summons to our mother city while you resided in Kreaha."

"Yes, I did."

"My son, Quinn, is to let your betrothed know you have at least reached the border, so he can be sure when to expect you."

She frowned. "Is there concern about my arrival?" What reason would there be to check in about her whereabouts if not a threat of safety?

"Quite the contrary. It's so they may prepare for the parade."

"Parade?" Corwyn asked, echoing her thoughts.

"Why yes, it is good fortune to celebrate the arrival of new blood in Donasela."

"Oh." She nodded. It wasn't her expectation, but it was better than hearing of a plot for her murder. "And you asked me inside for what reason?"

"To read you the standard procedure of your entry to Donasela, and the matters of the parade, but I suppose Sir Corwyn here can read them to you in your own time. I'll put the papers with him. You may go back to the area of your comfort if you wish, Your Highness."

"Thank you." She looked to the man, then to Corwyn, before stepping back into her carriage, and watching the faces pass as they moved forward, heading through the second wall and past the border.

She was in a new land now. Land that was soon to also be her own.

22

The Prince & the Knight

Throughout the night, Elena and Owen slept in shifts, taking turns to watch over the gates. Owen wasn't sure whether he should be upset or grateful that the only people to pass through were merchant carts and solitary travelers. Regardless, as soon as the gates reopened, he woke Elena with haste.

"Alright. I'll stay here, you go in. Ask only the king or queen about her whereabouts. If you see anyone you know, be cautious. They could be against us."

He nodded solemnly. "And when I find her?"

"Approach her carefully. From what you told me she could be emotionally volatile right now. There's no telling what lies people have told her in our absence."

Owen grabbed his things, wrapping the scarf around his head once again before leaving the camp and approaching the gate. Relaxing his shoulders, he pushed down the tide of paranoia rising in his stomach.

The guard was different from the previous night and looked even more of a stickler for rules. "State your business."

"I wish to attend the festivities."

"Today is the last day of the autumn festival, all of the main events have passed."

Owen did not have the patience for this. But he'd have to unless he

287

wanted to come off as more suspicious than he already was. "I understand that. I'm here to—" he paused, searching the garden behind the guard for an excuse. "I'm here to help my family pack up their stand."

"Last name?" the guard asked. He might have been fishing to see if Owen was pulling this all from his hind, but surely he was not concerned with checking his credibility.

"Smith. We're—" he paused again, clearing his throat to keep his voice neutral. What had he seen most common among the merchants last night? "Jewelers."

"Kingdom of residence?"

"They're from Kreaha. I moved to Trenvern five years ago to make money in a different setting. My younger brother was sick, you see. The taxes in the west are low enough for me to work and send back enough for—"

"Alright, Alright, I don't need your life story, kid, find your family."

Owen nodded, suppressing the giddy smile that wanted to rise in triumph of his clever sob story—stolen partially from Gwendolyn, of course. He slipped past the gate, making his way through the groups of people that socialized in the light of the morning sun.

The gardens around him were green, much greener than those at the training fort during this time of year. The amount of water it must take to supply them for one day could likely last a family an entire month.

Owen weaved his way through a series of paths, eavesdropping on the conversations of nearby groups in hopes that they might provide him with needed information. The soldier had no idea where he might be able to find the king or queen, as asking anyone was sure to arouse suspicion as to his intentions.

Upon reaching the marketplace, he made a beeline for the booth that appeared to have several Kreahan souvenirs. Flags, little wooden ravens, and maps of the kingdom's territory lined the table. The man behind it smiled at him as he approached.

"Good morning sir." Owen clasped his hands behind his back. "I was wondering, did you happen to have any maps of the castle?"

"Why might you have an interest in such?" Luckily, the question was posed out of curiosity rather than suspicion.

It surprised him how quickly he was able to make up fibs, given he had no history of lying. "I'm an architect's apprentice. The palace is so wonderfully built. I can't go home without some sort of keepsake to show him."

The man shrugged, taking this as an acceptable answer. "I might have an old hand-drawn map from last season's garden exhibition, give me a second, young man…" He ducked down, rifling through a box to the side of the table, bringing up a rolled parchment. "It's not perfect for your needs, but it has a bird's eye view of the structure at least."

Owen thanked him and hurried on his way, unrolling the map. The man was right: it wasn't very helpful to him, but if the labeling of the gardens gave any indication, he might find the Royal Court somewhere in the building next to the 'Private Royal Gardens'.

His intuition proved correct when he came across a long line of people heading into the Throne Room. A quick questioning of the person in front of him revealed that it was customary on the last day of the festival for the king and queen to accept gifts from visitors.

He followed the slow-moving line inside, where a chamberlain was announcing each party and their gift. The collection at the front was glittering with all sorts of goods. Foods, blankets, jewelry, fine silks—a plethora of things he was sure Kreaha already had a surplus of. Well, that and a bird that chirped in its cage on the side. Though such probably wasn't the most surprising gift there.

When he got closer to the front, Owen stepped away from the line. He stood to the side, sure to be in view of the guards just in case. The gift-giving period lasted for a long while, so long that even Owen, who was trained to stand and observe for hours as a guard, was growing less patient.

The room emptied, growing quiet as soon as the doors shut behind the crowd.

"I hope you know that there are servants who can answer any questions you have, young man, otherwise you may have just been waiting for nothing. Additionally, there is a waitlist for kingdom complaints until after the festivities are done," the king addressed him before he even moved forward.

Having been called upon, Owen stepped to the middle of the room, bowing to the thrones. "Thank you, Your Majesty, but my concerns are purely to fulfill an important royal duty. It is beyond imperative that what we discuss is kept in this room."

The queen waved her hand forward. Two guards stepped up to Owen. Aware of their intentions, he separated his arms, allowing them to check for any weapons besides the sword on his waist. After they were finished, a majority of the guards turned to leave the room through the doors on either side of the thrones. As they did, a particularly well-dressed man emerged from the left, leaning against the wall.

The king noticed his presence but didn't seem to mind it, motioning for Owen to continue.

"I am a soldier of Trenvern. I have traveled here with news regarding the fate of my kingdom. It is most important that I share this with the princess of Trenvern."

The queen looked over to her husband before turning her attention back to Owen, worry on her brow. "I believe Her Highness Alanitora—"

"What's your name?" The man against the wall interrupted, pushing himself from the surface and towards Owen.

Whoever this was must have been important if he was allowed to interrupt. "Owen."

The man nodded, crossing his arms. "Mother, Father, I can take care of this."

"I do think this information should stay between the king, queen, and I," Owen protested.

The king shook his head. "No need, Regenfrithu's information will be more accurate. He tended to Alanitora and her entourage upon their arrival."

Regenfrithu raised his eyebrows, signaling at the door. Owen hesitated, unsure of if he should trust him. After a moment, the realization that he didn't have a choice struck, and the soldier cautiously followed suit.

"We assigned Alanitora to a room upstairs next to my own. We can talk there where things are more private."

At first, Owen was nervous that this might be someone with malicious intent, someone who could be the very threat he was told to avoid. However, upon further inspection, he saw that the supposed prince held much less muscle than himself. As long as there was no one else against him in a match, the odds were in his favor. He would just have to be extra cautious.

On the other hand, the prince's suggestion of secrecy could have been a hint that he was an ally of Alanitora. Though the idea of her confiding in someone besides her ladies seemed a little odd. Either way, he stayed silent, hoping Regenfrithu would lead him to the princess.

After climbing numerous steps and turning a few hallways, they made it to a long corridor adorned with wondrous jewels and opulence. Just the furniture looked like it could be sold in exchange for a lifetime of a soldier's wage. At the end of the hallway, Regenfrithu opened another door to reveal a continuation of it. Owen peered over the prince's shoulder to be sure he wasn't in a trap, only to see a small young woman standing in one of the side doors, her collar unbuttoned further than what might be considered acceptable.

One of the knights Owen trained under had told him to avoid women who appeared in front of an unknown man with provocative manners. If they weren't members of a brothel, they were girls with malicious and unholy intentions. Now, he was not one to shame a woman for her choices in either wage or leisure, but this girl... had an untrustworthy air to her.

"Oh, you brought a friend, Raven?" she said coyly.

He did not like this girl.

"About that, Mira." Regenfrithu looked between the two of them, clearing his throat. "I'm going to have to cancel on you today, some things have come up."

A scowl appeared on her face for a second before dissipating. "Very well." She curtsied and moved past Owen on her way out, touching the prince's arm lightly.

Owen fought back a disgusted expression.

He really didn't like this girl.

"Right this way." Regenfrithu motioned towards the room.

If this was the prince's room, that meant Alanitora's was in this very hallway. He swiveled his head around, hoping to find any sign of her.

There wasn't much time.

Owen shook his thoughts. Patience was important, even in urgent situations. He followed the prince into the room, relieved to find it empty of strangers but disheartened to see no familiar faces.

Regenfrithu shut the door behind him as Owen took a survey of the room. "You're close with Alanitora, yes?"

Owen paused. Was he? What happened after their kiss suggested he wasn't. Then again, there always was the fact that the kiss even happened. She *had* kissed him back. "Yes."

Regenfrithu gave out a huff of amusement, shaking his head as a tight smile formed on his lips. He stepped forward slightly, about to pace around the room, but instead froze for a second. Then, he raised his right fist and swung it towards Owen.

Owen's face shot with pain as the fist connected with his cheekbone. That was certainly going to bruise. He braced himself. If the prince continued to approach him with malcontent, Owen would have to fight back, but the consequence of that would hang him. He held his position, mind buzzing from the blow and thoughts of what was to come.

Fortunately, that seemed to be the only blow Regenfrithu planned to make, as he shook out his hand, walking toward the table beside him that held two chalices and a bottle of wine.

"So you're the reason for my loss," Regenfrithu grumbled as he poured himself the wine, then tipped the chalice to send the liquid down his throat like a crimson snake.

Owen swallowed, fearing to say the wrong thing. "I'm— I'm sorry?"

Regenfrithu slammed the cup down, giving him a repulsed look. "Don't play dumb with me, boy. You're the reason Alanitora rejected a prosperous life with me, and you know it."

"I—" What in the world was he talking about? Did this arrogant prince think he was competition for Alanitora's hand? If so, he must not know much. "I believe you may be mistaken, Your Highness."

"Your name is Owen, no? The same name that ended our fate before it could begin."

Okay. Was he hearing this right? The prince's ignorance must have been just as large as his ego to think himself worthy of Alanitora. He might be a pretty boy, but his personality was lacking. Whatever it was that caused him to be so aggressive, Owen was glad Alanitora was now far from it. Good on her for rejecting his uneducated advances. He deserved it. And more.

At least his own affections for her were accumulated over time, and not in two days. Though... she had rejected him as well, so it probably didn't make much of a difference.

No. This had nothing to do with how Owen felt about the princess, it had to do with saving her. "Where is she?"

The prince rolled his eyes in annoyance, pouring more wine into his cup. "Gone. Left for her wedding." Owen cursed beneath a staggered breath, compressing any physical reaction. "Not that I blame her. A queen has to do what she needs for her kingdom, I suppose. Even if a just as good option was here," he grumbled, swinging his arms about.

"That you're right about. When did she leave?"

Regenfrithu scowled. "You seem awfully adamant about acquiring her whereabouts. Looking to confess your love?"

"Just answer the question!" Owen couldn't help but raise his voice. This random Kreahan royal who had spent his entire life with everything given to him knew nothing of the risks behind the walls of his pristine palace.

"Yesterday evening. My sister said she was summoned by her betrothed."

"Dammit." Owen pressed down his frustration again. His eyes scattered back and forth, trying to process how he could get to her fast enough. If she left the day before, that meant they had lost too much time. There was no telling where she was, especially since there were multiple roads that led to Donasela through this point in Kreaha. He stumbled across what to say. "Thank you for the information, Your Highness, I will be taking my leave." Elena would know what to do. He had to pray that she would.

Before Owen could even put his hand on the doorknob to the prince's room, Regenfrithu was there, holding it closed. "Where do you think you're going?"

Owen practically itched to punch this guy. "I have important business to attend to, if you could please—"

"And what is that?"

"Nothing that concerns you," Owen spat.

"Oh, I think not." Regenfrithu crossed his arms. "This is my domain, my kingdom. Tell me what it is that you are so keen to tell Alanitora about or I will cast a horrendous fate upon you."

Owen could tell the prince was at least tipsy and had been drinking all morning based on the bags under his eyes. Drunken royals were something he was willing to deal with, but ones who threatened his life… that he had a limited tolerance to. Unfortunately, this particular one did have the power he claimed, and that wasn't something Owen could risk, especially since Alanitora was getting further and further by the minute. He took a deep breath. "Respectfully, Your Highness, this is a matter of life or death regarding the royal crown of Trenvern. If I don't get to her soon, it may be too late to even save my kingdom."

The arrogant look on Regenfrithu's face dissipated. "Are you saying her life is in danger?"

He wanted so badly to bite his tongue. "Yes."

"Tell me everything." The prince stated, locking the door.

Owen looked at him and back to the door. There was no way he was getting away from this situation without telling him, was there? Owen didn't know if he could trust him, but he did know he wouldn't be able to escape Kreaha with his life if he defied him and the prince sent an order out for his head.

Elena depended on him. Alanitora depended on him. All of Trenvern depended on him. And if that meant sharing a dangerous secret with a potential enemy. So be it.

As he closed the rushed narrative, Owen watched the prince's face with anticipation, trying his best to read the expressions. Finally, Regenfrithu closed his eyes and nodded. "Very well." He unlocked the door.

Owen stepped forward, ready to bound himself down the hall and out of this godforsaken castle.

"I'm coming with you." Another set of damned words left the Kreahan's mouth. Owen's stomach tightened.

"What?"

"If what you say is true, then I'm coming with you." His whole demeanor changed in an instant, from a depressed drunkard to a valiant noble. "If her life is really in danger, then I can't risk it. I lost her once, I won't make that mistake again."

Owen scoffed. So he was back on the idea of being in love with her... But this time, amusingly, he wanted to be her savior. "Don't act as though you and she are meant-to-be."

"Why not? It seemed that way for her, too."

"You— what?" Owen couldn't help the curiosity, no matter how hard he tried to hold it back.

Regenfrithu laughed. "Do you believe you are the one entitled to her affections?"

"No, I—"

"You know nothing of love, do you? I would go to the end of the world."

"You would?! You've known her what? Two days?"

"Yes. and I have never been more sure of anything in my life."

"This is unbelievable, I'm not going to let some haughty prince come with me."

"You don't really have a choice."

"You've resorted to threatening me again, then?"

"No," Regenfrithu spat. "I can tell you actually care for her, too. I'm saying you don't have a chance to help her without me."

"What could you possibly do?"

"Don't think that just because I am not trained as a soldier like you that I do not have value. Without me not only will you be walking the entire way, but you also won't have the faintest idea where to go from here. I know the fastest routes to Donasela, and I know my kingdom like the back of my hand. Tactically, I'd say I'm a good ally to have."

"And if I refuse?"

"It'll be your loss. Kreaha holds the fastest horses from the kingdom of Neydel. If time is of the essence, then you'll need steeds that don't tire and can go the distance. Furthermore, I know trading posts on the way where we can get such steeds if ours do tire. The little money you have won't buy you any of that."

Though he hated to admit it, Regenfrithu was right. Even if they stole horses, there was no telling how fast they might be. With how far behind they were, he couldn't pass up the possibility. Conflictingly, even if riding with the prince meant access to the best resources, it also meant drawing attention to themselves. Either way, he was going to have to give this stubborn ass an approved response.

Owen huffed. "Fine. I'll discuss it with my traveling partner."

"Good. I'll meet you outside the front gates at eight tonight."

"Eight? Are you mad?!" So far, yes, yes he was.

"I have duties to attend to first, unless you want the entire kingdom to come after you for supposedly kidnapping me. If you wish to leave without the supplies I'd get you, then so be it, but I will be traveling to Donasela either way. With you or against you."

Owen left the castle wringing his fingers nervously. He didn't like the power that Regenfrithu held over him. If anything, it made him wish they never stopped at Kreaha in the first place. They didn't have time for this, for futile royal affairs. His gut was telling him that Regenfrithu was truthful about his intentions, but that didn't change his concern with divulging sensitive information.

Alas, Owen told himself not to worry, that Elena would know what to do. Or at least... he hoped she would.

The neutral expression that she made worried him more. As he explained the situation it was unchanging and never shifted until it was her turn to talk.

"We should leave now, yes?" Owen asked when she stood pensive for more than a few moments.

"...I don't think so, the prince is right. We won't get far on our own, especially if we are walking."

"Well, just steal some horses like last time!"

"I never said I stole that horse, and besides, it'll be too risky to get one this close to the capital."

"Well—" He searched for words, flabbergasted. "We can't just sit here idle for ten hours. Alanitora is already so far ahead since we've waited this long here."

"You're right." Those words were rare, and Owen was sure a 'but' would follow. "Which is why it's best we don't waste our time here. If the prince is genuine, then we will gain a good amount of supplies for our trip without expense."

"And if he isn't? Perhaps he's on their side and is plotting against us as we speak. You said not to trust anyone."

"Yes, and I don't trust anyone, but it seems to me he is as genuine as you are when it comes to helping Alanitora... much to your dismay. If he is feigning an alliance then we will figure it out when the time comes."

Owen narrowed his eyes, stepping back. "You seem awfully patient despite what you claim is about to happen in Donasela."

Elena narrowed her eyes right back at him, glaring at him in a way that, though not as strong as her daughter's, was undeniably powerful. "Acting rashly gets you nowhere, I've learned that in my years as a queen. And if we can't prevent the disaster that is coming, it's best we have allies beside us to help fight against the consequences."

Owen paused. "You don't think we'll be able to stop it in time, do you?"

She averted her eyes, a grim look casting darkness over her features. "It's best we try."

He threw his arms into the air. "Well, why didn't you start with that?!"

"Because I know you, Owen. I know you fight best when there is hope. Like how you think that by preventing this, Alanitora might fall for you despite her previous rejections."

"How do you—"

"Does it matter? The bottom line is: I'm willing to take the risk to get us an upper hand."

"Yes, it matters! One moment you say not to act rashly, but the next moment you are all about taking risks. How is that not acting rashly?"

She raised her eyebrows, it seemed for once Owen had led her speechless. "You'll learn the difference someday. I'll give you the same offer as Regenfrithu, and your last chance to leave your compliance to me and your complaints behind. If you want to go ahead and try and find Alanitora on your own, act so rashly. But do not be surprised when you fail and arrive too late to help me."

Owen grumbled. He didn't like the secrecy, the commands, but he supposed serving as a knight would have just as many issues. "Fine," he spat. "But don't ever blame me if your decisions go south."

"I am well aware our situation is my fault," Elena stated, the closest she would get to an agreement with him. He began to unpack some of his things when she spoke up again. "Oh, and Owen?"

"What?" He turned.

Elena smiled at him. "Always keep your questioning of orders, it'll do you well in coming fights."

Owen had planned to spend the rest of the day staring into nothingness and letting his thoughts brood, but Elena insisted it would do him good to roam the castle grounds, even if it was not with her. He was quite vehemently against the idea, fearful of anyone who might recognize him, but upon the third hour, he found himself too restless to resist.

The crowds were much less busy outside the second time around, and information from some of the booths suggested that there was an event happening in the Great Hall. Regardless, Owen still hid his face with the scarf as he scanned the booths, only showing interest when the word 'free' was suggested.

With the little coin he did have, he made sure to buy the cheapest meat and bread that he could find, knowing that they might go hungry without it.

Around five in the evening, there was a queue out the front gates for carriages to leave. It wasn't enough to be everyone that currently resided in the kingdom, but it was a considerable amount. He was able to slip out on his own without suspicion, heading straight towards the campsite where Elena had lit a small fire. Owen was grateful Kreahan guards had no issue with people camping outside of their kingdom.

By the time a quarter before eight came around, Owen was more than anxious, pacing back and forth with his eyes glued to the entrance gates. He still wasn't sure if they could trust the prince, but Elena's composure surprisingly helped calm him.

A few minutes before eight, Owen watched as the two guards standing at the entrance left their positions. He took this opportunity to step up and peer through the gate entrance from the side.

"Would you mind not looking like a begging vagrant? They'll come right back when they hear of it from a guest."

Owen jumped at the prince's voice, who stood in the shadows a few meters away from him. "You said to meet you at the gate!"

"I did. And I'm here." Regenfrithu stepped from his place. He held reins in both hands as well as a bag. All three horses swung their heads around impatiently, as though their proximity was uncomfortable. He looked around. "Where is she? We only have a few minutes before they finish their report and come back."

"She's—"

"Right here." Elena emerged from the woods, both her and Owen's bags slung over her cloaked shoulder.

Regenfrithu gave her a brief smile, holding out one of the reins. "Your

Majesty… You do look much like your daughter."

She mirrored his smile, taking it and passing the bags to Owen. "As you said, we don't have much time. Pleasantries can wait. Let's go." In a few swift motions, she was already on her horse, looking back at the two boys patiently.

Owen sighed, taking his horse from Regenfrithu. This was going to be quite the ride.

23

A Warm Welcome

It took another two hours from the border before the entourage stopped to set up camp for the night, leaving Alanitora's mind to spiral in the meantime. Perhaps it was the idea of finally crossing into her new kingdom, or maybe it was news of the upcoming parade, but things were beginning to feel *real*. She'd been so worried in the past week about the calamity of her kingdom and the assassination attempts that she hadn't fully realized what was coming.

She was going to be married within the next few days, and there was no changing it. Despite not having doubts in the past, something in her gut was telling her it didn't feel right. Alanitora tried her best to shake the feeling, to revert to her previous state of mind, but when she succeeded, she was left with a different issue entirely.

Sir Corwyn. Somehow he knew she would be uncomfortable going in with Jean Clarke on her own, and even went so far as to say such. But the princess had no idea that Corwyn knew anything about Devante since those who knew anything were sworn to secrecy. How many details about the border situation had spread?

Alanitora felt Corwyn to be trustworthy from the moment she met him, but she hadn't the chance to confirm her gut instincts. If there had been any sign of it otherwise, she must have willed it away. She might have simply ignored such signs in desperation to have a figure to look up to.

It was likely a misunderstanding on her part, but the paranoia that was slowly infecting her mind insisted she examine every possibility.

And the worst idea was that Corwyn was in on it— in on the assassinations, in on the Men of the Blood Dragon— in on any and possibly all of it.

It might make sense, Corwyn and Devante were the same rank. And someone must have sabotaged the carriage to divert its path back when it caught on fire. She was well aware of the possibility someone in her entourage, even if it was a single soldier, was plotting against her.

Corwyn was the one closest to her. If she let him get too close and he wasn't who he appeared to be, it could jeopardize any ability to save her kingdom now that her father was dead.

She never would have doubted her ability before, but lately, Alanitora's gaze of reading wasn't working as usual. Sagittarius was the key example of limited intimidation, but people like Zinaw and Regenfrithu she couldn't quite grasp. Maybe her abilities were limited to those from Trenvern, however that might be. Even so, was it possible that someone could use that against her? And perhaps project a different motivation onto her beliefs?

Originally, she had planned to go straight to sleep once her bed was ready, but Alanitora knew these intrusive thoughts would make their way into the space of the darkness, and further into her dreams if she even could rest.

Owen wasn't here to anxiously watch over her, and Diane wasn't here to warn her of the typical *'someone is going to assassinate you'* signs. However she went about this, Alanitora would have to do it carefully.

One solution—one word—came to mind.

"Sagittarius."

She turned her head at the call of the princess. "I'm not going off into the woods this time around so you know—"

"That's not what this is about." Alanitora stepped closer. She lowered her voice, taking a quick look around. "I just need to tell you where I plan to head."

"For what? An alibi against murder?"

"No, I—, well in a way, yes if the murder is my own."

Sagittarius raised her eyebrows. "I'm not quite following."

The princess let out a heavy sigh. "I'm about to talk to Sir Corwyn, and I can't help but have doubts about my safety. I think it's wise I tell someone where I'm off to in case I end up dead. I'm pretty sure I can—"

"Trust me?" Consternation struck the archer's features for a moment. "Alright. Though I don't know why you'd choose a stranger over your ladies-in-waiting, I'm honored and flattered either way."

"They don't know how to fight... And you aren't a stranger. Not anymore." Alanitora smiled.

Sagittarius' lips curved into a heartfelt smile much different from her typical smirk. She nodded.

Good, that was settled. She now had someone who she could lean on in times of calamity.

"Oh, and Dagger Eyes?" Alanitora turned back to her. "You can call me Sage. It's what my friends do."

"I might, if you stop insisting on giving me that nickname."

"Never going to happen."

It took a few deep breaths before Alanitora was able to step into Corwyn's tent, which held a cot on the floor and a rolled-out mat next to it with materials and notes.

He was sitting in a chair, hunched over a little desk comical in proportion to how large he was.

Alanitora watched him for a moment as he wrote next to the candlelight, his features calm. She cleared her throat, prompting the knight to look up from his work.

"Your Highness." He stood, putting down his quill and clasping his hands in front of him. "What brings you here? Is there an issue?"

"No, not really." She shook her head. Where was she to start? "I just wanted to ask you a few things."

"Of course." He was open and relaxed, with no trace of stiffness or nervousness. He also was without the boasting confidence that she found many Trenvern soldiers held.

Alanitora decided to come right out with it. "Back at the border, when Sir Jean Clarke suggested we go inside, you protested against it. Why?"

"As I said then, I thought it might make you uncomfortable." He frowned.

No. She saw it there in his eyes, that twitch. "You're lying." Alanitora quickly scanned the room for sharp objects he could use against her. His sword was off to the side. If he wanted to get it she would have time to run out, but between the two of them on the floor was a drawing compass. She doubted he was fast enough, but Corwyn could easily throw it at her if given the opportunity.

He sighed, stepping away from the desk. "No, I'm just telling partial truths," Corwyn said distraughtly. "I was nervous what might happen with Devante would happen again."

She crossed her arms. "And how did you know what happened with Devante?"

"Owen told me."

How ironic. The one person she had thought she could trust to tell no one turned around and did it.

As if he could read her thoughts, Corwyn continued. "Though I wouldn't worry, he was explicit that it stay between him and me. I assume your wishes were for no one to know of what really happened at the border. He needed help to cover it up."

Alanitora's shoulders relaxed. He was telling the truth, and there were no signs of a bluff. "And you complied?"

The knight frowned. "Of course. Owen is one of the few I was able to trust among the men I was assigned. That's why I put him in your carriage."

"You put him in the carriage?" She assumed he had made his way into that position on his own.

Corwyn nodded. "He was one of the few lads I trusted, always honest and eager to help. Nearly all of the other soldiers here didn't train under me, and those who did admittedly aren't the best batch. Uldin and Paul don't have that same integrity." She didn't know who Paul was, but if putting him in the same sentence as Uldin was any indication, he likely was not an upstanding guy.

"But I suppose I could have been wrong about him, too, given the carriage incident."

"What do you mean by that?" Alanitora asked.

"It became clear to me you were sabotaged, Your Highness, but I'm sure such isn't news to you. And since you relieved Owen of his duties, I suppose that means..."

"Oh, no, not at all!" she quickly refuted. Alanitora was certain Owen wasn't the one to plot against her. "We just had a... difference of opinion. There was nothing regarding a betrayal, and he's still as good of a man as you believe him to be.

"Well, that's a relief!" Corwyn chuckled. "I thought my judgment of character was off." Alanitora certainly knew how that felt, and it was good to hear she wasn't alone. All the anxieties that bubbled within her finally started to settle down.

"If I'm fully honest, Sir Corwyn, there is something I would like to discuss with you in regards to my safety..."

The next day was quite a bore as they rode through Donasela. They kept the same riding arrangement as before and both Alanitora and her ladies spent the entire time looking out the window at their new homeland. Though the weather and climate were similar to Kreaha's, wildflowers and fields in place of forests where they traversed. It was a lovely landscape, and for a moment, it felt like a dream of golden light.

They passed a few towns on their way, most of which must have heard of their arrival, for they flocked to the sides of the streets in a similar manner to those in the Kreahan-Donaselan town. Gwendolyn warned this would be just a precursor to the parade they would participate in when they finally reached the capital.

A good portion of the time before they left was Corwyn debriefing the logistics of said parade, before relaying the rest of the information about their schedule upon arrival to Gwendolyn, whose delegation to the task had her fret more than Alanitora was used to.

"I just think some of the ceremonies are unnecessary," she protested, reading over the plan once again.

"Well it's not like she's being dunked in water seven times and then having a series of runes drawn atop her forehead," Sagittarius scoffed in a rare use of her voice that day.

"Well, sure, but a chorus of schoolchildren singing prayers in her name? A formation of Donaselan soldiers performing some kind of... march?"

"I think it'll be wonderful!" Korena mused as expected. "Think of all the attention we'll be given. How many people will wave at us? Or how about the awe in little girls' eyes when they see their pretty new queen?!"

Alanitora shook her head in amusement. "I don't think it'll be wildly theatrical."

"Even so, we should be prepared for the most extravagant of celebrations anyway, if not to fit in, then to impress— Oh! I do wonder if we will have time to prepare beforehand."

"Um... Yes, I think so." Gwendolyn checked a series of parchments, her eyes flicking back and forth between a few of them. "Yes! It looks like we'll stop a short time beforehand to separate from our regular procession. Most of our wagons will go directly to the castle and start unloading while the two carriages and a series of soldiers will participate in the parade. There will be an extra unloaded wagon for you and me to sit, Korena." She nudged her friend slightly.

"Oh!" Korena nearly jumped out of her seat. "Sagittarius should take that chance to get dressed in something nicer if she's going to the parade too!"

Sagittarius gawked in protest. She looked like she was about to bite off the blonde's head before Alanitora put her arm out to stop her.

"Sage doesn't have to change into anything if she doesn't want to."

"Sage?" Gwendolyn asked.

The archer waved her hand about. "Don't worry about it, Apothecary."

"Regardless, in the company of Her Royal Highness, you need to dress accordingly!" Korena huffed.

"Can I wear something black?"

"This is a celebratory parade, not a funeral procession. You can't just wear black!"

Sensing a fight forming between Sagittarius and Korena, Gwendolyn intervened. "Regardless of what we wear to the event, there are other details to be sorted out…"

As Gwendolyn repeated the boring specifics, Alanitora rested her head against the side of the carriage. The thought of being in the public eye was tiring enough, but the possibility that she might fall asleep within it was what prompted her to accept the oncoming slumber.

The rest was greatly needed, as she could feel its effects when awoken for the preparation. Korena practically dragged her out by the arm and into a small tent sent up for them to change in.

Gwendolyn sat with her legs crossed on the floor, rifling through a chest of some of the princess' dresses. She looked up. "Oh good, you're here. I was thinking either orange or brown. They are the Donaselan colors."

Still stirring, Alanitora peered over at the orange dress Gwendolyn had set aside. She'd never worn it, and for good reason. "Do you really think I'm the sort of person to look good in orange?"

The lady pursued her lips in contemplation before throwing the dress aside. "Good point. Maybe just brown then?"

Korena blew a raspberry beside her. "Brown is a boring color… No offense, Gwennie. We should go with something bright and new. Like a pale pink!"

Neither of these options sounded good to Alanitora. There wasn't anything wrong with them, nor did they look bad with her complexion, but they didn't fit where she wanted to go with her first impression.

"Red." The princess jumped upon hearing Sagittarius, who had been hidden unmovingly behind a few chests. "It's both flattering for your complexion and bold. The right shade would suggest a sophisticated but warm manner. A dark green could also work."

"Ooh, green *is* Trenvern's color, it might be good to represent home!" Korena agreed.

"Both are good. If we go with the idea of representing Trenvern, it may have a polarizing effect. I like red. Gwendolyn, do we have anything between crimson and burgundy?"

Gwendolyn's wide grin was an indication that they had just that.

The dress they chose was a gorgeous deep red that fit her chest into a tight upright posture. Long translucent bishop sleeves hung over her wrists, and a large layered skirt covered her legs.

The second that Alanitora confirmed she was satisfied, her ladies turned in perfect unison to face Sagittarius.

"Nuh-uh. Hell no. I am not one of your dolls. If you really want me to dress nice, I will, but you aren't putting anything on me." The two didn't budge. "Okay fine! You can pick out three dresses for me to wear and then scatter. If I hate all of them, I'm staying in my clothes. Understood?"

Gwendolyn nodded. "Deal."

When Sage emerged a long while later, not only had she adorned a simple dark teal dress, but she had also removed her mask, which left all three girls in a moment of surprise.

Alanitora had thought the bandit to be the kind to even sleep with the damn thing on, but now that the mask and the dark black that surrounded her eyes were gone, she could better see Sage's features. A smirk pulled at the edge of Alanitora's lips. "No more hidden identity?"

Sage narrowed her deep-set eyes, waving her mask between her fingers. "You say that as though this flimsy piece of leather would make me unrecognizable to you. You know my voice and stature, and with your attention to detail, Dagger Eyes, you could probably spot me without a mask from a field away. No. Taking it off is to stop onlookers from recognizing a particularly charming southern bandit they might have run

308

into on the road."

"So… taking the mask off is what conceals your identity?" Gwendolyn asked.

"Exactly." Sagittarius smiled. "Don't worry, I'll put it back on after. It is a part of my appeal, after all." She looked between the three, then snapped her fingers. "Come on now, enough dwindling on my gorgeous appearance, you all best be preparing."

As the time for the parade approached, both Gwendolyn and Corwyn were running around the prepped wagons frantically.

Tathra, Zinaw, and the wolves had been set up in one of the more caravan-like wagons while Lorenalia sat at the front of a carriage.

The other carriage, as Corwyn soon explained to her, was to house Alanitora. He helped her up into the coach's seat, which had been decorated with a bed of flowers that framed a halo behind her head. He explained how it was an easy setup because Kreaha tended to use the same carriages for their festivals.

Sagittarius was to sit in the carriage while Corwyn rode on the back of one of the horses as means of security.

Despite her nerves, everything was getting settled. The pieces of the event were falling into place. The last touch came with Korena, who excitedly grabbed Alanitora's attention with her bouncing.

"Tora, look what one of the Donaselan captains gave for us to give you!" she exclaimed, holding out a golden wreath, adorned with perfectly detailed flowers wrapping around the leaves. "Supposedly, it's a staple of status in Donasela! Worn for ceremonies like this one."

Alanitora stood still as Korena placed the wreath on her head carefully. It was strange: It looked familiar, but she was certain she would remember seeing such a beautiful thing. Regardless, it was lovely and fell perfectly onto her temples.

"Good luck!" With a brief hug, Korena hopped down from the carriage, giggling as she went to go find Gwendolyn.

Alanitora took a deep breath as Corwyn made his way to the reins of the horses leading the carriage. He nodded to her as the procession ahead of them began to move forward.

Her insides felt like there were growing vines of morning glory that wrapped around her, blooming like the wildflowers they had passed to get here.

Cheers of the crowds could be heard as the capital city of Donasela came into sight. It was much more luxurious than the one at home, but she hadn't seen enough of Kreaha's to compare it to theirs. Regardless, most of the buildings had reinforced roofs, appearing to be both a commercial area and residential.

A few small children were the first to see her, having run in the opposite direction of the carriage to intercept them. Their eyes lit up like torches when they saw her, and she gave a small, polite wave back before watching as they ran off.

Their first stop was at the very front of the town, where the Donaselan soldiers gave a small performance while some watched in awe and others looked to her. She kept on a smile, waving at a few, but for the most part, looking forward to not give anyone the wrong idea.

The more they traveled into town, the livelier the crowds got. People waved handkerchiefs and held up offerings she couldn't accept. Dozens of flowers and loose petals were thrown her way, to the point where it almost looked like a snowstorm of spring color.

People stood on roofs to get a better view. Mothers and fathers held children on their shoulders.

She had never felt such joy in seeing a group of people together, especially those of a lower class. They seemed so cheerful, and it was infectiously spreading into her smile. A girl and her lover atop a balcony, a baker presenting his goods, a young boy holding up his play weapons.

There was so much life here in Donasela, and it flowed throughout the streets. To think her only interaction with large crowds was the gathering

310

of soldiers before war or a meeting of nobles to discuss new rulings.

She couldn't see either her friends or her ladies in waiting, but she was sure they would be having a good time. Korena was basking in the glory of eyes settled on her while Gwendolyn took a more humble approach.

She wondered how people might react to Zinaw with the wolves, though she did consider it could be seen as more of a festive show than the idea their new queen owned wild wolves.

The longer they ventured, the warmer Alanitora's chest became. Anyone with who she made eye contact looked genuinely happy to be there, and amid all the sorrow within her life, all the pain among her own home, and the loss of hope for her companions, she could finally see a light blooming in the distance. A light that would carry her far if she followed it.

After nearly a dozen stopping points, the castle walls themselves began to come closer and closer. There would only be a few more stops before she was there, and it became apparent to the princess that even if she didn't want this bliss to end now, it was her home. This could happen once again, this feeling of fulfillment in a place of brightness.

A large tavern had its doors open to her right. She watched as a bunch of burly men with tankards rushed out, raising their glasses to her. A laugh escaped her throat and she didn't even worry how unappealing it might look on her—though Gwendolyn had said that her laugh was the kind to bring a smile to everyone's face.

Not wanting to divert her attention unequally, Alanitora looked to her left among the crowd, giving them a wave as well.

That was where she saw it. A man. Aiming a crossbow at her. Before she could think, before she could react, the arrow was being sent in her direction.

She froze as it hit the wall of the carriage right next to her cheek, pinning her hair. Her heart pumped out of her chest. She had been caught completely off guard. Alanitora fumbled her hands around her skirt as a gasp swept the crowd, cheers turning to shouts of anger, fear, and confusion.

Not everyone realized what had happened, as only a few Trenvern soldiers drew their swords. Even those who did couldn't find the source. Without the clear vantage point Alanitora had, they looked around frantically.

Alanitora locked eyes with the man as he raced to reload his crossbow. He was faster at preparing weapons than she and would be ready to strike again before she could even send something his way.

She'd have to try to stop him. Duck out of the way, get one of the daggers from under her skirt, anything to prevent getting hit in the open for everyone to see and nothing they could do to stop it.

It didn't matter. Her body was rigid, hair tangled in the embedded arrow, hands shaking to find anything.

And then a swishing noise came from above. Then another, and one more. Three arrows stuck out of the man's chest, as screams filled the crowd around him. He fell backward, the crossbow collapsing onto the ground next to him.

The princess breathlessly looked up to see Sagittarius kneeling atop the carriage, her dress stretched awkwardly in her stance as she lowered the bow.

"Thank you," Alanitora whispered lightly, her heart still refusing to calm down.

Sagittarius nodded at her before jumping down from the top of the carriage and onto the road. "Move," she demanded, causing the crowd to split where the man lay dead.

All movement stopped at this point, the focus centering around the assassination attempt. Alanitora sat still in her position, dazed and demure as Corwyn came around to check on her.

She had no recollection of the words she exchanged with the knight, only focused on what Sagittarius was doing. The archer stood over the body. She then knelt and checked his pulse before pulling out the arrows. "He's dead."

Murmurs spread across the crowd.

"Your Highness, are you alright? We heard the commotion!" Gwendolyn and Korena ran up to the side of the carriage behind Corwyn.

"Oh yes, we saw Sagittarius kick out the carriage door and swing herself atop! It was quite theatrical. I'd think it was a show if not for the screams," Korena added.

Alanitora broke her gaze from the bandit. She stayed rigid, still unable to break her trance. "Yes, I suppose that would be the preference. I'd much rather say that was the deal than cause this panic, but it seems to be too late."

Corwyn cleared his throat. "Alright, we'll have to cut this short. If you will, Your Highness, please return to the safety of the carriage." He held his hand out to help her down.

She nodded, taking the arrow from her hair and following his direction. Alanitora gave her ladies-in-waiting yet another reassuring nod in regards to her life being on the line before shutting the carriage door.

Her heart was starting to relax, but her head still spun with an inability to process what had just happened. She didn't even have the capacity to consider what it meant.

Sagittarius climbed in after her moments later, sitting across from the princess with both her bow and the enemy's crossbow in hand. She could only assume someone else was taking care of the body.

"Are you okay?" the bandit asked, concern knitted into her eyebrows as she closed the curtain windows. It was strange, there was so much more expression on her face than Alanitora was used to. Perhaps it was the lack of a mask, or maybe something else entirely...

"Yes, thank you... for saving my life." She didn't think she'd ever need to say that to another soul.

The archer smirked. "I didn't. I just beat you to saving yourself. A few more seconds and he would have been dead anyway."

The words were meant to spark pride, but Alanitora's mind couldn't settle on the idea.

"I thought you said you didn't kill people."

"I don't." The dark gleam in her eyes suggested that today was an exception. Alanitora nodded, ready to show her appreciation again. "I brought you a present though." Sagittarius held up the crossbow.

"Why would I need—" She paused, an image on the wood of the weapon catching her eye. An image she couldn't ignore.

Engraved into the side of the crossbow was an elaborate dragon, a single ruby-colored stone sitting in place of its eye.

24

The Fox's Den

This was not good. In fact, it was far from it. Alanitora wasn't much concerned about someone's attempt to kill her—that had already happened enough times in the past week. She was worried more so for what this meant in regards to first impressions. Based on the happiness of the people, she assumed Donasela hadn't seen many assassination attempts in their time.

The crossbow indicated that this had nothing to do with them and everything to do with the "Men of the Blood Dragon", as Diane had called them. She had no idea they would be out this far and only thought them to be based in Trenvern. It was possible they had traveled with her, but she still had no clue as to their motives to initiate her demise.

The people of Donasela could see this as a threat to their lives. What sort of princess did she have to be for someone to wish to kill her in the public eye? And even worse, Alanitora hadn't been the one to defend herself against the attack. What did that label her as? She had spent all her life trying to be seen as someone who could fight, but now they must see her as just another fragile royal.

"Your Highness, it's alright to come out now. We are secure." Corwyn's voice sounded from outside as the carriage pulled to a halt.

She looked at Sagittarius, whose cautious vision held the same warning as her gut: Be careful.

Alanitora opened the door, relieved when she saw Corwyn standing there with a line of guards around them. "You and your companions will be escorted to the Throne Room. They've set up the area to ensure your safety."

"Thank you," she replied with a smile.

"Let us go. We shouldn't waste time."

Sagittarius and Alanitora followed Corwyn to the lord that was waiting for them, who in turn led them through the corridors to the Throne Room. Alanitora wasn't too concerned with taking in her surroundings, but she was well aware of the light that shone within the pearly walls.

As soon as they opened the door, Tathra and Lorenalia turned their heads. Zinaw stayed back, holding the wolves to her sides.

"Oh, thank goodness no one was harmed." Lorenalia grasped Alanitora's hands in her delicate ones.

"No one but the man who shot at her," Sagittarius scoffed.

"Where's Korena and Gwendolyn?" Alanitora asked, ignoring the archer.

"Meli is escorting them here. They shouldn't be too long."

"What's important is all visiting royalty is here."

The unfamiliar voice brought Alanitora's attention to the front of the room. There, a middle-aged man with dark brown hair stood confidently. His posture was only a small indication though, as he was adorned with expensive fabrics and jewels around his neck. This was the king of Donasela. Her soon-to-be father-in-law.

She approached, straightening her posture in the utmost respect. This was where first impressions truly mattered. Never mind the parade.

The man had kind, softened eyes, but there was a slice of sharpness in them, one that wasn't common for Alanitora to see. They were the kind of eyes that could stare an enemy down at battle, but like a sword serviced for years, had become weathered and dull over time.

His bone structure suggested that he had been handsome in his youth, but his demeanor showed a present sadness that counteracted such a lively past. He was the sort of person that Alanitora felt she had already met at some point, despite never having done so. As though he reminded her of someone else.

She presented a deep curtsy. "Your Majesty. It is wonderful to make your acquaintance."

He bowed in return. "And you, Queen Alanitora. My son should be here shortly, he's gathering information about the incident."

Alanitora nodded. She had to hold her tongue from apologizing and saying it was her fault, aware it would be best to only say so if directly asked.

"I'm sure you must be exhausted after a long day's journey though. As soon as my son comes back, I'll have him bring you and your company to your temporary rooms before the wedding. You may take a rest there until called upon for a meal. During that, if it's alright with you, I would like to discuss our plans going forward. Ceremonial practices and customs... All those things."

"Of course. Thank you for your hospitality."

The king—whose name she recalled to be Crevan—smiled for the first time.

He dismissed her, allowing Alanitora to turn back to her companions in the room. She needed to talk to them anyway.

Drawing a deep breath, she began, "Thank you, all of you, for coming with me on this journey in the past few days. I know some of you did not intend to stay here for the wedding, but I would indeed love it if you did, especially since it'll give you time to relax before a long journey." She looked to Zinaw and Tathra before turning her head to Sagittarius, who had put her mask back on. "If you would like to leave, I can arrange for some valuables to be given to you by tonight."

There was a moment of silence after she spoke followed by a chorus of voices all at once.

She chuckled. To think she had only known these people a few days now and already considered them friends. "One at a time please, I can't read your minds."

"I'll stay," Lorenalia began. "Might as well be an ambassador for Kreaha until I figure out my next move."

317

"Zinaw and I talked about it during the parade. We'll stay for at least the wedding."

"It's more for the wolves, they're awfully inseparable, and there's no way in hell I'm abandoning Becorath." Zinaw crossed her arms.

Sagittarius narrowed her eyes jeeringly at Alanitora. "I just watched someone almost kill you, I think you need me to stick around to prevent it from happening again."

"I—" Alanitora began.

"—*And*, I assume the longer I'm in your services, the more money I get, yeah?"

"Sure." Alanitora held back a laugh, nodding at the rest of them. "Then I guess it's settled."

It was then that the front door practically slammed open. Korena, Gwendolyn, and Meli came through with two men behind them. Korena bounded straight towards the princess in excitement.

"If I had known he was such a hunk, I would have swapped places with you!" she shouted in a hushed tone.

"I'm sorry?"

Korena violently nodded her head behind her, to which Alanitora followed. Surely enough, one of the men held a heavy resemblance to the king. He had brown curls and a jawline so similar to the king's that there was no way they *weren't* father and son. His eyes were sharp, dark brown irises resting in an almond-shaped setting.

He was certainly attractive, but not the most attractive man she had seen. Beside him was a man of about the same age, though taller and with blonde hair. She wasn't sure who he was, but there was no way he could have been the prince, considering the contrasting features.

The prince stepped forward, placing his hands behind his back and bowing cordially. "Your Highness, guests of the crown, I thank you for your patience. I am Prince Daruthel." He nodded past them towards the king. "I understand my father wishes for me to show you to your rooms and, well... there are quite a few of you. That shouldn't be much of an issue though." Daruthel stepped back with a smile, looking at the blonde man beside him. "My lord-in-waiting will go ahead to make sure the rooms in the west wing are ready. In the meantime, please follow me. We can take the scenic route."

Unlike with Trenvern or Kreaha, the Throne Room of Donasela was held in the very center of the castle, or the metaphorical heart, as Daruthel explained. They made their way into a private courtyard, where a large willow tree swayed in the center, surrounded by a bed of flowers. The prince paused for an exposition about its historical significance, though Alanitora was unable to pay much mind, as the thrill of her recent experience was just starting to fade, instead replaced with rising fatigue.

Luckily, a few others from their group—such as Lorenalia and Korena—took the initiative of conversation instead. This allowed Alanitora to ease her mind as they were taken up a series of half-paced stairs to a corridor of rooms.

Daruthel took them up to the rooms. He told them the entire hallway was for her party, but she would switch rooms herself just before the wedding based on tradition in Donasela that no one from the bride's side is to see her until the day of, save for select servants. She did hope such exceptions would be Korena and Gwendolyn.

"Now," Daruthel turned to the lot of them. "It would be rude of me to not know my future spouse's company. Please, take this chance to introduce yourselves without judgment." His eyes continuously shifted towards Sagittarius while he spoke.

Lorenalia, in her naturally gregarious fashion, stepped forward first. "I am Princess Lorenalia of Trenvern, accompanied by my dear friend and wait, Meli." She motioned to the guard next to her, then looked to the rest of the crowd.

"Tathra of Redanor."

"I'm her cousin, Zinaw. I'm from Kindar. The wolves are under my watch for now, if you were wondering."

Daruthel chuckled, tilting his head at the canines next to her. "I have to admit, I was curious. They seem pleased. As long as they have no plans to relieve themselves in the nicer parts of the castle there shouldn't be much of an issue."

Zinaw's eyebrows raised in surprise. She nodded in approval towards her cousin, who shrugged in return.

Now that the royal parts of their party were introduced, Korena and Gwendolyn looked to Alanitora expectantly. She stared in blank curiosity for a moment before the realization struck that they wanted *her* to introduce them.

"These are my ladies-in-waiting, Korena and Gwendolyn, they've traveled with me all the way from home."

Gwendolyn curtsied. "I believe we had the brief pleasure of interaction just before the gathering, but it is lovely to be formally introduced."

"Likewise," Daruthel beamed. "Well, it seems your gaggle has collected representatives from all over Mordenla!"

Alanitora let out a light laugh. It sounded forced, though she tried not to mind. "Yes, we did all come together quite spontaneously, though in good enough humor."

The prince hummed in contemplation of this, before speaking again. "And the mysteriously masked maiden?" Daruthel eyed the archer. "Another lady of yours?"

"Bodyguard." Sagittarius sneered.

"Lovely either way." He gave her a small bow. Alanitora watched Sagittarius' face turn to an expression of disgust. It was humorous, actually, how unrestrained her reactions were. He cleared his throat, turning to the rest of them. "I'll leave you all to it. Ladies, Your Highnesses, feel free to roam as you wish. There should be no restrictions on the town, and the castle is open, save for the more obvious areas, such as the Dungeons and the Royal Chambers."

"Prince Daruthel, there is no need to give them the exposition. That should be my job, not yours." The group of heads collectively turned over to the blonde lord-in-waiting they had seen in the Throne Room. He stood at the end of the hall with a pair of maids, appearing to have just finished preparing the guests' rooms.

He walked past them, nodding at Alanitora with a curt smile before patting the prince on the back. Daruthel laughed. "Thank you. Everyone, allow me to introduce you to my lord-in-waiting, Francis."

"Yes, I'm sure they are ever so excited to meet me," Francis retorted in a lightheartedly sarcastic tone. "We should get going. Your father needs help settling the plans." His eyes scanned the room, locking with Alanitora's and holding a steely glare before breaking away. It seemed the prince's servant didn't trust her.

"Of course," Daruthel replied, turning. He gave one last nod to Sagittarius on the way out, his eyes scanning her lightly.

The Donaselan maids followed suit, their footsteps fading before the majority of the entourage headed into their rooms in silent agreement.

"I don't like him much." Sagittarius shrugged, following Alanitora to her doorway. "I'll be in town. If I'm gonna stay here for a bit, I should at least get the scope on the common people. See if they're really happy or putting on a charade for goodwill."

It wasn't something she really thought about, but she supposed it was a good idea, not that she was sure she wanted to know before the wedding. It might give her doubts if she didn't already have them. "You may do such," Alanitora said.

The rest of her time before the private lunch King Crevan summoned her for was spent relaxing in her room. She dismissed Korena and Gwendolyn from her care until the next day, aware that they were just as tired as her from the long journey.

In full honesty, she just wanted to sleep for a few days, and not have to worry about anything anymore. Dreams were her best chance of escape from reality after all.

But there was one good thing to the side of it: she was finally where she had spent the past week dreading to arrive at, and it wasn't as bad as she anticipated. Sure, things could get worse from here, but at the moment there was a level of contentment that Alanitora had feared would never come in the entirety of her future. For once, she could stop running and focus on what mattered.

Right now, that was getting her kingdom out of the ashes.

At one point, Alanitora got up from her bed, which rested against the wall with windows, and peered outside. The afternoon sun shone through, casting shadows upon flower petals that lay in planter boxes just outside the window. Below was the public courtyard, where a few vendors set their things up and many people walked throughout. She had to stick her head out to see the end of the right side.

There was a collection of flowers in the center, giant beds with several plants and little stepping stones through them. It was a small garden. Not luxurious and tempting like Kreaha's, but rather wild and free. The kind of garden a young girl would dream of living in as a faerie among the birds and bugs that called it home.

A small boy caught her eye as he looked up at her among the adults that passed by unaware. He waved, beaming in excitement as if he had just found a glittering gemstone.

She waved back with a soft smile before stepping away from the window. It occurred to her that the golden wreath was still upon her head. She took it off, placing it on the bedside to smooth out her hair before picking it back up to look over the features. It was well crafted, looked almost as though someone dipped a real flower wreath in liquid gold itself.

The time for her to meet with her future spouse and father came not too long after. While finding her way to the Throne Room would be an easy task, she did not know the location of anything else. It took a bit of asking directions from the guards there to find where she needed to go.

Those she asked for help from were cordial, if not benevolent. So much so that Alanitora was beginning to think maybe Trenvern was the only kingdom with coarse servitude. She decided she would only conclude such if she came across another kingdom, which she doubted would happen anytime soon.

Upon arriving, she noticed two things. First, the private dining room she had been instructed to attend was fairly small and could serve a dozen individuals at maximum. Second, all four of the people in it were male.

She recognized all but one gentleman, who was the first to speak among them. "Your Highness, thank you very much for your punctuality. Allow

322

me to introduce myself." The man stepped forward. He had white hair and a slightly sagging face, which showed his age quite well. His hunched, shaky posture further contributed. "I am Sir Balgair, chief advisor to King Crevan." He turned to his employer, who nodded with pride.

"It is wonderful to meet you, Sir Balgair." Alanitora bowed her head respectfully.

"Please, Your Highness, join us for a meal, will you?" Crevan motioned to the table, pulling a chair out for himself and waiting for her to do the same. "Our food should be here any minute now."

Alanitora obeyed, seating herself across from the king at the table for six. Balgair and Daruthel joined them on either side, while Francis stood to the side, his arms folded in front of him.

As promised, the food came right after, and the men made no hesitation to eat. There was no room for small talk as they consumed a majority of their portions.

Alanitora had just finished the last spoonful of her soup when Balgair cleared his throat, taking a moment to dab a cloth to his mouth before speaking. "I believe we should get the heaviest of matters out of the way first. No need to dread the inevitable." He chortled, leaning back in his chair. "Typically, if there is a need for a new successor and the Donaselan kingdom is in crisis—whether financial, political or some other disastrous situation—the coronation of said successor is supposed to happen before anything else. Therefore, extending this tradition to cross-territorial affairs, the same should apply to the wedding."

Crevan nodded. "That's why we summoned you earlier. We currently know nothing about the situation of your home kingdom. As soon as you are wed to the Donaselan crown, you can properly pass your title down to one of your siblings without scandal."

"One of my siblings?"

The men looked between one another. "My dear," Daruthel's eyes filled with pity. "We thought you would have been informed... your father has passed."

"No, I understand that, I received such news..."

"Then why is there confusion?"

"I don't *have* any siblings."

"I'm sorry?" King Crevan stood. "Then who will the Trenvern crown go to?"

She froze. This question had been on her mind for some time, but for whatever reason, she had assumed she'd learn the answer when arriving in Donasela. "Perhaps my father intended for me to rule upon our marriage?"

"No, it was clearly stated within our arrangement that you were to be the Queen of Donasela. We explicitly stated that Daruthel was the only child of Donasela."

"Why would your father agree to a marriage between two kingdoms with only one heir?" Balgair looked between her and the king.

A silent pause filled the room.

"He likely wasn't expecting to be assassinated," Francis began, breaking his own silence and stepping forward. "But one thing is for certain: The arrangement said that Donasela couldn't supply their aid until after the wedding. If we want to help Trenvern, the wedding must proceed."

Daruthel nodded. "Francis is right. Once we wed, I will do everything in my power to be sure your home sees justice." He reached out, giving Alanitora's hands a quick squeeze. "But I understand if you don't want to go through with it. This must be heavy on you." She was to marry a kind man, that was for sure, and it brought comfort to Alanitora.

She took a moment to think. The Fonolis might have taken over, and with how limited her resources were now, Alanitora doubted the soldiers she brought with her would be able to fight for an entire castle.

The princess nodded. "I'm willing to go through with the wedding." There was no going back, but if it meant saving her people, she would never want to anyway.

"Well then, we'll set the date the day after tomorrow. Most of the preparation has already been dealt with, all that's left is the process of getting you ready." King Crevan moved himself from the table.

"Luckily, the ceremony itself is fairly simple. There is not much required for the participants, just a few repeated words and the ability to not fall asleep." Sir Balgair laughed at his own words, but it quickly descended into a cough.

"Do you have a proper dress for the occasion? If not, we'll have to get you fitted immediately," the king asked.

Alanitora recalled her ladies-in-waiting mentioning a wedding dress on the way here. "I believe I do."

"Good. It's up to you whether you would like to hear about Donaselan customs before or after the wedding. Either way, Balgair will explain the most important ones to you when you go over the matrimonial process."

"I look forward to it." She shifted her gaze from the king to his advisor, who smiled back.

"Alright, we will leave you two be. If you need anything, there are guards outside to call on." Crevan patted down his robes, leading his son and Lord Francis to the door before closing it behind them.

She turned to the old advisor, nodding for him to say what he needed.

But the man waved his hand at her. "Eh, don't worry, I won't bore you with trivial facts. But tell me your favorite dessert, I'll be sure to get it on the chef's menu." He laughed heartily.

She giggled at his answer. Serious business aside, Alanitora could tell Balgair was a man that could never bore her, no matter how trivial his facts might be. And with the weight of the world on her shoulders, she found relief in his smile, as it was a smile that had seen strife and struggle before, yet still stood.

His smile said that through the chaos, it was all going to be alright.

And she believed it.

25

What Once Was

Diane was tired. Given that getting home as fast as possible was her first priority, she had barely gotten any sleep in the last few days. This was fortunately made much easier with the horse the strange woman had given her—Diane was still confused why and was half convinced the woman was a witch ready to curse her at any second.

Then there was the issue of nighttime. Diane was so useless when it came to lighting a fire that she wondered why she thought she could make the journey in the first place. And thus she was forced to ride all during the night for fear of the cold biting her curled up figure had taken hold. In the mornings, she'd tie her horse up in a secluded area and sleep under a tree for however long she might need to. This was also uncomfortable, as the dew chilled the grass and seeped through her clothes. The autumn weather was not ideal, but at least it wasn't freezing.

Even worse than functioning on half her usual sleep was the paranoia that came with it. She took an unfamiliar route to avoid the checkpoint Devante had been in charge of, and even then her wariness kept her from stopping anywhere within a league of the area.

In fact, the only time she stopped after that was to trade her exhausted horse for a fully nourished one.

It was after such that Diane began to recognize her surroundings. Road markers and farm buildings, twisted paths she used to run along and tall trees she used to climb.

She was nearly home.

That nostalgic relief sank when the top of the castle came into view over the hill. Recollections of blissful childhood were replaced with the fearful feelings that surrounded her leaving during the fire. She tried to remind herself that it was distant from her control, that she did what she had to in those moments.

But the sight of the makeshift straw roofs and charred walls of Trenvern's capital stopped her heart. The entire south side of town was crumbling to ruins. Some houses were caving in, others held burnt, blackened items in the front.

Diane dismounted from her horse, tying him to a post out of view on the outskirts. The girl kept herself low, making her way around the back of the town and avoiding the castle's line of sight the best she could in case any Fonoli were on the lookout.

It was empty, eerie. The only motion among the streets were the tumbling bits of trash and the half-torn flags that hung mournfully over the entrances of abandoned houses. The smell of smoke still lingered in the air, but another pungent stench carried with it.

As she passed through a back alleyway towards the nicer part of town, her feet stumbled over a lump on the ground. Diane had only intended to look down to readjust her footing, but her eyes caught on the blackened corpse of an animal—either a cat or a small dog. She yelped in horror, covering her mouth to hold back the need to gag.

She stood back and slowed her breath, begging for her heart to slow with it, before stepping over the animal and making her way to the end of the alley with haste.

Unlike the outskirts, this part of the capital had generally better infrastructure. The foundation of the stone homes had been undisturbed, though the walls and a fraction of the roofing charred considerably. So much damage had happened in one night. So much change came about from one fire.

Her house was among those saved from the ruthlessness of the flames, and Diane made no hesitation to approach. To her bewilderment, the door to her old home budged open easily enough.

She peered inside. Torn furniture sat near the entrance, a few cupboards lay open with their objects on the floor. Someone had ransacked them. Diane didn't care much if there was destroyed property, so long as she wasn't about to find the bodies of her parents. She stepped around the broken pottery and spilled flour at her feet, listening closely for sounds of either familiarity or threat.

Something clattered in their storage room.

Diane withdrew her needled glove, placing it over her fingers as she stepped towards the door with light feet. She took in a deep breath, counting down in her head. Her fingers wrapped around the door's handle.

She swung it open. Her eye flew to a young girl curled up against the back shelf. Dirty blonde hair cascaded around her shoulders. She looked up with fear in her doe eyes, her face dirtied with ash that made her blue irises evermore bright.

"Jenny!" Diane pulled the girl into her arms, relaxing herself into the embrace. "Are you okay? What happened?" She separated from her, brushing aside a loose strand.

"M'fine. Mama told me to come here and hide. Said she'd be back soon."

"What happened?" Diane repeated, seating herself on the ground.

Jenny put the stale bread she was chewing on aside. "I was asleep when they came. Ms. Conlan came knockin' on our door, told us to round up." Of course Diane's mom would. She always had that caring and authoritative nature, dictating she take care of others before herself.

"And then?"

"There was fire and screaming. Mama told me to close my eyes, so I did. I was upstairs when all the ladies were talking."

"All of them?"

Jenny counted her fingers. "Everyone but Miss Thatcher, I think…" She frowned. "M'not sure. Most everyone rushed home after. Next morning they rounded everyone and took 'em all to the castle… I'm sorry, that's all I really know about what happened."

"That's okay." Diane ruffled the girl's hair. Jenny's face cheered at the affectionate touch. "Do you know where my parents went?"

She shook her head. "But I've been watching like you told me to! There was an arrow in Mr. Samson's violets."

Diane paused, her mind going over the signals, rules, and signs her mother had put in place for her. And then it clicked. She stood suddenly, looking around her home before rushing to collect a few things in her satchel. Jenny watched, her eyes darting back and forth to keep up with the ginger.

Once satisfied, Diane took a string from her pocket and tied back her hair, letting out a deep breath. She hugged the young girl again. "Okay Jenny, I have to go, but I need you to do one last thing for me. It's gonna need you to be super brave though. You think you can handle it?"

Sneaking into the castle was not something that Diane expected to be easy, but to her surprise, it was exactly that. The areas that typically held crowds of people were almost as barren as the town. The only indication that life resided were the brief moments where she saw groups of people move past a window or the distant echoes of voices that bounced from stone to stone.

Per her mother's cautionary instruction, Diane's visits into the castle were rare. This was not an issue though, as she had also been instructed to memorize maps and plans of it in the event something bad happened.

Like now.

She stuck her back to the walls, sliding her way across to evade any wandering eyes. At the sight of anyone or the sound of even a pebble shifting, she'd freeze, scanning the area. It was like being a rabbit surrounded by a parliament of owls.

In order to get where she needed, Diane would have to go to the one place she most dreaded: The Keep. She had never been, but the mere idea of being trapped in a place where inhumane conditions were set upon the vilest of people sent a chill down her spine.

Getting in and past detection would take some planning. There were two entrances to the dungeons, both of which were in areas of constant surveillance. With any luck, the left entrance would do her good, as it was further from the governed section of the castle.

Diane made her way to the entrance, checking her surroundings before locking the door of the hallway behind her.

That was strange. There wasn't a guard in sight. She was expecting there to be at least one. Who was protecting the prisoners from their escape? If the Fonoli had indeed taken over, where were they holding the Trenvern officials if not there? Surely they hadn't transferred everyone. Though, it might explain the emptiness of the town. This could be where they were keeping the residents of the town. Unfortunately, if that was the case, Diane wouldn't be able to help them. She had to find her parents first. And if there *were* people to save, she wouldn't do it alone.

With another deep breath and a shakeout of her sweating hands, the red-haired girl grabbed the torch from its stand next to her and approached the door with caution. She slowly turned the knob, further surprised it wasn't locked.

The nagging feeling that something was very wrong only grew. The air around her smelled rotten. Dried urine, mold, and decay wafted their way into her nose, and the girl felt another urge to gag. She held it back, putting her hand over her mouth and nose to filter the stench.

The room was dark and damp. The eerie sound of silence was only interrupted by small echoes of dripping water and scurrying mice. She held the torch in front of her to see some amount of the area, but the brightness of the fire counteracted such adjustment.

Though the cells rose high into the tower where there was more light, Diane knew she was to go deeper. According to her brother, that was where the more dangerous prisoners were kept. She shuddered at the thought of coming across them, but with all the silence, perhaps she would be lucky.

Diane descended the stairs, pulling her shawl in close. It was much colder in here than she anticipated. That, combined with the smell, caused intense discomfort.

She passed the first few cells, which were thankfully empty. As she went on, the torch reflecting her presence, that silence became much more foreboding. The further down she went, the worse it smelled, but no complaints or moans were heard from the prisoners. Curiosity prickled at her skin, telling her to look in the cells, to see the condition these beaten humans were in. But Diane kept her focus forward.

A fly buzzed around her head, and she swatted it away. She took another step and suddenly, the sounds of dozens of flies rose in a harmonizing hum. Her head turned to the sound.

Diane couldn't help but stare at the sight before her. Two eyes bore lifelessly into hers. Rot and decay were overtaking the corpse in front of her, and he looked more inhuman as she involuntarily scanned the body. One side of his face was burnt to a crisp. The other hung pale, dragging down the features that once adorned color and life.

She couldn't look away. She couldn't move. She couldn't stop the violent shaking in her chest.

Flies fed on him, maggots crawled out of the skin and fell onto the floor only to inch their way back to unburnt bits.

Diane tore her eyes away at the sight but was met with the corpses of others. Most completely burnt, others with only strings of flesh left.

They all looked so... fresh. If she was right about the process of decay, these people died very recently, within the last week or so.

The girl couldn't take it anymore as an acidic composition rose into her throat. She bent over, releasing it and watching as the putrid liquid seeped from one step to the next.

She sat there shaking for a few moments, the hum of flies joined by an undertone of fleshy movements from whatever non-flying creatures might have been feasting on the bodies. Diane wiped her mouth, stumbling to her feet and rushing down the steps. She didn't need to see these horrors. She needed to breathe. She needed to find her family. And if she just held

331

on to her sanity a little longer, she could get to them.

Focus. The bottom of the stairwell lay out in front of her not long after, which meant what she was looking for was nearby.

There were five cells in a circle at the bottom of the dungeon. In between them was a hallway that either led to more cells or the cesspit.

Luckily, these cells were empty and had been for a while. Their walls were crumbling at the foundation.

Diane took a deep breath, moving to pay attention to the details of her surroundings. She was looking for the cell with something different in it. Sure, there were some buckets knocked over in one, a couple of rat droppings in another, but she needed something more substantial.

And then she saw it. In the fourth cell, there was a string hung by a few nails against the right wall, leading to the corner of that cell. Diane went to open the cell door but found that the iron gate was indeed locked. She gave it a shake, frowning when it didn't budge.

She might be able to maneuver her pins to open a regular lock, but these were much more reinforced. Diane made her way to the right side, reaching her arm through the bars to grasp at the string. The iron was cold on her skin, but she pressed forward.

It was just out of reach of her fingertips, however, and no matter how far she pressed her arm through, she couldn't grab it. Diane took a deep breath. She was going to have to get her shoulder through the bars.

Diane bit her lip in anticipation, wrapping her fingers around the inside of the door's iron bars. Hey, who knew, if it didn't work, maybe the door would open instead. She took a few deep breaths, and then, gripping tightly, Diane jammed her shoulder into the gap of the bars.

She felt her shoulder nearly go through for a moment before popping back out. Heaving breaths of pain held her from screaming. Once more. Just try once more.

She gripped the bar tighter, her fingers tapping repeatedly as she counted down again. And then she pushed, with all her weight, all her effort, and as sudden as she could.

She heard it this time, pain shooting through her shoulder.

Diane's hand was shaking as she held back a cry. The bar now rested tightly between her shoulder blade and her collar bone. She raised her arm carefully, reaching out for the string again. Her hand quivered, but the pain was consistent. When Diane's fingers brushed against the end of the string, she smiled in relief. She pinched it lightly at first, slowly tightening her grip around it to not drop it. Diane pulled slightly, just far enough to reach her other arm out to grab it.

Now that there was no use of it, she dropped the arm that was stuck, focusing on the other. She tugged the string towards her and through the nails, wrapping it around her palm a few times. As she did, the wall beside her rumbled slightly, and a vertical rectangular-shaped section of the cobblestone opened to reveal a dark hallway. She pulled a little more until the door opened inwards as far as it could before she released the string back to its position. It hung from the last nail now, more string to grab onto than before.

Diane took a moment to free her arm from the door, grimacing as she did her best to jerk her shoulder back out of the bars. She yelped as it popped back out, relieved to have her arm free again. It was still throbbing, still sensitive and sore, ready to bruise... but it finally felt more comfortable.

The redhead picked her torch back up from the floor, stepping into the doorway. The stones looked natural among the others but were cut half the thickness and backed by a wood door that was rotting at the edges. She saw the other side of the string tied to the handle, pulled back to a small hole in the wall that connected this room with the adjacent cell. She carefully closed the door, pulling the string back into its place.

Diane turned, looking around the walls of the hidden hallways before she began walking. Luckily her memory of the route had only been needed for the location of the door, as this path had only one route.

She had no struggles until the series of ladders she came across about halfway to her destination. It was difficult to put her weight on her shoulder, so she did her best to bring herself up with one arm. This proved ineffective, and at times she was forced to momentarily use the bad arm.

There were times when she could hear muffled voices, footsteps above her, and occasional knocks on the walls. Each one made her jump, and Diane at one point found herself clutching her shawl so tightly that a small movement might rip the fabric.

A rat squeaked in the distance, echoing around the hallway as she turned another corner. Up ahead, she saw a soft glowing light at the end. Her heart fluttered in anticipation. Was it her parents? It had to be, right?

She placed the torch down so it wouldn't give away her approach and began walking cautiously towards the light. There was, of course, the possibility these weren't her parents but an enemy who were somehow able to get the coded message out of them.

Her first view of the room was the faint glow of a torch low to the ground. It illuminated two cots and a pile of blankets. A large, half-filled basket of food sat next to it.

Peeking her head in, Diane saw two figures with their backs turned to her, talking in low voices. Their figures were unmistakable. "Ma?" she whispered out into the dark.

The two turned, and she could see their faces clearly upon the soft firelight.

It was them. It was her parents. Tears sprang instantly into her eyes that matched that of theirs. Diane rushed forward, wrapping her free arm around her mom as both her parents held her close.

They held on for a long moment before separating. "Are you alright?" Her father smoothed out her hair.

"Yeah, I'm okay. Where's Owen?"

Her parents exchanged a worried look. "Hon," her mom paused. "Did you not see him when you followed the princess? He was supposed to be with her." Their voices were barely above a whisper and yet held so much emotion that the room filled with an air of their concern.

"No, we did travel together for a bit, but he was released from his duties. I thought I'd be able to meet him here."

"What?" Her mother's tongue was sharp.

"What is it, Alice?" Diane's father put a hand on his wife's arm.

Alice sighed, standing up straight. "Do you mean to tell me that neither you nor your brother are with the princess?"

"Yes, but you told me I only needed to make sure she got out of Trenvern. And Owen said his assignment was last minute."

"I know. We were relying on him to not abandon his post, but it seems things didn't go as planned." Her mother bit her lip, bringing a hand up to tap her chin in contemplation. A frown hardened her features as she paced.

Diane was lost. What was her mother talking about? She was used to being a part of the plan herself, but Owen? Owen was never a part of it. And if he wasn't here, where was he? Was he stupid enough to go through the border by Hearthshire? Or maybe he came to the castle to report to his commanding officer… Which meant—

"Oh no," Diane whispered. Her parents' heads snapped toward her. "He must not realize what happened. The Fonoli— they must have captured him."

"The Fonoli? No, they—"

"Shh!" Diane's father silenced them. "He's back." He waved them over to a spot on the opposite wall. Light shined through a large crack in the stone where grout usually went.

She peered through the crack. Diane realized now where exactly they were. It was the Royal Office. She could only see as high as the desk, but she knew simply by what was adorned upon it and the decorations that hung on the wall behind.

Alice smoothed out Diane's hair. "We can talk later. I'm glad you're okay, hon." She kissed her daughter's forehead.

"And the other asset?" a low, gruff voice asked. There was pride in it, the kind that, knowing their own situation, disgusted her.

"Sent message that they're leaving their post, following the princess as we speak," another voice said, this one much less aggressive.

Did they mean Alanitora? It made sense. If the Fonoli had taken over Trenvern, then they were likely to try and kill the last heir.

Unable to hold in her frustration, her fists tightened in anger. Her mother was right, she shouldn't have left Alanitora.

The first man grumbled as he made his way around the desk. She couldn't see his face, but the man was decked out in jewels fit for a king, Trenvern's king. He wore King Ronoleaus' robe with pride, happy to show off the murder of the monarch like a hunter with fur pelts. Diane may not have liked the king, but he was better than the Fonoli, who had burned down her home.

She wished she could burst through the wall and slice his throat herself, but her needles would not suffice in a satisfying sweep of the neck. Instead, Diane kept watching, her anger bubbling.

It was at this moment that this imposter king threw an object on the table. It took a strain of her eyes, but then she saw the dagger clearly. It was nearly identical to one she had seen before: a silver blade with a metal dragon wrapped around the hilt. There was a bloodstain on it, and when the imposter king picked it up to wipe it off, she could see that it was indeed fresh with how it shined in the light.

The imposter spoke again. "Make sure you get a report of the parade. With her perverted luck, I'm sure the princess will evade death once again. The attempt won't be in vain though, it should plant seeds of doubt."

"Yes, Your Majesty."

"Oh, and summon the new recruits for a meeting later this week. We will need to give them the motivation to carry out the plan."

"Yes, Your Majesty."

"Now go. I have private business to attend to."

It was the Men of the Blood Dragon. There was no doubt about it. And this man, whoever he was, was most certainly high up in their twisted cult.

A series of footsteps walked away from the room, and the imposter king sighed, collapsing himself into his chair.

No.

That was impossible. She had watched him die.

The night of the fire, she had seen him impaled by a sword up above, where everyone could see. He had slumped to the ground, a sword in his torso, his death was burned into her mind. She'd told Alanitora he was dead too. But now—

336

Diane looked to her mother in shock, but Alice's face was imperturbable. Had she known? Her head zipped back to the imposter king.

Well, *imposter* may not have been the right word.

The wicked grin on King Ronoleaus' face widened, as he turned the dagger in his hand. "You'll pay, Alanitora, your mother as well, if the bitch isn't already dead."

Ronoleaus stabbed the dagger point first into the desk, the glinting ruby eye of the dragon staring straight at Diane.

26

The Crone

T he next couple of days had been completely awful for Owen. First, there was the issue of his damned horse, who, on top of Owen's inadequate riding, seemed to dislike him. The steed always shook his head, stayed still on more than one whip of the reins, and consistently threw a fit when they rode at a steady pace. At first, he thought it was just his faulty riding, but soon after he found himself inclined to believe that the horse had it out for him. He pondered if giving him such a stubborn horse was intentional on Regenfrithu's part, though there was nothing to suggest such.

In fact, that was another of his issues. The prince didn't fit his expectation of being high maintenance, but he still held a haughty air to him that shouted superiority. Owen didn't need there to be a competition of masculinity between them, especially given the power imbalance, but that didn't stop his sour thoughts. Alanitora's fate should not be Regenfrithu's concern, yet he persistently pretended it was.

When Elena further explained the situation to the prince, Owen's role, and who she was, his attitude towards her changed. He treated her with respect, as though she was a colleague, all while ignoring Owen every chance he could. He was silent when the rest of them were, which was often, but if conversation was ever brought up, he was cordial to the former queen. Owen supposed it was only a headache to him rather than a hindrance.

Perhaps the prince felt the same way about him.

Lastly, and far from least, what bothered Owen most about their trip was the time. Sure, the journey was a bore, he was used to that. Looking forward and staying silent was the purpose of his job, but in this situation, he kicked himself at how slow they were. Whenever he brought up these concerns, Elena tried to pacify them, claiming they would get there in time.

It was frustrating. Why would she, who knew the situation better than anyone, be least concerned with their speed? Alanitora's life was at stake, and if she loved her as she claimed, she should be rushing to get to Donasela as fast as possible.

There was a feeling in his gut, a feeling that told him time was of the essence, and trotting casually was wasting it. Elena was hiding something else, he knew it, yet he had no way to get it out of her.

At this point, it felt like he was the only of the three who actually cared. Despite Elena's maternal relation, despite Regenfrithu's claim of connection, Owen knew he was the only one who understood Alanitora.

There had been a point not far from Kreaha's capital where they came across the remains of what at first looked like a carriage crash. Contents of traveling inventory lay left and right, whether it be torn clothes or splintered wood strewn about. The three were willing to ignore the scene until a more violent, messier one came into view.

"By the blackbird…" Regenfrithu gasped, pulling his horse to slow down.

Elena was the first to dismount, kneeling to observe the dried dark red liquid that pooled across the ground. There were similar spots of dark crimson riddled across the path. She picked at it with her fingertips. "A battle took place."

It was already the thought on their minds, but her words were what persuaded Owen to get off his horse and join her search of the area. There wasn't much. All the spots of blood looked like they were from nonfatal wounds, and none indicated a larger pool or any corpse.

"Oh no…" Regenfrithu was at the side of the road, peering into the forest with the little light they had.

"What is it?" Elena stood.

He plucked an arrow from a trunk. A scrap of fabric fell from it. Someone had been pinned to the tree. "Sagittarius was here."

"Who?" Owen asked.

"A lone bandit from around these parts. She attacked us during the ball the other night... Alanitora was there. Fought her off well."

"That's my girl." Elena smiled, her comment was quiet, but Owen couldn't help but smile as well.

A sense of dread suddenly overcame the soldier. "Do you think—" He frowned. "Do you think that she came after Alanitora? For a rematch?"

The same dreadful face struck Regenfrithu's features.

"No." Both their heads turned to Elena. "Multiple people fought here, if your Sagittarius attacked, she wasn't alone doing it. And since there are so many people in my daughter's entourage, they likely wouldn't have succeeded. It wasn't a personal attack."

"That's not like her, but Sagittarius was here. This is her arrow, I'm sure of it, and there isn't usually this much blood."

"Then she was likely raiding another party. It's not of our concern." Elena, finding no other evidence of importance to her, mounted her horse, ushering the men to continue on their journey.

The next day was spent gaining progress towards their destination. As Regenfrithu promised, there was an outpost for them to trade their horses in for new ones along the way. At night, the three of them lay around a small campfire. Owen found he couldn't bring himself to sleep. His heart constantly aching at the thought of what was to come, and who he could trust.

Regenfrithu was much too clueless about the situation to be plotting against them. And Elena, well, Owen felt it hard to completely believe her, but he was done with his blind faith in the opposing side. In the present moment, his best bet was to follow Elena. She knew what to do. She would be able to get them into Donasela. If anyone tried to blindside him, he'd just have to be sure he didn't die and warn Alanitora himself.

As they approached the Kreahan-Donaselan border on the second day, Regenfrithu fell back to converse with Owen for the first time. He started with simple questions about his upbringing, home, and family, which Owen had no problem answering so long as no vital details were shared.

He talked about growing up in two worlds at first, sometimes roaming the castle as a lady's son, other times frolicking among the capital town like any other common kid. He restrained himself from speaking of his relationship with Alanitora, as well as his training with the Trenvern soldiers.

"And you? I don't know much about Kreaha, especially the royal family. Do you find yourself at peace with your relatives?" Owen hoped this wasn't too personal for Regenfrithu, but at that same time, he was digging no more than the prince had mere minutes ago. Besides, this was the first courteous conversation they'd had. Something told the soldier it wouldn't last.

"I am. My mother and father are good people. I wasn't always raised by them in the way you were, but they did their best when they weren't busy. My sister might say different."

"Oh, you have a sister?" That was right, Regenfrithu had mentioned her briefly in their meeting.

"Yes, Princess Lorenalia. She's much more… rebellious than I. I'll admit I've never been too close to her. She's heading to Donasela with Alanitora as well. And you, do you have any siblings?"

"Diane. She's fifteen and quite rebellious herself. Well, I'd say more on the bratty side."

Regenfrithu perked at the mention. "Say, I believe I met your sister. She was a part of Alanitora's entourage, was she not?"

So much for keeping Alanitora out of the conversation. "Yes."

"Well, I regret to inform you that she did not leave with the rest of Alanitora's party."

"I'm aware." Owen looked up to Elena, unsure of how much detail should be shared. The former queen was not paying attention to them, however. "We encountered her on our way towards Kreaha, she was heading back home."

"And you didn't go with her?"

"No."

"Well, why not? Nothing is waiting for you in Donasela."

Was he serious? Was this him trying to heat him up? Prompt him to become angry? There was no smug grin on his face, but nothing to indicate innocence either. Owen controlled his breath. "There may not be, but I still intend to play my role as defender of my kingdom. If you have an issue with that, perhaps you should return home."

"She's not going to love you for this, you know. If you think being her valiant knight in shining armor will win her affections, I would try reevaluating your perspective."

Owen could agree. He could act nonchalant, or ignore him. But the ruffling of his feathers was too persistent for him to not fight back.

"And if you think she won't see through your selfish intentions, you clearly don't know her well—"

"Enough. Both of you," Elena called out from ahead. She didn't have to turn for Owen to know she was talking to them. "I can practically feel your over-compensation from here."

Queen Elena turned her horse perpendicular, stopping at the road in front of them. Regenfrithu's horse came to a stop. Owen had to pull at his reins repeatedly to gain control of his.

She gave them a steely glare. "So that you are aware, I understand the driving motivations of young men, I've been the victim of their antics. But you two. Oh, you two are something else." Elena raised her head, looking down at them. "I'll say this once, and don't think about dismissing it because my daughter would agree in a heartbeat. Alanitora is not a prize. She is not a golden fleece, nor is she the kind to be only interested in romantic endeavors. The two of you may think yourselves worthy of her affection but I raised that girl since she was a small babe and I have watched her grow more than either of you can comprehend.

"You think you know her? You think you can win her heart? Think again. There is nothing to win of that girl's heart, I've made sure of that. She will know what she wants and she will be the one to decide. But understand me when I tell you that if I find her choices to be faulty, I'll make sure *myself* that you have no chance to pursue whatever it is that your mind fantasizes about with my daughter. Now silence. If I hear one of you start any kind of quarrelsome behavior I will not hesitate to continue this journey in solitude."

One might hear the scurrying of a mouse fields away in the silence the three of them were left with.

"Are we clear?"

"Yes," Owen stated.

"I apologize, Your Majesty." Regenfrithu bowed his head slightly.

"And to think I had hoped you'd emerge from the conversation with a close companionship of your own." Elena turned her horse back to the road.

Owen and Regenfrithu exchanged a look before the soldier nodded forward, prompting the prince to ride ahead of him.

They made their way into the bordering town as night fell, stopping just before to discuss the plan. Owen was set to do the communication since Regenfrithu would be recognizable as the kingdom's prince and if an enemy recognized Elena they might do anything in their power to stop them from crossing into Donasela. Owen held back a smirk as Regenfrithu spent time spreading dirt across his pretty face to make himself less noticeable. He also had to change out of his clothes, as even though they were set for an excursion such as this, they were still too flamboyant to flaunt around as a commoner. Without a word, Owen gave the prince the cloak he bought at the Kreahan capital. If not to disguise him, then to be sure he didn't freeze in the night air.

They made their way through the village itself without any complications, though the soldier wouldn't be surprised if someone could feel the palpable paranoia that surrounded the three.

Regenfrithu explained how this particular border worked, with the village having been established as neutral ground between the two territories. When Donasela reinforced their borders two decades back, the city agreed to be the main passing point to gain both commercial success and compensate for the split. According to what he had heard, many residents have an inking in their skin that shows they are a native and can pass through without routine checks, but most of the time patrol is familiar with their faces, and such is not needed.

Owen led the three of them at the crossing point, before being instructed to halt by a guard that stepped in their way.

"Apologies, sir," she began, clasping her hands behind her back. "But the border is closed for the night. There was a recent attack, and we cannot accept anyone else onto Donaselan soil for the time being."

Owen exchanged a look with Elena. She gave him a nod to reassure him before he turned back. "We do have urgent business to attend to, is there any way for us to get through?" It was worth a try.

The guard shook her head. "You'll have to wait until tomorrow morning to pass through."

Aware there was nothing more he could do at that moment, Owen turned his horse around, prepared to withdraw.

Regenfrithu, however, had a different idea, stepping forward himself. "And, just out of curiosity, when will the royal wedding be?"

Owen had half a mind to kick his mouth shut before he was recognized. Luckily the young guard paid no mind. "Likely two or three days from now. I'll have you know it is a private event if you were thinking of attending."

"No, no, just curious." Regenfrithu flashed a charming smile, thanking the woman before following Owen and Elena to the side of the road.

Owen sighed, running a hand through his hair in frustration. "Well, what do we do?"

"Should we try to sneak across?" Regenfrithu suggested. "It seems residents are still going between. If we fake the tattoos—"

"That won't work, not if the same guard is on patrol."

"Then I'll get us in. They'd let the Prince of Kreaha pass."

"No! That's too risky." Owen's rebuke summoned a frown on Regenfrithu's brow and a look that said he was ready to swing his fist at the soldier again.

"Owen's right." Elena subsided their glares at one another. "It's too risky to try and sneak across. We'll have to wait. The last thing we need is to draw attention to ourselves."

"Now that you mention it, maybe we should." Regenfrithu looked aside pensively. "Draw attention to ourselves, that is. If the palace gets news of our presence, either of us, surely they'll put the wedding on hold."

"Absolutely not," Elena snapped, it took Owen back for a moment, hearing her with a sharp tongue directed at the prince. "We do that and Alanitora is dead. They will kill her without hesitation if the wedding doesn't go as planned."

"Dammit," Regenfrithu spat.

Sighing, the soldier looked between the two. "Then we stay the night, and cross tomorrow morning."

For the first time, Regenfrithu agreed with him.

It seemed that fate was not on their side the next morning, as even though they chose an inn that looked right over the road, none of them had anticipated the long line of people who had queued to cross as well. Some were there to attend the wedding celebration, and others were leaving the events that had taken place in Kreaha, making it even more complicated that they were not to be recognized.

A large majority of the morning was spent pacing around the inn room, waiting for the activity to die down, for if one of Regenfrithu's suitors recognized him, everything would turn over.

The idea of *"better safe than sorry"* was something Owen thought might apply to this situation, if being safe hadn't meant Alanitora's life was on the line.

By noon the border had cleared up significantly, and the trio made their way into the queue without difficulty. The stableman in which they gave their horses to the previous night was delighted to learn that such steeds were branded by the Kreahan government, and was happy to trade them for new horses and a few rations of food to compensate.

Adding a small streak to their luck, they were able to pass through the border with no hesitation nor abnormalities and were soon on their way. They stayed quiet for most of the ride, either preoccupied with their surroundings or their thoughts.

As the afternoon sun began to dip closer to the horizon, Queen Elena veered off of the main road. Owen didn't question it at first, assuming it meant they were just avoiding a crowd of opposing travelers. However, when it became apparent that they would diverge further from the capital if they remained off of the main road, Regenfrithu was the one to bring it up. "Where is it that we are heading, if I may be so bold to inquire?"

Elena looked back at the boys, and her expression read as though she'd either forgotten they were there or hoped they'd be gone. "The home of a friend."

For what felt like the hundredth time in journeying with the secretive woman, Owen felt the urge to question her. And for the first time, he held back from doing so.

It was late afternoon when their destination came into view. They had been riding across fields of farms and wildflowers alike before it was clear they were making their way behind the castle. Its towers were well in view over the hills a league away.

Elena dismounted her horse, signaling the end of their journey. There was a small quaint cottage on the top of one of the hills. A welcoming glow of firelight cascaded onto its windows. And in this brightness, Elena held a fond smile on her face. One Owen hadn't seen from the queen since he was a boy.

Rows of brilliant flowers paved the way as they got closer. Each one was unique, and all were cared for with a great deal of love.

A gray-haired woman stepped out of the cottage, her hands clasped to her heart, and her smile so wide Owen could see the creases of her face from where he was.

Elena handed her reins to Regenfrithu at this moment, before walking towards the woman with determination in her step.

"Is she—?" Regenfrithu began.

"I have no idea," Owen responded, dismounting his horse as well and following the former queen.

"Oh, El…" He could see the woman's features quite well now: She was older than Elena, but not enough to be the age of her mother. Her wrinkles were slight and formed into a loving smile, and despite such signs of old age, she looked young in a way. Jubilant. The woman's eyes were glossed with tears as she pulled Elena into a hug.

"Hadiya." Elena returned the hug with joy. "It's been too long."

"Too long? Now that is an understatement dear. And getting your letter was quite the surprise." The two separated. Hadiya looked up at the prince and the soldier, a questioning look on her face.

Elena followed her gaze. "Oh, they're here to help. This is Prince Regenfrithu of Kreaha, and Owen, a trusted soldier of Trenvern."

The woman's smile pressed into a thin line. She nodded at the two of them. "Very well. there's a place for your horses in the barn. Once you boys deliver them, come on in through the back door. I've prepared the water for tea."

After putting away their steeds without exchange of words, Owen and Regenfrithu entered the cottage. It was warm and cozy, the kind of place you might want to spend the rest of your old life at. A clutter of blankets and pillows lay in front of the small fireplace, which held a bubbling iron pot. Countertops lined the edge of the walls, allowing the windows to cast the light of the evening sun onto the ingredients of a stew. Dried herbs and flowers hung from the ceiling, while a more lively bouquet rested in the vase at the table where the two women sat.

"Nonsense dear, what a mother does to protect her kin is forgiven above all— Oh!" Hadiya jumped out of her seat at their entrance. "Please, sit. You're lucky I made enough food to feed El five times over. Blame it on such a tiny figure." She gave a hearty laugh and made her way to the fire stove to mix whatever concoction was in it.

Owen, for one, had no idea what was going on. He exchanged a silent look with Regenfrithu, who was unsurprisingly just as confused. There were so many questions in his mind, but something kept him from asking them. This Hadiya seemed a kind woman, but also had an aura to her that

347

suggested she would curse anyone who said anything disrespectful.

Perhaps she was a witch. It would explain the plants.

Elena, on the other hand, was completely relaxed. Her posture was the least tight he had seen since the start of their travels, and she was sipping her tea comfortably. "I must ask, how is Balgair?"

"Oh, you know Thomas. Insistent he isn't overworking himself, then constantly complains about how much sleep he's getting."

"It's nice to know that nothing's changed." Elena placed her cup down, looking over at Owen and giving him a nod and a smile as if to say it was alright for them to relax.

"He'll be home tomorrow morning. That's when we will tell him. Thomas will be able to help get you to your daughter before the wedding."

"And you've told neither him nor anyone else of the predicament?"

Hadiya frowned, dropping her ladle back in the soup contents. "Absolutely not. I very well know the severity of what could happen had I done so."

Elena's face softened. "I apologize, my friend. I find that I can never be too careful these days."

The woman grunted. "Well, you can relax for the night." It was ironic, how the woman who told Owen to have patience, relax and trust her was being scolded for not doing such. "I wasn't expecting your companions though, they'll have to take the barn."

Regenfrithu whipped his head to Owen in a hardly concealed shock. Clearly, he wasn't too used to sleeping on the floor with hay and bugs.

"It's fine. I'll stay there with them. Someone should keep watch of them anyway." Yeah, Owen would rather be under Elena's sharp eye than wake up in the middle of the night with Hadiya holding a knife over him... not that it would happen.

"Well. You all should eat. There are some arduous challenges ahead.

Despite being wrapped up in several wool blankets that the kind—albeit terrifying—lady had provided them, the draft that came from the dilapidating ceiling of the barn cooled his cheeks. He lay on his side with his eyes closed for a long while, hoping to let sleep him take over.

There was no bliss in the darkness. No peace in his turmoil. There was, however, a whisper in the night that caused his eyes to flicker open, the sight of Elena looking up in the moonlight imprinting on his mind.

She stared up through the hole in the barn as though the stars were all falling. Her eyes shone in somber awe at the sky above. A certain peace settled on her face as she whispered words lightly into the night. He couldn't make out much of what she said but the end of her prayers was most distinct. "You are strong, my love, I only hope our separation has made you stronger, for I fear breaking you."

Owen watched as a tear rolled down her face, and even though such a sight might typically be saddening, there was a certain indescribable beauty to it.

27

Human Nature

The day before the wedding was spent with so many preparations that Alanitora could hardly keep track of them in her memory. Right as she woke up, she was bombarded with questions by her ladies-in-waiting, who were eager to hear of a possible budding romance between her and her betrothed. She explained that while she had no love for him necessarily, there was nothing wrong with the man. That he had, in fact, been quite kind to her.

Korena was quite insistent that things were to change, as "who wouldn't fall in love with the great Princess Alanitora?"

"Queen," Gwendolyn then corrected.

Queen still felt strange to her, as she only associated it with thoughts of her mother upon hearing it.

In ironic contrast to Korena's comments of a budding romance, the three of them saw the Prince of Donasela leaning into a conversation with Sagittarius not much later that morning. Alanitora couldn't help but wonder if he had already fallen for the other brunette. Well, as much of a brunette Sagittarius was with the scarlet ends of her hair.

She observed them for a moment before Sage shot her a glance, one that asked to be saved from the interaction.

"Good morning to you two," Alanitora said cordially.

"Ah, Your Highness. I apologize, I did not see you there." Daruthel separated from the archer, greeting Alanitora with a bow. "How was your first night?"

"Quite fine, thank you." This, of course, was a lie. She hadn't slept very well despite her exhaustion. Too much to think about.

"Your beds are quite comfortable, I might note. Why, I think the most comfortable I've lain upon ever!" Korena cheerfully took up the conversation, and Daruthel listened attentively. Alanitora wondered how long he might hold polite affairs to her bubbly friend before giving up like most others.

He engaged actively in the time being, the flow of conversation as easy as a riverbank. He asked questions with genuine intrigue, brought others into the discussion, and went far enough to repeat back their answers.

This went on for a short while, allowing Sagittarius to lean back and take inventory of Alanitora instead. They had their own silent exchange briefly before Daruthel asked the four of them if they would like a tour of the castle.

"Yes, of course. That would be wonderful—" Alanitora looked between the prince and Sage, who was fidgeting at the prospect. She sputtered to give her an excuse. "Sagittarius, could you do me the greatest favor and find my weapons chest for me? I'll be needing it in my rooms." She would have to ask Sage about it in a later interaction. See if she was uncomfortable around Daruthel for any particular reason.

"Of course." Sagittarius smiled, walking past the prince before mouthing, *"Thank you."*

The tour was excellent, as not only was Donasela grand in size, but also in lightness. It wasn't overly bright and opulent like Kreaha's palace, nor dark and damp like her own. It was, quite honestly, perfect. A word she hadn't thought she would ever associate with a castle, yet there they were.

There was a lot of walking, some general gestures by Daruthel to halls they'd rather not waste time going in, and ultimately an extended show of the essential parts. The biggest, most impressive room by far was the armory. She hadn't been allowed in Trenvern's, but there was no doubt that Donasela's was much larger. It made sense, given that their main export was weapons and armor.

Daruthel spent some time explaining the history of the castle, taking them to certain points that he had attached memories to. Saying the man was sentimental would be an understatement. He talked about his friends growing up, how his mother passed when he was five, and how he took on a number of responsibilities as an adolescent.

"Sounds like you're quite prepared to lead your kingdom," Alanitora commented softly.

"Yes. Though, let me be clear that I am not in any way saying my father is incapable of it. He just found himself in an awfully low spot after everything we had been through, and though he did not need me to, I felt I should help. I find that two minds, especially if they contrast, are better than one." He winked, and for a second she saw something so familiar in his eyes. Something she had seen often but couldn't quite place her finger on. "He focused on the logistics, I focused on our people."

"Is that why the people love you and your father so?" Gwendolyn asked.

Daruthel laughed. "I suppose you could say such, yes. Compassion has often been a strong suit of mine. I can't imagine ruling people without considering their good health."

This was not at all what Alanitora was taught a leader should be, especially by her father's standards. Being above others and highlighting that difference was what led one to respect, especially in times when things got rough. Respect for authority meant cooperation and understanding of what was necessary for the good of the kingdom. She could tell her mother, on the other hand, was less inclined to the idea, but Queen Elena rarely talked of ruling with her daughter anyway.

Their meeting came to an end at the entrance hall, where a large coat of arms was chiseled into the wall. A statue of a fox stood on its hind legs in front of it.

That was right... Alanitora had completely forgotten that Donasela's animal was a fox. She smiled at the statue's glinting eyes. It was wonderful craftsmanship. There was a humane amount of detail to it. Fine hairs along its stone coat, realism in the features of its face. Enough to catch her attention for more than one glance.

With one last line of exposition, Daruthel explained the speculative tale of how the fox came to be their symbol. She didn't pay much attention, already tired from walking and talking, but Alanitora endured each and every word with feigned interest.

She was relieved when they were released from the binds of social banter, which might be good to have with her future spouse if she weren't so exhausted. Regardless, the fate of the day had another plan for her, and it was just when she was ready to collapse on her bed that Korena and Gwendolyn whisked her from relaxation upon finding her wedding dress.

They jumped about excitedly, swinging her arms around and squealing with anticipation, begging her to at least look at it. Reluctantly, Alanitora agreed. She wanted one moment away from the wedding ordeal, but things were not so easily escapable. Perhaps it would be better to get this last thing over with.

It was a wonderful dress. A white gown cascaded across the floor, layers and layers of fine materials of satin, silk, and chiffon wrapped around. The bodice was the most eccentric to any she had seen before. Embroidered flowers with thin gaps mimicked a traditional lace in appearance but held thicker bonds. The texture was wonderful to run her fingers over, as the grooves of flowers and leaves cascaded from the bust to the v-shaped waist.

"Where did you get this?" she asked, holding it up to her chest. It was nearly the perfect height.

"We came across it a bit back in Trenvern while going through some old possessions."

"Well, it's absolutely gorgeous." Alanitora gaped at the dress. She could hardly believe this had been locked away somewhere at home for... who knew how many years.

"Oh, won't you try it on!" Korena clasped her hands together. "I'll need to alter it as best I can before the big day, and I'd rather get a head start now than stay up at night. I have to look pretty for the grand event."

"Of course." She was far from opposed to this being her dress for the occasion, and the excitement around its beauty was enough to snap her awake for a little longer.

It took them a while to find the proper undergarments that would not reveal themselves under the shape of the dress, but once they did, Alanitora slid it on with ease, quite surprised it already fit her well. She looked in the large mirror of the room, spinning herself left and right to get a look.

It wasn't often that Alanitora thought of herself as beautiful. She had always acknowledged it, but never really felt like it mattered. Yet in this dress, she felt as gorgeous as a golden sunset. The slight cream color complimented her skin and contrasted with her hair equally. The curves of the dress followed her hips and the skirts were not too large nor too constricting. It highlighted her figure, glowing in the specs of afternoon light.

Korena had her stand still for another hour as she went around and altered the dress while it was still on the princess. This was not normally their process, but Korena did it with ease, as there weren't too many changes to make.

"The stitch work really is incredible," she commented, taking a close look at the hem between her fingers.

Gwendolyn, who was there to supply her with whatever was needed, stopped to look as well. "Oh, certainly!" she exclaimed.

It was at this point that the door burst open, giving the three a shock, only to find Sage standing there.

"Hey, so I—" She paused, taking in the sight. "My stars, Dagger Eyes, you dress up quite well." She looked her up and down before entering the room, a wide smirk upon her face.

"I agree wholeheartedly." Gwendolyn smiled. "What do you have there?"

Sagittarius looked down at her hands where she held two fine leather boots. "Oh! I got them from Daruthel's room, aren't they nice?"

"Ooooh," Korena cooed, a needle between her lips. "So you and Daruthel...?"

Sagittarius raised her eyes in quiet confusion before she realized what Korena was insinuating. "Hell no, I stole them!"

Alanitora let her mouth agape. The princess supposed that she shouldn't expect her to end her thieving ways just because she was under her employment. It may not have been the best business to let her steal from her future husband, but in an honesty she wouldn't admit, she wasn't too motivated to correct her.

"You—" Gwendolyn began.

A gasp sounded from Korena, and Alanitora might have jumped back if she weren't consciously standing so still.

"Tora look! There's a little hidden dragonfly in the corner of your skirt!" In her general flightiness, Korena popped up to show her, forgetting about Sagittarius' situation as soon as romantic endeavors were no longer a part of it.

Alanitora chuckled, running her fingers over the embroidered dragonfly. It was an endearing little detail. The thread was the same color as the skirt, making it easy to miss, but when taking in the actual details, she could see that each strand was perfectly placed. Curling wings and a sectioned thorax.

Gwendolyn put down the pincushion she was holding. "How are our other companions, Sagittarius? Are they faring well with their arrangements?"

"Lorenalia, Tathra, and the other one? I wouldn't know. I mean, I saw them, but I have no idea how they are. I didn't bother to ask."

Gwendolyn sighed, a slightly annoyed scowl on her face.

"I *did*, however, bother to ask the townspeople if they were content with the actions of the crown. Surprisingly, they were." Sage took a moment to move aside some of Alanitora's hair to get a better look at the neckline. She gave it a shrug of approval. "And get this: their satisfaction was even to the point where when I asked if there was anything the crown could do to improve as better rulers, they only ever gave me boring and mundane requests. Like, a new theater, or better sewage management. Seriously, where's the fun in that?"

Alanitora shook her head. She'd never been one to pursue adventure herself, but employing Sagittarius did just that. The archer paced around for a bit longer, either judging the contents of the room or examining

Korena's work.

The rest of the day in itself was, while busy, fairly uneventful. Alanitora and her ladies separated for the majority of it, as while the two were to direct the moving of her possessions into new chambers, she was to meet with Balgair and continue their discussion from the previous night.

The old advisor brought some light to her mind by telling her stories and jokes as they made arrangements for the wedding. When it rolled into the afternoon, she offered to eat lunch with him, which he graciously accepted. Balgair was able to put her at ease as they dined. It was such small actions that labeled him a good source of tranquility. His warm presence reminded her that through difficult and unclear times, the sun could still shine through.

The only other man who had given her that same comforting energy was Corwyn. In light of this revelation, the princess found herself making a detour across the castle afterward to find the knight. She found him among a collection of Trenvern soldiers in the Great Hall, who toasted her presence. It was warming to see that a majority of their attitudes towards her had changed from confused hesitance and the blank stares they gave her not a week ago.

She smiled at the lot of them before asking Corwyn if he was able to step away for a while. He obliged, and she led him to a secluded corner of the room.

"Is everything alright? I cannot help but still feel awful about the other day. I promise you we are doing everything we can to investigate with the local authorities about what happened. If there is anything I can—"

She placed a hand on his arm to stop him. "Sir Corwyn. It is all fine. Truly. That wasn't what I wanted to speak with you about."

He readjusted his footing. "Alright then. What can I do for you?"

"Nothing necessarily. I just wanted to take a moment to..." To what, exactly? Alanitora wasn't entirely sure what she had wanted to tell him, only that she'd had the urge to hold tight to his positive light. "To thank you again. For your dedication and guidance. For your resolve and kindness."

"I'm just doing my job, Your Highness." He laughed, averting his eyes in the humble manner that was so true to his character.

"No, you aren't." She tilted her head to the side. "I've met many a men who are just doing their job. You, Sir Corwyn, bring more than that. You bring altruism and grace to your name. You embody loyalty and clemency."

He closed his eyes pensively, nodding as he took in her words. "Then I have to disagree with you again, as I am only doing my job as a human upon this earth."

Alanitora considered this. Perhaps that was who he was. The personification of humanity. Though not all of it, for she had seen too often the nefarious aspects of humanity. Corwyn instead was the epitome of humanity's capability in her eyes. And if he saw that as his role in life, so be it.

She hummed in agreement. "I will admit, I have been curious—Now that your task of accompanying me safely here has come to an end, what will you and your men do?"

Corwyn's smile brightened, his eyes creasing so far above his grin that they nearly disappeared. "Well, we may not be on Trenvern soil anymore, but we are within jurisdiction to receive orders from what may be our newfound leader. In any case, it's up to you where we venture. Protocol might be to return to the capital to await further instruction, but serving you is our first priority, so if you require our assistance here, we will grant it."

Alanitora looked back over to the table of soldiers within her entourage. "If I'm being completely honest… I would prefer it if you and I did not have to say farewell. You've proven yourself to be the most amazing of allies. I could use your guidance and knowledge in the forming cloud of confusion. But I also understand that a number of our entourage—and perhaps you as well—have families at home they could be worried sick about. If they wish to leave, they should be able to." She turned her eyes back to Sir Corwyn. "We can wait until after the wedding to figure all of that out. When the time comes, you and I can talk to the troops together."

"Very well, Your Highness." He bowed, crossing his arms behind his back in preparation to bid her a good day.

"Sir Corwyn?"

"Yes?"

"Would it be alright if I gave you a hug?"

His eyebrows raised in surprise, but a smile soon replaced his shock. "Of course."

She wrapped her arms around his core, and as he embraced her back, she rested her head on his shoulder. Alanitora closed her eyes. "I really do appreciate you."

She felt his hand at the back of her head. "And I you."

It was late in the evening when all of Alanitora's companions came back together for supper. Lighthearted conversations arose among stressful times. It seemed the other three nobles were having a wonderful time in Donasela, which was all Alanitora could have asked for, as their host of sorts.

Lorenalia recalled her time on the outskirts of the capital, where she struck up a conversation with passing citizens and surveyed the landscape. Meli broke their silence for the night to detail how the two of them also took some time to pick a number of flowers for Lorenalia's outfit the following day. It was no surprise that Lorenalia was the type to decorate herself with a flourish of color.

Zinaw admitted that she'd spent a majority of the day locked in her rooms begrudgingly trying to train Silver Moon before she and the wolves paraded around the castle. Apparently, people were, "overjoyed to give the canines an undying amount of attention."

Then there was Tathra, who spent her time in the town, just to see what it was all like. She offered to let Alanitora know what her impression was at a later time, given that a second course was about to be served.

Though not their intention, the reported activities of each of them helped ease Alanitora's rising apprehensions. All seemed well so far, and it was already exhausting to be here without thinking of other aspects of Donasela's capital.

As supper continued, Alanitora found her energy increasingly spent, even without conversation. Everyone else was preoccupied with one another, particularly Gwendolyn and Korena, who enjoyed laying out the gossip they'd heard thus far.

The only person not in attendance from Alanitora's party was Sagittarius, and the princess found herself wondering where the bandit was. She'd seen her earlier that day, but her absence caused increasing boredom among everyone else. Strangely, Alanitora didn't know why. It wasn't as though Sagittarius had anything particularly interesting to bring to the table. Additionally, she had already checked in and given her a debrief of her findings earlier. There was no need for Alanitora to speak with her.

The rest of the evening was just as uneventful and even more tiring. Alanitora did not have time to catch a break until all of her things were moved into her traditional pre-ceremony quarters. She wasn't sure if they would be her personal quarters *after* the wedding, but after all of that, she desperately did not want to have to move her things again.

At last, after waiting an excruciating amount of time to be alone, she could relax. Just her and her thoughts in a silent room. Alanitora lay there upon a new bed, in a castle where she would spend the rest of her life, letting her thoughts run so wild that she nearly feared she was going mad. And even when those damning thoughts dissipated, her heart began to ache more than she could deal. The pain in her chest would not allow her to sleep.

She was so fatigued, and yet, rest was not allowed. Alanitora stared into the abyss of the room, moonlight casting its way onto the chests filled with belongings, making the metal binding glint slightly in the corner of her eyes.

She felt empty. Hollow. Though different from before and for the first time in Alanitora's life, guilt infected her mind for reasons unbeknownst.

"I love you." the voice was faint, but it sprung her from her pillow. She looked around frantically to check for any intruders. There were none.

359

She really was going mad.

And then the scent of something familiar came across her, something that she grew up close to. It was the smell of lavender.

The smell of home.

Tears sprang to her eyes instantaneously, flowing down her cheeks without her control. That stream of liquid salt brought her heart forward. Silently, the princess cried, curling herself back into the bed.

She felt so trapped. She felt so alone.

And she felt like all of it was her fault.

What was the feeling? This feeling that pained her so much. A feeling unyielding that foreboded much worse.

Tomorrow was the day she traded herself for the sake of honor. Tomorrow was the day things would change forever.

Tomorrow was the end.

28

Bound

Alanitora woke up with dried tears on her face. Tears she had no memory of shedding, and tears she wished had never stayed as a reminder of what she was concealing the feeling of.

This was it. Today was the day.

She sat up and looked at the clock on the wall. It was one of the few things the room was previously furnished with. That, the bed frame, and the fireplace. All of her other things had been consolidated into one corner for the time being, as even though the guards offered to set things up, she'd much rather place everything with her ladies.

Two hours. Two hours from now she would be wed.

She did not wake with a note from her ladies, and when she instinctively called out for them there was a cold silence. Her dress lay across a chair, ready for her to put on. And at the foot of her bed, Silver Moon raised his head to look at her.

Alanitora had no issues dressing herself, though it certainly wasn't ideal, as most of her clothing fit best when someone helped her.

Taking a deep breath, the princess pulled the blankets from her legs, swinging her feet down onto the carpeted floor. She might as well get started.

Alanitora stopped by the table where the singular Kreahan rose lay. She'd put it there in the evening yesterday when it came with the rest of her stuff.

It seemed much lighter now, and although the color was starting to slip from the petals, it still held its magnificent scent.

Getting ready was relatively easy up to the point of the wedding dress itself, which held laces on the back that she could not see well enough to tighten.

Once it was on for the most part, she grabbed her shawl to wrap around her shoulders. The morning air was cold, though not unwelcoming. As she brushed out her hair, Alanitora looked out the window at the courtyard below. It was buzzing with people, and the sun shone especially bright on the flora.

A few people noticed her and looked up with bright smiles, waving at their soon-to-be queen with delight. She smiled in return, meeting their greetings with a wave of her own.

"What do you think you're doing?!" A hand grabbed her wrist, jerking her around. She was met with the glare of Francis. Alanitora, after a passing moment of shock, narrowed her eyes at the man. "I thought you were told no one is to see you before the wedding. Such is a violation of tradition."

Silver Moon jumped off the bed, the hair on his back raising as a low growl released from his throat. She wondered if the wolf had noticed him entering as well, or if he had only become alert with Francis' aggression. The latter seemed more likely. Seeing his hostility, Francis threw her hand down. Silver Moon stayed tense, though calmed his protests.

"And you?" Alanitora moved to put her brush down on her vanity, using the reflection of the mirror to look back at the lord-in-waiting.

He scoffed. "It's not as though I am a part of the common folk. There's an exception to high-rank *servants*." He held indignation in his voice with the word. "Move your hair."

Confused, Alanitora gathered her hair over one shoulder, the mass of brown waves covering a large portion of her bodice. Francis strode behind her, and taking her acceptance of his request as permission, tightened the laces of her dress aggressively. She stood her ground as the constant tugs swung her with the motions.

"They say bad luck is bestowed upon the Donaselan bloodline if tradition is not followed." Francis tied the strings together, one hand snaking to her waist and the other placed coldly around the nape of her neck. It was faint rather than forceful, but enough to send chills down her spine. "That includes the process of conception."

She stared straight into his eyes through the mirror, his perversion enough that she was surprised the looking glass didn't break. Alanitora raised her chin. "And what do you mean by that?"

"I mean, that ill fate falls upon a queen who cannot conceive a royal child within the first few months of marriage." A threat. A warning. His hand moved from her waist to her stomach.

Alanitora caught his wrist with her hand, letting her nails dig lightly into the skin. Had she an accessible knife on her she'd slash his fingers instead, but her dress was both white and without folds for weapons that she had been so used to. She pried his hand from her, tossing it aside as she turned to face him.

"I've no need of your assistance, thank you. My ladies will do just fine. Are they not, after all, the *high-ranking servants* you speak of?" She sent a steely glare into his eyes, and he held it firmly. This time, Alanitora could tell that her weapon was not faulty, that instead, he was deliberately holding a shield against it. Taunting her with the idea that she could not break him. His gaze said she was futile in even trying. He was trying to scare her.

Alanitora didn't care. She'd had enough of this. All of it. She'd had enough of the word of a man tying her down to a certain fate. That was for her to decide. If Francis was not the close advisor to her betrothed, she'd incapacitate him then and there. But instead, the princess would play the long game. Ruin him in a slow and suffering path. Getting married was the first part.

Without surrender from her, he yielded. A snarl formed on his face before he broke the stare to head for the door. Silver Moon beat him there, growling much louder as the lord reached for the handle.

"On your way out, be sure to summon my ladies here. I'll be needing their assistance," Alanitora announced.

He hesitated a moment before looking back at her, barely meeting her gaze, as his intimidation had failed. "Yes, Your Highness."

Alanitora nodded, and Silver Moon backed away slowly. The two watched as the man left, closing the door behind him. Once he was gone, she let out a long-held breath. The encounter reminded her it would be important to arm herself just in case. Without the pockets, it might be hard to access quickly, but having blades hidden under the skirt would feel safer than nothing.

Alanitora rustled through her weapons chest, trying to find the perfect blade. Once all this was over she would have to spend time cleaning her weapons, as too many of them were not in the visual condition to be worn to her own wedding. She owned plenty of ornate daggers given to her as birthday presents, but years without use diminished their shine.

Her hand slid across an object and a jab into her finger caused her to withdraw her arm. A wood splinter rested in the pad of her ring finger. She picked it out with frustration. Strange, it wasn't the wood the chest was made of.

She looked back in the chest, pulling out the toy sword from the bottom and chuckling at the idea. It was ironic how the one thing in the chest that wasn't an actual weapon was the one to hurt her.

Wiping off the tiny bead of blood that emerged from her finger and tossing the play sword back in the chest, Alanitora picked out a pair of steel daggers. The tips of the blades curved slightly and the hilts each held an engraved sign, but other than that, they were nothing fancy.

A somber wave washed over her in the next moment, and Alanitora seated herself on the floor of her room with her back against the bed. Silver Moon came over to comfort her. She ran her hand through his thick fur to get her mind off of... well, her mind was blank. Almost numb. There was an empty feeling in her, and she knew she had to release those feelings that caved her chest in.

By the time her ladies had come to her aid, she was no longer wallowing in it, but it still followed her every move like a shadow. This seemed to be a shared sentiment between her, Gwendolyn, and Korena. They too, could feel that she was battling something and as a result, that morning's conversation was as they normally would be had they still been at home: observations about the weather, castle gossip that Alanitora doubted they knew anything about, and constant compliments about Alanitora's appearance, which she accepted with a smile.

But a majority of her mind was elsewhere. She was truly giving up her heart for this, wasn't she? Tales of love and romance had never really concerned her, but now that she knew it wasn't something she could have, Alanitora wanted it. She feared losing it. She was well aware that in the grand scheme of things, this was not what the marriage was about, and it was selfish to want otherwise, but a part of her was fighting so hard.

The princess had to focus on the future. For this was necessary, was it not? The people she had met along the way, all of them, got to choose their fate, didn't they? They got to craft their path, did things their own way without having to worry about responsibility or consequences.

But she did. She held the responsibilities of her whole kingdom.

Alanitora sat still as Gwendolyn wrapped her hair into the golden leaf crown, letting particular curls fall to frame her face. She stared into the emptiness of her reflection, the gaze of hazel irises boring into her own. And at that moment she saw what she could not feel: A sadness, an unfulfilled void.

Alanitora looked away. Soon.

"Get up, now!"

Owen shot awake at the slamming of the barn door. The light of the morning sky blinded him momentarily. He blinked it away, trying to gather a sense of his surroundings.

Hadiya stood above them with a fearsome expression on her face and a parchment clenched in her hand. "Up, I said! No time to waste!" she repeated, waving her arms about.

Elena stood, brushing off the dress that Hadiya provided her the night before. "What is it? What's happened?"

Hadiya shook the papers in her hand out towards Elena, who took them. "I should have known something was wrong when he didn't show up at dawn." She began pacing around the room as the former queen read.

Owen brought himself to his feet, moving to read over Elena's shoulder. "What is it?" Regenfrithu asked, rising as well.

There wasn't enough time for him to read the letter in its entirety when Elena let out a frustrated grunt as she buried her face in her hands. Owen watched as she moved back, her hands fell to her sides with the paper gripped lightly in her fingers. Her eyes darted back and forth, as though she was reading something in her mind. And then, after a few moments, she handed the letter to him and moved towards her satchel.

Owen brought the letter up to read as Regenfrithu walked over and stood next to him. "What's it say? What's going on?"

He skimmed over the words so fast that his eyes tripped off the edge of the page, confounded by the content. Owen moved the letter between him and Regenfrithu so the prince could get a better look. "It's from Hadiya's husband. He says he's sorry that he's been kept at the castle, that there's been an unexpected amount of preparation for the wedding that has held him up day and night in discussion with Donasela's future queen—"

"That must be Alanitora," Regenfrithu commented.

"That's not all though—he says that luckily he should be home in time for supper as they have decided to go through with the traditional Donaselan wedding this morning…"

"Shit," the prince breathed. "We're too late."

Elena swung her cloak over her shoulders, clasping it in a swift motion. "Hadiya, do you still have a map to the temple passage?"

"Of course I do, but the entrance is all the way on the northern side, it would take less time to ride directly to the castle—"

"Do you think that gives us a chance? There is no way we could sneak our way in over the plethora of citizens eager to see their new queen!" Elena's voice rose with bubbled anger. Owen watched Hadiya shrink at her words.

366

She had a right to panic, they all did, but taking it out on someone who was trying to help wasn't the way to go about it.

"It wouldn't be an issue if we hadn't wasted time!" He couldn't stop the reprimand from escaping his lips.

She turned to him. "You think I wanted to waste time? Do you have any idea how cautiously coordinated all this had to be in order to even get this far?! I'm no use to her when I'm dead, but I'm even less of use if they are using a traditional wedding. It all ends at the vows. There is no undoing it. No changing it. No way out."

"Well, you should have told us of that possibility before we even got here!" Owen had told them. He had told them that they should hurry, that they didn't have enough time. But Elena hadn't listened, and now it was coming back to bite them.

Elena's expression went dark as she stepped towards him. "You—"

"Oookay." Regenfrithu moved between them. "How about instead of arguing and wasting more time, we get going. We have a wedding to stop, no?"

Pinching the bridge of her nose, Elena was the first to yield. She relaxed her shoulders with a deep breath. "Right. Get the horses ready. Leave your things here, we don't need the extra weight."

The wedding procession—which started with Daruthel, continued with a series of lords and ladies, and ended with Alanitora—made its way from the Throne Room to the Temple. A large veil had been put over Alanitora's figure to maintain the idea of her not being seen, and in doing so, she could only see the outline of figures ahead of her. Korena and Gwendolyn walked with her per request, guiding her with each step, and making her look far more graceful than she felt.

Despite how slow she was walking, time seemed to pass so fast. It was too soon that she stood at the front steps of the Temple, where the veil was removed from her face. As they entered through the front doors, rows of eyes lay upon her, most unfamiliar. Her gaze made its way to the front of the room, where she at last saw the faces of her companions. This eased some of her worries.

Prince Daruthel stood at the center next to Balgair, who gave her an encouraging smile. She decided to focus on that instead of the whispers and comments from the crowd, plenty of which were about her dress and appearance. The soft murmurs surrounded her like storm clouds not yet ready to release the crackling energy. Only low rumbles and small flashes of light to warn of the inevitable.

She pushed her feet forward. This was the right decision, it had to be. She held her chin high in assurance of that. If this were a battle, this was the move that gave her the upper hand. Everything else that had happened: the violence, the losses, the destruction… All of it be damned if she didn't fight back.

"Swallow your pride," she whispered to herself.

Alanitora reached the front of the room before looking back at where she had come. Korena and Gwendolyn arranged the train of the dress behind her before turning to their seats in the front row. Silver Moon sat patiently next to them with Zinaw. It seemed the girl had trained him quite well in the last few days.

Alanitora turned her gaze back to the prince, but her eyes were distracted by the look on his father's face behind him. King Crevan was completely aghast, something she surmised was the result of the reality that his only son was to be wed, but there was something else that she couldn't quite grasp. He sputtered his mouth open and closed when their eyes met, before forcing a smile and averting his vision.

Corwyn, who must have thought her hesitance was due to a fear of tripping, stood from his seat and helped her up the steps to where she was level with Daruthel. She thanked him with a smile, and the man squeezed her hand before returning to where he was.

Balgair cleared his throat, waiting for the shuffling in the crowd to cease. "If you may, please join hands."

As she did so, Alanitora finally met eyes with Daruthel. There she saw herself reflected back. She wasn't sure what exactly it was that had his eyes mimic hers. It wasn't sorrow or hardship, it was something else entirely, though in the same realm of pain.

"Under the keen eye of the fox, and the lords and ladies that represent it, this fine morning is a celebration of the union between two. One soul of our own in that of Prince Daruthel, and one from afar in that of Queen Alanitora of Trenvern," Balgair spoke of this with pride, that was one comforting thing. "I must ask that we rejoice in this union. That it brings fortune to both families, and by extension, both kingdoms. May it crash down any divide between our lands, and forever hold peace for future generations."

Her mind was drifting away to thoughts of everything she stood for. If all of the assassination attempts said something to her, it was that her life was of value. She would not waste that value. She'd rise above it.

There was nothing set about her future, nothing but her will to move forward. To discover the bounds of the world and to change the way it worked. For if there was one thing she knew, it was that she was capable. Alanitora stood proud at that moment. Of how far she'd come, and how far she would go.

It was the mention of her name that brought the bride back into focus. "Do you, Alanitora, accept this union of marriage willingly and in your own regard?"

She looked between Daruthel and Balgair. "Yes."

"And do you, Daruthel, accept this union of marriage willingly and in your own regard?"

His answer was not without hesitation. "Yes."

"Then, with honor, I ask that you each take this cord and tie your fates together." Balgair turned with a gold rope and handed it to her first.

They had gone over the symbolism of this moment the other night: she would tie her end of the cord around his right wrist, and he would tie his end to her left before the two of them tied said hands together with the remaining rope. Such was the way of a traditional Donaselan wedding, which Balgair claimed had not been used since his grandfather was a child. It was a symbol of binding that would last forever even after the rope was removed, and promised her soul to his for eternity until taken by death. Her future would forever be connected to the man in front of her, and there was no way out of it. Nothing in the universe could break it.

Alanitora took her rope and tied it snugly around his wrist with a nod before giving the other end to him. She had made her final choice. This was how she was going to save her kingdom.

Daruthel began to wrap it around her wrist, nearly folding it over into a knot when there was a loud rumble behind him. He paused, looking up at her.

Unsure if they had been the only ones to hear, Alanitora shifted her eyes around the room. The audience had their eyes focused on one of the fox statues at the front of the Temple. It was moving away from the wall, scraping against the carpet beneath. Something was pushing it, and then it stopped.

The room stayed still, silent in uncertainty. People from the crowd began to stand up, craning their necks to see. Alanitora, too, turned her head in curiosity. She could just barely see the dark of a passage previously covered by the base of the fox. She watched a hand emerge from the passage and curl around the stone.

A figure stepped out from behind the sculpture, taking the hood of their cloak down to reveal long dark brown hair and a fair, structured face. "Cease this wedding at once."

Alanitora nearly couldn't breathe. It was as though she had seen a ghost. With a shaking breath, she pressed one word out of her mouth.

"Mother?" The sound of it reverberated in her head, deeper, more clear, and at that moment she realized she had not been the only one to say it.

The princess looked up at the prince before her, whose eyes met hers in the same moment. And she saw what had been so familiar about them. They were exactly like her own in likeness.

There was no doubt about it. They shared the same blood.

29

The Truth

Alanitora jumped back, the cord tugging at her wrist before falling to the ground. Her eyes shot back and forth between her betrothed and her mother, who stepped closer as two other familiar figures emerged from the statue.

"My love?" Her eyes next hit that of King Crevan, who was stepping down from his spot and towards Elena.

Alanitora watched in near horror as her mother's features softened. No.

No, it couldn't be.

She was dreaming, was she not? This wasn't right, it couldn't be. It made no sense.

She looked past her mother's shoulder, only to find both Regenfrithu and Owen standing there. They stared at her, a different surprise on their features. She couldn't speak, but if she could, she would have called out to them, called out to anyone. Her gut was swirling and she felt as though she might vomit.

"Mama?" The second time Daruthel confirmed it, the crowd began to flurry with whispers.

A smile erupted on Elena's face. "My loves, all together at last." Her mother's eyes began to water.

Alanitora opened her mouth to speak, but before her voice could rise from her chest, a hand grabbed her arm, pulling her back tightly. Before she knew it there was a blade at her throat and a warm, uneven breath against her cheek. In the corner of her eye, she noticed a familiar dragon's head peeking out from the hilt within her apprehender's grasp.

"Nitora!" Owen shouted. She watched him step forward at the same time as half a dozen others.

"Don't!" She recognized Francis' voice in her ear. "Anyone moves and I'll slice her open before she can even scream."

Alanitora froze, scanning the crowd. All eyes were on her, panic was everywhere, and through all the commotion she locked her gaze with one individual in particular.

One who sat still among those who had jumped back from the action. One who held no fear.

Sagittarius stood furthest to the right at the front bench, her hand reaching behind her skirt where she must have held a knife.

Alanitora shook her head ever so slightly. Things would get messy if the bandit tried.

"Francis, what are you doing?" Daruthel asked.

"You stupid, foolish idiot!" If she weren't in a compromised position, she might tell him that was a terrible string of words. "What did I tell you? Go on with the marriage and everything would be fine!"

Alanitora didn't understand much, but she knew this was a very real threat. Her daggers, as she'd also regretted that morning, were out of reach. She was stuck with her opponent undistracted and pressing a blade against her throat that threatened to spill her blood in one movement. There was no way she could get out of this now.

Tears that had been melancholic only seconds before bled from Queen Elena's eyes with anger. "Let go of my daughter."

"Your daughter? I don't understand. Lord Francis please, let the queen go." King Crevan looked between Alanitora and her mother.

Elena gave him a sympathetic look. "She's your daughter too, Crevan."

Alanitora looked at the king. He stared back at her with wide eyes. He was... her father? But—

"The family reunion can wait, can't it?" Francis interrupted. "The princess' time here is running out."

"Wait." Elena took another step forward, holding her hand out. It was shaking. "Take me."

Francis chuckled, clicking his tongue. "That's not how this works."

"Yes, it is. He wants both of us dead eventually, doesn't he? Alanitora knows nothing. I do." She pressed her hand to her chest, taking another step forward. When Francis seemed unconvinced, she continued, "You take her out, you know I'll let out everything I know. There's a reason the plan was to have her live. Right?"

Plan? What plan? Who was *he*? What was going on? Everything was happening far too fast for her to keep up.

He thought about this for a moment, tapping his thumb against the side of her neck. "Very well, her life for yours. If you try anything I'll kill both of you."

"No!" Alanitora instinctively called out. Her throat pressed forward into the blade, the sting of a small cut causing her to bite her lip.

"Shut it!" Francis growled in her ear. "Unless you want to lose your ability to speak for good. Now... Let's go about this slowly, shall we?"

He shuffled her closer to Elena, the dagger pressed thinly against Alanitora's neck. She could feel the anxious twitch of his muscles, and the uneven quickening of his breath. The man was nervous without a set plan.

But so was she. Alanitora made no effort to hide her fear as she looked into her mother's tearful eyes. Eyes that she might be seeing for the last time. And despite all she knew—or thought she knew—of her mother's transgressions, she desperately wanted to hug her one last time before the end.

Elena simply smiled reassuringly to her daughter, blinking away her tears to show nothing but love. She reached her hands out, grasping Alanitora's forearm tightly. "Remember what I've taught you." She smoothed her thumb over her skin.

Alanitora nodded, squeezing her mother's hand as she slipped her arms away. She turned her head ever so slightly to catch Francis at the edge of her vision.

He took one arm away from her chest, keeping the dagger to her throat and reaching out to grasp Elena by the elbow. Yanking the queen closer to his side, he looked between the mother and daughter, prepared to move the blade as fast as possible.

Alanitora let out a deep breath. She was not ready to let her mother go, not with so many memories behind her and even more questions in front of her.

In the moment that Francis removed the blade from her neck and towards her mother, Alanitora jabbed her left elbow backward with all her might, connecting it with his torso. She ducked, pivoting her foot and punching him in the gut.

The force caused him to stagger back, allowing Queen Elena to move away from him. Still holding his dagger, Francis growled as he struggled to rise to his feet.

"Sage!" Alanitora yelled out. She turned just in time to catch the dagger the bandit threw to her, flipping it in her fingers before charging at the man.

He just barely dodged the slash towards his face before thrusting his own dagger at her. She jumped back, allowing herself to breathe, to focus. Alanitora stepped forward to strike again, their daggers meeting in the middle. She kept hers pressed, hoping for him to withdraw first.

But he did not. Francis grinned as the force of his blade overpowered hers. His stature and strength pushed down on her, causing the princess' arms to shake.

Unable to hold much longer, Alanitora pushed off, attempting to readjust. Francis did not let her, though. He took the opportunity to attack, thrusting and slashing as she tried her best to block his quick incessant offenses. Nonetheless, he had power over the fight, and one swing caused her to fall back off her balance.

Her head and back hit the floor, aching from bruises inflicted earlier in the week. The next thing she knew, Francis' foot was on her right wrist, forcing her to release her dagger.

Aware every second in this fight counted, Alanitora took her other hand and swung it into the back of his knee.

He buckled, catching himself over her. They came face to face, his sweltering huffs apparent against her cheeks. It was when that abhorrent heat left her face that she became concerned, for Francis now held his arm high above her, ready to plunge the blade into her heart.

Alanitora, still with one arm pinned under his weight, frantically reached her left arm over and grasped at her dagger. She then hurled the hilt up and into his face. The impact on his cheekbone reverberated into her wrist.

As Francis bellowed, Alanitora slipped herself out from under him, using her freed legs to kick him in the stomach. She scrambled to her feet, grabbing his left arm and twisting it around and behind his back. With all the strength in her left arm, she held on, digging her other elbow into his back to force submission.

Still holding himself up with his shaking right arm, Alanitora raised her foot. It took only a moment of contemplation. She stomped down on his elbow, forcing it to bend the other way. There was a loud crack, and he released his weapon. With one last cry of pain, he finally submitted, the echoing clang of his dagger the only other noise to combat his voice.

Alanitora dipped her head down, disarrayed strands of hair swaying in the gust of her breath. "Tell the Men of the Blood Dragon I said hello," she snarled before kicking him forward.

Sir Francis blundered away from her, narrowing his eyes at the crowd before him. "This isn't over. We will see each other again."

"I'm counting on it," Alanitora spat.

Before anyone could make another move, Francis yanked a chair from its place with his uninjured arm and launched it through one of the stained glass windows, jumping out among the shards of glass.

King Crevan was quick to his feet. "Sound the warning bell, close off the perimeters of the castle. No one gets in or out until we search this place in its entirety." The guards—who likely should have jumped into action *without* being told—did such, rushing past the crowd and out the temple doors.

"Father, it's Francis for goodness sake! He knows the grounds far too well, never mind the fact that he practically invented our search protocols. It's more than unlikely we'll catch him," Daruthel sputtered.

A frown deepened on Crevan's face.

"That's alright, Your Majesty," Alanitora spoke. If what the last few minutes had suggested was correct, *Your Majesty* was not the only thing she could call the man. She picked up Francis' dagger from the floor. "If he does escape, he'll be sending a long overdue message."

Though he looked intrigued by her comment, King Crevan stopped himself from asking around their present company. Instead, he cleared his throat and looked towards the bewildered crowd. "Lords and ladies, I must apologize profusely for the distress inflicted upon you. Please remain calm and return to your rooms. We will update you as necessary. If you have any questions, ask a commanding officer. You can identify them by the medal on their uniforms." He tapped his breast with two fingers, then lowered them and bowed.

As though there was a mystical call to obedience with his words, the crowd looked around at one another before making their way towards the entrance doors. The whispers did not cease, instead allowing for the blanket of murmurs to slowly decrease with their exit. Of Alanitora's traveling companions, her ladies-in-waiting and Sagittarius were the only ones to stay behind. She saw Lorenalia give her brother a small wave before Sir Corwyn led her out. The knight looked back to Alanitora and nodded before shutting the doors behind him.

Time stood still. Not one of the dozen people in the room spoke or moved.

Many of the people who mattered most to Alanitora were within this room, and none of them were sure if they should draw her attention first. Their focuses shifted among one another, exchanging questioning glances.

After a few more quiet moments, Regenfrithu was the one to speak up. "I believe we all may need to sit down. From what I *do* know of the confusing situation, the complications and complexities of the narrative are something we should brace for."

Queen Elena looked between her daughter and the king, nodding in agreement.

As the others silently set up chairs around the empty ceremonial table, Alanitora stood to the side. She could feel the lingering glances of everyone's eyes on her skin, but she dared not return them. Too much was happening with too short of time to process. Her mind couldn't articulate even the smallest portions. So many questions swam around her mind, all useless to ask unless she wished to bring up a dozen more.

So instead the princess looked silently down at the dagger clutched in her hands, her fingers tracing over the spine of the dragon wrapping around the handle.

"Don't, she doesn't know the situation yet." Alanitora glanced at Owen through the veil of her eyelashes, who was holding Elena's arm firmly, stopping the queen from approaching her.

As soon as the area was ready and everyone else had seated themselves, Alanitora made her way to the spot between her ladies and Sagittarius.

Elena let out a long sigh, then began, her eyes unafraid to wander around the room. "I know you all must have a lot of questions, and I will do my best to answer them. But first, I would like to make a few things clear... without interruption." In agreement to such terms, the rest of the table remained silent. She continued, "I tell only the truth when I say I never made any attempt to betray anyone at this table. Had the lives of my loved ones not been in danger, my truth would have come out long ago."

"It's alright, they'll understand," Owen said, resting his hand on the table in reassurance to Elena. She relaxed her shoulders slightly at this.

So the two of them had traveled here together, that was certain. Yet Alanitora had no idea how such came to be, or why Regenfrithu was brought along as well.

She wanted so desperately to believe her mother's words, but with everything that had happened, such was more difficult than it seemed on the surface. Knowing that Owen—who had been more closely aligned with the crown over Elena a week ago—was siding with her now? It assuaged at least a portion of her doubts.

"Secondly, I understand if any of you feel hatred towards me because of this. You don't have to believe me, I just ask that you listen." She turned to the king of Donasela "That being said, yes Crevan, it is me, and the woman that sits before you is your daughter."

Alanitora looked up at him. So it was. The shape of their eyes and their noses held similarities. His full eyebrows and curled hair had been given to her over that of her mother's sparse brows and straight hair. And while her face shape was like her mother's, her chin jutted out slightly like his.

Crevan's eyes melted onto hers as he realized their likeness as well. But if this was true, then... "Ronoleaus—" The name slipped from her mouth.

"—Has told you nothing but lies since the day you were born," Elena finished.

"Elenora..." Crevan's eyes were beginning to well with tears. Elenora. Was that her name? "We thought you died."

"I know, my love." Her eyes flicked to Daruthel, who had been quietly picking at the sides of his thumb. "And I needed you to think so until I was sure you were safe. But that day never came. Not until today."

"If I may—" Balgair was the next to speak up. "Queen Elenora, for those of us that know neither of the narratives, could you elaborate?" So *he* knew her too.

"Of course." Queen Elena took a deep breath. She looked around the room, her eyes stopping on the bandit to Alanitora's right. "But I need to know that I can trust everyone here."

Right, if what she said about Crevan and Daruthel was true, and if she came with Regenfrithu, then the only person she wasn't familiar with was Sagittarius.

"Mother, this is Sagittarius. She's a friend, and I trust her."

"Yeah, I have no idea what kind of royal drama is going on, I'm just here for the benefits." The archer shrugged.

"The monetary benefits?" Regenfrithu hissed.

"No, the benefits of getting to spend time with the lovely princess here." The two narrowed their eyes at one another.

"Well, if my daughter trusts you, then I have no reservations." The former queen took in a deep breath, preparing to lay everything out. "Nearly twenty-four years ago, I was married to Crevan in this very temple. It was a marriage of love, one we rejoiced in for a long five years. In that time, I gave birth to a son, Daruthel, and became a diplomatic figure for Donasela.

"It was the end of autumn that I was scheduled to meet with royalty from the Mariane capital to discuss an adjustment of our tariffs. As I departed, though, I carried a secret I had only recently discovered myself: I was with child. The only other person I divulged this to was my dear friend Hadiya, who accompanied me on the trip. While on the road, we were ambushed by ruthless, bloodthirsty bandits that did not hesitate to slaughter our men. In what I presumed would be her last moments alive, Hadiya mounted me on a horse and sent it running as far and as fast as it could."

Balgair exchanged a look with Crevan before speaking, "I remember Hadiya's return from that trip well. She came home severely injured: lacerations on her torso and arms, and a deep wound on her head. Said no one else survived the attack... Are you insinuating that my wife lied to us?"

"No, I don't believe she knew of my survival at the time."

"But you could have come back. Couldn't you?" Daruthel raised his head, his voice held resentment. Alanitora hadn't a clue what his life was like since losing their mother, but she knew exactly how he felt. The anger. The disdain. The pain that came after all hope was lost. She felt it all too recently when Elena disappeared from Trenvern. When she was told she was a traitor. Part of her still believed she was that traitor, but the princess knew better than to ignore the words of the woman who raised her. Daruthel did not have that same faith.

"Everything in me wanted to, my love. You *have* to believe that. If I had any choice in the matter, the last thing I would ever do is abandon you. But I passed out on the back of the horse without food or water, without any means of survival. All I had was a sack of my belongings. I didn't know where I was or what was happening until a royal hunting party came across me a day or so later. I was malnourished, and the baby within me was asking for more than I could give. It was then that I met King Ronoleaus.

"In my confusion, I at first believed him to be kind." Tears were freely flowing from mother's eyes now. She felt a sharp pain in her heart at the sight. "He fed me, put a blanket around my shoulders, and let me ride in the carriage on the way back to his home: the capital of Trenvern.

"He placed me in the West Tower for the next week so I could be nursed back to health. I was kept in solitude, save for visits from him and a couple of maids. The cold had caused me to fall violently sick and delirious. While I told no one of who I was, I must have let something of my baby slip, for soon Ronoleaus' entire demeanor changed. I think he planned to let me go until that point.

"But then he insisted to me that the child was his, and I was to be his new wife. That I was to bring his son into the world and get to rule beside him. I did not want this. I told him I was already sworn to another, but he didn't care. To stave off his attempts, I made my second mistake: I told him who I was sworn to in hopes that Donasela's power would intimidate him into letting me go. It didn't. I refused adamantly, but the life within me needed food, and he wouldn't give it to me until I agreed to his terms. As much as I despised the idea of betraying my family, I could not bring myself to let my child perish.

"We were wed a week later, in front of a small audience as witnesses. It was then that he introduced me to the only maid of my company. A woman, who happened to be a month further along than I, was to be my midwife. This was your mother, Owen."

The orange-haired boy lifted his head, smiling at the prospect. Alanitora smiled too. She knew at least some fragments of this story. How she'd been born prematurely on the same day as Owen. How they had grown up together under the watchful eyes of both mothers. How the two women spent much time together themselves.

"I told her my story. The only person I ever would tell the entire story. And she swore upon her children's lives she would protect mine. That is why we raised you two so close, and when that failed, why we pushed you into the role of a soldier. By encouraging you to be a loyal defender of the crown, we knew you would be trustworthy enough to gain sensitive knowledge while still maintaining your morality. Your sister, on the other hand, was to keep a far distance from the situation, watching from the shadows, able to see the harm that Trenvern was capable of. I understand you got to meet her recently, Alanitora."

The princess nodded. It made sense now how Diane had known so much about her despite Alanitora never even knowing of her existence. Her instinct had told her to trust the girl, and she was glad she did. Otherwise, there was no knowing whether or not she would believe her.

There still was a pending curiosity. Something that wasn't quite adding up. "Though, I can't help but wonder—" Alanitora intervened. "If Diane knew everything, why didn't she tell me? Would it not have saved us all of this insanity?"

"As I said, Alice is the only one that knows my full story. She taught Diane to not trust Trenvern but never detailed why. Those discoveries were up to her to find. I doubt she's still in the dark, though. It's safe to assume she's found her way to her parents and is helping lead the defiance we began."

Elena cleared her throat, continuing her narrative, "Regardless, all of the stress I was under is what I believe to be the cause for your early arrival. The day that I went into labor, there were stars in Ronoleaus' eyes. His temperament shifted to anger the moment he learned you were not a boy that he could pass on the crown to. A heavy resentment that caused your so-called father to beat me senseless day after day, claiming it was all my fault. Through his charm, through his aggressive front, it was then that I saw just how deranged he was. There was a malignant sickness in his mind that bent reality to what he wanted it to be.

"Losing interest in you was his biggest error. I knew I could raise you close to me, teach you to be your own person, to see things the way they were without telling you anything that could get you killed. All your life we were watched. I could never tell you the truth, no matter how much I wanted to. So instead, my love, I taught you other things.

"The art of combat—something I wish I had known if only to defend myself from such a life—puzzles and riddles to keep your mind sharp and cautious of who to trust, and the keen and powerful gaze bestowed to you

381

through the blood of your true father."

Alanitora looked to Crevan. While their eyes physically looked similar, there was an additional depth to them that she only saw in the mirror. Like a world of glass beneath, with an expanse of both vivid colors and ebbing darkness. But his gaze was withered and weakened.

Daruthel interceded to explain. "Donaselan royalty has been known to be blessed by the sly eyes of the fox, allowing them to observe situations and people better than the average person. One hundred years ago, some thought this made us the superior bloodline."

"Indeed." Elena nodded at her son, who smiled in return. She turned back. "The moments I did not spend with you, I spent in his bed. He believed me to be blessed enough by his twisted God to have more than one child where the other women had failed, insistent that the fault was not his. For years he tried to put the seed of a son in me, and for years he failed. Now that we were bound by marriage, Ronoleaus saw me as a possession, his completely.

"When it didn't work with me, he continued with several other women. I tried my best to intervene, stop him from doing the same harm to others, but the second he realized that the life of my baby girl was the only thing I was living for, all threats turned from me to her. Despite my distaste, I had to stop actively resisting him for that reason. When he separated you and Owen, I became more and more obedient to his commands. After all, it was better to be closer to his secrets than far. My passive defiance allowed me to gradually connect with the community, see what sort of lies and propaganda he might be spinning to the public.

"As long as he had even the slightest influence in your life, I had to stay silent and follow his desires. In these last few years, his demands meant keeping you at an arm's length. By the time I learned of his plan to marry you to your brother, he had already been sure to falsify evidence that framed me for conspiring with the enemy. I was going to be killed before I could explain anything to you. That's why I had to leave. I had hoped to cross paths with you outside of the walls as soon as he sent you on the trip, but I believe my disappearance caused him to set things in motion prematurely."

Alanitora frowned. She was confused again, stuck on a discrepancy. "Things were set in motion because the Fonoli attacked, not because—"

"The Fonoli are on his side!" Elena slammed her palms to the table in frustration, worry across her brow. "That's part of his plan! He made a deal with the crown prince to stage a war and flip the power. All of this has been staged from the beginning."

"What?" Alanitora's eyes widened in horror at the mere idea. The fire... the fire that burned down her home, that devastated her people... was ordered by Ronoleaus? No, that couldn't have been right. It occurred to her that maybe her mother was lying about such an outlandish theory, that maybe she *was* conspiring with the other side.

Korena raised her hand. "I don't understand. Ronoleaus perished in the fire. Alanitora is the queen of Trenvern now."

Elena turned her gaze to the blonde, unsurprised by the statement. "No, I can assure you he is alive and well. The man may be deranged, but that sick bastard is more clever than I'd like to give him credit for. I promise you that he is sitting comfortably on his throne at this moment, crafting a different narrative for his survival."

Gwendolyn's eyebrows furrowed. "This is absolutely insane. Surely he couldn't have orchestrated something so complicated and expected it to go exactly as planned?"

"You should never underestimate a man hungry for power, just as you should never underestimate a mother's love for her children." Elena sighed heavily. She knew how unbelievable this was. "I'm well aware of the insanity of the plan. I also assumed my own counterplan to go south. It was necessary to consider such things after spending years around that man. I was hoping Alanitora's dress might make it clear to Donasela who she was."

King Crevan shook his head lightly. "She looks like the spitting image of you in it, but— I had assumed someone found the dress here and gave it to her."

Alanitora's vision snapped to Korena and Gwendolyn. "Where *did* you find this?"

Korena shrugged. "It was in one of your chests before we left. Gwennie was having me check the inventory and we just... found it there."

"How did you get it to Trenvern—?" Balgair asked.

"Your wife. I had Alice send a message for her to meet me covertly in Elisan ten years or so ago. Given it was my first and only time out of the kingdom, I knew it was our only chance. Ronoleaus would have someone check our inventory coming back. I needed to be sure that whatever she brought could both be hidden among the other items and a sure confirmation of my identity. Hence the dress and my wreath crown."

Alanitora reached her hand up to the gold wreath upon her head. No wonder it looked vaguely familiar. She examined it with her fingertips as her mother continued.

"I did hope you'd find the dress, Korena. It was the last thing I did before leaving. That, and the warning note I left for Alanitora."

"Note?" She contemplated for a moment, memories of her mother's personal chest cultivating in her mind. Along with her mother's wreath crown, there had been a slip of paper, but it wasn't of concern to her at the time and was missing when she went to look for it later. "I believe I came across it, but I never had the chance to read it—"

"Then how did you know about the dragons?"

Alanitora frowned in confusion, placing Francis' dagger on the table. There were only three other people in the room who knew about the Men of the Blood Dragon. "How did—" No. That didn't make sense, it couldn't be right, could it? "King Ronoleaus..."

Elena nodded. "His personal spies. I had a feeling they would be following you to be sure you married Daruthel. That was his plan, you see. He knows the ways of the Old Kingdoms far too well. He knows that the ceremonial wedding binds are followed by conceiving the next heir."

"And if Alanitora and I were married, we'd have to—" began Daruthel.

The princess thought she might be sick at that moment. She hadn't been made aware of this from Balgair, and she had staved off Francis' earlier threat as something else entirely. But if there was truth to it, that meant...

"With such a similar mix of blood, the child would be of ill fate."

Elena nodded. "It does not make much logical sense, I am aware. I'm not sure anything does with him. I believe Ronoleaus thinks himself immortal. Not only would he have the use of the Donaselan army to defeat his enemies, but he'd also have a snag at making the kingdoms merge with his choice of heir in charge."

"Like I would let that happen!" Crevan stood in fury, the scratch of his chair on the floor echoing on the temple walls.

"I assume he was to have Francis put an end to your life, and advise Daruthel in a certain direction."

"If he wanted power over Donasela, then why were the Men of the Blood Dragon trying to actively kill her?" Gwendolyn asked.

"What?" Elena spat.

"They've tried to kill her three times now, possibly more according to Diane."

"What?!" Elena repeated, looking from Gwendolyn to Owen. So it seemed her mother didn't have all the answers. "I wasn't informed of this."

"Once at the Trenvern border, once when I arrived here, and just now," Alanitora explained.

"That doesn't make sense. Killing you would ruin the Donaselan plan, wouldn't it?"

"Maybe he didn't think it would work?" Daruthel suggested.

The queen's frown deepened. "I thought I had known his entire plan… But that may not be true." She turned to Owen again. "If your sister knew anything about it, she was supposed to tell your mother."

Owen threw his arms up in defense. "Hey, don't look at me, I only just found out Diane was your little spy. She's been known to be quite rebellious though. Probably thought she could take it on her own or something of the like."

"Well that's not very helpful, is it?" Sagittarius shrugged.

Elena bit her lip out of frustration. "It's not. It also means we have to adjust our counterplan. Damn. I thought I had finally gotten ahead of him after all these years. I thought we could beat this." She looked up and around the room. "I know things are crazy, but I ask you to have faith. I'll need to hear everything anyone might know. We can still stop him."

"Can we?" Alanitora stood. She'd heard enough. She'd heard enough to know her mother was telling the truth. She'd heard enough to be angered by the deception cast over her throughout her entire life. And she'd heard enough to feel more motivated than ever to put an end to the madness. "I had no clue the Men of the Blood Dragon were connected to King Ronoleaus. I let Francis get away. He'll know the wedding didn't happen. He'll know you've told us everything. We won't be ahead anymore."

Elena raised her chin. There was pride in her eyes when she looked up at her daughter. Despite the dire situation, the hope she had in her kin was stronger than anything. "But we are ahead. We don't have secrets and deceptions anymore. All we have to do is unravel his web of lies and let the truth shine through. Besides… We're all together again. And that makes us unstoppable."

Words never rang more true in Alanitora's ears. She looked around the room, focusing on every person who sat with them, who stood by them, and who had an honest faith in her. In each other. These were her people. These were the people she'd stand by and stand up for. There was a storm coming, and chaos with it. It became clear to the princess that the crashing waves would soon surround them and make it ever more hard to keep their heads above water.

"Then let's be prepared."

30

Loyalty Within Lies

Alanitora sighed, resting her elbows on the railing of the balcony that looked over the woods behind Donasela's large castle. Her mind was fizzing with questions, but none that she had enough energy to ask.

This was insane. All of it was. In no way was her life normal. In no way had she *thought* it was normal, but all of this was far beyond anything she could have imagined. Where she was standing right now was meant to be her home. Her mother had practically been abducted by her so-called father, and her entire life in Trenvern was one of lies.

It was heavy enough without tying in the fact that she had nearly married her full-blood brother. When they had debriefed, Daruthel had told her not to worry. That they would take care of any immediate repercussions within the kingdom, but her worries didn't cease with that, for no longer was she thinking of royal customs or the responsibilities of a leader. She thought only of the people who had been with her in that room a few hours before.

About how every one of them had sacrificed so much to follow her, and now she had no idea where she was going. Part of her wanted to give up, to stay lost in the trepid waters. To let the tides wash over and decide her direction. Nevertheless, it wasn't possible. Not when they were depending on her. And if Ronoleaus was alive and truly as awful as her mother described, then the entire kingdom of Trenvern was lost, too. She didn't know how long things had been this way. She didn't know why Ronoleaus sent the Men of the Blood Dragon against her, but Alanitora *did* know that things were going to change. They would regret not being able to kill her, that was for certain.

"Hey." The princess turned. Owen was standing in the doorway of the balcony, the setting sun cascading a golden glow to his bright hair.

"Owen," she greeted. He had cleaned up since the meeting and was now wearing a white tunic that was a little too small for him. She smiled, looking down at her feet. What was there to say to him? After the way she'd left things—left him—her pride prevented her from an apology, but her morality prevented her from anything as simple as a thank you.

She didn't need to worry, for the soldier spoke first, "I'd ask if you're alright, but I think we both know the answer to that is more complicated than a few words." Alanitora chuckled at the remark. "Instead I'd like to say I'm sorry."

"For what?" She frowned, looking up. None of what had happened had been his fault, at least not out of the things she was worried about.

He shrugged, looking between her and their surroundings as if the landscape held an answer. "For the mistakes I've made, for whatever conflict I may have added to, and for not trusting your judgment." Owen paused for a moment before adding, "You were right."

Alanitora held herself back from asking about what, not wishing to sound like an overly curious and naive five-year-old. Instead, she raised her eyebrows in amusement. "You'll have to be specific, I fear I have the tendency to be right."

He stepped up to her in return, standing next to her on the balcony. "Your mother, for one. My blind faith in Trenvern for another." Owen looked down, regret striking his features.

"None of that was your fault." If what Elena had said earlier was true, Owen had been set up to have faith in the crown as much as she'd been set up on the path she was on now.

"I find it hard to know that. You've done good by your people, I put that at risk."

"Maybe." She paused, aware her words might be sharper than intended without notice. "But none of us could have known the insanity of the situation. Much has changed in the past seven years, for both of us. We shouldn't take the blame for the situations we were put in by others."

He chuckled, looking up at the sky. It was getting darker by the minute, hues of sunset painting the sky in a variety of colors. "Who would have known—the two kids we were, blown over into this?"

She looked up at him, examining his features. "We knew. Did we not? The entire time as kids, we knew we were going to be a part of something, Perhaps we forgot with time though."

"I mean, technically, we are still kids."

Alanitora narrowed her eyes. "You'd be surprised how much assassination attempts age you."

"If that were true, you'd have gray hair." He nudged her with his arm.

The two of them, here, it was nice. Sure, everything was still absolutely insane, but in that moment, with the sun setting, with the stress of everything dissipating, it was good to have a friend. A friend who she felt knew the most unmasked version of her, even if from forever ago. And Alanitora could tell that no longer was Owen holding onto the fantasy of what they could be.

He thought the same too, at that moment. The soldier recalled his panic that morning when Hadiya rushed into the barn. He remembered the dread that overtook the three of them before Elena rushed them into a long, dark, secret passageway ever so similar to the ones he'd learned about back in Trenvern. And as they neared, the worries went away, and something told him everything would be alright, a little light of hope in the darkness.

Owen looked up. "Do you remember when my mother would take us out into the courtyard at night, and point her hand up to the stars? Tell us all the stories of the creatures that made their way into the sky?"

"Yes," she responded, looking up as well. Their eyes locked on the same star ever so high up. It wasn't the brightest, but it was the first one she saw. Polaris.

"Do you think that—" He paused momentarily, "Do you think that she taught us that stuff intentionally? Your mother did such with the nursery rhymes and poems, it would make sense if…"

"I think it's certainly possible. The stories she told us were about adventure and hope. Even if not intentional, your mother was—from what I remember—the kind to put faith into other people. But who knows, I suppose you'll have to ask her yourself."

He smiled back at her, a sadness creeping in. She could tell part of him feared he may not see his mother again, but she had thought the same only a day before. Alanitora rested her hand on his, looking up at the north star.

For a moment, they stood there in silence, aware of each other's presence and what it meant, making no move to change that. Owen spoke first. "Nitora." She didn't correct him this time around. "I want you to know that I am here for you. Not just as a friend, but as a loyal soldier, if you'll have me. I understand my judgment has been clouded from doing what I should have, but I see clearly now, and I'm willing to follow you as far as to the end."

It was her turn to smile at his comforting words. She turned to him, accepting the duty he had bestowed upon himself, upon the two of them. Alanitora then withdrew her hand slowly, stepping back to re-enter the castle. "I'm glad to have your support, we can discuss the extent of it another time. If it's alright, I'll need to get going. There are some things I would like to clear up."

"Of course." He bowed at her exit.

She paused just before entering the castle, turning to face the soldier once more. "Oh, and Owen?"

"Yes?"

"Thank you. For many things, but above all, thank you for helping get my mother back to me, and thank you for fighting alongside me."

He nodded at her, watching as she left before turning back to the darkening sky. She had said *alongside*. Not for, but alongside. One word said so much to Owen. The two of them might have a lot of growing to do after the faults made on either of their parts, but for now, there was peace in knowing she was open to the change.

Unbeknownst to either Owen or Alanitora, below them in the darkness of the forest a man had been watching with a grin on his face. He looked up at them in astute and keen observation, unable to hear their words but still delighted in the idea that the two were vulnerable and close enough that he could kill them, if only he had a ranged weapon.

His interest was soon lost, however, as the princess departed. Focus instead shifted to the pain in his arm, a persistent reminder of his failure earlier that day. In addition to Alanitora rendering his right arm useless, his hasty escape led to a particularly large piece of stained glass having lodged itself into his bicep. Francis had put his arm into a sling and wrapped it where the cut was, but he feared the wound might become infected without proper care. He had been trained in many things; attending injuries was not one of them.

So instead he sat there in the shadows of the trees, waiting patiently as the sun set so he could slip out of the capital boundaries and regroup before his next orders. Out of everything that happened, Francis focused on the satisfaction that he had escaped. He thought the princess would be naive, he didn't think she would be an outright fool.

Escaping, of course, had been far too easy. One would assume Donasela of all kingdoms would train their soldiers better in pursuing a suspect. But slipping out had been both satisfying and boring. If he was gonna go out, Francis would have much rather gone out with more exhilaration.

"They very well know now, don't they?" Francis withdrew his spare dagger, turning to face the voice in the darkness, settling when he realized the woman was no foe of his. "Should we report back?" she asked, leaning against the tree opposite of him.

"No need, news will reach him soon. We're supposed to keep our positions and await new instruction."

"Damn. I really did want to see his face when he learns Alanitora figured it all out," she chuckled. "You really screwed that one up, didn't you? Nice job blowing your cover. Probably would have been more useful in the long run if you'd kept it."

Francis looked at the woman, barely able to see her through the shadow of the trees. "Daruthel has seen my dagger, They would have figured it out sooner or later. Besides… you're the one to talk," he sneered. "I thought your orders were to stay in Kreaha."

"Orders and all? Blah blah. Doesn't matter. Those two princesses left for here too, thought it'd be fine to follow."

"You sure it wasn't so you could stay with your beau?"

"You sound jealous."

"I'm not."

The woman let out a long sigh. "It's going to be a tough one anyways. I think he has an interest, but he hasn't taken the bait."

"You need to be careful," Francis said sternly.

"I will, I will." She threw her hands up in defense before crossing them again. "All I gotta do is tell a sob story for the girls and raise my chest a little for the boys."

"And Alanitora? She's got the Donaselan fox's eye."

"Please, I thought that was a myth."

He quirked an eyebrow, tilting his head at the remark. "As did I until I came face to face with it myself. It's stronger than her father's and brother's. That's for sure."

"In any case, I've got her fooled so far. Everything is under control."

"Don't get too comfortable," Francis growled. He flipped his backup dagger, sending it through the air and into the bark next to her head. He pushed himself from his tree and walked towards her. "Make sure you give that to our new member since you're the one with the inside pass now."

"New member? I thought she didn't even know she was our little traitor."

"In due time." Francis stopped, glowering over her. He placed one hand next to her face. "Begin with flames?"

He could see her facial features much better now, and a wicked grin, a grin he loved ever so much, spread across her lips.

"Seal with blood," she responded, taking her own dagger and flipping it around in her fingers playfully.

Pulling his dagger out Francis backed himself from the tree. He took the blade to his skin and sliced through the palm of his good arm. The girl did the same, extending her hand out before the two of them joined their palms together, the warm liquid spreading within their grip.

And with that, he pulled her forward swiftly into a kiss so deep that neither felt their wounds. The two intertwined effortlessly: lies may have riddled their lives in every other moment, but now there was a true passion.

In the folds of the forests, two lovers joined together, fueled with a desire not only for one another but for vengeance.

Walking around Donasela's castle felt strange, to the point where Alanitora wondered if it ever might stop being strange, now that this was her home. She hoped to have familiarity with it in the future, but after so long in Trenvern's castle, the walls of Donasela felt unnerving. She kept to the inside, avoiding the open courtyards as much as she could, knowing how many people frequented there. That, of course, didn't stop the stares.

After all, people knew it was her, the girl from Trenvern, that had come to marry their prince. Furthermore, rumors about the situation were beginning to spread. Though there were a number of false claims, among them was the truth, and it was terrifying to think how many people could know.

It was the curiosity of what was being said that led Alanitora to the Throne Room that night. A shift in the narrative was needed.

She had just turned into the room when her eyes rested on the two figures in the center. Elena and King Crevan stood, holding one another with such a softness that Alanitora couldn't quite believe it was her mother standing there.

Well, not just her mother, but her *father* too. Her parents. By blood at least, and she wished it could be by a bond that Ronoleaus had not stolen.

Her mother's head was nestled under Crevan's neck, their hands clasped together in front and their free arms wrapped around one another. The king of Donasela rested his head upon hers, his eyes closed as though this was a moment he believed to only be a dream.

And then she saw it: Her mother was crying. Alanitora may not have been able to recall the last time she had seen her cry before this morning, but it was perhaps the first time she'd ever seen her cry out of joy.

She waited patiently in the entryway, hesitant to interrupt a moment neither the king nor former queen thought they would ever have. To think that her mother had been happy before giving birth to her, to think that she had been in love: it made her heart melt. That was all she could ask for, the happiness of her closest loved one. And that happiness was here and now, in this room on a night where the moon was full and shined its light on the world.

What she was witnessing now was a true love, and Alanitora would do anything to keep it so.

Elena's eyes opened softly, and her smile widened at the sight of her daughter. She made no move away from her first husband, instead welcoming Alanitora in. "Hello, my love."

Crevan seemed less relaxed, but she couldn't blame him. Alanitora was a familial stranger to him. It couldn't be easy to stand in front of her, knowing that she was his daughter raised away from his nurture.

"Good evening," Alanitora greeted, making her way closer to them. "I was wondering if I could talk to you… King Crevan, about the official statement."

"Right, of course." Crevan released himself from the embrace, standing tall. "We should send out a notice to the capital tomorrow."

"Saying what, exactly?"

"The truth."

"The truth? You can't be serious," Alanitora repeated. All of it? Complete clarity? Total transparency? Surely the people of Donasela didn't need to know *everything*, especially if it was about something as severe as royal affairs with a possible war.

She and Crevan didn't share such sentiments. Elena looked between them before stepping forward herself. "I think what Alanitora is saying is that if you do this, there will be no turning away from labeling Ronoleaus, and potentially Trenvern, as your enemy. It is something that can't be taken lightly."

"I'm aware of that, Elenora," he began. "But lying to them isn't an option, it never has been. Your life may have been prone to its secrets, but here there is not such. If Alanitora is my daughter, then people should know that, just as people should know my wife—their queen—is alive and well."

"I understand that, my love, but—"

"A large number of our nobility saw you in the Temple today. Not all of them fit the pieces together about our daughter, but they at least know about your return. If we wait to say something, or—even worse—if we lie about it, they may antagonize you for not returning sooner."

"You're asking them to join a war, one they may not be ready for," Elena replied. Alanitora stayed silent, paying close attention to both sides of such an argument. It might have had to do heavily with her, but the princess had no experience in making such firm decisions. It would be best to weigh both sides, even if she was leaning towards her mother at the moment.

"A war that was started when Ronoleaus took you from us. I'm not igniting the flame, I'm fighting against it. As you've said, it doesn't matter what we say, that bastard will find out regardless."

"You're right, but we have to find a way that conceals enough of what we know, right now that's the only advantage we have over him. If we let it out in the open, it might expose his treachery, but it might also dissuade people from our story based upon the radicalness of the truth."

The way they spoke. It was much more a discussion than an argument. One where no one held more power, and both listened. They were working together, not against one another.

"Then we tell them only part of it," Alanitora said. When the two turned to her to show they were listening, she continued, "Tell them that their formerly presumed dead queen and her unborn child had indeed been tragically torn apart from her family, and had no choice but to remain hidden to ensure the safety of Donasela. Tell them many unforeseen fortuitous events has unexpectedly brought both the queen and princess back home where they belong, and that the crown is doing everything it can to avenge the injustices bestowed upon its own flesh and blood."

Her parents stayed silent for a few moments before looking at one another. Elena quirked her brow. "I told you she has your intelligence."

"My intelligence?" the king chuckled. "Elenora, my love, it's your keen intellect she inherited, not mine."

Were they... flirting? In front of her? Alanitora made no move to be honored or offended by the comments.

The queen's smile settled. "Nevertheless, she has a point. And if the war is as inevitable as you claim it is, then such a declaration will work in our favor. If there is anyone who might wish to aid us in such 'avenging', they'll come to us. It makes testing loyalty much easier and leaves any citizens who may not want to be wrapped up in a war out of it.

"Besides, I have no doubt in my mind that Ronoleaus is rallying up large crowds and spreading lies into their ears about his supposed daughter and wife as we speak."

Her mother was right. "If he wishes to work from the shadows, then so will we."

Crevan gave an affirming nod. "So we do this discreetly. We should let the messengers know now."

Elena began to follow her husband, but Alanitora reached out, stopping her. "If it's alright, King Crevan, could I speak to my mother alone? Just for a little."

The king nodded, his lips thinned into a tight line at the mention of his name, and Alanitora could tell the man was conflicted over what she was to call him. She had thought of the predicament herself earlier and decided that while *Your Majesty* was too formal, *father* was far too casual for a man she had just met, regardless of their relation. "Of course." He made his way out, leaving them the large room.

Alanitora stayed silent. It had only been a little over a week, and yet it felt like years since she had seen her mother. So much had changed. For the first time in her life, she had felt she stood on her own, without the woman in front of her to hold her hand. And now, she no longer needed her help to stay above the water.

"Nitora." Elena's eyes softened. All of the walls that Alanitora saw blocking her from reading her mother came down, and the full range of her emotions could be seen. It was like there were new colors in the rainbow. Fascinating, beautiful, and indescribable.

"Mama," Alanitora replied. She hadn't called her mother that for a long time, just as the nickname her mother gave her had been equally unused.

The eyes of both women watered. Alanitora moved forward, wrapping her arms around her mother and holding her close, the warmth of her embrace enveloping her entire body.

"You've been so strong." Elena's breath quivered for a moment. She stroked her daughter's hair, then pulled back from the hug. "And you've grown so much."

Alanitora took a deep breath. At last, she felt safe. "Everything you've done. My entire life. Was to train me for this?"

"It might be a lie if I were to say absolutely *everything*, but I did as much as I could to prepare you for the inevitable fight, yes. I know it is a lot, and I understand if you have any doubts—"

"I don't. You've always been the one person I depended on. I know you had to make tough calls, and while I may not agree with or understand all of them, you did what you had to do."

"As did you." Elena smiled, touching her hand to Alanitora's cheek.

"Not like you. You spent all that time trying to protect me, while Ronoleaus did such awful things to you. Awful, unforgivable things. I won't let him have the satisfaction of knowing what he did without paying for it."

"But can you do that? Can you face your father?"

"He is not my father. He is not your husband. And he is no one's king. I'll make sure people know that. If Ronoleaus wants a war, then he will get

397

it." Alanitora raised her chin with pride. She would make sure that tyrant of a man was brought down, and she would make it clear to all who ever heard his name just the kind of person he truly was.

"That's my girl." Elena brought her into another hug, jubilant smiles at their reunion in truth. "And you are not alone in this. Always remember that."

"I will," Alanitora said, finally stepping back from her mother. She was home. Perhaps not in location or comfort, but her heart. After all, her idea of home had never been separate from the woman who raised her in every sense.

"Now." Elena relaxed her shoulders. "I know we have a whole lot to catch up with and talk about, but you've had what I imagine might be the longest day of your life. We can speak tomorrow. Go get some rest."

"Will you?" she asked with a light laugh, her mother was certainly right about it being a long day. Though it didn't quite feel as long as the day her mother went missing that started all of this.

"Alanitora Nayana Vulperis of Donasela, for the first time in eighteen years, you are finally safe. I think my sleep tonight will be better than ever."

Alanitora Nayana Vulperis of Donasela. So that was her true name, was it? Elation filled her chest at the sound of it. There were so many things she wanted to ask her mother... How she came to name her such, how she and Crevan met, and just about any other questions pertaining to all of the things her mother had taught her all these years. Nevertheless, now was not that time. She had the rest of her life to share those stories.

Giving her mother's hands one last squeeze, Alanitora left the Throne Room, intending to retire to her quarters.

31

Redemption

She didn't make it very far from the Throne Room when her name was called from behind.

Regenfrithu waved to be sure she saw him, then made his way to intercept her. "I've been looking all over for you." The prince rested for a moment to catch his breath.

"I was just heading back to my rooms, care to escort me?"

"Of course." He smiled, offering his arm.

She took it, and the two began to walk side by side through the corridors.

Out of the three people that popped out from behind the fox statue at the wedding, Alanitora least expected to see Regenfrithu. She had pushed aside the idea that she might see him again, along with whatever sparks of intrigue she'd had. Now, those feelings were coming back ever so slowly.

"I assume you are staying the night here?" she began, breaking the silence.

"Yes."

"And you've got your rooms set?"

"Indeed, despite the short notice."

The next question she wanted to ask was why he had come all this way, but Alanitora had an inkling of an idea why, and she wasn't sure if she was ready to hear that answer. Instead, she brought up something from the same realm. "There is no way you would have been able to leave your home on such short notice, though."

He laughed. "I may have snuck out." Regenfrithu gave her a wink.

She feigned shock. "Crown Prince Regenfrithu, you what?!"

"Don't worry, I left a note. There is no reason for anyone to worry."

"Oh, but that doesn't make it any less scandalous. Why, you were the centerpiece of the ball, the main attraction!" She dramatically pressed the back of her hand to her forehead, pretending to faint.

"That's... a reach. There are still celebrations going on, even without me."

"Then I suppose you'll be heading back tomorrow to continue?"

"Actually... about that. " Regenfrithu met her eyes as they turned the hallway to a partially outside corridor, lanterns lining the edges. "I canceled my search for a bride after you left." His words hit her in the chest. They were the words that she hadn't wanted to hear because of the possible reality they presented to her. "But that's not what I needed to talk to you about."

"Oh?" She raised her eyebrows. She hardly expected the prince to think something else was more important than the implications of what he had just told her.

"I've talked to your friends." He paused, realizing the term *friends* could be both specific and broad. "Your ladies, the princesses, Owen, and the knight who was in charge of your journey here... As well as Sagittarius." There was a certain degree of disdain in his voice when he mentioned the bandit's name.

"And?" Alanitora did her best to keep her voice level. Her stomach was tying itself into knots at the mention of all the people she considered herself close to talking without her. Whatever Regenfrithu was going to tell her about, it was big.

"And we've all agreed that we want to fight with you."

Alanitora stopped in her tracks. "I-I'm sorry?"

He let go of her arm, turning to face her. "Alanitora, this is bigger than just you and your family, we know that. If Ronoleaus is as bad as you say he is—which, from what your mother told me on the way here, he is—then this affects all of Mordenla. He's power-hungry. If he had succeeded in taking down Donasela into his command, then we would all be, for lack of a better word, doomed." Regenfrithu paused, pinching the bridge of his nose as if he could feel the pounding headache that was forming for her. "If he had that much ambition to pursue such a plan in the first place, I doubt he's willing to give up."

Alanitora nodded. She was following him so far. Regenfrithu was right: this did affect all of Mordenla. It wasn't something she had realized, perhaps because she was at the center of it all.

The prince continued, "Which is why we all talked. All of us are in to help however we can."

"But—" She thought of all the things that worked against them. Most of them weren't kings and queens, and nearly all of them were mere teenagers. They couldn't possibly hold the resources to start an army.

"I know it sounds insane, but hear us out. I'm not asking you to make a decision, nor am I asking you to take this all on for the lead, but please meet with us tomorrow. Or— later this week if you at all feel like tomorrow is too much."

She paused, looking up at his eyes. Genuine. Supportive. That was something that must have been in each and every one of her companion's eyes as well. But at the moment she could only see his, and the dedication in them.

"Please? We are all here for you."

She thought for a moment, going over everything in her mind as fast as she could. The positives and negatives, the different possibilities… all of it. After a few seconds, she nodded, continuing down the hall. "Alright."

She opened the door to her room, not bothering to close it behind her in case Regenfrithu did want to come in. She did hope he made his departure soon, as her exhaustion was only piling up.

The prince stepped in.

He stayed silent for a long while, and she thought he was ready to bid her farewell when the prince released a soft gasp. Alanitora turned to see him looking down at the rose. "You kept it," he remarked.

"I did." Part of her wanted to say that the reason was that it was too beautiful to throw away, but that was not quite true.

He reached out, touching the petals tentatively, as though it were ready to crumble under his fingers at any second. "I—" he began, before pausing. "I wanted to apologize. For the way I acted back home."

"You don't have to…" Her heart skipped again, this time she feared it might jump out of her throat. So they came back to this. The topic she so desperately wished to step around for the time being.

"I do. I do because in no way was it right of me to act so harshly to you. My entire life, I've gotten what I want, so when there is a possibility that something I want will slip away, I can't help but grasp at it. And if that doesn't work, then I detach myself completely."

He was being so raw, so open. She knew the words he was speaking of because she did the same thing. In order to keep going, she had to. Owen, her mother, and just about every other thing she had lost along the way. And now that the calamity was settled, it was her time to pick those things back up. But what she had with Regenfrithu was new and fragile, and the idea of dropping it again might make it break forever. Finally, she spoke, "Then why did you come?"

It was a question she thought she knew the answer to, but she needed to be sure.

He chuckled. "I couldn't not." The prince looked up at her, and for once, she let her own thoughts be clear. He read them well and knew she was not ready. "I know nothing about you, and yet I *feel* like I do. I came because my curiosity got the better of me. You are a mystery I have yet to solve… That and when I found out what was happening, I thought it would diplomatically be best if I helped you out."

"So… you decided to travel without guards and accompany a known fugitive queen from a neighboring kingdom?" She chuckled. She was grateful he had trusted her mother in hindsight, but if she had been in the prince's situation Alanitora certainly wouldn't have.

"Hey, you're one to talk. You teamed up with Sagittarius. She *did* try to kill me."

"She did not." He raised his eyebrows at her. "If she had wanted you dead you would have actually been shot."

"Right, but instead she shot you. In the arm. Which might I add, looked incredibly well mended this morning." Alanitora looked down at the spot in question, which was now covered by the long sleeves of the dress she changed into. The princess hadn't realized that her wedding dress showed it, and now that she thought of such, the sleeveless gown likely showed quite a few of her scars.

"What can I say, I'm good at healing," she said. After a moment, she added beneath her breath,"And hurting others."

"Don't worry, the only thing of mine that could be wounded is my pride, and I brought that upon myself."

Alanitora recognized his attempt to console her. "Thank you, Raven—" She froze. "If it's still alright I call you that?"

"It is," Regenfrithu noted. "I said it was for friends, you are one... I assume you are fine with just Alanitora?"

"Yes, Alanitora works best, the other nicknames have been taken. Tora by my ladies and Nitora by—"

"—by your mother and Owen, I surmised such. Owen was telling me what you were like as a kid earlier today."

Alanitora smiled. The idea of the two of them talking was foreign to her. "Owen, huh?"

"Yeah, though I'm not sure I believe him about the whole mischievous hijinks stuff."

Who would have known? Regenfrithu and Owen being friends. What they shared with one another about her might've made her anxious... if she cared.

With all of the chaos, she was beyond the point of worrying about two boys.

She decided to diverge from the subject nonetheless. "Can I ask you something?"

"Go for it."

"You're the crown prince. You've been conditioned to rule your people. How are you always so relaxed?" Relaxed wasn't quite the right word, but she knew he'd understand what she meant.

"In which way? Because up here—" He tapped his head. "It's far from relaxed."

"I mean, the way you live, the way you go about your life without constantly looking over your shoulder."

"I don't need to. I've never had to worry about what were to happen to me because the people of Kreaha support the crown to the point where they would riot had we been dethroned. I'd say that's why I'm so sociable. I know that getting people on my side is going to be helpful if I ever need allies in the future."

"…Because you're stronger with the people who support you." Realization struck her. Everything that had happened, she wouldn't have been able to get through without the people around her.

Alanitora frowned. And now they were going into a war. All of them were there for her, risking whatever lives they'd had before to help her, and for what? A thank you? A chance to do something right? Or because it was *her*?

Regenfrithu cleared his throat. "I should probably get going. I need the sleep, and you have a big day tomorrow."

"Goodness, I hope to someday never have to hear that I have a big day coming up."

He smiled, making his way to the door. "Goodnight, Alanitora."

"Goodnight, and oh! If you come across either of my ladies, please let them know I would like to see them within the next hour if possible."

Raven nodded before shutting the door behind him.

Alanitora knew that though she was tired after all of what happened, tonight would be one with little sleep. She finally held the chance to breathe. She let her thoughts occupy her mind when sitting at the edge of her bed staring at the fire in front of her, for any attempts to block things out would be futile and frustrating.

She didn't know a lot of things. Ronoleaus' true intentions, who the Men of the Blood Dragon were, nor did she know the separation of truths and lies from her childhood. But she knew one thing: She was home now.

Home was where her family was, and after so many years of denying such, she'd finally found them.

They were the people who stood with her when any sane person would not. They were the people she could smile and laugh with. They were the people she could depend on.

The thought of them summoned Korena and Gwendolyn, appearing not long after Raven's departure.

Though she might normally be exhausted at the thought of socializing with her ladies, her mood brightened when seeing them enter. "How did you—?"

"We were already on our way here when he passed us," Gwendolyn replied.

"Can you believe he traveled all this way just to stop the wedding? I know he's a prince but he seems a lot more like the knight in shining armor that adorns all those stories about wayward maidens!"

Alanitora laughed, standing to meet her companions. She pressed her lips together in a smile to let Korena finish before speaking herself. "For once, if it's alright with you two, I don't want to talk about other people."

"Is something wrong?" Korena tilted her head.

"No, quite the opposite." Alanitora hesitated. The closest she had come to this had been the day before they arrived in Kreaha. Deciding upon it, she grasped one of their hands in each of her own. "I want to say thank you. For everything."

"Tora, you don't—" Gwendolyn began.

"No, I do. I really do." She nodded. "The two of you have spent more time with me than anyone else in my life, especially in the last week or so. And it's taken me far too long to realize how important you are to me. I know I'm not one for sentiments, but neither of you asked to be brought into this, and yet you have been here for me in more ways than I can count."

"Of course we have." Korena smiled.

"I know we'll be talking about it more tomorrow, but... Trenvern is your home too. The way things are going isn't right, and I'm going to change that. For my mother and I, but also for you." She gave their hands an extra squeeze. "We're gonna get our home back, I promise."

"Tora..."

She let go, raising her arms out towards them for an embrace. The ladies accepted the notion gratefully, stepping to her touch and wrapping their arms around her like a warm, comforting blanket.

Alanitora held them tight, resting her head between their shoulders. "I'm not sure what I would do without you two."

"Probably kill a bunch more people," Gwendolyn noted sardonically.

She let out a light laugh, followed by a resonating chuckle shared between the three of them.

The door opened behind them, and she raised her head to see Sagittarius—and a very happy Silver Moon—in the doorway. "I uh, sorry to interrupt. He wouldn't leave me be."

Korena and Gwendolyn looked up as well, and the wolf came bounding towards them, rubbing himself between their legs to get in on the group hug. The three were forced to separate as the mass of fur interjected, and Alanitora looked at the two of them with a bright smile, holding back a laugh.

"I'll see you two tomorrow. Get some sleep, I know you've had just as long a day as I."

They nodded and said their goodbyes before moving past Sagittarius on their way out.

"Alanitora," she acknowledged.

"Sage." The princess watched as the bandit smirked at the use of her nickname. When she didn't make a move to speak, Alanitora opened her mouth instead. "Thank you for helping with Francis today."

"Of course, what are friends for?"

"Friends?"

"Why not?" Sagittarius pushed herself off from the door frame and stepped in, taking a good look around Alanitora's quarters. "You didn't need me, though. You handle things pretty well on your own."

Alanitora sighed, sitting in the chair to her left while she ran her hand through a content Silver Moon's fur. "That's what I thought too until I realized these aren't things I can do alone. Not with the insanity of what's happening."

Why she was sharing these sentiments and insecurities out loud—and to the one companion she'd known the least amount of time—was unbeknownst to her, but it was out there now, and she felt no need to put the wall back up tonight.

Sagittarius looked her up and down before stepping forward again. "You know what I think?" The archer kneeled in front of her. "I think that while you do need to depend upon your friends, you also need to have equal faith in yourself."

Alanitora raised one of her eyebrows. "And why do you say that? It's not like I express much self-doubt."

"No, but you and I are a lot alike." The princess narrowed her eyes at this remark. She and Sagittarius, alike? Hardly when it came to their situations. The bandit sighed, bringing her hands to the sides of her mask and removing the string that held it in place. She put it on the table next to her. "We're leaders, and not by choice."

Silver Moon, apparently tired of their serious talk, raised from his seat and walked over to the edge of her bed, curling up in a ball with a sigh. She watched him settle before turning her attention back to the bandit, who waited patiently.

Sage looked up at her. The eyes so hard to read, suddenly soft and wise beyond her years. Her playful attitude and rebellious nature had been pushed aside. "You are going to have to make tough decisions, not for you, but for the people that you think you depend on. There are going to be times when those decisions ask you to do the impossible, and you have to make those very things possible. There will be days where you'll want to stop because it's all too much, but you mustn't. In those days you will stand alone, and you will stand stronger than anyone else.

"So yes, while it is imperative that you recognize the need for your allies, it is also important that you continue to fight by yourself as you have been. You have to lead them into this battle, but you also have to protect them. Let them support you but don't let them fall because of you."

"How do you know this?"

"I don't steal for myself, Dagger Eyes, I never have. Just as you never hurt others for selfish reasons." Sage's hand reached for hers, and she squeezed it.

Alanitora looked down from the hand and up to the unmasked bandit. Her gaze held respect and understanding. Sagittarius was the kind of person who would be honest with her when no one else would be.

"So. The man who wronged you and your mom? You're gonna take him down. Him and all of his followers. And then you'll save the day. That's where we do differ... You won't have to work from the shadows to take that son of a bitch down."

Alanitora felt a smile spread on her face. She nodded in affirmation, standing with the bandit, and feeling much more confident.

"Now," Sagittarius stated, taking her hand away. "Get some actual sleep. I'll know if you haven't."

She narrowed her eyes mockingly as Sage picked up her mask, heading to the door. Alanitora followed, shutting the door behind her, leaving the princess alone at last.

She looked around the room, the only sound a crackling fire dying out, the flames flickering low as they became glowing embers. The candles around the room flickered slightly, casting a shadow onto the furniture she had grown up with.

The change had come, and it was still twisting its way into her life, moving bits and pieces of her core around with it. She supposed this was not necessarily a bad thing, but a chance to change into someone else as well.

She made her way around the room, smiling as Silver Moon lifted his head to follow her pace. One at a time, she blew out all but one candle, then undressed, taking both daggers from their place on her legs and organizing them neatly on the center table.

After a moment of hesitation, Alanitora picked one up and instead set it down on the vanity of her mirror, running her fingers across the blade. This was her fight. It was the beginning of something she would forever remember. Here and now, her life would shift for good.

She sat down in the chair and slowly looked up into the mirror. There she met hazel eyes, bright and full of hope. Even in the dim lighting, she could see the green peeking through.

But something else in that reflection stared back at her. Something she hadn't seen before.

Something new.

She smiled at it, and for the first time in her life, Alanitora saw completion in her own eyes.

Epilogue

The Great Hall of Trenvern was crowded with anger. People filled it as well, but it was their anger, their madness, that expanded across the space. And Jenny stood at the edge of it. The girl was among the few children there. At first, she worried this would be the thing to make her stick out, but it seemed no one minded a small girl in the corner when their attention was focused on something else entirely.

Someone else entirely.

She recognized a lot of the faces there. Many of the people nearer to her were her neighbors and acquaintances of her parents. None of them were the kind ladies she knew to be a part of her mother's group, nor were any of the friends she used to play with there. They were all somewhere else. A different part of the castle, or maybe they had been lucky enough to escape.

Regardless, she did her best to stare ahead and not make any eye contact. Jenny had always been the type to daydream, but now she put all her focus into being in the moment. People were depending on her, and she wasn't going to let them down.

Closer to the front of the room were nobles who sat in chairs patiently, murmuring to each other in hushed tones. Whatever was about to happen, it was likely big.

She thought of Diane's instructions for what felt like the hundredth time, trying to ease the bubbles in her stomach and the tears that kept pressing to the surface of her eyes.

At last, a cheer erupted across the crowd. People in front of her stood, and Jenny had to crane her neck from side to side to peek through any gaps.

"Settle down please, everyone!" A loud voice boomed through the walls reverberating until people took their seats. King Ronoleaus stood at the front of the room. He was standing atop something, holding his arms out so everyone could revel in his presence. She'd heard his voice before, though scarcely. It still terrified her every time. This made her more nervous.

A procession of the royal guard marched their way from the doors of the room to the front. In a perfect formation, they lined up behind the king, standing still as though the universe had frozen them in their positions.

"I know you are all angry. I know you have all suffered losses," the king began, captivating every set of eyes in the room. "But it is now that I show to you why you should have to suffer no longer."

There were a few shouts from the crowd in support of this statement. Once again, Jenny stayed silent.

"Just a week ago, the Fonoli set our capital ablaze. Destroying our livelihoods, killing our innocents. I understand there is a vast difference between those who live in the castle and those who live in the town, but I can tell you that all of our belongings burned together. But we rise from the ashes."

"We rise from the ashes!" The soldiers behind him shouted collectively. Even their combined voices did not match his volume.

"Though I have debated telling you these things for long, we can no longer have any secrets among us, if we are going to beat the forces that sparked this... I, too, was lost in that fire."

There were a few murmurs in the crowd. People turned to one another, whispering to check they had heard him right. Others continued to look up at the king, willing for him to continue.

"I do not mean my spirit, nor my title. I mean I truly was lost." The king pulled up the sleeve of his shirt, taking off one of his gloves to show the bubbled skin of fire. "When they found me the next morning, I was not breathing. I'm sure many of you have heard such."

A few people nodded. Jenny had not heard this.

"But as our Lord willed, He knew my fight was not over, and before the sun set the next day, I rose again, full of life, and full of clarity."

This time the sounds of the crowd's comments could not be contained. People no longer bothered to whisper about it, and Ronoleaus let them, raising his chin in satisfaction.

Jenny held back a frown. The people around her looked awed by his words. Persuaded by the lies he so clearly told. She could see his charisma, but they couldn't have been that dull, could they?

But as she searched with her eyes, she found no face that held more than a pinch of doubt. How could people be so naive? She was a fraction of so many people's age in this place and yet they seemed less intelligent than her five-year-old cousin.

"I know you all blame the Fonoli for this." Ronoleaus continued. Many nodded, others shouted out verbal agreements. "But they are not to blame... I am."

There was a flutter of hope in Jenny's heart that he might be telling the truth finally. Nevertheless, she knew better than to believe it.

"I am to blame for letting someone whose only goal was to take over my kingdom into my home. Yes, that's right. The woman I loved, the woman who was your queen... betrayed us." When the crowd's sentiments changed to an even stronger rage, Ronoleaus furrowed his eyebrows in what looked like worry. "Please, I ask that you settle down. I understand your anger, I felt it too, but as I am trying to say, I am not without blame. Which is why I've called you all here today... To listen to my story and make your own decision.

"I found out very recently that my wife had been secretly corresponding with the Fonoli. I debated what to do for a long while. After all, no one wants to think the person they love could betray them. By the time I decided to take action, it seemed it was too late. She had told them how to get into the castle, using a secret entrance, and fled the kingdom before anyone could catch her. As we stand here, I know that she is spreading lies about me across Mordenla, trying to start a war against a kingdom I have spent so much time trying to maintain the peace of."

This wasn't true. Jenny knew that for sure. She even tried to consider that there might be something the queen had done wrong, but she had met Elena herself numerous times when she held her mother's hand at the meetings. The woman Ronoleaus was talking about was kind, gentle, and strong. She protected others. He described someone cold-hearted and vicious. And everyone around her believed him.

"The worst part is," Ronoleaus paused, an effective tear rolling down his cheek. "Not only has she corrupted the minds of innocents, but also that of our daughter, Alanitora." More whispers rose. "This is what breaks my heart more than anything. I thought my daughter was safe and strong, I had no idea that her ideals had been twisted for years... And now I fear that she, too, is spreading lies. I sent her to Donasela to marry the prince and hire them to help us against the Fonolis, but now I believe they have become our enemies."

This wasn't good. Jenny had never met the *princess* of Trenvern, but from what she remembered, her mother's friends were all putting faith in Alanitora to lead them in a new age.

"I have no idea what she has done to ruin our people, but I know that in the coming days, we have to be prepared. We mustn't believe their lies, and we must rise from the ashes like dragons in flight!"

"We will rise from the ashes!" The soldiers behind him called out.

"We will rise from the ashes!" The crowd echoed. Their anger had turned to pure hatred, and it was becoming more and more suffocating to stand.

"So now you all know the truth." Ronoleaus stepped down from his stand and into the crowd. He crossed his hands behind his back, stepping through the aisle and towards the back of the room, looking around at everyone in there. "I'm not asking for you all to fight. Only those who wish to. Dinner will be served in the courtyard a few minutes from now. You may eat if you wish, or stay behind if you would like to volunteer for the fight."

He stopped at the end, his eyes sweeping over the people in the back until he settled on the corner she was in. "That is all, thank you."

Thankfully, his eyes never met hers, for Jenny feared she may crumble under the sight of such a cruel being. Ronoleaus turned, walking back to his stand as people filed out of the room. Most of the women and children

413

left, joined by a few of the men. By the time Ronoleaus made his way to the front of the room and sat on his throne, a little over half of the people were gone.

Jenny stayed where she was. No one had paid attention to her thus far, and she prayed it would stay that way. Diane needed her to be here. Her family needed her to be here. And though it might be a bit ambitious to say, Trenvern needed her to be here.

As folks moved closer to the stand, she reluctantly followed behind, edging herself to the confinement of one of the large green curtains to conceal her small figure but still allow her to see. If someone did find her lurking there, she could feign innocence and get away with it as the young child she was.

Ronoleaus cleared his throat once again now that those who decided to volunteer had made their way to the front. "I cannot express how grateful I am for your service," he announced. "And to show such, I will demonstrate our league with one of our own." He turned to the line of soldiers, beckoning one in the center forward. "Everyone, this is an exemplary member of our cause."

The boy couldn't have been more than eighteen or so, his face was young but the frown on his forehead had been aged with fortitude. Pride brought his chest out.

"He not only has trained for the crown his entire life but has served us for the past few years diligently. His courage and resolve helped greatly to put out the fires our traitors started and has sacrificed much for Trenvern." The king rested his hands on the boy's shoulders, giving them a confident pat of approval. "It is with great honor that I promote you to our circle." Ronoleaus turned, signaling at a chamberlain to the side, who brought up a box and placed it on the table.

King Ronoleaus removed his arms from the boy, opening the ornate box and pulling out a beautiful, intricate blade that curved a few times from tip to hilt. There was an iron dragon wrapped around the handle. Jenny stared in awe. It was beautiful, the silver color shining in the firelight with a gleam of mystery. She nearly stepped forward with everyone else to get a better look.

"With this weapon, I give you, William Tabyer, membership of the Crimson Draconia." He pressed the dagger into the boy's hands, and Jenny watched as William weighed it within his palms, before turning to the crowd in front of him. He seemed nervous under the pressure but was holding extremely well, keeping his chin high.

Ronoleaus continued. "William has suffered a loss from my daughter like many of us. With her deception, she has warped the mind of one he has held close, persuaded his love that her cause was of good intent. And now, William has very well lost what he once held most dear."

The crowd sent out whispers and grunts of frustration, angered by the idea the king was planting in their mind. It seemed William believed it just as well. Jenny wasn't sure this love they had talked of, but she knew that whoever it was had the right mind to not side with such terrible propaganda.

"However, as those of you in this room will learn, to truly be admitted, you must prove yourself for once and for all. Alanitora has stolen the love of your life, do you know what you must do?"

A darkness settled over Williams's eyes as he looked up and across the crowd, his lips parting. "I have to kill her."

Jenny watched in horror as cheers erupted from the crowd, a flurry of people pressing their way towards the front to be the next appointed by their precious king.

Ronoleaus' eyes gleamed with pride. So this was war.

Acknowledgments

I'd like to start off by thanking my mother, whose words, wisdom, and years of encouragement are what prompted me to start writing this journey in the first place. Thank you for being the one I complained to the most about my writer's block or my frustrations with the year-long delay in getting it out. Thank you for reminding me of my brilliance and creativity when I doubted myself most.

Just as importantly, I want to thank my editor and sole confidante, Sage, for being my number one fan since the very beginning of Dagger Eyes. I have no idea how you handled the first draft, but I'm glad you stuck around for the rest. I cannot express how grateful I am to you for answering my late-night calls where I fantasized about the release and babbled ideas about books 2 and 3. This book would not be where it is without you.

I'd also like to thank my additional beta readers Leah and Sebastien, as well as early readers like Karlee, Tee, Becs, Octavia, Samiya, and Sylvie for your feedback and support in these last couple of years. Special acknowledgment to my friends and family for being there for me, and my community on TikTok who provided an amazing amount of boosting on my videos to get the word out in the first place. I never anticipated that Dagger Eyes would sell more than 15 copies, but here we are.

And last but not least, in remembrance of two very special souls who are no longer with us. Jayden, one of the most loving people I have ever encountered. Although we never met in person, I always looked forward to seeing you come into my lives and send your flurry of pink hearts. You would have been a wonderful surgeon, and although you were far too young to be taken away from us, your impact on the people around you was so incredibly strong. And my grandfather, "Uncle Bob" Santos, for being one of my biggest inspirations. Thank you for teaching me to speak my truth, to spread my voice, and advocate for my beliefs. I was told too late that you wanted to write a book with 13-year-old me, and even though that never got to happen, you are one of the biggest reasons I kept working on this one. Keep making them laugh up there, and I'll keep telling the stories down here.

Of course, through all of these thank you's, I have great gratitude to you, reader, for giving this aspiring author a chance to share her work, her imagination, and her life from the past seven years. Just the fact that someone is reading these words means that my dream has already come true. To many more.

-Tarin Santos

Q&A with the Author

Q. You've been writing Dagger Eyes for seven years. How has it changed over time?

A. I would be lying if I said there weren't any changes made. The funny thing about starting a book when you're eleven years old is that your view of the story and its characters is from the perspective of a kid. As time has gone on, those perspectives and what I truly wanted out of the series changed, yet at the core, it's still the same 15 thousand word book that I wrote in middle school.

I think one of the best things to look back at is how I viewed my main cast. They're all teenagers, and as an eleven-year-old, I wrote them how I viewed older kids. I wrote them as this collection of cool teens that I wanted to look up to. Now they're younger than me, and while I still look up to some of their traits, they seem so much more immature.

Alanitora, for example, I wrote as a seventeen-year-old. As a kid, everyone older than me was more mature, but I found over time that Alanitora *rarely* changed, and she still held that naive, unknowing, and sometimes stupid energy that a seventeen-year-old has.

As mentioned, the first draft—finished by the time I was 13—was much shorter than it is now. My writing methods on Wattpad weren't about depth, they were about shock value and telling the summary of a half-baked story. With time, the characters grew up with me, they became a part of me. No longer was it a fun little story with plot twists: it was a story of real people with wants and wishes. The book became centered around how these characters acted and reacted. How they felt, what made them angry and what drove them to their decisions.

Q. When can readers expect books 2 and 3?

A. I've been asked this question a few times, and it's just as difficult to answer now as it was then. Dagger Eyes has been a vital part of my life for years. The brainstorming, the writing, the editing, the perfecting. I'll be completely honest when I say I need a break from this haphazard family that has developed in Alanitora's presence.

Given that I am releasing this book the first year of university, I know that if I were to rush the release of the next ones along with trying to obtain my degree, they wouldn't have the same soul they do now. So I think I'll have to take that break.

What this means for the time of release? I don't know. I know that I have so much left to share, that these characters won't let me rest until I tell their whole story, but I don't know when or how long that'll take. I plan to take it one step at a time, but also, I know that feedback from my readers will have an effect on my motivations, as much as I don't like to admit it. Though not necessarily likely, if a strong community (I don't like the wording of fan base) were to develop with the release of this book, I could see myself dedicating extra time to getting books 2 and 3 out. Whether or not there will be other stories in between? We'll have to see...

Q. Will you write anymore after the Dagger Eyes trilogy, whether in the same universe or different?

A. It never fails to make me laugh when the question of other stories is brought up. Simply because... I have 19 other book ideas and counting. All with their own universes and characters. Different genres, different audiences, just generally different stories to tell. From demons and monsters and magic, to historical fiction, to monsters and magic IN historical fiction. Mystery, romance, fantasy, comedy, drama. All the things, really.

I've always said that Dagger Eyes is not going to be my best work, but it is my first book. I know that I would rather like to get those stories actually published (we'll have to see how trying to get that up and running goes). It's also always possible for me to revisit the world of Dagger Eyes after the trilogy is over to share the stories of my favorites.

Q. Alanitora is a tough, no-nonsense character. Where did you get that inspiration?

A. Well, Alanitora is pretty much everything I'm not. Sure, I'm strong-willed and considerably clever, but in no way do I have the ability to shut up and focus on the task at hand, nor can I beat up half a dozen assassins. In regards to her temperament, I drew that up in opposition to my own. Where I am empathetic, caring, and overly anxious, she is apathetic, serious, and assertive—helpful for the things she has to do, but destructive for the relationships around her. I felt as though it would be a good way to step into the shoes of someone I'm not so that both of us could learn from one another (regardless of one of us being fictional).

In the first draft, these traits were scarce. She didn't have as much depth to her. In full honesty, besides being grammatically written terribly, Alanitora was a bit of a Mary Sue. In time, I changed that by giving her some faults, but I did keep *her belief* that she was perfect.

Her strongest and coolest traits, however—the fighting, the royalty, the wit—was inspired by my own fantasies I had as a kid. My parents used to call me ninja princess because while I wanted to be girly with pretty dresses and fairy tales, I also wanted to kick ass like a comic book superhero. By drafting up Alanitora, I had a way to live that out. Often when you see a kick-ass woman in media, she's physically rough, buff and sword-driven. But who says she can't still have long flowing gowns and (non-sexualized) femininity?

Q. What character do you connect to the most, then?

A. That's a tough one, for sure. I did unconsciously inserted my compassion and heart into the characters of Gwendolyn and Korena. That choice was sourced from a need for balance, but in essence, I think I'm a combination of Alanitora's ladies-in-waiting. That aloof, hopeless romantic, daydreaming excitement that Korena has, mixed with the empathetic, caring intuitive energy of Gwendolyn.

As time has gone on, I have found myself connecting more and more to the character of Sagittarius, however. Her sarcasm and flirtatious nature are two things that I find myself often resorting to when I wish to hide my wounds, which is the exact reason she does that. Readers have only just grazed the surface of Sagittarius' personality, but I think it won't come as a shock that she has a big heart that's been hurt time and time again. And *that* is something I relate to

Q. What was your favorite scene to write?

A. 100%, without a doubt any of the high-stake scenes, but specifically the scene in (Spoiler Warning) Chapter 7, where Devante poisons Alanitora, and she is incapacitated from fighting the way she normally would. It's the scene that I always read as an excerpt, and I can't completely tell you why. I think there was something about the fact that for the first time, we see Alanitora in a compromised position, that the real dangers of life and death come to her. We see her at her lowest, defenseless as she tries to figure out just how she's going to get out of this situation.

And let's not forget to mention just how *maniacal* Devante is. He's one of the only characters that is demented and proud of it. So much so that some of my early readers were not happy about his ~~supposed~~ demise.

Q. Favorite character to write?

A. Asking who my favorite character is would be like asking me to choose my favorite child (it's Corwyn BTW), but asking who my favorite character to *write* is a whole other level of difficulty. Especially since they all have their quirks that are fun to experiment with. It's a close call between Sagittarius, Korena, Owen, and Zinaw, so I'm gonna just go with Gwendolyn instead.

Gwendolyn is the kind of person that I want to be more like. She might be anxious and timid, but she has so much compassion and heart. Where the other four are fun to write because they have fun eccentricities that make hilarious character interactions, Gwendolyn doesn't share parts of herself as much. There are very key parts of her character that are never directly stated, but any reader that takes the time to get to know her can pick up on it.

Q. There are a few queer characters throughout the novel, how did the decision to have a diverse set of characters come about?

A. I will say it wasn't exactly a decision for me. I always wanted Dagger Eyes to exemplify a diversity of stories, but there was never an active "I have decided there are going to be x amount of queer characters". The characters have an identity that is true to them, I just fill in the gaps. Of course, in actually writing them I tend to draw from my own experiences as a queer woman. Certain characters' exploration of their sexuality is a reflection of how, in the years writing this, I discovered my own.

Of course, in a universe different from our own, it is hard to identify diversity without establishing systems of oppression as well. The land of Mordenla doesn't have a set queer history, but the majority of the land has a heteronormative mindset. It is easier to explore homophobic prejudice, than say, racial prejudice when labels like 'Asian', 'Black', and 'Latino/a/x' don't exist. With race, *I* might see certain characters by our world's standards (Alanitora being part Asian on her mother's side or Zinaw being half black), but it's not something that I can properly convey in the text all the time, especially since ethnicity is not just appearance, it's also culture. Given that, I understand that readers will picture characters differently than me, and that's okay.

Alright, that might be a little off-topic, but we are talking about diversity here. Going back to the queer example... Regardless of worlds and their different cultures and prejudices, I wanted to recognize that sexuality and gender are fluid. I never really chose characters' sexuality for them, but I have chosen how they are seen because of this. Hence, I decided to make it so that Alanitora was most used to a heteronormative viewpoint but open to the idea of other genders and sexualities. That way, readers who aren't as familiar with such have the opportunity to learn and understand these things along with our protagonist. I'm super excited to further explore those identities in books 2 and 3 because I think readers will be intrigued by the direction they go. In a story where compassion is a key lesson, I think it's important to bring up diverse narratives. (And hey, I'm still learning things myself! I'm no expert, and this allows me to explore a new understanding too.)

Q. Do you have any advice for young aspiring authors?

A. Aaaah! This is such a broad question sometimes! I feel like there are hundreds of tiny bits of wisdom that I could share from the past seven years.

I think one of the bigger ones that I wished I'd followed more is this: Don't overwork yourself. Creativity takes time, and if it is time between school and work and friends like it was for me, you gotta slow down. Take some deep breaths. For a long while, I thought that the longer it took for my book to be finished, the worse of a writer I was. I thought that every time I had free time, I should have been working on the book, and not laying around or watching shows. But that's the thing— you need free time. Free time is how that creativity blossoms. It's important to take a break from your work.

I feel like, especially if you're a young writer, it's a really cool thing to tell people "Yeah, I'm writing a book. It's this long". And a lot of people *will* praise you for it. It might get to your head or it might motivate you further. But the thing is, what's better than getting a book out when you're super young is getting a book out that you know is your best work. I feel like *this* book is not my best work, but it is a work I'm proud of. It's a work that I'm willing to put out there because I'm ready, and from a creative standpoint, it is complete.

Don't give up, too. Not giving up is very important. And trust me, you're going to want to. It's okay to take month-long breaks. If you have writer's block, one thing I will advise is to just *sprint*. Don't worry about details, don't worry about grammar, just get it out—you can always edit and rewrite later. I find that writer's block is usually just when you're tripping over one specific detail again and again. Getting that mental image out of your head and onto the paper is how you destroy it. Saying "screw that detail" and moving past it.

Ultimately just be patient with yourself. Remember that you have a life outside of writing, too. It's okay to live while you're in the middle of a project. In fact, taking time off of writing to live is where the best inspiration and experience come from. (I will have a notebook I carry around or the notes app for whenever I have a tiny little idea. Always write down little ideas and dreams and scenes because they can come back and be turned into something elaborately beautiful).

You got this, you do. If you're in it for the right reasons, your work will flourish. Try not to get caught up in the ego of it. Don't write a book because you want to be known for writing a book. Write a book because you *want* to tell a story. In those first stages, your writing should be for yourself and your characters before anyone else. It's about who is telling the story and who the story is being told about, not who the story is being told to. That can come later. You don't need to look for anyone else's approval of your work. Worry about the audience and people's perception of your writing when **you** are ready to release it.

Dagger Eyes Tracklist

A tracklist consisting of thirty-one songs— one per chapter. Songs on this list were ones I felt expressed a particular deeper understanding of the chapters' story, themes or characters. Some are easier to interpret than others, but ultimately, the reasoning behind them is for me to know, and you to speculate. Enjoy!

1. **The Mother—** "Valkyrie I: Bloodshed" by Varien, ft. Laura Brehm
2. **An Old Friend—** "Lilith" by Ellise
3. **The Duel—** "Castle" by Halsey
4. **Shifted Fate—** "You Don't Own Me" by SAYGRACE, ft. G-Eazy
5. **Escape—** "I See Fire" by Ed Sheeran
6. **The Girl With the Red Hair—** "No Roots" by Alice Merton
7. **Of Blood & Wine—** "Blood // Water" by grandson
8. **Silver Secrets—** "Start a War" by Klergy with Valerie Broussard
9. **Unbroken—** "I'm Running with the Wolves" by AURORA
10. **Path of Destruction—** "Survivor" by 2WEI ft. Edda Hayes
11. **Amethyst Gardens—** "Spider in the Roses" by Sonia Leigh & Daphne Willis
12. **Raven Crown—** "Dangerous by DeathbyRomy", ft.blackbear
13. **The Maiden—** "Valkyrie II: Lacuna" by Varien ft. Cassandra Kay
14. **A Question of Love—** "Fiending for a Lover" by DeathbyRomy
15. **The Archer—** "Do it Like A Dude" by Jessie J
16. **Priorities—** "City of Angels" by Em Beihold
17. **An Absent Farewell—** "Assassain" by Au/Ra
18. **The Crooked Flickers—** "Me & My Girls: by Selena Gomez
19. **Wolves & Hares—** "Seashore" by the Regrettes
20. **Crossroads—** "Soldier" by Fleurie

21. Honor Among Thieves— "Ain't No Rest for the Wicked" by Cage The Elephant

22. The Prince and the Knight— "Fairytale" by Alexander Rybak

23. A Warm Welcome— "Fighter" by Christina Aguilera

24. Fox's Den— "The Kid I Used To Know" by Tori Kelly

25. What Once Was— "Kingdom Fall" by Claire Wyndham

26. The Crone— "Valkyrie III: Atonement" by Varien, ft. Laura Brehm

27. Human Nature— "still feel" by half alive

28. Bound— "lovely" by Billie Eilish & Khalid

29. The Truth— "Oh Mother" by Christina Aguilera

30. Loyalty Within Lies— "Black Sea" by Natasha Blume

31. Redemption— "Wings" by Birdy

Tracklist picture credit:
Anna Doezie

Please note that while I do not have explicit permission to use the songs listed, the purpose of this tracklist is purely for the entertainment of Dagger Eyes' readers, and not intended to be profited off of. All rights remain reserved to their respective owners :) — Tarin Santos.